SPENCER BLACKWELL IS

GREED

GREED

BOOK TWO OF THE SEVEN DEADLY SERIES
FISHER AMELIE

Oh, Grandma. I will never forget you. Not your ridiculous Chesterfields, nor your "yule-ry", not your magnificent, albeit, expensive taste, or your garden honoring Our Lady. I will never forget your stacks of catalogs, your perfumes, your millions of picture frames full of your children, grandchildren and great-grandchildren. I will never forget the "bobas", the detested highway bridges, your saltines with ham and mayo. I will never forget your generous heart, nor how you never said an unkind word about anyone. I will never forget your "benefits of the doubt" or your hope for the seemingly doomed souls around you. I could never forget you, Grandma. Ever.

GREED FURY LUST IDLE BINGE ENVY VAIN

7D

PROLOGUE

GREED IS a strange, strange sin.

All you want to do is acquire. Acquire money, acquire material, acquire time, acquire energy, acquire attention. The running mantra is "I want, I want, I want" but that quickly turns to "I need, I need, I need."

Suddenly there just isn't enough time for friends, for family, for anyone. Your goal is to acquire and to make sure what you acquire stays acquired. Your life depends on it. You don't see truth because the truth is shadowed by enormous homes, incredibly fast cars, in lavish spending. Your life no longer belongs to you, but you are blind to it all because those around you are seeking the same.

So you shuffle along at an impossible rate, and you pass the real world around you.

GREED

But what you'll come to realize, altogether too late, is that it's never enough.

It's simply never enough.

"I CAN'T do that," he said, exhaling sharply and staring out the glass into the street.

"Why not?"

His face softened. "I need his money."

Spencer looked at me, and I couldn't help but stare back. We were all in the same boat, prisoners to greed.

—VAIN

CHAPTER ONE

"It's confirmed. Peter Knight of Evergreen won't approve the acquisition. You know what to do," my snake of a father told me, not two steps into his front door.

"I just got off a seven-hour flight. You can't let me settle in? Possibly say hello?"

He stood, watching me, a slight tick in his square jaw. He tucked his hands into his Italian silk pants. His six-foot frame followed the steps up to the foyer and stopped a few inches away from my own. We were face to face. Although I fell an inch shorter, he no longer intimidated me. I knew if I had to, I could kick his ass.

"Hello, Spencer," he said, a serpent's smile spread wide across his mouth before falling flat. "Get to work. I don't pay you to sit around. I don't care if it is your Christmas break."

We stayed where we were, each waiting on the other to back down. The tension was palpable. In the end, his face relaxed and he began to chuckle, stepping aside and making way for me. I picked up my bags and headed for my room, giving myself plenty of space to pass him without touching him.

When I got to the bottom of the stairs, I changed my mind and threw my bags on the second to last step, intending to pick them up later. I stretched my muscles, loving the feel of my back popping, and started for the kitchen.

"Where the hell do you think you're going?" he asked, still standing in the foyer, watching my every move.

"If I don't say hi to Mom and Bridge, they'll think something's up," I told him and continued on.

He didn't respond, but I felt his stare burning into the back of my head.

I knew my sister and mother were in the kitchen because I could hear their laughter from across the immense modern monstrosity that was my parents' home. My dad picked it out because he picked out everything, and my mom went along because my mother always goes along with what my dad says.

My mother was a beautiful woman, though she doesn't realize it. In fact, she was gorgeous, inside as well as outside, but she shared the physical characteristics of a woman in her forties who'd had two kids, and for some reason, she thought that gave my father carte blanche to be a cheating, lying asshole and get away with it.

As soon as I entered the kitchen, my seventeen-year-old sister, Bridget, or Bridge as I call her, squealed, jumping off her stool and threw her arms around my neck. Her eyes burned with moisture when she pulled away to look at me.

"My Bridge," I told her, squeezing her cheeks together, puckering her lips.

"My Spence," she garbled through goldfish lips.

I released my grip, kissed her cheek, then hugged her. "I missed you, Bridge."

"I missed you, too, bub. What are you doing here so early? We weren't expecting you for another two days."

"I know. After I finished my exams, I thought I'd surprise you, decided that last dorm blowout wasn't worth it."

Bridge's hands met her hips and one brow arched over a grey eye. "You're lying, but I don't care," she said, smiling.

My mother, Jessica, stood, straightening out her crisp apron and smoothed her hair before making her way over to me.

My mom was a former Tennessee beauty queen, all Southern drawl and breeding. In my younger days, I'd done a lot of "yes, ma'ams" and "how'd ya do's" to get me labeled the freak in my Cali private school. Needless to say, I'd lost my inherited politeness by age seven.

"Mama," I said, tugging her small shoulders to my chest.

"Baby boy," she said, her smile wrinkling the laugh lines around her eyes. She smacked my cheek with a kiss then immediately tried to wipe away her lipstick residue with her red manicured fingers. "Merry Christmas, Spencer honey."

"Merry Christmas," I told her.

She pulled away and joined Bridge back at her stool. I leaned over the counter, examining their Christmas cookie progress.

"How were your finals?" my mom asked, steadily rolling the dough with a pin over the cold floured marble. Bridge's eyes followed the movement as well.

"Fine. I aced them all," I said, popping a piece of dough in my mouth.

"*Cha*," she tsked, but smiled anyway. "So cheeky, boy."

I was majoring in business. I had a mind for it, yes, I just didn't enjoy it. My dad picked my major. He paid for my life, so I complied, just as I would comply with the "job" he had for me that evening.

I raised my head from my mom's task and noticed Bridge looked a little green. "You okay, Bridge?" I asked.

"*Wha*?" she asked, her hand going to her throat. "Excuse me," she said, swallowing, "I'm not feeling well. I think I'll go lay down."

"Go on, buttercup," my mom told her, her hands methodically rolling the pin.

I watched Bridge unsteadily get up from her stool and walk to the door, but when she reached the entry, she leaned a little on the jamb, a hand going to her mouth.

"Need help?" I asked her, standing from my leaning position.

She turned and smiled but shook her head. "Nah, think I just ate too much raw dough."

I nodded and she retreated from view.

"You're not staying," my mom stated, her eyes trained on her task.

"Yeah, uh, I gotta meet up with a couple of friends."

She stopped rolling and looked up at me. "Sure you do, love," she said, patting my face with a flour-covered hand, her eyes devoid of emotion.

I studied her for a moment, wishing we didn't have to play these little I-know-what-you-do-but-I'm-going-to-pretend-I-don't games. I watched her face, wishing I could be honest but instead of coming clean with her, I squeezed her shoulder briefly, noting how bony it was, and smiled before trotting off toward the stairs.

I yanked my bag up and over my shoulder, climbed to the third floor and wound down the window-lined hall, the sun still beaming through, warming the cold stone beneath my sock-clad feet, to where my bedroom was. The door swung open and I took in the room—pristine, dark and my own private sanctuary. I really missed it. It was where I would go when I needed to escape my father. He never bothered me in there. In fact, I don't think he'd even set foot in mine or Bridge's wing of the house.

I threw my duffel on the bed and watched how it sank into the billowy down comforter. I stood still for five minutes at least, memorizing the silence, possibly procrastinating my dad's *task* a little.

Brown was nice, but I had a roommate named August. Something I'd never experienced before. I mean, he was cool as shit, but I'd never had to share a hall, let alone a room. I tried to convince my dad to pay for an apartment for me, but my mom stepped in and said I needed to "experience college life." Whatever that meant. If she really wanted me to experience it fully, she would start questioning why her husband called me back home every few weeks for a day or two only to send me back with no explanation whatsoever.

College life isn't interrupted with twice-monthly flights back home. I love my mama more than you could possibly imagine, but she was one of my dad's pawns. Then again, who the hell was I to talk? Maybe it's why I didn't ever defend her from him like I should, because how could I call her kettle black when I was the biggest fucking pot in our house?

I grabbed my cell and dialed Lola, whose name, by the way, wasn't really Lola. I pulled my t-shirt over my head, entering my bathroom, which was bigger than my dorm room back in Providence. I started the shower as it rang.

"Hello, Spencer," Lola purred.

"Drop whatever you're doing," I told her, leaning against the sink counter, my back to the mirror. I crossed my free arm against my bare chest, gripping my shoulder. It stung like a mother since the previous Thursday's impromptu football match.

"I have a very important client expecting me tonight,

Spencer. I don't think I can do it."

"Cut the bullshit. It's your regular rate plus a ten-thousand-dollar bonus if you do a good job."

She was silent, baiting me, waiting for a larger offer. I kept my mouth shut.

"Fine," she conceded, making me smile.

I slipped the piece of paper my dad had his valet, Frederick, lay on my bed out of my pocket. "Seven p.m.," I read, "Sofitel Bar." I closed my eyes, vomit threatening to make an appearance. I hesitated at the next part. "He's a family man so dress seductively but not obvious." I swallowed down the bile.

"Got it. See you then."

I pressed end to the call and stared at the surface of the phone. My reflection, the one I'd hoped to avoid for the evening if I was going to be able to do what I needed to do, stared ominously back at me. I threw the phone through the doorway and onto the bed, sick of looking at myself, and undressed. Standing in the shower, I washed the flight off my body and hair. I let the hot water run over my sore shoulder for half a minute. I made a mental note to have Bridge rub it out for me. *Hope she's feeling okay. Poor kid*, I thought.

When I got out, I wrapped a towel around my waist and headed for my closet, sliding the large doors across half the length of the room on each side. Immediately, I grabbed my three-piece tailor-made suit from Gieves & Hawkes in London and a crisp, starched shirt and laid them on the bed. I took a deep breath and entered the bathroom, situating myself at the sink, and looked in the mirror. I averted my eyes quickly and laced my toothbrush with toothpaste. I brushed my teeth without looking at my reflection and applied deodorant, but shaving and waxing my hair was a different story. I didn't have a choice but to face myself then. I let the Bvlgari

10

after shave sting, a self-imposed penance that didn't touch the surface of paybacks for the sins I'd committed or was about to.

I dressed, took a quick look in my closet mirror, acknowledged that I was as ready as I would ever be and grabbed my keys, jacket and wallet before tucking in my Kiton pocket square.

I strode down the hallway, the sun hidden now, hidden from exposing me for what I truly was, a walking contradiction. I twirled the keys to my Aston Martin, a habit that feigned how carefree I wanted people to think I was. I'd just made it to the second level stairs when I did an about- face to check on Bridge before I left.

I knocked on her door. "Who is it?"

"Housekeeping," I said, straining my voice in much too high an octave.

"No, thank you. I'm all right," she said.

I smirked to myself. "Housekeeping."

"I'm fine, thank you," she said more sternly.

"Housekeeping. You want head for pillow?"

It got quiet and I stifled my laugh.

"Come in, David Spade," a weak voice commanded.

I swung the door open, expecting her to be crouched on the bed with one of her ridiculous books. Bridge could party with the best of us, much to my dismay, but she was a complete nerd at heart. But instead of her nose buried in the pages of the latest, I found her lying pathetically slumped over the edge of her bed, her silver bathroom trash can perched just below. My heart sank for her.

I sat next to her and shifted my baby sister's hair away from her shoulder. "You okay, dude?"

She ignored my question and took me in instead. "Where do you think you're going, Tom Hardy from *Inception*?"

"Funny. I'm meeting someone. You watch too many movies, by the way."

GREED

She smiled at me but barely. "You look sharp. Lots of effort for whomever she is."

I didn't correct her misassumption. "Thanks. Can I get you anything before I jet?"

"A time machine?"

"No can do, kiddo. Whatever you ate has to take its turn. Don't worry, though, there's a light at the end of the tunnel." She nodded, but looked unconvinced. "If you need anything, ring my cell."

"Yeah, I'm sure your date would appreciate that," she teased.

I smiled the best I could and stood. "Bye, Bridge."

"Bye, Spence."

I closed her door behind me, and reminded myself to check on her when I got back.

GREED FURY LUST IDLE BINGE ENVY VAIN

7D

CHAPTER TWO

I whipped my Aston Martin into Sofitel, but dodged the valet, choosing to park in the back of the lot. This is one place where I didn't need to be remembered. I only wanted to blend in. I got out and locked my door, taking out my cell and ringing Lola as I made my way to the Sofitel entrance. She answered on the second ring.

"I'm here. Room five-seven-eight."

"Lobby," was my only response.

I hung up. I'd reimburse her for the room as I always did, to avoid a paper trail.

By the time I entered the lobby after walking the remainder of the lot, Lola sat secreted in a corner next to the cool steel sculpture at the room's center. She stood when she saw me, devastatingly beautiful as always. She inclined her head and I reciprocated. She eyed me with appreciation but as always, she did nothing for me. Uncommonly pretty but not much else. Also, never dip your pen in the company ink, gentlemen, even if the company isn't necessarily aware she's stocked.

We entered the hotel bar. I, casually with my jacket unbuttoned and a single hand in my front pocket and she, seductively as any femme fatale there ever was. I spotted my target, Peter Knight, waiting at the bar, studying a whiskey neat twirling in the glass before him. *Damn*, I cursed under my breath. He'd beaten me there. He didn't notice Lola either, though, making my stomach clench a little in hesitation. I hoped he was distracted instead of the stand-up guy I suspected he was. I fought the nausea.

Lola and I sat together in the darkest corner of the bar, as out of sight as we could possibly get. Peter Knight kept glancing at his watch, waiting for the meeting with an executive that would never come. He ordered one more whiskey and that was my cue. I glanced at Lola, nodding once and she stood, making her way toward Peter, choosing a seat two down from him.

She ordered the same drink Peter had because we'd done our research and her hand covered the rim of the glass, the drug she'd held in her palm fell to the bottom. I could tell it had already begun to dissolve. Her hands moved to the sides of the glass to cover the effects.

I knew when it was fully mixed because her hands fell flat on the bar top. She leaned back into her stool and displayed her breasts, her arms moving to rest on her lap. Every man with a pulse, including Peter this time, took note of her. She was effortless. She smiled lasciviously at him.

"Hi," I heard her breathe.

Peter only nodded once and turned back to his drink. Confirmed. He looked but he didn't touch. My jaw pressed tightly. *Damn, he didn't take the bait. Plan B.*

Lola quickly glanced my way and imperceptibly shook her head once. I stood, coolly removed a handkerchief from my front left pocket, patted my neck and forehead, replaced it, smoothed out my jacket, tugged at my cufflinks ensuring the cuffs were stiff and made my way to the bar top, sliding into the stool right next to Peter. He smiled at me then glanced at his watch once more. I was running out of time. The bartender approached me.

"What'll it be?" he asked.

"What are you drinking?" I asked Peter.

He smiled. "Macallan, eighteen, neat."

"The same," I said with a grin, oozing charm. *Open up room for conversation.*

"Popular tonight," the bartender said simply, making my adrenaline spike.

"It's a great vintage," I hedged.

We silently watched the bartender pour me a matching glass and walk away to attend another customer. I internally breathed a sigh of relief.

"Jonathan," I lied, extending a hand.

I was always Jonathan. I don't think "Lola" knew it as anything else during our little charades.

"Peter," he answered, taking it.

I took a sip then set the glass down, nervously twisting it back and forth in the palms of my hands. I sat up slightly, checking my actions and angled myself toward him, making eye contact. *Establish trust.* I breathed deeply, taking yet another sip. *Don't waste time.*

"Are you were from the area?" I asked.

"No, actually, I..." he started but before he could finish, I faked a clumsy movement, sweeping the pen he had sitting on the bar top next to him onto the floor.

"I'm so sorry," I said, as we both made a move to retrieve the pen.

I grabbed it first and awkwardly fumbled with it, distracting him further. *Hope he buys this.* I watched through my peripheral as Lola subtly switched her roofie laced whisky with his glass. When she righted herself, I

15

handed it back to him. He sat back in his stool.

"Butter fingers," I joshed.

He took a swig, a third of the glass' contents gone.

"Nervous?" Peter asked, more astute than I previously gave him credit for.

I went with it. "Uh, yeah. I'm meeting a girl here. Blind date." I noticed Lola smirk.

"Well, that explains it then," he laughed, slapping me on my sore shoulder. I took the pain. I deserved it. "Get out early, I always say. Dating is the pits," he joshed.

I cleared my throat and followed his lead as he took another swig, unaware of the poison streaming down his gullet.

"Married then?"

"Yes." He sighed. "Thirty years next week, actually."

I felt beads of sweat pour down my back at the declaration. He took yet another sip. I narrowly stopped myself from swiping the glass from his hands. *Even if he drops, which he will, you can still back out. Just help him to his room. He'll think he'd had too much. He'll only wake up with a great night's sleep.*

"And you're still happy?" I asked, ignoring my conscience, grasping for anything terrible, anything that could justify what I was about to do.

"Oh, you know, it's not easy, not all the time anyway, but I can honestly say I am genuinely happy with Maggie. She's my everything, if I was being candid." He laughed at some private joke. *I hated jokes. My punch line would destroy him if his wife ever found out.*

My gut began to ache so terribly, my hand inadvertently scrubbed at my neck. He mistook it for nerves.

"Don't worry, son. I'm waiting for someone, too, though it looks like he's a no show and I flew in all the way this close to Christmas for nothing. Anyway, I'll wait with you."

"That's so kind of you," I told him honestly as he finished his drink.

He ordered another.

I glanced at Lola and she lightly tapped at her wrist but avoided eye contact.

Peter and I spoke of nothing consequential over the following fifteen minutes, but when that time came to a close, he appeared totally inebriated. So much so, that the bartender stopped by.

"Is he staying here?" he asked. "Wish I'd known the guy couldn't hold his liquor."

"It's not a problem. He's got a room here," I told him. "Don't worry, he's a friend. I'll take him back to his room."

He nodded in answer, setting our tabs down on the bar top. I paid his as well as my tab in cash to avoid trace backs or, for that matter, waiting any longer. The drugs were seriously taking effect, and I wasn't sure I'd be able to handle his dead weight despite my daily reps of two-eighty-five.

I made a move to stand as Peter slumped forward a little. *You waited too long.* "Come on, dude," I told him, throwing his arm over my shoulder. We made our way toward the elevators.

"You're a good man," Peter slurred. "That's rare... someone so young."

I didn't respond, *couldn't* respond, really.

We barely made it to the elevators. I pitched him inside and sat him against the sidewall then held the door open with my hand, praying no one else would come. Lola quickly emerged ten seconds later without a word spoken and we let the doors close.

"We waited too long," Lola finally said, when we reached her floor. She stuck her head out when the doors opened. "It's clear," she said.

I swung middle-aged Peter Knight onto my shoulders

17

with only a little difficulty, glad for the minute rest I'd gotten between supporting his weight during the walk through the lobby and reaching Lola's floor. "Lead the way," I told her.

Lola took me to her room, quickly unlocked the door and we entered. The entire ordeal couldn't have taken more than five minutes, but it felt like an eternity. I pitched him onto the bed. He laid there, clothes in disarray, hair mussed, and snoring.

Lola and I watched him for a good thirty seconds, waiting for him to stir but he didn't, he was dead to the world.

"Shall we get started?" she asked.

I vacillated back and forth between right and wrong, willing myself to just walk away, begging myself to figure a way out but no argument was more convincing than the mil' I was getting paid. *Besides*, I thought, *as long as he complies, this is not a big deal at all. He can go back to his wife and kids and I can go back to Brown a little bit wealthier.*

"Yes," I finally answered.

Lola slithered from her dress and stood in her lace bustier and garters, let her curled hair down and went to the mirror, leaning over to freshen up her lipstick. I went to the bag on her bathroom counter and removed the SLR, slid on the power button and waited for her at the foot of the bed. I watched her, taking in her beautiful body, admiring her, internally acknowledging why she was the most expensive call girl I knew. She caught me staring in the mirror and smiled with perfect white teeth.

That's when I noticed it. She was breathtaking, yes, but if you *really* took stock of her, took in her little flaws, she was revolting. Nose tinged red from recently snorting. *Of course,* I thought, *how else could you do what you did.* Slight bruising expertly covered up with makeup around the throat and arms, evidence of her profession. I thought of my sister and wondered if Lola had a brother or even a father. Ribs protruding, proof to the naked eye that she starved herself to stay thin. Another product of our society. Another otherwise gorgeous girl made ugly by the pressures and influence of an L.A. life. I turned my head and observed the man sleeping in front of me.

And how are you different? I asked myself. *You'd do just about anything for money. You'd risk this man's wife and family. And for what? So that your dad can manipulate another business deal to make him even more cash than he already has? More cash to spend in places where cash needn't be spent?*

Lola crawled across the bed, yanking at Peter's tie, and licking the side of his face, posing with her leg wrapped around his.

Click.

Another million can give you better security, ensure you can live within the lifestyle you're accustomed, eventually give you freedom from him.

Lola switched it up. She unbuttoned his shirt and spread her lacquered nails across his chest, pressing closely to him and smiling a viper's expression at the camera.

Click.

It's not likely this Maggie woman will ever see these photos anyway. It's low risk and you get a cool mil out of a night's work.

Lola straddled him, unbuckling his pants and threw her head back in mock satisfaction.

Click.

GREED FURY LUST IDLE BINGE ENVY VAIN

CHAPTER THREE

"Here's your blackmail fodder," I told my father as he sat at his desk.

He clapped his hands together in excitement, rubbing his palms quickly back and forth and grasping at the flash drive like he was the devil and I'd just thrown down sin, which is a little too spot on. I turned to walk out the door.

"Stay right there," he ordered. I obeyed, standing where I stood but didn't turn to face him.

I heard him pop the drive into his laptop then a few clicks of his mouse.

He groaned. "These are good," he giggled like a toddler. "These are fantastic." He paused. "Wow. I might have to give Lola a call—"

"Stop," I said, refusing to face him. "I did your dirty work, but I don't have to listen to another damn word."

"Fine," he said, like I'd slapped him. "One day you'll get it."

"Trust me," I said, "if ever the day comes that I 'get

you,' that day will also be synonymous with my death."

"Come here," he said.

I faced him at his desk.

"Come around here," he ordered.

He was logged on to an online banking session. It was a wire transfer. A million dollars made out to me. My heart began to race in anticipation. He slowly hovered the mouse over the send button and pressed. The click resounded through my head. It was different this time. Too reminiscent of the clicks that earned me the pictures. This transfer didn't quite feel the same as all the others though, and my stomach dropped.

"You're too afraid to accept it," my father began, leaning back in his chair, "but I'm gonna say it anyway. *That* transfer. *That*, among the many others, is you 'getting me'"

I backed away slowly. "No, it's not."

"Yes, it is," he answered with the same serpent's smile, elbows on the chair's rests, hands steepled in front of him.

"I'm nothing like you," I told him. *Who are you trying to convince?* "Nothing," I repeated.

"Son," he said, leaning forward, "you *are* me."

I turned and bolted down the hall, away from his cackling laugh, away from his accusations, desperate to leave my own suspicions behind. I ran up the stairs, shedding pieces of my suit as I went, determined to shower, resolute in washing away what I'd just done, who I really was, but I was certain there was nothing that could cleanse me, to launder my poisoned blood. This was who I was. Hopeless personified.

I vomited twice, showered and brushed my teeth, but it did nothing to appease my unsettled stomach. I threw on a pair of Adidas pants and laid on my stomach in bed, curling my blanket over my head after turning on my stereo. I'd left one of The Cure's albums in there.

Knock. Knock.

"Come in," my voice cracked. I cleared my throat. "Come in," I said with purchase.

My door opened and I lifted my head to see Bridge. "How was your date?" she asked, hopping on the bed and laying next to me. I shifted onto my back, the blanket falling between us, and tucked my hands behind my head.

"It was okay," I lied.

"An untruth," she said, throwing her hands behind her head as well. "But I'll let it go for now."

"You're doing that a lot lately," I teased. "How are you feeling?"

"It passed," she said, getting quiet.

We shared a moment of silence.

Finally, I studied her, my brows creased. "You okay?"

"Yeah, fine," she hedged, hopping up. "Hey, want to get dinner Friday? Just you and me?"

"Sure. Mom doesn't have dinner plans for us?" My mom usually had every minute of our days planned when I came home.

"Nah, she and dad are going to his office Christmas party."

"Okay. How's school?"

She rolled her eyes at me. "You're only four years older. You act like my freakin' father or something."

Someone has to. "All right, simmer down now. Simmer down."

She rolled her eyes again but smiled. "Want to watch *It's a Wonderful Life*?"

Hell to the no. "Absolutely not."

"*A Christmas Carol*?"

It's like she has a window into my conscience. "No, let's try something funny."

"*Elf*," she recommended.

"*Elf* it is."

That night I opened my laptop and set it on the bed beside me. I toggled between wanting to log on to my Swiss account and wanting to throw the whole damn machine across the room. I settled on logging on. I couldn't help myself.

Seven million two hundred ninety-three thousand eight hundred fifty-nine dollars and seventeen cents.

A burn of satisfaction radiated across my chest and I couldn't help the smirk that appeared after, but that burn turned into a different kind of heat, an uncomfortable heat in my stomach when I thought of the imaginary image I had of Peter Knight's wife.

I imagined Peter's face when she opened the envelope of pictures. I imagined how he would fluster and struggle to explain images he had no recollection of. I imagined her slapping the innocent man, imagined her packing up a bag and the kids and leaving him.

I slammed my computer shut and ran to the bathroom, vomiting once more. But it did no good. I still felt like the piece of shit I was, and there was nothing I could do about it. My only choice now was to sit there and pray that he would choose the merger route, to save his family.

My only consolation was that he seemed like the kind of man who would pick his family over his career.

Besides, he'll get rich off this merger...Nevermind that he didn't want the merger in the first place because he thinks your father is a dishonest prick.

And yet, despite the fact that I knew it was wrong, I was going to keep the money because the idea of letting it go was more painful to me than the sin I'd committed against Peter Knight. I was deathly afraid to admit it out loud but I was *exactly* like my father. And it felt like I could do nothing about it.

GREED

The greed was more powerful than the will to do right.

I've got to get out of here.

GREED FURY LUST IDLE BINGE ENVY VAIN

7D

CHAPTER FOUR

I took my dad's private jet without asking. I did this often whenever I would do his bidding. He never questioned it. The pilot would return to L.A., and I'd call him back when I needed him.

A limo sat at the bottom of the airstairs. I immediately climbed in just as my cell began to ring. I stared down at the name displayed across its face. My mother. I hesitated for a moment, trying to decide whether I should answer it.

Get it over with.

"Hello?" I asked.

"Spence, honey, where in the world have you gone?"

"I'm in Vegas, Mom, what's up?"

There was a long pause.

She sighed. "I know your daddy can be a little much sometimes, but that's just his way. He loves you, darlin'."

I stifled a bitter laugh. "Yeah, okay. Listen, I'm sorry I didn't tell you, but I need a day or two to catch my breath.

I'll be home soon. You won't even know I was gone," I charmed.

She sighed yet again. A guilt tactic that usually worked, but my desperation to be away from my father trumped it. "Bridge is very disappointed," she plied.

I sighed. "Shit. The dinner. Tell her I'll be home Friday morning. I promise."

"Fine," she conceded. Her voice was weak, reminding me of all the times she spoke to my dad the same way.

"I love you," I added, narrowing my eyes. "I've got to go. There's something troubling in the car with me."

"Okay, honey, love you too and be careful?"

"I will," I lied and hung up the phone, laying it in the seat next to me.

I ran my hands over my hair and smoothed my pants before resting my palms on my thighs. I cut and lit the Gurkha HMR cigar, courtesy of the hotel, in the tray next to my seat. I took a long, silent drag, letting the smoke out slowly and filling the car with an intoxicating scent. At fifteen thousand dollars a box, it better taste and smell like fucking heaven.

I settled a little deeper in the leather. "Who are you?" I asked the silent girl on the bench across from me.

She cleared her throat but spoke smoothly. "I'm Piper."

"Is that your real name?" I asked her, rolling the window down an inch to watch the lights and let a little of the smoke out.

I turned back to her. She was beautiful, without a doubt. Shiny burgundy hair curled to meet her waist, her eyes were brown and bright and her skin was flawless.

"Yes," she told me, and I believed her.

"Piper, why are you in my car?"

"I was sent."

"By whom?" I asked, staring straight at her.

"I'm not at liberty," she explained.

"Ah," I said, letting it lie. "What are you here for?" I asked, knowing full well what she was there for.

"I'm here to do whatever you want for however long you want."

"That's vague," I replied.

"Consider me your own private *attendant*."

"That clears it up, thank you," I teased with a smile.

She smiled back and it wasn't all too unpleasant a look. I decided she could stay, but I wasn't sure what all I was going to do with her. I'd decided to play the night by ear.

"We'll eat," I told her.

"Naturally," she flirted.

I shook my head and smiled at her then rolled down the divider. "Joël Robuchon, please," I told the driver.

GREED FURY LUST IDLE BINGE ENVY VAIN

7D

CHAPTER FIVE

OH MY *God, my head*. The pounding was intolerable. My eyes felt heavy, too heavy. I began to move my arm, but it felt pinned by something, making me crack open an eye. I glanced to my left. *Shit. Shit. Shit.* The back of Piper's head rested on my wrist. I slid my arm out from underneath her but she only groaned, dead to the world, it seemed.

I practically jumped from the bed, staggering back a bit from the pain in my head. *Oh, God. Oh, God. What have I done?* I asked myself, bringing my hands to my head. *Remember. What happened? You went to dinner...*

Dinner. It was standard. Steaks, liquor, *lots* of liquor. More liquor than I thought two people could possibly drink. Random memories of Piper moving to my side of the booth, her hands sliding up my thighs, her tongue in my ear. My stomach lurched and I turned, only to stumble over a random guy sleeping at the bottom of the villa's master stairs. I felt ill, and not from the liquor. I made my way to the kitchen, meandering around the leeches asleep at my feet. I needed water. I staggered a little, still a bit drunk. I threw open the freezer door and stuck my head inside.

"Fucking leeches, all of them," I said, thinking on all the assholes littering my villa floor. *She's the worst*, I thought of the burgundy headed vixen in my bed. I lurched into the cold air, ready to spill bile, but closed my eyes and swallowed instead. I breathed deeply through my nose several times and the nausea subsided.

I closed the freezer and opened the fridge, grabbing a bottle of water and chugging it. When I was done, I threw it on the floor and looked around me. Thirty or so people laid about scantily dressed.

"You have no purpose!" I yelled at them, but they slept on. "Did you hear me?" I slurred. A few of their eyes opened, so I kept yelling until they were all awake. "You all have no purpose! You're worthless leeches! Every single one of you is a worthless leech!"

I stumbled forward and rested my hands on the cold marble of the island facing them. They all looked frightened, their eyes wide before standing and gathering their belongings, tripping over themselves in a sleep-induced hangover to get out the door.

"That's right! Get the fuck out!" I screamed, making my head pound worse. My hands went to my hair and I tugged, desperate for the ache to disappear. I looked about me and spotted an empty bottle of wine. I grabbed it by the neck and threw it at the wall to make them move faster. They stopped short when it shattered then kicked it into a higher gear, clambering stupidly.

I watched them all with an eagle's eye and spotted a girl near the bottom of the stairwell trying to drape a piece of clothing over a bottle of L'or De Jean Martell.

I launched myself at her and yanked the bottle out of her hand. "I should have you arrested, you little thief."

GREED

Her eyes widened and her breaths quickened. I balanced the bottle on the banister and shoved her away from me. "Fucking leeches, all of you!" I shouted at her as she ran for the door, but I caught her and clasped her around the upper arms and turned her around. "Always looking for the handout," I gritted in her face. "Do you know what this costs?" She shook her head in answer. "More than you're worth, trash. More than you're worth."

Her eyes narrowed in anger. "Let go of me," she ordered.

I peered down and noticed my hands were digging into her flesh. I released her immediately. "Get out of here," I barked. She ran and I picked the bottle back up, twisting off the top and taking a gulp. It made my stomach turn, so I spit it out and let the bottle spin to the floor, its contents spilling onto the tile as the bottle rocked slowly back and forth. Thousands of dollars of deep burnt orange cognac seeped into the grout and I shrugged my shoulders. *Oh well.*

I ascended the stairs once more, running my hands over my face. *One more person to kick out.* I dragged my foot over the last step, heading for the master but changed my mind at the last second, opting for a shower instead, hoping it would sober me up. I muddled around several empty bottles of liquor strewn about the hall leading to the closest shower and locked myself in the room.

I never did well with sex. I always felt sick later, and I wasn't really sure why. Yeah, in the company of friends, I'd brag about my fair share of conquests, pretending that girls didn't mean shit to me because that's what guys do. Pathetic as that is, I admit, but the reality of it was my stomach felt heavy with guilt, my chest beat painfully afterward, and all I wanted to do was run away, much like I always did when I made bad decisions. Hence, Vegas.

Ask yourself something. Have you ever thought about why guys want you gone the next day? It's not because they've got things to do, though I'm sure there are a few assholes who think like that, either because they repeated the folly so often they learned to bury the guilt or because they didn't have a conscience to begin with. But, truthfully, it's because they can't *stand* to look at the reason they feel a hole in their chest. They don't like reminders of who helped put that sick feeling in the pits of their stomachs. As long as they had a decent mama, the guilt is always substantial. Always. If they say differently, they're liars. I'm not sure if the feeling goes for chicks, but I'm willing to bet it might. I mean, they're human, right? They have the same little voices in their heads we have.

Girls, I'm gonna tell you something that I could probably get my ass kicked for copping to, but what the hell, here it goes: Waiting to have sex with someone until they say they love you is a trick, a device, a deception...a *game*, if you will.

Now, before you lose your shit or something, listen to me. I'm not saying that it's not possible for you to have sex with someone you're dating who loves you, but I *am* saying if they loved you like they said they did, they wouldn't put you in *the* predicament to begin with. I won't lie, I've had plenty of sex with plenty of girls, and it rocked. Well, it rocked until the next day, anyway. Hell, I've even lied to a couple and told them I felt more than I did. Shocking, but, baby, we all do it because guys love sex more than they love you, trust me.

There are two things I've found with the act. One, guys love sex because they love the feeling. Nothing more. Two, girls love sex because it feels good as well but, whether or not they want it, there's also an emotional tie. I can't imagine a girl having sex with a dude she didn't really know and not feeling almost psychotic afterward

31

because she will forever be tied to this guy she barely knows.

Damn, I just realized why so many chicks I've slept with lost their shit afterward, why they become a little desperate to call and connect and search for something that will never be. Almost makes me feel bad—almost.

I started the shower and leaned against the marble at the sink until the water began to steam. I scrubbed my face with my hands, frantic to sober up, noting the stubble that'd grown and trying to decide whether I wanted to shave. *Screw it*, I thought.

I closed my eyes.

Piper moved closer to me, pressing her body closely to mine as the beat of the music permeated our skin and vibrated against every sense we possessed. Her mouth moved on mine. I could feel the corners of her smile lift against my lips. Her eyes lit with amusement like she'd won something but I didn't care as long as she let me touch her more. I realized briefly I didn't know where I was, but I was too happy, too sloshed to give a shit.

"Want some?" she asked, extending the palm of her hand. A tiny pink heart sat in the center.

"What is it?"

"Ecstasy, of course," she said, popping the pill in her mouth.

"Can't," I told her, shaking my head. "I have drug tests at school," I slurred.

"Who cares," Piper offered, swinging her body tightly against mine, making me forget about school altogether. She brought her face in close to mine. "Come on, all the cool kids are doing it," she taunted.

I smiled at her and that was all the answer she needed. She kissed me and I realized she'd placed another pill on her tongue. I swallowed, uncaring...for the moment.

"Stupid fool," I told the mirror, disgusted with the memory.

I shook my head, hoping to evade the flashback and began to undress. When I lifted my shirt over my head, my ribs felt sore as shit. I inspected my reflection, wiping the steam off the mirror first. On my lower left side, my ribcage felt like it was shattered. It was a dark black and blue. I lifted my left arm over my head and tentatively traced the massive bruise with the fingers on my right hand, wincing at a particularly sensitive spot.

"Have you ever felt free?" she asked.

"Never," I answered truthfully. I could barely keep my eyes open. "I live in a cage," I embellished.

"Poor baby," Piper cooed, swiping her crimson lacquered nails down my face. She wasn't sincere, not even in the slightest. Anger briefly flashed across her face.

"I know what you're thinking," I rumbled through a thick tongue, "but you'd be wrong."

"No I wouldn't," she whispered. "You live a life of privilege."

"It's not half what it's cracked up to be. Do you know how hard it is to be a good person with money?"

"Do you know how hard it is to be a good person without it?"

We were quiet, watching the fountains below my twenty-story villa.

"Do you want *to feel free?" she asked.*

"Of course," I admitted.

She grabbed my hand and we stood. She dragged a chaise to the edge of the concrete balustrade and perched on top, almost toppling over she was so inebriated. She giggled then braced a hand on my shoulder before balancing one high-heeled foot on the balcony edge.

"You're crazy," I told her.

"I know."

But I followed her. For some reason, I followed her. My mom's voice of reason popped into my head, something about friends and bridges and jumping, but I ignored it. I anchored my dress shoes from Church's in London on the cushion of the chaise. I stared down on the foot, seemingly unable to move another inch. Fear crept into my stomach, securing me where I stood.

"Come on," she whispered in my ear.

I steeled my stomach and lifted onto the chaise. I turned toward the world around us and breathed deeply of the cool air that can only be found at the height we stood. I let the wind rush through my hair and took one more step onto the edge of the balustrade before lifting my entire body.

I stood on the precipice of twenty stories, of exhilaration, of adrenaline, of stupidity, but most importantly, I stood on the precipice of death. I turned to Piper, her eyes were wild as the wind whipped her hair around her face and plastered her gown to her body.

She grabbed my hand to steady herself and turned toward me.

"Do you feel it?" she asked.

"Feel?"

"Do you feel alive yet?"

"No."

She ignored me and faced the fountains below.

"I wondered what would happen if I jumped," she stated matter-of-factly, but I could tell she didn't care if I answered her. She was contemplating.

"You're insane," I told her.

"I know," she admitted, lifting a Cheshire grin my direction.

She faced the wind and screamed, making my adrenaline spike further than it already was.

"You're burning my buzz," I told her.

She turned to me but it was too quick a reaction for her drunk body, and she stumbled. She began to fall forward but did nothing to stop herself. Instead, she closed her eyes as if she sat at the top of a roller coaster, ready to drop.

I tossed her back and she fell on top of the chaise, unharmed.

But I lost my footing. My arms wound around, as if that could balance me. This is it, *I thought.* Poor mom. Poor Bridge.

My feet slipped from underneath me and I began the fall but at the last second, Piper pulled hard at my arm, drawing me back toward the villa decking. It wasn't far enough and I caught the middle of the balcony solidly on my side.

My left arm dropped to my side, but I kept my right hand on the growing bruise. *Oh my God,* I thought. *I could have died.* I lifted trembling hands and ran them through my hair then down my face. I stared at my reflection, wondering if I kept it up if my poor mother would have to bury me in the family mausoleum before I even finished college.

I entered the shower and sat at the tiled seat, letting the steam swarm around me, hoping it would hide me away forever. My heart beat erratically in my chest, thinking back on what I'd barely survived. My skin blazed in anger thinking on the redhead, thinking on her whispers, her gentle coaxing. She was so convincing, so alluring, so *persuasive.*

"That one," she said, pointing at the Bugatti.

My personal steward, a gentleman named Lawson, approached us as we lingered near the Bugatti. I took a deep breath to clear my head of the alcohol and ecstasy, hoping I could pull off the rental without a hitch.

"The Bugatti, sir?" he asked.

"Yes, thank you, Lawson."

"Just sign here, sir," he said, offering me the clipboard and the licensing agreement I signed every time I came here.

I took the board and pen and tried to steady my hand, but I wasn't very convincing.

"Everything all right, sir?" Lawson asked, his brows furrowed.

"Of course," I said, smiling. "Just tired, I guess. I'll take it until Monday, Lawson."

"Yes, sir," he said, studying me for a moment longer, then taking the board from my hand.

He turned and walked behind a wall to wherever they kept their keys. Piper ran her hands down the side of the car with a gleam of satisfaction in her eyes.

"So pretty," she whispered.

I placed my hands in my front pockets and leaned against the exterior. "It's a Bugatti, Piper," I told the wall.

She stopped and stood, narrowed her brows at me. "I know that!"

I sighed. "Calm down."

She obeyed. "Can I drive it?"

"No."

She walked the entire perimeter of the car running her hands along its length, coveting every inch. Pathetic, I *thought.*

"Your keys, Mister Blackwell," Lawson said, appearing out of nowhere. He handed me the keys and I opened the door for Piper before getting into the driver's side.

Lawson slid open the large glass accordion doors to allow me through. I placed the key in the ignition, then pressed the start button just underneath the stick shift. The engine rumbled low, but inside the cabin, the Bugatti had the distinct sound of being in a wind tunnel. The engine was that powerful. She purred so smoothly, I imagined it similar to laying on the belly of a content lion. She was beautiful.

I tentatively drove her out and onto the street. I could feel Lawson's eyes on me. He would never dare question me further than he had, but I think he knew something was wrong. If he didn't then, he definitely did later.

I shook my head, unable to remember anymore. "What happened?" I asked the thick, humid air in front of me. I searched and searched but couldn't remember...but it felt like I should.

I stood, desperately trying to remember, and began to wash my hair, feeling overwhelmed, feeling like it was imperative I remembered what happened next.

I began to rinse and looked below toward my feet. The water ran red. *What in the hell?*

"Faster!" she yelled, and I felt powerless but to obey.

I punched the gas, earning me a fiendish, almost inhuman grin in return. She removed her belt and leaned into my neck, breathing me in deeply, making the hair there stand on end. She traced her red lacquered nails along the goosebumps there before running her tongue along the length. My eyes rolled back into my head.

I felt the car pull a little to the left and I whipped my head up then righted her despite my intoxicated, swimming head. Whoa, *I thought. I turned to tell her to put her belt back on but was struck mute, distracted by her sliding onto my lap and threading her fingers around the back of my neck.*

"What are you doing?" I smiled into her mouth, muddled by a combination of the liquor, the ecstasy and how unbelievably sexy she was.

Every single touch from her felt indescribable. She ran her fingers through my hair and I shuddered at the enlightened sensation. She breathed on my neck and I felt the muscles in my stomach tighten. She crushed a grip of hair at the back of my head in her hand and pulled down before kissing me.

The tingling in my lips exploded and my response to her was immediate as my hands abandoned the wheel

GREED

"Oh, God," I breathed. "I love this."

"Me too," she whispered back before biting my earlobe. "Do you know what would make it even better?"

"What?" I asked, suddenly and carelessly willing to perform whatever she asked.

My eyes rolled into the back of my head again when she ran her lips up my throat.

"This," she said, her eyes blowing wide and her smile growing serpent-like before her heel jammed into my foot on the gas.

I sucked in a breath as we surged forward. She brought her mouth in closer to mine and kissed me deeply, distracting me yet again and bit my lower lip hard, drawing blood. The iron coppery tinge filled my mouth and woke me up, reminding me to steer.

I tried to pull away from her venomous kiss, but she held fast, driving her lips more firmly against mine.

"Stop," I spoke into her mouth but she continued to ignore me. "Stop," I said again, more emphatically, but she refused to move.

I yanked her hair back, making her squeal in delight, and peered over her shoulder while attempting to get her heel off the top of my foot but it was too late.

"Oh, shit," I breathed.

As if time stood still, Piper glanced over her shoulder, her hair whipping around with her to see the damage she'd done before turning back toward me and leaning into my neck. "Do you feel alive yet?" she whispered.

I breathed in sharply.

Time sped up once more and the car made purchase with something substantial throwing us forward then back. Glass spun around our heads in colorful jagged shards reflecting the lights of the Strip. I held onto her with everything I had, cradling her head against my chest, while our bodies lashed brutally toward the passenger side, then back toward the driver's side window where the back of my head cracked the glass.

Blackout.

"Come on," she whispered into my left ear.

I groaned, in terrible pain, wishing I would die and soon.

"Come on," she insisted, dragging me by my arms out of sharp splintered piles of glass. "We have to go before the police come."

"What?" I asked, still coming to.

Sirens split the perpetual horn blaring from the car. She helped me to my feet and wrapped an arm around my waist. We stumbled away from the crash, much to the confusion of onlookers.

I startled from the memory and shook my head, examining the top of my foot and noticing a deep gash where the heel of her stiletto had bore through. My hand went to the back of my head and I winced at the soft spot where my skull had met glass.

"Oh my God," I said.

I watched red imbued water swirl around the drain and suddenly felt dizzy.

"What in the hell have I done?"

I sat back down and ran my hands down my face once more, once again recoiling from the ache in my bottom lip from where she'd bitten me.

"Spencer?" I heard her deceivingly angelic voice call out.

Fists clenched at my knees.

"Leave," I ordered.

Her slim, blood-colored lacquered hands wiped away the condensation built on the glass shower door. Her smile was the first thing I saw, and I trembled at how disturbing I found it in the light. Her eyes burrowed into mine, and I noticed how soulless they looked now that I saw her for what she was.

"Leave," I demanded again.

She moued her counterfeit pout and opened the shower door before stepping inside in her gown. She watched me and began to tug down one strap but I stopped her.

I snorted in disbelief. "Absolutely not. Get the hell out of here right now."

"Oh, Spencer, I don't think you want me to do that."

"Like hell I don't! You're certifiably insane, you know that?"

She sighed and leaned against the shower wall as if she wasn't wearing a satin gown. "It's coming back to you then," she stated rather than asked.

I gulped. "I remember it all."

She studied me with furrowed brows. "*All* of it?" she asked. I watched her. "Even the money?"

My heart quickened. "What money?"

"So...*not* all of it."

She seemed to get some sort of sick thrill out of knowing this part of the night I couldn't recall.

"What happened?" I asked her.

She began to laugh, cackle really, and escaped the shower. I jumped up and tossed a towel around my waist. I followed the wet trails of her dress all the way into the bedroom but couldn't find her.

"Piper," I called out, searching the room. "Piper!" I called again, scouring the closet, but she wasn't there.

I ran from the room, sprinting down the hall to the top of the stairs and peered over the edge. "Piper!" I shouted down, but she didn't answer.

I descended the stairs and inspected the living area as well as the kitchen. She was gone. I threw open the villa doors and scanned the balcony, but no Piper. I ran back through the living and practically tossed the front door off its hinge.

"Piper!" I yelled into the empty hall.

I stumbled back into the room and closed the door, resting my back against its flat surface. "Where in the..."

My hands began to tremble as a thought came to the forefront of my mind. Slowly, ever so slowly, I walked back through the living room, hesitating to step over the threshold of the balcony. My breaths deepened.

"Oh, please, God. Please, God," I prayed under my breath as I reached the balustrade.

I placed both my hands on the edge and leaned over.

"Come on," she whispered. "It'll be fun."

She dragged me by my tie to the gambling floor, the private floor just for whales.

"I'm too drunk to gamble, Piper. Besides, my head hurts like a mother," I slurred.

"Shh," she quieted into my left ear, "you'll do fine."

I followed her to the concierge and he stood when he saw me.

"Mister Blackwell, will we be joining a table tonight?"

"Yes, please," I mumbled.

"Your account is up to date. Here is your card," he said, offering me the digital readout of my winnings for the past year.

I'd won close to two million, hoping to add it to my total in Switzerland. My seed money. The money I would use to get away, to feel free...finally.

"This way to the baccarat tables," he said, pointing me toward the left on the floor.

He knew me well. Baccarat was my game because the game favored neither the house nor the player. The odds were almost fifty-fifty. That's why I liked it. It was a safe, simple game, and I won more than I'd lost. I gambled with my father's money, but the two million was pure profit and all mine.

"No, this time we'd like to play Black Jack," Piper chimed in.

"Of course," the concierge complied, leading us in the direction of the tables.

"Black Jack?" I asked her.

"Yes, Black Jack is much more fun."

I didn't respond. My head was pounding so furiously, I just went along with it. Just play a few hands and get gone, I told myself.

Nothing. There was nothing below. She hadn't jumped.

I staggered back into the villa and shut the balcony door, locking it behind me before dragging my feet to the sofa and falling on top. My face hung near the edge, forcing me to acknowledge the mess, the chaos, around me.

I watched a still bottle of Jack underneath a shattered glass coffee table. It had maybe an ounce of liquor left inside and it sat, the perfect gold liquid inside its clear glass coffin, waiting for its fate, waiting to be consumed or discarded...much like myself.

I was so tired of nights like those. So tired of fearing the unknown, of discovering near-death experiences, exposing myself to dangerous things I wouldn't remember until it was usually too late. That night may seem out of the ordinary, but not for me. Not for Spencer Blackwell. That was fairly typical for me. That was my life or, very likely I knew, soon to be the end of it.

"Just get your cash, send it to Switzerland and call it what it is." I turned and laid on my back. "Get out now, while you still can. Run."

I ran up the stairs, dressed and grabbed my bag before heading to the lobby to check out, but first I needed to cash out. I visited the new concierge, a woman this time, someone I'd seen before but couldn't remember her name.

"Good morning, Mister Blackwell," she greeted cheerfully, her hair clean and kept, her teeth bright and white.

"Good morning," I told her, my voice rough. I looked down at myself, fully aware that despite my designer digs, I looked as to be expected.

"What can I do for you?"

"I'd like to cash out, please."

"Not keeping your balance here?" she asked.

"No, I've decided to take a-a breather for a bit."

"Just a moment," she said, secreting to some area in the back.

I leaned against the counter, ready to beg loudly for her to return quickly that I was in so much pain.

She returned a minute or two later but it felt like an eternity.

"Mister Blackwell, it appears you don't have a profit balance."

My mouth went dry. "Excuse me?"

She peered at a computer screen in front of her. "Yes, it seems you lost your balance. There's actually a settlement owed of five million seven hundred thousand."

My heart leapt into my throat. "That cannot be," I insisted, bracing my head in my hands. I didn't think it could take much more pressure. "Okay, uh," I breathed. "Charge it to my father's account," I told her.

"Of course," she said.

When he found out, he would remove my signing privileges.

"Thank you," I muttered before heading toward the lobby and sitting down in the nearest chair to catch my breath.

GREED

I lost it all. I was relying on that two million to fund part my freedom. Now, I knew I was going to have to live another year under my dad's thumb to make it up.

The very thought made me want to wretch. So I did. All over the expensive marble floor.

GREED FURY LUST IDLE BINGE ENVY VAIN

7D

CHAPTER SIX

I HELD out her chair for her and she tucked herself within it as I pushed her in place. I glanced around me. Every eye in the place was peeled and staring a hole through the miniscule dress I begged her to change out of but she didn't. Bridge never listened to me when it came to that stuff. Ever.

"*Assholes,*" I spoke between gritted teeth toward all the leering eyes.

When I sat myself, I immediately shot a blazing look at the fifty-year-old idiot at the next table. He was sporting a wedding ring and was undressing Bridge with his eyes. When he caught me staring, his eyes popped wide for a moment. Embarrassed, his bright red round face found the ceiling. Apparently, it was fascinating. I had something just as fascinating—my fist. In his stupid face. My hand closed, the skin at my knuckles pulling tight, the blood fighting to reach my fingers. After Vegas, I was in the mood for a fight.

GREED

"I'm pregnant," I heard at my left, shocking me. My gaze whipped back to her face. My heart pounded in my chest. My hands fell open.

For a brief moment we sat there, quiet, unmoving, the asshole forgotten. My breath rushed in and out of me, hurried and burdensome.

My hand shot out and my water glass shook, the water sloshing violently as I brought it to my lips.

Suddenly, I'd never been thirstier.

The entire contents poured down my throat in one fluid spill. I set the glass down slowly, using both hands to steady the shivering glass, and I sat up a little. I'd unwittingly slumped in my chair. I wiped at my mouth with the linen napkin laying to my right. The pressed, starched, perfect napkin that I absently noted my father would have complained about simply because he could.

"How?" I asked, swallowing hard.

She raised a single brow. "Well, you see, when a man and a woman get together—"

"Bridge," I nearly shouted, slamming my hand on the table. The utensils clinked and rang, sliding into the china setting. "This isn't a time for jokes." I gritted my teeth, reminding me of my father. Her eyes clenched tightly and her bottom lip began to quake. Right away, I pulled my lips apart. I relaxed my fist and let my hand slip off the table. I asked as kindly as I could, "How, Bridge?"

She took a deep, wobbly breath and turned her stare away from mine. "I don't know, to be honest." Little bits of moisture began to gather at the corners of her eyes. She examined her water glass, running her finger along the base of the goblet.

"Who?" I asked, ignoring the tears.

I didn't have time for tears. I didn't have time for sympathy. We were in deep shit. She knew it. I knew it.

"I don't want to say," she said.

Her eyes moved to her lap as she absently meddled with the napkin laying across her knees.

"I'm your brother, Bridge." I leaned toward her over the table and narrowed my eyes. "I need to know who I plan to kill."

Her eyes trained themselves on mine. "Don't be an overdramatic idiot. And I won't say a single word anyway. I told the father and he wants nothing to do with it." My blood boiled to a dangerous temperature. *Asshole.* "I asked you to dinner for one reason and one reason only."

I closed my eyes and took a good, solid breath. "What do you need?"

"Help telling dad."

I nodded, still absorbing it all and attempting to bring my heart rate down. Then it dawned on me.

"The nausea," I said, recalling the day I'd arrived.

She nodded once, tears threatening to spill again.

Bridge didn't eat much. Nor did I, for that matter. I'm not exactly sure if it was the fact that she complained of feeling sick again, which set my heart beating an abnormal pattern, or the fact that we were about to drop the biggest bomb on my parents' shoulders. We left it unsaid. Memories of Vegas kept invading my thoughts, and I felt nauseous myself.

"Wait, I forgot my purse," she said when we reached my car.

"I'll get it," I told her and opened her door for her.

I watched her seventeen-year-old body hop in. She strapped herself to her seat then tucked her leg beneath her, the way so many young teenage girls do, and twisted a strand of her long blonde hair around her finger while texting someone with the other hand.

All I could think as I looked on her was that she was so young. She was way too young to be pregnant. She was

GREED

my baby sister. My little Bridge. Granted, she was only four years younger, but that never mattered to me. When she was ten, I was fourteen, and I recalled scaring off the bullies who pulled her pigtails. When she was fifteen, I was nineteen and I would yell at her to stop wearing those freaking shorts around my friends. And then she got pregnant, and I still felt very much like the older brother I was. I just wished I could have protected her better, but instead I led by the worst example ever. Piper's Cheshire grin popped in my head, and I flinched.

I grabbed Bridge's ridiculously oversized leather bag from her forgotten chair and headed for the door. I jumped into my car.

"The Holes?" I asked, so pissed at myself, I could've kicked my own ass.

"Of course," she answered, her gaze staring out toward the busy street.

"The Holes" were where fifty or so of our most elite group would gather together at the home of one our parents' because it was inevitable that someone's folks would be out of town. We would "hole" up for the weekend, binge on drugs, sex and booze.

I slammed the palm of my hand into the steering wheel. I leaned forward and started the car. I fell back into my seat and ran a hand down my face.

"Jesus. I just-Bridge, we need a plan."

She turned my way. She looked so lost. "Thanks for helping me, Spence."

"Please, Bridge. Your problems are my problems," I said, hitting the gas.

We sat in the car at the end of our street, staring at our parents' monstrous house. I listened quietly to Bridge's crying. I tried comforting her, but it did no good.

"We'll get it over with," I said.

"I want to wait until after Christmas. It'll kill Mama."

"No, we tell them tonight. The sooner, the better. I'll be able to defuse it better the more time I have."

"So you're going back to Brown after all this?"

I looked at her like she'd gone crazy. "Why wouldn't I?"

"Well, I just thought you'd want to stick around for a little while."

"Bridge, Dad's not gonna let you keep it."

"I don't give a shit. I'm going to."

"Let's see what happens." He would never let her keep it.

"No, I need us to be united on this front, Spence. I need to know that when I stand up to Dad you'll be there to back me up. I need support." He still wouldn't let her keep it.

"Fine, Bridge."

I parked in my spot and got out, Bridge following right behind me. When I opened the front door, Mom and Dad were in the main living room. Mom was on the floor sweeping up shards of a liquor decanter, and Dad was on the sofa with a paper in his hands. Something had transpired, and Dad had won as always.

Mom stood up, quickly swiping under her eyes. "Oh, kids!" she said with false excitement. "How was dinner?"

"Okay," I said. "You all right?" I asked.

"Fine. Fine. Just fine," she spat out quickly, standing and leaving the glass in the pan on the floor.

"Uh, listen," I said, shoving a nervous Bridge into the seat opposite from Dad.

I sat next to her, but Mom didn't make a move to sit next to him. He was obviously ignoring all of us. She picked a chair to our right and sat. My dad got up, his nose still in the paper, and started making his way to his office.

"Dad," I said, and he turned around, stunned I'd

disturbed him. "Yes, I know, but you need to hear this."

His scowl would have burned holes through me if I wasn't so used to it and if we didn't have something so dire to tell them. Plus, around the age of sixteen, I noticed he'd become aware of my size and he'd stopped manhandling me. I could be a serious threat if I needed to be, and he knew it.

He sat, crossed his legs and folded the paper across his lap.

"Bridge," I said, opening the floor for her.

My mother, distracted before, finally noted Bridge's puffy eyes and red nose. "Bridget, honey, are you all right?"

The tears started streaming anew, but she stayed my mom with a hand when she attempted to comfort her. "I'm fine, well, not fine, but I have something to tell you both."

She took a deep, cleansing breath and I sat forward, fists clenched, preparing for the inevitable blowup from my father.

"I'm pregnant," she said.

The quiet was deafening.

"This isn't a problem," my dad said, with eerie softness, pressing the creases of the paper over and over.

"It's not?" I asked, bewildered.

"No, this is an easy fix, especially since it's over Christmas break."

"No," Bridge said, realizing what he meant.

"Excuse me?" our dad said, breaking his cool exterior and uncrossing his legs.

"*No*," Bridge said strongly.

"Dear, lovely, stupid, whorish Bridge," my dad said, sliding forward and staring right into her eyes, his face pinched with the most evil expression I'd ever encountered, reminding me of Piper yet again. "You will get rid of that thing, or I swear to God I will have you killed and make it look like an accident."

My mother gasped.

"Dad!" I said, jumping up.

He stood and met me nose to nose.

"She wants to keep it," I said.

"I don't give a shit. This will not be tolerated. I'm in the middle of the biggest merger of my life and I will not have our family name tarnished!"

"Oh, but having her murdered won't bring unnecessary awareness? Possibly negative awareness?"

He considered what I'd said, the sick bastard.

"Perhaps," he agreed, "but it's got to go to save this merger."

"Give it up, old man. This family name is soiled beyond redemption and you know it. It's why Peter Knight said no. It's why they *all* initially say no. It's why I'm always called home to *fix* it."

His neck turned beet red.

"Shut the fuck up, Spencer!"

My fists clenched tighter and my chest met his. "Make me, you lousy piece of shit!" I yelled in his face.

Bridge stood and pulled me away. "I'm keeping it, Dad," she said, charging past me toward the stairs.

Mom stood with her hands over her mouth, unable to speak.

"Stay right there!" Dad yelled, and she, like I, was powerless to disobey. "Come here," he said more steadily.

She descended into the sunken living again and stood beside me once more, this time trembling.

"I—" she began.

"Shut up." Her mouth shut tightly. "You forget," he said, with frighteningly quiet intensity, "I have a lot of political pull in this city. I've got a handful of doctors sitting in my back pocket right this minute. So, I'm only going to say this once. You will take care of this of your own volition and immediately, *or* I will have you deemed of unsound mind and get one of my judges to approve any medical procedures I see fit. Now, think about this for a moment, Bridget. Imagine how difficult I could make your life if I had this kind of power over you."

My heart pounded in my chest. "You wouldn't," I said, scared by him for the first time in a very long time.

"Wouldn't I?" he asked me and only me, a devilish smirk across his face. And, of course, I knew he would. "I consider it your job to make sure she goes through with this," he told me.

He walked out of the room, never looking at Bridge or my mom again.

"Bridge," I said softly, edging toward her.

Her eyes became glassy. "No," she whispered. Tears spilled over. "No," she said again.

"Bridge," I said, reaching for her, "we have to."

My mom wrapped her arms around her, and I wrapped my own around both of them.

CHAPTER
SEVEN

BRIDGE AND I talked all night and I finally convinced her that going in was the best thing because either way, dad would make sure it was done. Going in voluntarily would at least save her the punishment of my dad controlling every aspect of her life for the rest of her life. He would do it too, just to punish her. I didn't trust the man before, but I never thought him capable of the threat against Bridge until I saw the expression in his eyes. He showed me how truly heartless he was, how he was willing to take down his own daughter to achieve what he wanted and any miniscule feeling I had left for him was snuffed out the second he proclaimed it.

She agreed that her friends and classmates would desert her, judge, and mock her as well. She didn't think she'd be able to weather their torment. She remembered a classmate of hers getting knocked up and the hell she was put through. She decided she wouldn't go through that.

GREED

The next morning was cold and bleak, as the sun had yet to rise. The early morning noises felt overgrown and ominous, leftovers from an unusually black night. I opened the car door for Bridge, the chill in the air seeped deeply into my bones, the weight of our decision, of what we had to do, heavy on our hearts. The sadness emanating from her made me hesitate opening my own door. I would have given anything not to sit inside the car with her. Maybe it was the fact that I knew I was forcing her to do something she didn't want to do. Maybe sitting next to her was a reminder of that. Either way, I was a selfish asshole and I knew it.

The chill in the air made me shiver. I got in, started the engine and blasted the heat. Bridge had curled up into herself, the leather creaking beneath her, a little ball of a girl, her long blonde hair in a messy bun on her head, not a stitch of makeup on her face and her eyes red from crying the entire night.

"It's okay, Bridge," I assured her, pulling out onto the long drive that led from the house to the main street.

She curled up tighter, resting her head against the freezing window, staring out into the dark morning. Six in the morning and we felt so alone on the road, only the occasional city truck or passerby would grace us with a roar as they crawled past us, their tailpipes puffing into the frosty air. It was a farce that California was seventy year round. In the winter, we occasionally got fifty- or sixty-degree temperatures, which doesn't seem that low, but when the sun is vacant, it *feels* like it could snow and the cold bites your fingers with stiffness. That morning it felt like my entire body was numb with that same stiffness.

My stomach ached and my mouth went dry when we pulled into the clinic's parking lot, a seemingly opaque haze fell in a fog over its surface. I pulled into a space near the front and got out, wrapping my jacket tighter around my chest and walking to Bridge's door. When I opened it for her, she just sat there. I had to lean in and unbuckle her belt.

"Come on, Bridge," I said softly, her dazed eyes stared ahead of her into nothing. Her expression gave away that she saw the same.

I grabbed her upper arm gently and guided her out of the car. She leaned into me and I locked it with my key fob.

When I opened the door to the clinic, it appeared, for lack of a better word, used. The chairs were old, fading and peeling their pleather cushions. The walls were, at one time, white but had dulled and stained yellow. The ceiling was missing a few fiberglass tiles; some were present but cracked or missing large chunks where protruding wires fell at strange angles. The floor was a checkerboard pattern of light blue and white vinyl tiles. A bronze trash can from the seventies rested near the door beside a low fiberboard table full of magazines whose subject matter contradicted the very purpose of the clinic itself. The chairs lined the walls, and there was a row of two seats in the center.

There were four people already in the waiting room, a couple who sat against the wall nearest the door and two girls around the same age on the opposite end of the room from them. I sat Bridge in a chair toward the center, facing the couple, and approached the window. An older woman in her fifties slid back the glass partition.

"Yeah?" she asked, smacking her gum.

"Uh, we had an appointment today at seven a.m."

"Name?" she asked, picking up a clipboard.

"Bridget Blackwell."

She checked a list then grabbed yet another clipboard and handed it over. The pen was attached to the top with a chain. "Yeah, fill this out. We'll call you."

She pushed the partition closed without a second glance and I sat next to Bridge.

"I'm sorry we couldn't do this at a hospital, Bridge," I told her. "The whole point of this is to be discreet so people don't find out." She nodded. "You need time to recover before school starts too."

"I know, Spencer," her worn voice told me.

I looked at her then noticed the guy in front of us. He was laughing at something on his phone while his poor girlfriend looked terrified, her arms pressed tightly against her abdomen. He looked up at me and smirked, gesturing with his head toward his girl before rolling his eyes, an attempt at camaraderie. When I didn't bite, he went back to his phone with a picture of a naked girl on the cover, and obnoxiously laughed at whatever text he'd gotten. All he made me want to do was kick his ass and tell the girl to run as fast as she could.

I began filling out the paperwork while Bridge sat bent into herself on the chair. Halfway through the tedious process, I looked over again to check on her and looking at her hair triggered something. For some reason, I was bombarded with memories of when she was little. She had this ridiculously curly hair, and it was always wild about her face, regardless how hard my mom tried to contain it. She'd put it up in some sort of clip but sure enough, five minutes later, it was a blonde halo around her face.

I remembered her being four or five, her melodious little squeaky voice with a lisp inviting everyone she could within a five-mile radius, stranger or not, to her ballet recital. She wore her leotard, ballet flats and tutu every single day for two weeks, practicing every opportunity she could, dancing to imaginary music throughout the whole house. I thought she was so goofy in the head but, and I'd never had said it out loud, especially at the time, I thought she was adorable.

I remembered summers when I felt too cool to stay at home. I'd leave around ten in the morning, head out to the pool to say goodbye to my mom. Bridge would've already been swimming two hours by then, a two-toned, thin, little nothing of a kid constantly yelling out for us to watch her make the same dive over and over again. Her lisp gone by then but her falsetto "please, Spence" got me every time. "Fine, Bridge," I'd tell her. She'd dive in and come up; her eyes round with anticipation. "Amazing, Bridge!" my mom and I would always say, clapping.

I remembered skinned knees, birthday parties, school plays. I remembered when boys first started noticing her and that protective part of me warning off every one of my friends. I remembered the first time she came to the Holes. I marched her off to my car and drug her ass home. She was furious at me, yelling the entire way, but I'd be damned before she attended one of those things. Never mind the fact I went to them every weekend. But then I went off to college and there was nothing I could do to stop her. And then there was this. This awful, shitty thing my dad was doing to her...*I* was doing to her.

"*Shit*," I said under my breath, crumpling up the paper I was filling out then throwing the freaking clipboard onto the seat next to me.

"What's wrong?" Bridge asked.

"Let's go," I said, standing up.

"What-what do you mean?" she asked, confused.

"I mean, let's get the fuck out of here."

"No, we stay."

"No, we go. You don't want to do this anyway."

"It doesn't matter. Dad will—"

"Dad won't do shit," I told her.

"How're you gonna stop him?"

57

"I just am, okay? Let's go."

She stood up hesitantly. "What's your plan?"

"I don't know," I said, "but I'll figure it out."

I walked to the door but stopped when I noticed the young girl and her douche boyfriend. I dug into my back pocket and pulled out my wallet, grabbing every bit of cash I had.

"Seven hundred fifty dollars," I told the girl, "all yours if you leave this dickhead right now, go home and tell your folks. I can even give you a ride home if you want."

"I'll take it," she said without hesitation, standing.

"Wait a minute!" the jackass said, moving to stand himself.

I glared at him. "Sit your ass down," I ordered in my most fierce voice.

The guy backed down.

"Need a ride?"

She looked over at Bridge and Bridge nodded. "Yes, please."

When we reached the car, her eyes widened.

"Where'd you get a car like that?"

"My dad bought it for me," I told her, cringing at how obnoxious that sounded.

"Damn, he buy one for you too?" she asked Bridge. "You're brother and sister, right?"

"Yeah," Bridge admitted, buckling herself in.

"You guys look exactly alike."

Bridge and I smiled at each other.

The girl's name was Valerie; she was a junior in high school and had only been dating the guy at the clinic for three months. He told her he'd loved her, told her he would "take care of her," that if she got rid of the baby, he would marry her later. I told her he was lying and an asshole. She asked how I knew that, and I told her, "I'm a guy, Valerie." She took that as explanation enough, or maybe I'd confirmed what she already knew.

Valerie's house was tiny and in a bad neighborhood but was clean with a decent car in the drive. Her parents obviously didn't have a lot of money, but from what I could tell, they worked hard for what they did have.

When we pulled in front, her dad was leaving for work, I assumed. I got out of my side of the car and pulled back my seat to let her out.

"Valerie?" her dad asked, hesitation in his voice. "Who's this?"

"Just a friend," she said. "Can you come in for a second?"

"I'm late for work already."

"Please, it's important," she said.

"Fine," he said, heading back up their wood porch. Valerie began to follow.

"Wait!" Bridge got out of the car and ran up to Valerie, throwing her arms around her. "Don't be afraid," she whispered. Valerie let a tear slip and nodded her head before climbing the steps herself.

We both got back into the car and drove a little bit in silence before Bridge started to break down. She faced the window, but I could see her pained expression through the reflection.

"We pretend we got rid of it," I said.

"Okay," she said, her hand going to her belly.

"I have an idea, but I need some time."

"Fine."

CHAPTER EIGHT

I KNEW I only had a few days before my dad figured out that Bridge was still pregnant, and I had an idea of what I needed to do, but I was looking for the perfect opportunity to do it.

Christmas Eve morning, two days after we left the clinic, I woke early, throwing on a t-shirt because it felt a little chilly. Our house was pretty much floor-to-ceiling windows, and the floors were stone. In other words, it didn't matter how much money you had, it was damn near impossible to warm the place.

I dialed August, my roommate back at Brown. Ladies, hands over ears. This is how dudes talk and I apologize.

"What's up, fucker," he answered. Told ya.

"Hey, asshole. What are you up to?"

"Oh, you know, a little of this, little of that. This is named Ashley, that is named Farrah."

I laughed. "You're a sick bastard."

"I learned from the best, douche."

"I taught you much, young Jedi, but I never taught you that. Guess I'm just a higher breed of human."

"I'm gonna take an axe to that fucking pedestal, nuckfut."

"Still couldn't knock me down to your level." I laughed before turning serious. "Listen, uh, I'm sort of in a jam out here. Think you could do me a favor?"

"Yeah, whatever you need, dude," he added, all joking aside.

When I got off the phone with August, I padded over to Bridge's room and knocked on her door.

"Come in," she grumbled.

I opened the door and found her hunched over a trash can.

"*Yeah*, we're not going to be able to hide this for long," I said, shutting the door behind me.

"Shut up," she complained uncharacteristically.

"Why don't you keep crackers by your bed?" I asked, repeating something I'd overheard somewhere.

I noticed her face looked pale and her eyes were watery. I wanted to kick the ass who did this to her.

"I do, but nothing works. Nothing. I mean, *nothing works*. All eating crackers gives me is something more substantial to throw up. God," she groaned, "I wish I'd never let this happen."

"Dude, it's pointless now. What's done is done."

"Thank you, Spence," she bit sarcastically.

I hid a smirk.

"What's the plan? Send me off to our cousin's? Pretend my nonexistent husband died in the war?"

"Funny, but not *too* far off."

"What does that mean?"

"I mean, we have to hide, Bridge."

"Maybe I can, like, take a semester off, have the baby here, give it up or something."

"He'll never go for that. He'd never risk being exposed."

"Well, maybe-maybe we—" she began, the backs of her hands against her cheeks.

"We can't *anything* other than leave L.A."

"I can't," she answered desperately. She stood, then realized she could barely stay upright so she slumped at the edge of her bed. "I can't leave L.A. All my friends are here, school. What about Mom?"

"Mama's afraid of Dad, Bridge. She'll only stop us."

"Maybe she'd come with us," she added wildly, wringing her hands.

"She won't. She'll try to stop us and you know it."

Bridge's hands pushed her hair out of her face. "I can't do this without Mama, Spence."

"Yes, you can. I'll be there."

"It's not the same," she said honestly.

My heart broke for her a little. "I know, Bridge, and I'm sorry for that, but this is what we have to work with."

"What are we going to do about money? Where are we going to go?"

"I've got some money," I hedged. "August is helping us with the rest."

"August knows?"

"Yeah, I had to tell him."

She huffed, reminding me of the teenager she was and making me cringe a little. "Fine."

"Okay," I said, stretching across the carpet that laid at the foot of her bed. My feet hung over a few feet but I didn't care. I tucked my hands behind my head. "Okay," I repeated, trying to remember everything August and I talked about. "August's grandparents own a remote cattle ranch in Montana. He's going to talk to them and let us know if we can hide out there, at least until you turn eighteen and Dad can't touch us."

"Dad can find us anywhere. This seems pointless," she said, hanging her head in her hands.

"Not this time, trust me." She didn't believe me, but she wasn't going to argue. "You know how Dad always yells at us about how he doesn't want the liability if we ever got drunk and killed someone driving?"

"Asshole," she said under her breath.

"Well, Mom told me he put our cars in our names to release that liability."

"No way," Bridge said, her eyes widened as she caught on.

"I know exactly where he put the titles in his office."

"He'll know you've been in there."

"So what? We'll be long gone before then."

"So we sell the cars and live off that money."

"Yeah," I said. "Well, that and I've got some money saved up."

"How much?" she asked, crashing back down on the bed, her legs still hanging off the end.

Seven million two hundred ninety-three thousand eight hundred fifty-nine dollars and seventeen cents. I hesitated. If I was honest with her, she'd have to know *everything.* "Enough," I evaded again.

"How much is enough, Spence?" she insisted.

"Enough to get us to Montana and to feed ourselves, pay for baby shit, all that. We wouldn't have to worry."

"Okay," she said, satisfied enough with that dodgy response. "When will you hear from August?"

"Tonight most likely." Bridge got really quiet. "What's up?"

"Will we ever see Mom again?"

"I'm sure of it."

"When?"

"As soon as we can, Bridge. We can call her as soon as you turn eighteen, if you want."

GREED

This seemed to ease her mind a bit.
"What do we do now?" she asked.
"We wait."

GREED FURY LUST IDLE BINGE ENVY VAIN

CHAPTER NINE

CHRISTMAS MORNING went by in a blur. My dad wasn't there, and my mom was picking up on our strange vibes. She didn't dwell on them too much. I think she figured it was residual emotion from Bridget's ordeal and didn't ask too many questions. That, or she didn't want to face what she thought our dad made Bridge do. Yeah, I was disappointed, but either way it worked out in our favor.

The night before, August called and filled me in on the plan. His grandparents lived in Bitterroot, Montana, and would be expecting us within the week, if we could get away. They had a trailer prepared for us and knew our predicament. They were willing to host us for however long we needed. I felt grateful.

I'd searched the distance between Los Angeles and Bitterroot and come up with a freaking nineteen-hour drive. It was going to be a bitch to drive a nauseous Bridge for that long, not to mention that once we arrived there wasn't going to be much for us to do. I shit you not,

GREED

Bitterroot consisted of a fire station, post office, school, and a single Exxon. I am not screwing with you. *Bridge better believe how much I love her since I'm doing this crap for her.*

My mom and dad would be leaving the day after Christmas for some party my dad's lawyer's firm was having in New York City. It was also supposed to be riddled with some sort of business deal that I had no interest in hearing about, but I did know they were leaving early the twenty-sixth, three-in-the-morning kind of early, and on his private jet to make it in time to check into their room and attend whatever bullshit meeting my dad had scheduled. They would attend the party that night and return the twenty-seventh around five in the evening our mom told us. We had thirty-nine hours.

Thirty-nine hours.

I stayed up until two in the morning waiting for them to leave, and then I went into survival mode. I'd already packed two bags and hidden them under my bed, and Bridge had done the same. Since we'd graduated junior high, my mom stopped employing live-in help to reduce the temptation my dad had with "messing" with our nannies and occasional maids. (Like I said before, douche.) So, Bridge left a note on their entrance door letting them know they could have the next two days off and wished them a Merry Christmas, which allowed us thirty-nine clear hours to erase our existences as we knew them...at least until Bridge's baby was born.

"Bridge," I said quietly at her door around four in the morning.

"Yeah," her sleepy voice rang out.

"You ready?"

"As ready as I'm ever going to be."

She opened her door for me and was dressed, though her hair was wet.

"Where are your bags?" I asked, checking the room.

"In my closet."

I made my way through her room to the closet and took in just how many clothes she was leaving behind. She only had a single bag of clothing.

"What in the hell, Bridge? This isn't going to last you."

She met me inside.

"None of my shit fits me anymore. None of my jeans will even button. It's infuriating. It's, like, I'm not showing really but the buttons refuse to close."

"Probably because they were too small to begin with," I said in frustration.

"What the hell is that supposed to mean?"

I sighed. "Nothing, Bridge. We'll find you some clothes later."

I grabbed her small bag of t-shirts and a few jeans and another she had packed with shoes and whatever else girls need then threw it next to mine at the bottom of the stairs before making a quick sweep of my room to make sure I got everything I needed. I turned to leave but stopped at the door, examining everything. I knew there was a very good chance I was never going to see that room again.

As it turns out, though I thought my local bank opened at six in the morning, in truth that was only the drive-thru, which was frustrating as crap because they wouldn't issue a cashier's check without checking ID in person. The lobby didn't open until seven-thirty, so Bridge and I went for breakfast at a twenty-four-hour place to pass the time. We were losing valuable hours, and that made me exceedingly nervous.

"Can you just, like, I can't stand the silence," she said, shivering opposite me in our fiberglass booth.

"Cold?" I asked.

"No, nervous."

GREED

"Okay, well, Bitterroot, the town they live near, is in the northwest portion of Montana. Today's high's supposed to be thirty-one degrees and the low should be around twelve."

"God," she said, wrapping her ski jacket tighter around herself. I stopped. "Keep going," she added when the waitress brought orange juice.

I pulled up a map of Montana on my phone. "August's grandparents' ranch is called Hunt Ranch." My finger searched the map. "Right there," I said, pointing to an area outside of Bitterroot, Montana. "He says there's approximately five thousand acres to hide ourselves in and that it butts against the northwest tip of Lake Gossamer then spreads west, it lies west of the city of Bitterroot. I did a little research and figured we'd have to drive south," I said, my finger following the highway on the phone, "into Kalispell for anything important though."

"Why?"

"'Cause Bitterroot is smaller than any small town you've ever been to."

"Oh, Christ. That's depressing."

"From what I can tell, though, the scenery is probably some of the most beautiful we'll ever see," I offered.

She considered this. "Beautiful, huh?"

"Yeah, colder than a witch's titty, though."

She shook her head at me but smirked. "Classy."

"I know. The ranch is owned by August's grandparents, Emmett and Ellie. He's got a cousin there named Cricket. I think he might be a little older than you. He graduated from high school a few months ago, apparently. Anyway, Cricket and August are pretty close."

"Well, at least there might be someone to talk to there."

"There'll be more than just someone. It's a working ranch, Bridge, which means there will be at least twenty people there on a daily basis."

Our food arrived but neither of us ate much for a myriad of reasons. I slapped two twenties down and we left right as the bank's lobby was opening.

The bank was where I kept any liquid funds I needed. It only had about two hundred thousand in it. My remaining fortune was kept in a Swiss account for obvious reasons. My stomach flipped when I thought on the two million I'd lost in Vegas. I knew my dad well enough when I opened the account to understand that if he could manipulate my funds, he would. He's transparent like that. I needed an account he had zero access to and the Swiss provided that for me. So that meant that any local funds needed to be removed immediately and the accounts closed.

"Hello, welcome to Wells Fargo. I'm Kelli, how can I help you?" a young blonde banker asked as soon as we walked in.

"Yes, uh, I need to close my accounts."

"Oh, well, that's a shame. Take a seat," she said, gesturing to two chairs in front of her desk. "Do you have your account number?"

I handed her all my information, including my license and debit card. She clicked a few keys on her keyboard and studied a monitor in front of her. Her eyes widened a bit before she checked her expression.

"It's unusual to see someone so young with a balance like this."

Bridge looked at me, no doubt wondering how much I had. Little did she know. You see, it wasn't that I didn't really want her to know. I just didn't want her to know how I got it.

"Uh, yeah, I'm a good saver," I evaded.

She smiled. "Oh, well, is there anything we can do to keep your business?"

"Unfortunately, no. The bank's been great. I just-we're moving."

"Oh, I see. That's nice. Where are you moving to?" she asked. *Nosy fool.*

"Virginia," I lied quickly.

"Oh, going to school there?" she fished.

"I am," I lied again.

"All right," she said, turning back toward her computer. "This is your balance." She discreetly wrote the figure on a piece of paper and slid it over to me. I glanced over at it to make sure it fit the number I remembered. The number was correct, but underneath she'd added another message of her own, including her phone number.

I slid the piece of paper into my back pocket and smiled. "Thanks," I said. The last thing I needed if my father waltzed in here asking if anyone had seen us was this ridiculous girl squealing.

Kelli handed me a withdrawal slip and I began to fill it out, shielding the amount from Bridge nonchalantly with my forearm. I'd done some math and research before we left and knew exactly how much cash I needed to purchase a modest truck with, as well as the essentials, like gas and food for the trip there.

"The remaining in a cashier's check?" she asked, smiling at me like she'd won something.

"Yes, please," I smiled back.

She stood and walked to the teller's station.

"What are you going to do with a cashier's check?" Bridge asked.

"I can't very well walk around with thousands of dollars in my pocket, can I?"

She eyed me, one brow raised precariously over her eye. "I don't know. It depends on how many thousands you have."

I sighed. "You think you're so clever."

She laughed. "I know I am."

I grinned at her. "It's a lot of thousands."

Her gaze narrowed on me, her arms locked around herself. "What the hell did you do?" she whispered.

"Nothing," I said, leaning back into my chair but turning my own stare out the window to my left.

"Bull. Complete bull," she said, calling me out. "No more lies, dude. Spill. What is going on?"

"I may have been a sort of a *lackey* for Dad."

She sat up a little. "No, Spence," she said, sounding more than a little disappointed.

"I'm sorry," I bit back. "Did you just cast the first stone, preggo?"

She balked aloud and punched my shoulder. "Please. This is *not even* in the same ballpark, buddy."

I sighed. "I don't want to talk about this right now, Bridge."

She sat up even straighter. "Too bad, Spence," she began, but the banker returned, saving me from any immediate beatdown.

"Here you go," Kelli said, sitting down. "You're all set," she continued, handing me an envelope. Her hand lingered on mine and I tried not to pull away too abruptly.

"Thank you," I said, smiling.

"If you visit the teller station on the far right, she'll be able to count your cash out for you."

"Thanks again," I said.

I got up and Bridge followed me to the station. The teller greeted us and began to count out the cash. I nodded when she laid down the last hundred. She tucked it into another envelope and handed it over. I placed both envelopes in the inside pocket of my coat. We left and got into our vehicles. Bridge followed me to one of the upscale dealerships off the highway and I'd never been more grateful for the silence. I was starting to feel I was in over my head.

CHAPTER TEN

"Welcome to—" the girl at the front desk began, but I cut her off, frustrated, overwhelmed and feeling like we'd wasted too much time already.

"Is your manager in?" I asked.

If she was taken aback by my abruptness, her expression didn't show it. "Of course, just a moment," she said, removing herself from her chair and click-clacking over to the manager's office.

"Can I help you?" an overweight gentleman with a buzz cut asked.

"Spencer Blackwell," I said, offering my hand.

My name registered with him. "Ah, Mister Blackwell, you can call me Jeff. How are you this morning?"

"I'm well, Jeff. I need to unload these two vehicles," I said, pointing to my Aston and Bridge's SLS.

"What are you looking for them?" he asked.

"No less than one-point-two." His eyes lit up. They were worth half a million more resale.

"I can't do that," he said, already chiming in with a cliché.

"How about this, have your men check them out. See if they meet your standards, then we'll talk."

I didn't really have time for this. I was already getting antsy. We'd wasted hours.

"Fine. Martin!" he shouted toward the girl at the desk. She nodded and pressed a button.

A man in blue coveralls came out.

"Martin, can you check out these vehicles for me."

"Yes, sir," Martin answered.

Twenty minutes later and Martin returned with a thumbs up, saving Bridge and me from ridiculous small talk with the car salesman. "SLS needs some realigning, but other than that they're perfection."

"My office?" Jeff asked.

I nodded and followed him back before sitting before him.

"And you have the titles?" he asked.

"In my pocket."

"Why do you want to sell?" he asked.

"Unnecessary," I answered. "Are you interested or not?"

"I'll take them for one."

"Not in a million years," I challenged, sliding deeper into my chair, my right hand casually resting on the side of my face. "I've offered one-point-two. It's more than fair. They're in almost perfect condition, and their commercial resale is close to one-point-seven. You know it. I know it. But if you feel like you need to win here, how about we meet in the middle?"

"I'm listening," he said.

Fifteen minutes later, Bridge and I walked out the sliding front door and stood, another check next to the one I already had, and our bags at our feet.

"Where to?" she asked.

"We walk," I said pointing to a dealership half a mile south, "to that truck dealership."

"I can't walk that far carrying these bags. I'll stay here and you can come get me when you're done," she said.

"I'll carry the bags," I said.

"You can't carry all these bags, Spence. I'll stay."

"You don't understand. When Dad finds out we sold the cars, he's going to ask around and these guys won't forget buying two luxury sports cars in one day, especially when they see what the guy who sold them to them picked you up in. You have to come."

"Fine," she pouted.

I gathered as many bags as possible and pushed on toward the dealership.

"I can't believe you can carry all that shit. You're not even breaking a sweat," Bridge commented halfway there. "I can't even keep up."

"Yeah, well, I have to do this kind of training for rowing at school. Upper body strength is number one for that team."

"Damn, that must suck."

"Tell me about it," I laughed, spearing her with a look. She laughed. "Sorry."

I took a deep breath. "Although, it doesn't suck when we race at parties."

"I'm afraid to even ask."

"We toss a girl on each shoulder and race down the street with them."

She rolled her eyes.

"The girls love it."

"Anyone in particular?" she asked.

"Does it matter now?" I quipped.

"I suppose not, asshole."

"Sorry," I said, realizing I was taking my frustrations

out on her. "I'm still getting over Soph," I said, referring to my old prep school friend.

Sophie Price was the most beautiful girl you'd ever met. Seriously. Take it from someone who's met Bar Refaeli in person. Soph was even more stunning. Especially since she'd had a personality makeover. I'd never regret anything as much as not making her fall in love with me.

"You can't make anyone fall, Spence. Either they do or they don't."

"I said that out loud?"

"Duh, and it's been two years, Spencer. You seriously need to get over her. She's with that Ian guy anyway, right?"

"Right."

"That hot South African guy named Ian," she concluded.

"Thanks."

"That hot Saffy named Ian who gives his life to mutilated Ugandan orphans and worships the ground Sophie walks on."

I stopped and glared at her. "That'll do, Bridge."

She pretended to zip her mouth closed and we kept walking.

I'd researched the truck dealership beforehand and knew exactly which vehicle I wanted. A black Ford F150 crew cab.

"You're kidding me," Bridge deadpanned when she saw it.

"I'm not," I said. "We're moving to a ranch. In Montana. I'm not kidding."

I started to fill the bed with our bags as a salesman came barreling toward us.

"How you doing, folks?"

"I'm going to make your life easy," I told him, settling

in the last bag. "This is the truck we want. I'm willing to pay fifteen hundred below asking price and in cash."

He grinned from ear to ear. "Let me talk to my manager," he told us before running back toward the main building.

"Stay with the bags?" I asked.

"Sure," she said, pulling the tailgate down and settling in for the wait.

"I'd take this opportunity to say goodbye to your phone."

"You're crapping me."

"Bridge, you're a walking blip on Dad's radar with it. Come on."

"Fine," she huffed.

"And don't contact anyone you know letting them know what's going on!" I yelled back as I followed the salesman.

"I know, idiot!" she yelled back, making me laugh.

Another fifty-seven minutes later, and I had the keys in my hand. The title I had mailed to Brown and put it in August's name. I'd told August to expect it.

"We're done, Bridge," I said.

She hopped off the tailgate and I began filling the backseats of the cab with our luggage. Bridge lifted the tailgate and hopped into the passenger side. I followed suit and got in the driver's.

She looked around her, inspecting the interior with her hands. "It's actually pretty comfortable," she admitted.

"'Merican made," I said, exaggerating the drawl a little.

"What now?" she asked.

I grabbed my GPS from my bag and mounted it to the dash.

"That's not built in?" she said.

GREED

I laughed my response.

"We're done," I told her, settling into my seat.

"This is it," she said, an obvious lump in her throat.

I didn't want to say it but I had to. "Can I have your phone?"

She studied it in her hands and looked sad. I knew she wasn't unhappy about the phone itself, but the phone represented a lifeline to our mom.

"Bridge," I said softly, reaching my hand out.

She put it in my hand and I took it with mine to find the nearest trash can. On the way, I rang August one more time, letting him know we were about to head out and I'd ring him at the nearest payphone when I could. He assured me everything was in place and we hung up.

I slipped both phones into a sturdy plastic bag then placed it on the ground. I raised my booted foot and beat the ever-loving hell out of the contents in that bag. When I was done, I peered inside and found nothing but mutilated pieces of glass and plastic, microchips and two batteries. I dug through the mess and found the SD cards. I took the lighter in my pocket I'd brought just for such a reason and burned them into charred unrecognizable pieces, letting them cool before throwing them back in the bag and then into the garbage.

Goodbye, Los Angeles. Goodbye, Dad. Goodbye, life.

It's for Bridge, I kept chanting in my head over and over as I headed back to the truck.

CHAPTER
ELEVEN

WE'D GOTTEN on the road by noon, just in time for Bridge to feel "starving." We stopped at some fast food restaurant and got her something. The entire nineteen-hour drive turned into a two-day fiasco of her feeling ill, me stopping to feed her what seemed like every hour, getting a crappy room at a hotel that would take only cash, filling up the bottomless tank (the truck, not Bridge), staying within the speed limit to avoid getting pulled over, getting Bridge clothes when we got to Salt Lake City and all the while driving by myself.

Yet, I wasn't looking forward to reaching Bitterroot because it meant a life I wasn't prepared for, a life I didn't really want. I'm aware how selfish that sounds, but the thought of not being able to return to Brown, despite the fact I didn't want to go when I first graduated, was brutal. I'd grown to love Brown, the people there, even my professors. I missed my teammates already. I missed the girls. The glorious girls with their short shorts and bright smiles.

I needed to get Brown out of my head. I was never going back there, and I needed to get used to that.

"How much longer?" Bridge asked. I hadn't known she'd awoken.

"We're about an hour away," I told her, the sinking realization that we were too far gone now.

"Mama's probably panicking right about now."

I nodded my reply.

Bridge started tearing up. "I'm afraid, Spence."

"Bridge, it's seriously going to be okay."

"I hate being judged. What if everyone there judges me? I don't think I can handle being judged...at least not without Mom there."

I sighed.

"Did you know I wore glasses when I was younger?"

"Of course," she told me quietly through tears.

"Okay, but listen. I was five years old, sitting in my assigned seat at the back of the classroom. My teacher called on me, asked me to read something she'd written on the board. I didn't know what to do. I couldn't see what she'd written and thought it was because of some insufficiency on my part that I couldn't see the board. I thought I wasn't as smart as the other kids. So I sat there, quiet, adrenaline pumping through my little body at a rapid rate, eyes burning, on the verge of tears. The class had turned to look at me by this point, fifty eyes studying me, waiting. She asked again, her tone laced with impatience, but I had nothing to tell her. A few kids started snickering around me, some accused me of being stupid; others giggled with each other. Although it was only a handful, an adrenaline-filled fear kicked into high gear and affected me more deeply than I had ever remembered feeling affected. My pulse strummed feverishly from the tips of my ears to the ends of my fingers. Hot tears betrayed me, spilling over onto my cheeks, making those who were laughing, laugh harder. I was humiliated."

"How sad."

"Yeah, but then my teacher did something I hadn't expected. She stood up for me. Hushed the other children, came to my side, took my hand and whispered in my ear. She asked me if I could see the board and I answered her honestly."

"What did she do?" Bridge asked.

"She picked me up, wrapped her arms around me, walked me closer to the board and just like that, the words appeared clearly to me, the judging sounds of the other children grew quiet, and I knew exactly what they were, could read them perfectly. Where once I had no answer, suddenly I had one, and that fear, that anxiety, that adrenaline turned to calm. I realized that all I had to do to solve my problem was to get close to it, approach it, to see it more clearly. I had nothing to fear after all." Bridge's tears fell harder. "I know the answer feels cloudy right now. I know we can't read what our future is because we feel so far away from it, but I promise you, Bridge, we're getting closer to the blackboard. And when we get there, all that fear, all that *overwhelming* fear of not knowing what lays ahead for us will dissipate. In the end, we'll have a beautiful little soul to take care of, and we'll discover that we had nothing *really* to fear. We'll discover that our problem wasn't genuinely a problem after all, not after we've seen it for what it actually is. In the light of day, when our adrenaline wears off, we'll discover that all we *truly* feared was the unknown."

"And the children who laughed? Judged you?" she asked. "What did they have to say?"

"By recess, they'd forgotten all about it, moved on

to the next poor sap. You see, all my problem was for them was something to focus on simply because they enjoyed it. They relished scandal just as much as the girls you pal around with, just as much as a lot of people we'll encounter on the way, but they forget, Bridge. They always do. They move on with fiery intensity, hungry to latch on to their next victim. They're constantly searching to kick those who are already down. They make it impossible for you to make a clear-headed decision. We're all so afraid of what everyone around us thinks that we risk ourselves to desperation. It's utterly stupid. It's utterly frightening. But it's utterly *human*."

"I hate being judged, though," she said.

"Who doesn't, Bridge? *Who doesn't*? But I ask you this, huh? Why in the hell do we care what others think about us?"

"Because we're human."

"But as humans, we're also capable of forward thinking. I consider myself fairly progressive. I'm choosing right now to rise above those self-righteous assholes. I'm choosing to live the life I want to live, splintered prying eyes be damned."

She wiped the tears away and laughed. "Yeah. Screw 'em."

And all the while I bolstered my little sister...I also found that I'd bolstered myself. *Come on, Bitterroot.*

CHAPTER TWELVE

WE PULLED onto the little dirt road off the highway, the only indication we were in the right place was the little rickety sign, hanging off its side that read HUNT RANCH, which was difficult to read because of the snow piled so high against it. It took us a little longer than I'd anticipated to travel the five-mile trek to the ranch because I'd never driven in snow before, not this kind of snow anyway. It wasn't an issue of traction but visibility.

"You weren't lying. This place is incredible," Bridge said, her face plastered to the frosted window.

Mountains capped with white glittered in the setting sun amongst cotton ball clouds. A million diamonds appeared to reflect in the surface of those caps before your gaze bled down to a dark ebony rock—a dichotomy of nature. It was pure magnificence. If you followed the mountain line to the base, a sea of powdered snow-covered pine trees meandered their way toward the road we were traveling.

GREED

"*So* beautiful," Bridge breathed. A tad bit lighter of heart, I thought.

"Yeah, makes me want to drink a beer," I teased.

Her head whipped my direction, she laughed and shook her head. "You're an idiot," she said before returning her eyes to the sights.

I laughed.

A song rang from the stereo, making our surroundings feel even more breathtaking, if possible.

"I'm suddenly not so scared," Bridge said.

We rounded the bend and came upon the ranch. It was everything I imagined an old-fashioned cattle ranch deep in Montana would look like. Nothing but a myriad of wood buildings alive with people.

We wound around to what looked like the main house. It was a two-story cabin with one large wall of windows jutting up and out in the center, but the roof over those windows extended out, covering a large wide deck and was supported by two huge trunks of what looked like very old trees.

The home was set a little farther up on a hill with its back to the mountains. A wide wood staircase ascended to the deck and met the broad wood front door underneath the overhang. There wasn't a cut board in sight, just weathered logs shined to an impossible sheen thanks to time, weather and many, many hands.

Our tires crunched the snow and we came to a slow stop in front of the stairs next to five different rusted trucks, dusted with random boots, gloves, the occasional tool and scattered hay. One even had a saddle straddling its bed wall. I cringed when I pulled in next to them, knowing our new truck probably stuck out like a sore thumb.

"I take that back," Bridge amended.

"No shit," I said, a little bit intimidated myself.

This was farther from home than I'd ever realized. This was friggin' Mars.

I got out and planted my foot in snow that was made icy by footprints and tire marks. I took a step and I almost bit it, catching myself on the bed wall before righting myself once again. I shook my head. *Don't drop, dude.* I started my way over to Bridge's side and opened her door for her.

A high-pitched whistle caught our attention. "Hi there!" a tall guy a little older than me yelled.

He waved his hand to stay us then jogged our way. I took the guy in. He was six-foot-two or -three, maybe one-eighty, his shoulders told me he was a manual labor kind of dude and that, if he needed to, he could knock you the shit out.

"Cricket?" I asked.

The guy laughed, which I thought odd, but he didn't explain himself.

"No, Cricket's my cousin. Jonah Hunt," he introduced himself, his breath freezing midair. He removed a red-blistered hand by biting his leatherwork glove and held it out to me.

"Spencer Blackwell," I said, shaking the offered hand.

"I'm one of Emmett and Ellie's grandkids."

"Nice to meet you," I said.

Jonah turned to Bridge and his eyes widened before he cooled them to a forced apathy. I narrowed my own gaze.

"Jonah, this is my sister, Bridget," I said, introducing her.

"You can call me Bridge," she said.

He stuck out his hand for her and she took it. "Nice to meet you," he offered with a smile. His straight white teeth were stark against his windburned red cheeks.

I hadn't noticed, but a few other ranch hands had

begun to get curious. No doubt they were anticipating us today and had seen our truck pull in. An older couple was making their way toward us and Jonah gestured toward them.

"There they are," he said.

When they were just a few feet away, Jonah yelled out. "Pop Pop, this is Spencer," he said resting his hand on my shoulder briefly before angling himself a little closer to Bridge, "and Bridget Blackwell."

"A pleasure, sir," the older gentleman said, offering his hand as well. He was tall and stood with a strength I'd rarely seen in a man of his years, a product of his profession, I suspected, with salt-and-pepper hair and sagging cheeks. "Emmett Hunt," he continued. "This is my wife, Ellie."

The older woman's clear cerulean blue eyes squinted in the sun and a weathered hand shadowed her stare. "So lovely to meet you," she said before getting closer, her eyes showed deep laugh lines.

Her cool hands found my cheeks and she smiled before moving to Bridge, doing the same for her but her hands lingered there.

"Welcome, brave girl," she said simply.

Bridge's eyes began to glass and she smiled back. "Thank you."

"Well, you've caught us at the end of our workday," she said, stepping back to stand with her husband. "Although, the work never really stops, but you've come just in time for dinner, which is a grand thing because we're preparing something a little extra special for you." She winked. "Jonah will show you to your trailer so you can settle in and rest a bit while I get it all sewed-up."

"Thank you," Bridge and I said in unison.

"Welcome to Hunt Ranch!" she said, before bounding up the steps behind Emmett.

"Hop in your truck and I'll show you the way," Jonah said.

We did as he instructed and I rolled down my window for him when he jumped on the truck's step bar.

He bent down slightly. "Back up a bit and head in that direction," he said, pointing at a cluster of wood buildings. I did so, slowly. "That was the main house, as you can guess. This here," he said pointing again to a tall wood structure to our left. It was open but covered. "This is our hay storage. Next to that is our main barn and the pen's attached to that on the other side." We rounded a small bend. "Carriage house to store all our machinery. A few of us ranch hands live above the carriage house, including myself," he said, glancing at Bridge. I felt like clocking him, but he was just trying to be nice. That didn't mean I had to like the attention he was giving her. "Horse barn," he continued. "We've got a few other little buildings a hundred yards or so that direction." He pointed east and I saw a peppering of buildings. "Those were original to the ranch in the late eighteen hundreds. Here we are," he said, gesturing to the left. "All of these weren't built until nineteen-twenty or so. They don't look that much different, do they?" he laughed.

We came upon a little silver Airstream tucked below some pine trees at the bottom of the sloping hill parallel to the main house. Bridge looked at me and I shook my head to keep quiet until we were alone. Jonah walked off the step bar as I came to a stop near the trailer and ran around to the passenger side, opening the door for Bridge.

"Thank you," she said, taking his hand and stepping down.

I opened the back doors and started grabbing bags. Jonah followed suit by opening the back door nearest him and grabbed the remaining. I nodded my thanks.

GREED

He led us to the trailer and walked the small stairwell to the round pocket door and opened it. I stepped inside after him, directly to my right was a built-in sofa that butted against the width of the trailer, save for a small wall of cabinets that lay perpendicular against the wall farthest from the door. Along that same wall, was a small fridge, closet, and across from those was a small sink and stove. There was also a small laminate table in front of the sofa. Past the center accordion doors laid two small twin beds on opposite ends of the trailer walls and beyond that, a small bathroom with toilet, sink, and tub with shower. The entire place was a trip back in time to the seventies, complete with gold laminate floors and countertops, but it looked and smelled clean and had new mattresses and bedding. *I hope they didn't buy that for us*, I thought. I felt bad enough imposing on their hospitality as it was.

"There's heat, electricity and running water," Jonah mentioned, setting our stuff on the sofa. "Although, you might want to keep a few extra blankets around when a blizzard comes 'round, and they will."

"Thank you, Jonah," Bridge said, studying her surroundings. "We're very grateful," she added.

Jonah smiled and nodded. "I'll leave you to it. Dinner's in an hour. See you there?"

"Of course," Bridge answered waving at him before closing the door.

We stood in silence, taking in our surroundings.

"It's-It's definitely different than L.A.," she said, breaking the quiet.

I was used to living in confined spaces living in a Brown dorm, but this was all very new to her.

"You're going to be okay with this?" I asked.

She stiffened her upper lip. "Of course. I wasn't lying when I said I was grateful. Besides, maybe they've got a shop in town. We can, like, spruce it up a bit?"

I laughed at her. "That's cool, Bridge. I'll give you some cash."

"Can we afford it?" she asked.

I pretended to calculate in my head. "I think we can swing it. Besides, I need to go into Kalispell for a few things anyway. Find a bank, somehow open an account without Dad finding out, find a doctor for you."

Her face dropped. "I almost forgot," she said, a sad smile gracing her face. "The whole reason we're here."

"Exactly," I added, inspecting the trailer, "which means boys aren't even an option out here."

"What the hell?"

"I saw how Jonah looked at you. I'm just sayin'."

She rolled her eyes. "Which bed do you want?"

"Bridge, I mean it, no boys."

She stiffened her back. "Spencer, you really know how to piss a girl off, don't you? Trust me, my focus is a little preoccupied at the moment."

CHAPTER THIRTEEN

WE UNPACKED as best we could and I noticed there wasn't a TV or pretty much anything of convenience really.

"We're going to have to make a list," I said, stepping back out into the cold.

Bridge closed the door behind her and ran to the truck. We drove back to the main house when Ellie asked us to. The ranch seemed pretty quiet from what we could tell, except for a few guys here and there. One in particular was on a horse and heading toward the barn. He looked like he might have been Native American, but his features appeared mixed. The only confirmation I could get was that he had a long ponytail at the base of his neck wrapped in leather.

"Hummina-hummina-hummina," Bridge joked.

"No," I reiterated.

"I can look," she laughed.

We parked where we had before and made our way up the wood stairs. I dragged my hand over the smooth wooden handrail. I couldn't believe how smooth the wood was. We knocked on the main door and stood hopping in our boots while we waited for someone to answer. We saw Ellie run toward us and swing open one of the double doors.

"Sorry, we usually enter through the side door. It's closer to the dining hall."

We walked in and took in the expanse of the main room. It was larger than our own main room back home. I'd failed to gauge just how large the home was from the outside because it was overshadowed by the surrounding mountains. The walls were covered in Indian blankets and stuffed animal heads. In the middle of the thirty-foot ceiling dangled a large antler chandelier.

It's all Petticoat Junction and shit in here, I thought as I looked around. I unknowingly slapped my hands together and rubbed them back and forth. I let Ellie think it was about the cold. *Now, if I could only find a Bobbie Jo.*

Just then, across the main room, entering from some sort of back door, a small figure emerged. She closed the door behind her after a large German shepherd mix shook out his coat and sat panting beside her. Time seemed to stand still as she stomped the snow off her rubber riding boots and removed her large jacket and gloves, revealing the shapeliest body I'd seen in years. She had these long gray socks under her boots that rose to just below the knee over her skintight jeans. My eyes traveled up.

I took in a red plaid button-up fitted to her like a glove. My stomach clenched waiting for her face, but she seemed to take forever unwrapping her scarf. Round and round and round her hand went, but she turned right when I could have gotten a good look. I cursed her under my breath. I felt this inexplicable urge to run over to her and turn her around.

GREED

She hung up her scarf next to her jacket and pulled her cap off her head. She shook out chin-length straight dark black hair then ran her hands throughout its length, smoothing out any knots. She bent over, sending me reeling and unzipped the long zippers on the backs of her rubber boots, stepping out of them and landing on the floor in her socks.

I discovered that she was the cutest, sexiest little thing I'd ever seen, and I hadn't even seen her face yet.

She began to turn and I held my breath in anticipation.

Holy. Shit.

The full sight of her nearly blew me over. I felt this punch to my gut and chest I'd never felt before, not even with Sophie. My hand went to my heart as if I could stop its pounding. This girl was beyond stunning. A French cut bob on a heart-shaped face. Her cheeks glowed a bright pink from the cold, highlighting her high cheekbones. Her eyebrows arched perfectly over big, bright round eyes with the longest lashes I've ever seen on a chick. Her mouth formed a perfect moue. Her pouty lips were fuller on the bottom. Her button nose was straight and so soft looking I wanted to kiss it more than anything in the world. I would have paid a million dollars in that moment to do just that. I felt like a perfect tool just for thinking it.

She was pixie-like in her stature as well, standing, maybe, five foot three. She stepped forward, no, stretched forward like a dancer, and smoothed her hands down her hair once more. I sucked in a breath, not realizing I already hadn't.

That's when she noticed us and smirked a little, betraying a cleverness I didn't think could be conveyed with a single facial expression. She stalked toward us looking altogether innocent yet at the same time *very* dangerous. She was punk met West, like Christina Ricci met *Annie Get Your Gun*. This girl *looked* feisty.

"Ah, Cricket," Ellie said, wrapping her arm around the girl's shoulders.

This *was Cricket?!* I felt bowled over. This *girl* was August's cousin? I'd always assumed she was a dude. *No wonder Jonah laughed.*

"Grandma," she acknowledged, eyeing me with a hooded tiger's gaze. She had her grandmother's cerulean eyes.

"Cricket, this is Spencer Blackwell and his sister Bridget."

"Nice to meet you," she purred.

Roll that tongue up, buddy. Drool is unattractive. Cricket winked at me like she could read my thoughts and I almost fell backward. I smiled. *Cheeky little minx.*

Yeah, feisty was a perfect word for her.

I watched her bounce on the balls of her feet, smiling, and fiddling with the bottom hem of her shirt. She gestured with her hands a lot. Her fingers were slender and topped with a deep purple. She kept them short. I liked girls with short nails. They looked more feminine to me than when worn long. Her hair shook back and forth when she talked, her short bangs resting across her brows. She would occasionally blow at them then smooth them back down with her hands. When she laughed, she laughed with her entire body, throwing her head back and revealing dimples at her cheeks.

My God, I was so attracted to this chick. I couldn't even pin it down to one thing. If you took everything I'd ever found hot, beautiful in a girl and piled them into a corner, you'd get Cricket Hunt...standing in a corner.

I stood, staring at her for God only knows how long until Bridge elbowed me. "Did you hear that, Spence?" she gritted.

"I'm sorry?" I asked, genuinely lost.

GREED

Her eyes bugged a little at me, silently telling me to get my head in the game. "Ellie was saying that Kalispell's close by. I was telling her we'd need to go into town for a few things, find a doctor and a bank."

"Yeah," I said, clearing my throat, then glancing my way back to Cricket. I couldn't keep my eyes off her. "We need to find a bank and a doctor for Bridge," I said absently, my eyes finding Ellie then moving immediately back to Cricket.

Bridge rolled her eyes.

"Well, dinner's right through here," Ellie added cheerfully. She took Bridge's arm and guided her down a wide hall, leaving Cricket and me alone.

I smiled idiotically because this girl sucked all the mojo out of me.

"I-uh-I..." *Smooth.*

Cricket's eyes widened in disbelief, probably because I couldn't string a sentence together. She walked the direction Ellie and Bridge had gone.

"Come, boy!" she said, snapping her fingers. I jumped at the order, scrambling to her side as quickly as possible. The large mixed German shepherd fell into stride next to her. She bit her full lower lip to keep from smiling. I nearly facepalmed myself but held back. Now *you have restraint? Charming.*

"August said you row?" she asked. Her voice spilled over me like warm syrup. I closed my eyes and enjoyed the drugging sensation, then realized she'd asked me a question.

"Yeah," I answered belatedly. *Good. A short answer, but it's better than mouth diarrhea.* "I row...a-uh-boat...with-uh-my teammates." *Superb! Just-uh-superb.*

"Do you use an *oar*?" she teased, biting her lower lip again. *I found myself fantasizing I was the one that bit that lower lip.* Her mouth distracted me. *Answer her!*

94

"Yes, smart ass, I use an oar," I flirted, grinning from ear to ear because I couldn't help it.

She smiled back, making me want to worship at her feet. *Stick a fork in me!*

"This is Useless Eugene," she said, patting the side of her dog's neck. "But I just call him Eugie."

"Where'd he get a name like that?"

"When he was puppy, he took a liking to me and would only follow me around. We couldn't get him to work unless I was there, and I was in school then. They'd take him out into the field, but he'd just come running back to the house looking for me. My pa called him a Useless Eugene and it stuck."

"How old is he?"

"Thirteen."

I looked down at the old boy and noticed a little hitch in his step. I could tell his bones were aching.

We walked into a large dining area with a long wood table and long benches instead of chairs that could probably sit at least thirty. The ceiling was lower in this room, making it feel more intimate. Along the center of the table laid a banquet. Platters full of chicken fried steak, fried chicken, actual piles of grilled steak and biscuits. There were bowls full of mashed potatoes, creamed corn and green beans with bacon. *These people's cholesterol must be through the roof*, I thought, but looked around at the few already seated. There wasn't a single overweight person there.

"If you worked twelve hours a day, burned approximately three thousand calories in those twelve hours with the sheer labor involved, you'd need dinners like this," Cricket said with a smirk.

That smirk I could tell was her signature trademark and I loved it already. *God! She was feisty!*

"I didn't say anything," I teased.

"You didn't need to. Your eyes said it for you."

"I'm just not accustomed to this. I eat differently is all," I explained.

She snorted. "Okay, sushi boy, take a seat," she jabbed, heading off toward what I assumed was the kitchen.

I watched her walk away and thoroughly enjoyed the view.

"Spence, over here!" I heard Bridge call over.

I joined her at the head of the table and sat to her left, on the edge of the bench.

"Oh my God, I'm so hungry," she said, eyeing everything before her like she hadn't just eaten a box of crackers in our trailer.

"Chill out, kemosabe," I laughed.

She glared at me. "This thing in me is like a freaking bottomless pit. It's always hungry."

I smiled at her and she smiled back but rolled her eyes.

"Happy?" I asked.

"I have a feeling I will be," she answered with a smile. She looked down at her hands in her lap then over at me. "Cricket seems nice."

"Shut it," I demanded, trying to hide my smile.

"And *my God* were you smooth," she teased, furrowing her brows. "I mean, I've never seen someone so charming before."

I laughed. "Was it that obvious?"

"No, coolio, you convinced *everyone*. The bug eyes were a nice touch." She clicked her tongue and formed an okay with her hand.

I ran a hand down my face. "How humiliating."

"I have to admit, I've never seen you trip over yourself like that, not even with Sophie Price did you lose your cool. This is a nice side of you or whatever."

"Maybe I'm tired," I offered by way of explanation. I

don't know who I was trying to convince—me or Bridge.

"Maybe."

More people kept pouring in. It felt like a scene from *Bonanza*. Men and women of all ages came in from the cold, sporting their horse gear. I couldn't believe people still lived like this. It felt so foreign to me, so fascinating.

Cricket followed her grandma into the dining hall, with another large bowl of potatoes. She looked at me and rolled her eyes but laughed. I watched her set the bowl down. She was so tiny she had to reach a little for the center of the table and it exposed her stomach slightly, sending me reeling. *Oh, please God, let her sit across from me.*

She moved slowly, painfully slowly, too slowly for me toward our end of the table but chose the part of the bench directly across from me. I tried with much difficulty to settle my rapidly beating heart. I smiled at her and she smiled back. Eugie, who was on her heels the entire time, curled up at her feet.

Emmett and Ellie sat to my left, Cricket's right, at the end of the table. Everyone sat chatting. I didn't know what we were waiting for. Every spot was filled at the table except the spot directly next to Cricket. My brows furrowed in curiosity until the door banged open with a cold breeze and the Native American guy I saw on the horse earlier came in. He removed all his gear and threw it on one of the hooks.

No, I realized as he made his way toward Cricket.

He braced a solid arm on the table and leaned into her, kissing her on the mouth before sliding in beside her. She smiled at him, turning toward him as he sat, and threaded her fingers through the top of his hair. They were talking, but I had no idea what they were saying. I was too distracted by the stabbing pain in my gut and chest. *Damn.* She laughed while he kissed her once more. I wanted to rip him off of her. I was so damn disappointed. I'd never felt more disappointed. I felt Bridge's eyes on me, but I refused to return the look, too obsessed with watching them.

They turned toward us.

"Spencer, Bridget, this is Ethan Moonsong," Cricket said, cheerfully introducing the bastard.

"Nice to meet you," Bridge said, a shiny smile on her face.

I nodded. "Hello." It was all I could muster.

He returned the nod. "Spencer, Bridget, a pleasure," his deep lulling voice responded.

Bridget leaned forward a bit and asked Ethan a question. He answered with vigor and my eyes shot to Cricket. She was watching me, gauging me, trying to decipher if my flirting earlier meant anything. I secretly smiled at her and shook my head, letting her know I was crestfallen in that moment but that it didn't mean shit. I was cocking my metaphorical gun. Her eyes widened for the briefest of moments before cooling. She turned and feigned interest in what Ethan was talking about but she wasn't fooling me. *Click.* My eyes never left her face. She periodically glanced my direction, and I knew from experience there was only one reason anyone would do this. She was trying to hide her own interest in me. *Click.* She turned to face me again and this time I winked, making her visibly squirm.

"Right, Cricket?" Ethan asked her.

Her gaze was riveted to mine. "Hmm?" she asked, shaking her head to focus.

"You okay?" he asked her.

She turned to face him. "What? Yes, sorry, what was the question?"

Click.

CHAPTER FOURTEEN

"Everyone! Everyone!" Emmett said, standing and clanking the side of his spoon against his tea, a canning glass I'd only seen people in movies drink from. He raised his hands to settle the rowdy table. "'Fore I say grace, I'd like to take this moment to receive the Blackwells." He turned toward us and the others stared our direction, making Bridge blush. Jonah smirked at her, attempting to ease her, simultaneously making me very nervous. "We are all happy to have you both here and wish that you'll be very comfortable. We welcome you into the fold."

"Here! Here!" a few rang out over the clinking glasses.

He sat and leaned toward us. Quietly, he said, "We've all been made aware that your security is a priority. None of mine here will ever expose you, my dear." Bridge's face fell toward her lap, her eyes turned glassy, her cheeks flashed deep red. She was embarrassed. Emmett chucked her under the chin. "None of that, miss. You done good, girl. No one here thinks any less of you. Fact is, my Cricket's the product of my middle girl, God rest her soul, in just the same way, and we wouldn't trade her for anything in the world." *Cricket's mom was dead?* He glanced at Cricket and sighed deeply. "Yup, I'd give just about anything to keep her around forever. She's my sweet angel."

"Thank you," Bridge said, raising her head and swiping quickly below her eyes.

Cricket winked at her, a silent declaration of camaraderie.

Out of respect, no one asked us a single question about leaving our parents. They asked many questions concerning us, but aside from asking when Bridge was due, which we weren't aware yet, the conversation geared mostly toward what interested us.

"Ethan," Bridge asked after everyone's plates were cleared, "if you don't mind me asking, what tribe are you from?"

"I don't mind." He smiled. "I'm from the Echo River tribe. We've been in the Bitterroot Mountains for more than three hundred years. We kept the mountains and the mountains kept us."

"Fascinating," she said. "I wonder how you survived the cold."

"We are made for this weather. We were made for those mountains."

Bridge smiled and nodded.

"What made you want to work here?" I asked Ethan, not able to help myself.

"My dad got me in. He works here," he answered. Bridge and I looked around. "Him. Right there." Ethan pointed to a large white man at the opposite end, a solitary-looking figure who didn't join in much conversation but seemed agreeable enough, grinning occasionally at the others around him. Ethan shared his eyes and nose. "My mom is Echo River," Ethan explained.

I nodded. "Where is she?" I asked.

Cricket shifted uncomfortably. Ethan's face fell to his plate. "She, uh, died two years ago."

"I'm so sorry," Bridge said.

"It's okay. She loved and was loved. I miss her, but I know where she is." He lifted his face toward us once more.

"And who are your parents?" Bridge asked Jonah.

Jonah's eyes widened as if in disbelief that she spoke to him. "My dad's Charles or Chuck as everyone calls him. He lives in Butte with my mom."

"Cool," she responded. He grinned like a fool.

"My mom was Chuck's younger sister by a year," Cricket added, fiddling with her napkin. "I know no one asked, but I figured I'd tell you anyway. Her name was Sarah." Ethan squeezed her shoulder and she winked at him, making my stomach churn.

"So how is August as a roommate?" Jonah asked.

Should I outright lie? "He's cool," I said truthfully but left it at that.

"Not chasing tail?" Jonah laughed.

"Maybe," I eluded.

"I'd be willing to bet there's no maybe about it," Cricket said, laughing.

"He's *popular*," I gave in.

Both Jonah and Cricket laughed. Ethan shook his head.

"What about you?" Jonah asked me. "You gotta girl back home? At Brown?"

I looked straight at Cricket and grinned. "Nope. Free as a bird." Cricket visibly swallowed. *Click.*

"We've gotta bunch of cute girls around here," Jonah continued. "Every Saturday night except during calving season, we all go into Kalispell. You should join us then."

"I bet the girls would be glad for a fresh face," Ellie chimed in happily.

"I'd love that," I said, sitting back a little, still watching Cricket, but she was ignoring me. *Click.*

"Are you good on a horse, son?" Emmett asked, changing the subject.

It took me awhile to turn my gaze away from Cricket. "Yes, sir," I answered. "I used to play polo in prep school." Our half of the table laughed. "What?" I asked, slightly offended.

"Not quite the same," Ethan said.

I leaned a little toward him, not sure why I was letting him get to me, I was usually very schooled at playing the upper hand. "I bet I'm a little better than you think."

He nodded as if he didn't believe me. *Let's go, dude.*

"Well, I guess we'll just have to see then," he added.

"You've got good arms and shoulders," Ellie said, appraising me. "You'll be handy come birthing season and that's just around the corner."

I exaggeratedly flexed my muscles, imitating a bodybuilder, making Ellie laugh. "Point me the direction of your nearest cow," I joked.

She slapped the table and actually hooted. "Boy, you are cuter than a button!"

"Thanks," I said, my cheeks feeling peculiarly warm.

Someone entered the room, another young ranch hand, but he appeared out of breath. "Emmett, we've got a heifer gone into labor and she's having some trouble."

"What in the Sam Hill!" Emmett exclaimed. "She's two weeks early!" He stood and Cricket followed.

"I've got it, Pop Pop," she told him.

He nodded and sat back down, picking up the drumstick he was still working on, thinking nothing of her offer.

She started for the room with her coat and boots,

Eugie nipping at her heels. *They're going to let this tiny nothing of a girl deliver a calf by herself?!* I jumped up and everyone's eyes turned toward me. Bridge eyed me strangely. I stood there a good minute, debating whether I should chase after her like a goon.

"Would you like to go?" Ellie asked me, saving me.

"Is that too weird?" I asked.

"Not at all. I didn't think you'd be able to see this for a while, but the ranch is fickle and the heifer had different ideas. Go."

I followed Cricket but not before noticing Ethan's furrowed brows. He was catching on, but I couldn't seem to care.

I grabbed my coat and gloves and opened the door to freezing temperatures. The cold was so bitter; it made me step back slightly. I pushed through the frozen wind and saw Cricket's little frame entering the barn, Eugie right behind her. The wind whipped against my face and I raised my scarf higher against my mouth and nose, reveling in the warmth from my breath. I made an immediate mental note to buy a cap of some kind.

When I entered the barn, it was several degrees warmer than the outside, the cows and hot lights brought it to a tolerable temperature. I looked around and noticed Cricket crouched in a corner messing with something. "Yoshimi Battles the Pink Robots" began to play. *Oh my God, could she be any sexier?* She stood and did a little shimmy dance move and my jaw went slack, but then she left out the other side of the barn. *Where in the hell is she going?* I started to follow but she quickly came back into the barn leading the heifer by a rope. She still hadn't noticed me. She guided the animal into a metal stall and it tried to ram itself through to the other side. It was caught by a hinged gate butting against its shoulder blades and enclosing its head. The gate prevented the heifer from stepping back, most likely to stop her from trampling Cricket. I stifled a shudder.

"You gonna just stand there?" I heard, startling me. Okay, she *had* noticed me.

"Uh, no, Ellie said I could come down? Is that cool?"

"Sure," she said, shrugging her shoulders.

I walked over to her corner of the barn and carefully made my way around the heifer.

"She's early," Cricket said.

The cow kept shaking her head up and down, side to side, snorting through what I could only assume was labor pain. She had a shiny auburn brown coat and the heat from her skin permeated in clouds above her from being so long in the cold, but she didn't look at all uncomfortable in that respect. It was as if she was made to survive those temperatures. The heifer saw me and stilled. I placed my hand on her head but she didn't flinch.

"How now brown cow?" I asked seriously.

Cricket snorted but stifled a smile, shaking her head. "You're a troublemaker. I can already tell."

"Can you?"

"You're inciting Ethan's wrath. Yes, you're a troublemaker."

I lifted my shoulders in question, feigning I had no idea what she was talking about. She rolled her eyes and started making her way around the barn. I followed her, keeping pace with Eugie. *Hey, lapdog, looks like you've got some competition.*

"Do you do this a lot?" I asked.

"About ten percent of our cattle will need help birthing during the season. I've gotten pretty good at wrestling a calf from its mother when I have to."

I looked her up and down in appreciation, but she mistook it for skepticism.

"I may look small but I'm capable," she huffed.

"Oh, I believe you."

She furrowed her brows but continued walking. She grabbed some wicked chain thing with metal-handled grips covered in black rubber as well as two metal bars and some strange contraption I couldn't put a name to. The barn was made of wood, much like all the buildings on the property, but this one had a concrete floor, sloped slightly to meet several drains at the base of the slant running through the middle of the barn. There were approximately twenty other cows inside, each in a stall lined heavily with hay.

"So you like The Flaming Lips."

"That I do."

"And you have a mixed breed German shepherd named Eugie."

"Yup, he's German shepherd and Australian Cattle Dog."

"That explains the face."

The dog had ears a little longer than a standard German shepherd as well as large patches of peppered white hair on his face but around his eyes were two large spots of black.

"Hey, watch it!" she said, waving the large chains at me.

I lifted my hands as if in surrender. "I didn't say he wasn't awesome."

She let the chains fall in acceptance and kept walking.

"Calving stall," she said, waving her hand in a circle toward the trapped heifer. "Head catcher," she continued the lesson, pointing to the hinged gate thing. "It's open all the way to the floor so if she wants to lie down, it can't bind, and won't suffocate her."

"And these," I said, gesturing to the chains in her hand.

"Chains?"

GREED

"Oh."

She took the chains and dropped them on a bale of hay next to the stall. That's when I saw that the calf's front legs were protruding out, covered in the sickliest-looking shit I'd ever seen. I nearly gagged.

"What's the matter, city boy?" Cricket asked, when she took in how wide my eyes had gotten.

I checked my expression. "Nothing." She laughed anyway.

The cow or heifer or whatever it was cried out.

"Poor thing, she's distressed. The heifer's not pushing," Cricket said.

She bent for the chains.

"What's the difference between a cow and a heifer?" I asked.

"A heifer is a cow who's yet to give birth."

"Ah."

She wrapped the middle of the chain around the calf's legs.

"You're really doing this," I stated.

She looked at me like I was a moron. "What else should I do? Let her and the calf die?" She began pulling on the rubber-lined grips. "See if we can incite her to push," Cricket grunted. She pulled a little harder, but the heifer didn't seem to want to cooperate. Cricket sat down and positioned her legs against the stall for leverage and began pulling a little harder. The animal cried out. "Come on, girl."

Several minutes passed where Cricket would pull then release, pull then release, but the cow wouldn't help at all.

"I'm gonna need to do all the work, I guess. Stubborn little thing."

Cricket pulled, her face tight, her eyes crinkled. She pulled until the tip of the nose was peeking through. She kept pulling but wasn't making the progress she wanted, I could tell. She looked up at me, appraising me.

"No," I said.

"Why not, greenhorn? You got something against getting those pretty digs dirty? Listen, I can call Ethan down here, but it'd be easier if you volunteered. This calf's pretty big and the heifer's pelvis is really narrow. I'm going to need some help."

When she mentioned Ethan, I'd already stepped forward, pushing up my sleeves. "What do I do?"

"Just position yourself like I did and gently, keyword *gently*, pull. Try to wedge the calf back and forth. We don't want anything tearing."

I nodded and sat on the floor, bracing my feet against the metal stall and gripping the handles. I gently pulled, shifting the calf back and forth steadily until the head popped out. I breathed a sigh of relief.

"Keep going," Cricket prodded.

I repositioned my hands on the handles to get a better grip and pulled once more. I was trying to be gentle but the calf wasn't budging.

"Be a little more aggressive," she encouraged. "Give it a little more."

I pulled harder and the shoulders started appearing, then the belly, and finally the entire calf spilled out and into my lap. I'd never experienced anything like that before and it was incredibly exhilarating. I smiled down at the baby but it wasn't breathing.

"She's not breathing," I said, panicking a little.

"Hold on," Cricket said calmly.

She took the calf and dragged it to a stall lined with hay. She sat down with it and stuck pieces of straw up its nose. I'd stood and followed her in by then.

"What does that do?"

"It stimulates breathing. Gets him to hack up any junk

in his upper respiratory tract."

She rubbed the little thing's chest back and forth, massaging, and encouraging it, speaking softly to it. Sure enough, the calf started breathing, its eyes dazed with little control over its muscles. Its little head bobbed back and forth, the muscles unpracticed. Cricket tucked its legs underneath it and propped it against a wall of hay.

"There you go, baby," she said.

"It's a boy, you said?"

"A little boy."

"I don't think I've ever used this word before, but that thing is cute as shit."

Cricket laughed out loud.

She cleaned up the cow then released her into the stall with her calf. She began sweeping hay from the birthing stall. I saw a broom in the corner near her stereo and pitched in. She locked eyes with me and nodded. We swept it all up and tossed it in a huge barrel for trash. I thought we were done, but she went to one of the long sides on the inside of the barn and started uncoiling a large hose. She began to spray down the stall and tools, the remnants washed down the drains. She then replaced all the tools back where she had gotten them. When it was all said and done, you couldn't even tell the heifer had given birth. Until, that is, you looked down at my clothing.

"Disgusting," I said truthfully.

"Just a little blood and guts," she explained.

"This all cost me around five thousand dollars," I said, gesturing to my clothing.

At this, she burst out laughing.

"Greenhorn, I don't even know where to begin."

She turned off her music and started toward the door we'd entered before coming from the main house.

"What am I supposed to do?" I yelled out.

"I suggest you wash up and get some rest. Work starts at five." She stopped and turned my direction. "I also suggest you wear something else, if you catch my drift."

"These are the only kind of clothes I own."

Where most girls were impressed by my clothing, by her expression alone, Cricket seemed to believe I was insane.

"Then I guess we'll have to buy you some new ones. Ones that, I don't know, don't cost more than my annual salary?"

She closed the door behind her and I stood there feeling like a first-class asshole...as I should have felt, but all that really made me want to do was check the balance in my account. I was going to start counting down the days, no, the minutes, until Bridge turned eighteen. I wanted out of there. Five thousand a year for grueling, thankless work? No, thank you.

CHAPTER
FIFTEEN

"Forget all *about little old me?" Piper pouted.*

"What?" I asked.

She ignored me. "You flirt with that girl but you don't really want her. You want me."

"Get the fuck out of here, Piper!" I demanded, descending the villa stairs.

She smiled at me, but it wasn't a beautiful smile, it was chilling. "Lost all your winnings," she giggled, digging in the blade.

My blood ran cold in my veins and I stopped at the bottom of the stairs. "Yes, you bitch, thanks to you, it's all gone."

She laughed, throwing her head back. "How are you going to leave him now?"

"Joke's on you. I already did."

She shook her head. "My darling, you only think you did."

"What are you talking about?"

"You have to share what you have with your sister. You don't have enough now. You'll go back to him because you know he'll take you back even after what you did, and he'll take you back because he can't trust anyone else. You need him. You need what he has to get you what you need."

"Shut up."

"He's your dealer!" she squealed.

"No, we'll be okay," I desperately denied. "I don't need him anymore," I cooed, an attempt to appease myself.

"Liar," she sang, bobbing her head back and forth as if she was insane before tossing herself onto the sofa.

I walked past her and into the kitchen. She popped up off the couch, ran over to me and lifted herself up onto the counter beside where I stood.

I studied her. "Why are you even here?"

"I'm Piper," she said, as if that explained everything.

"Get out of here," I demanded, but she didn't move.

I ignored her and opened my laptop on the coffee table, logging into my account. I could feel the pent-up pressure release from my chest as I read the balance. So close, I thought.

"Yet so far," she needled, giggling a little at the end.

My alarm clock went off at four thirty in the morning and I woke startled, confused and more than a little creeped out by my dream. I looked around and had forgotten where I was. My surroundings were nearly pitch black.

"Stupid alarm," Bridge whispered, her voice broken from sleep.

Dear God. Trailer. Bridge. Pregnant. Cattle. Ranch… Cricket.

It all came rushing to me in that instant, overwhelming me but the last image, the image of Cricket's smiling face, made me chill. I smiled to myself. *I want her.*

GREED

Bridge turned on the light and the smile fell. I threw the covers over my face and groaned.

"Four thirty a.m. was invented by God to vex me."

"And me," Bridge chimed in.

"I guess it's no more than we deserve," I laughed.

"Speak for yourself," she said before closing the bathroom door. I heard her vomiting on the other side.

I forced myself to get up and brushed my teeth at the kitchen sink, looking out into the drive. It was pitch black. The only light was from the window I sat at, and that only extended a few feet.

Bridge emerged and laid back down, moaning. I passed her, quickly smoothing her hair out of her face, then headed to the bathroom to shower. While I was in there the night before, I discovered I had only about three different positions I could make to wash myself. I had to angle my head to rinse my hair. It was a bitch.

I rummaged through my stuff the night before and found that I didn't have anything to wear that wouldn't be scrutinized by Cricket, so I picked my oldest pair of jeans, a thermal and a button-up. I donned the boots I'd worn the day before.

I opened the door, passing the afterbirth-covered clothes I'd worn and thrown on the ground. As I mourned their loss, I was interrupted by a four-wheeler's lights meandering down the snow-covered dirt drive. My hand immediately shot up to protect my eyes from their brightness, so stark against the black morning. The vehicle came to a stop and the lights were switched off. It was Jonah.

"Everything okay?" I asked.

"Uh, yeah," he said, avoiding eye contact. "I just thought Bridget would like a ride up to the main house."

"That was nice of you," I said, taking in Jonah.

"Yeah, well, I figured she wouldn't want to walk

through the cold and snow in her condition."

I opened the door and leaned in, keeping Jonah outside. "Bridge, are you decent?"

"Yeah, I'm dressed. Why? What's up?" she asked, edging her way down the narrow center hallway, only looking a little green.

"Jonah Hunt is here to give you a ride up to the main house."

She bit her lower lip. "Oh, that was kind."

I let the door shut behind me. "It was, wasn't it?"

"Hush, Spence."

She edged past me and opened the door for Jonah. "Come in," she invited. Jonah climbed inside. "That was nice of you," she told him.

The idiot smiled a shit-eating grin and removed his cap from his head. I waited for the "aw, shucks," but it never came.

"Just let me grab my coat and I'll be right with you."

Jonah and I stood in absolute silence.

"Ready," she said, wrapping her scarf and putting on her beanie.

I watched her climb on the back of the four-wheeler and wrap her hands around his torso.

Yup, gonna need to nip that in the bud, I thought. Jonah slowly edged them out onto the snow-filled road and drove up toward the house at a snail's pace. *At least he's being careful with her.*

I shut off all the lights and applied layer after layer of clothing, knowing how freaking cold I'd be getting as the morning wore on. Luckily, I was in a little better shape than Bridge was, attending a college in Rhode Island. I had two pairs of wool socks on, and my boots felt tight as shit, but that was it as far as double coverage. Everything else I improvised.

I started toward the barn and was grateful that the

wind was still. About halfway up the drive, my heart began to beat an irregular rhythm as I caught sight of Cricket coming toward me. My breath caught in my throat. This girl. This tiny little girl had *such* incredible power over me with her big, blue, round, sad eyes. Her unusual face, her unusually *striking* face. Her pert nose. The faint laugh lines around her eyes and mouth. And I didn't know her, didn't really even know if she and I were anything alike, but that didn't stop me from wishing we shared a future...even if she did belong to someone else.

"What are you doing in my neck of the woods?" I asked her.

"Just wanted to make sure you found your way all right. Jonah told me he was getting Bridget this morning. Thought it'd be rude if we didn't also help you out a little," she joshed.

"Sure you just didn't want to see me?"

She rolled her eyes. "This blatant flirting? You know you're courting Ethan's wrath again, right?"

This made me smile. "Am I getting you in trouble, little lady?"

"No, but—" she began, but I cut her off by grabbing her upper arm, stunned, truly stunned for the first time in my life.

"Holy shit! Are you wearing chaps?" I asked, pulling her away from me so I could get a good look.

"Excuse me?" she asked, looking at me like I was crazy again.

"You are. You are wearing *chaps*." My stomach dropped to my feet. *God, she's sexy as hell.* "Turn around for me," I teased.

"*Excuse me!*" *Is she mad?* "What is wrong with you!" she yelled, yanking her arm away. *Yeah, she's mad.*

"I just-I've never seen a girl in chaps before," I said, staring, a hand involuntarily ran the length of my face. I clamped my lips to prevent drool.

She haughtily brought her fists to her hips. "Listen, you're here to work not to flirt."

"I can't work *and* flirt?"

"Of course not, you're here to—"

"I'm pretty sure I can do both. I've tried it before. I was very successful."

"Stop it. You're—"

"And you look delectable in those, if I say so myself. I wonder if I could get you to wear those at all times," I mused.

"No! I-I...*ugh!*" *Click.*

"Are you flustered?"

"I'm getting Ethan."

"You *are* flustered. I fluster you. Huh, quite a change of pace since yesterday." She huffed ahead of me, her glorious backside facing me, rushing toward the barn. "Beautiful!" I said, stopping to appreciate it. "Now was that so hard?"

She immediately covered her ass with her hands and turned around, her eyes narrowed at me. She began to walk sideways like a crab, and I burst out laughing.

When I finally entered the horse barn, Cricket was plastered to Ethan's side listening to Jonah. I jogged over to them.

"...her," was the only thing I caught of whatever Jonah was saying. The group went silent. *Bridge. Bridge was their topic of conversation. Damn.*

"Hey, guys," I said.

Ethan nodded but seemed civil. *Cricket didn't tattle as she'd threatened.* I couldn't have cared less, but I found that interesting. I discreetly winked at her and her eyes shot wide before narrowing in promises of lethal force.

Jonah said, "Hey, Spencer! You're with me right now. We'll take this half of the stalls, and Ethan and Cricket will take the other side."

Damn. "Cool."

"So what's on the docket today?" I asked him, taking in my surroundings.

The barn was about fifteen-feet high, and had approximately ten horse stalls running half the back length of the barn on either sides, creating twenty stalls in all. The front half was a giant open space, though I wasn't sure what it was for. I could see from the road the day before that the horse barn was the biggest building on the property, and it was obvious once I was inside that was the case. I took in all the rustic wood surrounding us and couldn't imagine how many man-hours it must have taken to forge each log and plank.

The horse stalls themselves were made of wood as well. Their doors easily slid away on tracks from the opening. Each stall had swinging doors leading to the outside as well, but I could tell those were hardly used, at least not in the winter.

"We're going to be mucking out the horse stalls," Jonah explained. "We do this about once a day, unless the horses have been kept inside for some reason, then we'll hit them twice." He walked toward a wall, picked up two pitchforks and handed one to me. I followed him into the nearest stall. "Okay, so you'll want to wedge the fork underneath the pile of manure. With the fork low to the ground, tightly shimmy it back and forth, freeing any loose pine pellet bedding. We do this so the manure doesn't break up and we save clean bedding."

Together we cleaned the stall in around five minutes, moving to the next with the wheelbarrow, tying up or "racking up" the horse outside the stall, then returning the horse, dropping a new bale of hay, and filling its three-pound feed bucket with grains. We went from one stall to the next and the next until all ten stalls on our side were done. We didn't talk much but fell into an easy rhythm. In about forty-five minutes, our stalls were clean and our horses fed. I'd never worked like that with someone, and it felt like I'd actually accomplished something.

"Good job, greenhorn," Jonah said, slapping me on the back.

"Dude, what in the hell is a greenhorn?" I asked, eyeing Cricket as we made our way toward the main house for breakfast.

She and Ethan had two stalls left. I reveled in the fact that she watched me the entire way.

Jonah laughed. "You're a greenhorn. It's essentially a newbie, Spencer."

"Ah, guess there's nothing I can do about it then."

"Nothing," he said, but smiled and slapped me on the shoulder again. "Hungry?"

"Starved."

CHAPTER

SIXTEEN

AT BREAKFAST, Cricket came in a little too late for my taste. In fact, I knew for a fact they should've been in shortly after Jonah and me. I studied them from across the room. Cricket's raw lips gave away her little game, and Ethan's fucking grin pissed me off beyond belief.

"Hello?" I heard to my left.

"Huh?" I said.

"I was talking to you, Spence," Bridge said, rolling her eyes when I finally made eye contact.

"Never mind," she huffed. "I'm going to pee for the seventh time this morning. I hope Ellie didn't think I was trying to get out of work." She got up and headed for the restroom.

Cricket looked at me from the corner of her eye. I raised my brows in question but she ignored me. I began to stand up to join them, but Bridge rushed back into the dining room, startling me. There was a look of panic on her face.

"I'm bleeding," she whispered.

"*What?*"

She shook her head up and down, her eyes glassing over, biting her thumbnail.

My heart jumped into my throat. "Okay, okay, let's not panic. Uh, let me think," I said, running my hands through my hair. My eyes searched the table and met Cricket's.

She read something in my expression, jumped up and crawled over her bench, practically sprinting over to us. "What's wrong? You okay, Bridget?" she asked, reaching up and running her hand over my sister's hair.

"I'm bleeding," she whispered again.

"Oh, God. Okay, don't panic. I'll be right back."

Cricket approached Ellie and they spoke in hushed whispers.

"Hey, Spencer, do you have your keys?" she asked.

"Yeah."

"All right, we're going into town. Grandma's got a doctor she's going to call for us."

"What about all the work I need to help her with?" Bridge asked, an edge to her voice.

"Don't worry about that, darlin'," Cricket smiled. "Let's go figure you out."

Bridge nodded.

"You both stay here," I said. "I'll run down and get the truck for you."

I stood and made my way toward the door.

"Everything okay?" Jonah asked.

"Yeah, uh, well, Bridge might be having some complications. I need to run for my truck to take her into town."

Without thinking, Jonah ran across the deck, down the stairs and started his four-wheeler.

"You'll get there faster on this thing!" he said. "Just leave it down there with the keys in the ignition. I'll fetch it later."

"Thanks, Jonah." I was grateful to him.

I raced down the drive, passing the cattle barn and carriage house, rounding the horse barn, then winding down the trailer's drive. It was still pitch black, but the four-wheeler had headlights. It would have only been a seven- or eight-minute walk, but I was so anxious, walking that would have felt like a lifetime. I turned off the engine but left the keys in the ignition as Jonah had asked then propelled myself into my truck, started the engine and threw the gear in reverse before I realized I'd probably need some cash. Then I thought it would probably be a good idea to take all of it. I placed it in park and went inside, stuffing the wads of bills in a small pack.

I drove like a banshee, but it felt like it took forever to get to the main house. I sat idle for a moment, the exhaust from the truck billowing out around me when they finally emerged. I jumped from the truck and ran up to them, helping Bridge get in, then tiny Cricket right after her. Bridge insisted on sitting in the back so she could lie down if she wanted to. We were bumbling down the road in less than a minute.

"Thank God the roads are clear today and there's no snow," Cricket said, buckling herself in.

"Is your heater working?" I asked Cricket, placing my hand over Bridge's vent in the back to make sure hers was also heating up.

She looked at me strangely. "Uh, yeah, it's fine." She cleared her throat. "Thank you."

She peered behind her. Bridge was resting her head in her hand, her elbow sat on the armrest.

"You okay?" Cricket asked.

"I-I don't know. We'll see, I guess."

Bridge tried to sound cool but terror laced her voice.

"Do you mind me asking? Was there a lot of blood?" Cricket asked.

"Uh, no-yes...I don't know."

"Okay, that's okay. We'll see what Dr. Harmon says."
Bridge nodded.

Cricket turned toward me and I looked at her. We didn't speak. I hated to have to turn back toward the road. I wanted so desperately to know what she was thinking. I wanted to blurt out all my questions, but I also didn't want to alarm Bridge. So we drove the half-hour drive southeast into Kalispell in almost complete silence. Bridge would chime in occasionally to see how much longer or to ask if we thought everything was going to be all right. "Not long," we'd tell her. "You'll be fine," we'd offer with no real idea if that was the truth.

Finally, we entered downtown Kalispell. It was incredibly charming. Brick buildings built in the early nineteen hundreds, original cobblestone streets and the sidewalks filled with shopping people. The streetlights were still strung with garland and ribbon. It was beyond picturesque and looked like one of the last places on Earth you could photograph in black and white and people wouldn't be able to discern whether it was turn of the century.

"Here it is," Cricket said, as I turned onto Main. "This is Dr. Harmon's."

Bridget peeked out her window. "This looks like a drug store straight out of a Victorian-era film."

"Probably just a little after," I corrected.

Bridge speared me with a look, silently beckoning me to shut my trap.

I got out and ran to the other side and let Bridge and Cricket out. There were two entrances, one for the drug store on the first floor and another with a narrow staircase leading to the second floor doctor's office. We all climbed the stairs, our boots echoing in loud booms in the small enclosed space. The top of the stairs had a small landing and a frosted glass door. It read *Marshall Harmon, M.D.* and centered underneath his name it continued, *Obstetrician-Gynecologist.* Everything in me as a dude screamed to run.

We walked in and approached a little metal desk. It looked like something you'd find in a teacher's classroom in the fifties.

"Cricket!" the little receptionist with the beehive chirped. Her eyes slid to Bridge and she stood. "You must be Miss Blackwell. Come on back. Dr. Harmon's been expecting you."

Bridge followed her, the wood creaking beneath their feet.

"You're going to be all right?" Cricket asked her.

"I'll be fine," Bridge offered with a small smile. She stopped. "I don't know how long I'm going to be. You guys should run those errands, Spencer."

"Oh. Okay," I said.

I watched her walk to the room by herself, and I felt so heartbroken for her going in there alone. My mom should have been here. I hated my dad for that. I hated the boy who did it to Bridge, even if he wasn't all to blame.

I thought back to all the times I'd slept with a girl and not thought twice about it and my gut ached. If a girl doesn't safeguard herself, who will? I'd always had the mentality that men will change when women change, but I never thought about how safeguarding the girls around me was just as much my responsibility as it was theirs.

I looked over at Cricket. I studied the girl before me. She was beautiful beyond belief, but she wasn't some object to conquer, she was someone to be cherished, someone to be loved, someone to be revered. I wondered if Ethan did all that for her. I wondered if she gave all that in return to him, and that made my blood burn in my veins. That initial attraction between us was apparent, no doubt, but I wondered if I should give up on trying. I wondered if my infatuation for her even had a future, especially because she was with Ethan.

My mama would always say, "Whether they're aware of it or not, if their heart beats your name, answer the call." Stupidly, I always thought that meant any girl was pretty much open game, but I understood in that moment that it meant that nothing was ever final.

Did I want to rock the boat, though? Her whole family loved Ethan, and everyone was being so generous by letting us hide out there. *What are you doing?* I asked myself. *This whole thing is about Bridge. Get out. Make your future. Stop obsessing over this girl. Focus.*

"I know an outfitter just down the road. Close enough to walk," Cricket said. "We can get you some decent working clothes if you're up to it."

"That's fine," I said, feeling deflated.

I followed Cricket out, knowing that although I wanted her more than I'd ever wanted anyone else, she was far too out of reach. I had goals.

I constructed a hundred-foot steel wall between us and sealed all the bolts, leaving only Bridge and myself on my side. Who cared if I could still hear Cricket's heart beating my name loudly as a drum on the other side?

CHAPTER SEVENTEEN

AT THE outfitter, Cricket helped me find a couple pairs of decent jeans. I refused the Wranglers because I looked ridiculous. She also found a few shirts, long johns (I'm not shitting you), a wool-lined suede jacket, which seemed pretty standard among the other hands, and two pairs of sturdy work boots. I'd noticed most of the ranch hands would wear a bandana-like scarf instead of anything long. I assumed this was for practical reasons and told Cricket I'd like the same as well.

She came up with a couple of cowboy hats, but I couldn't bring myself to wear one. I looked comical in them. I tried one on and did a little jig, trying to lighten the moment. Cricket laughed and my gut twisted. I took it off immediately, desperate to get her lovely voice out of my head.

I settled for a fleece-lined visor beanie instead. She said those were pretty common around the ranch, so I wouldn't stand out or anything, to which I was grateful. I didn't want to stand out anymore than I already was.

"What about chaps?" I asked.

She looked at me, waiting for a cheeky remark, but I held a stoic expression. She cleared her throat. "We've got a million pairs back at home. Ellie makes them herself."

"No shit! She's pretty talented."

"At everything she does."

I nodded.

"I'll pay for these then," I said, dragging the rest of the stuff toward the front.

While I paid, in cash of course, I heard Cricket's phone ring.

"Hello?" Her breathing picked up, making my heart race. "Okay. Okay. Sure." She brought the phone to me. "It's August."

"August?" I asked, nervous. "What's up, dude?"

"Dude, your dad is crazy," he began.

"Shit. What happened?" My lungs deflated.

"I get home, right? I walk into the room and this guy with weird old-fashioned spectacles is sitting at my desk like he fucking owns the place."

"My *dad*?"

"No, dumbass, this big scary-looking fucker with fucking black leather gloves on and shit. Like he's getting ready to blow my ass away or some shit. Man, it was intimidating."

If I hadn't seen him ace his last engineering exam with my own two eyes, I'd never believe August had two brain cells to rub together.

"Well, did you say something? Am I going to have to haul ass out of here with Bridge?"

"No, no, dude. You won't *believe* it! I told him he could go fuck himself. Told him I had no idea where you were!"

I breathed a sigh relief.

"You're going to have to lay low for a while," I told

him. "Don't go to a lot of places if you can help it. Live your life mellow. Don't send a lot of packages here or call a lot. My dad will pick up on an increased pattern."

"I feel like James Bond and shit."

"Yes, August, that's exactly what you remind me of. James Bond."

He laughed. "How are you adjusting? Cricket's cool, right?"

I looked up and noticed Cricket was perusing the aisles.

"Why didn't you tell me Cricket was a chick?"

"I just assumed you could tell by the way I talked about her."

"How? How would I have been able to tell? You'd only say hick things like, 'Cricket can rope a calf like nobody's business' or 'Cricket can spit fifteen feet' or 'Cricket pantsed the school quarterback and got suspended for a week.' It isn't conducive to girl-type behavior."

"At my house it is," he explained.

"You could have warned me she was fine, though."

"She is a popular little thing," he laughed. "I decided to surprise you with that." We both got quiet. "Oh no, Spencer," he chimed in, "you can't. I'm ordering you, bro. Stay away from Cricket. She's different from the girls we chase."

"I won't," I said. "I have no intention of going after her." Except that felt like a lie. It didn't matter; I was determined.

"Good," he said, calming down a bit. "Besides, she's with Ethan. They've been together since they were kids."

That weird gut ache invaded my body again and I tried to check it. "Really? I'd no idea they'd been together that long."

"Yeah, they're childhood sweethearts and shit."

Maybe this will make it easier to ignore her. So why

does my whole body hurt thinking about it?

"Okay, well, remember what I said, cool?"

"Yeah, I've got you."

"Thanks, August, you're like a brother to me, even though I want to kick your ass sometimes for being such a douche."

"I love you too, man."

"Adios."

"Peace," he said and hung up.

I pressed end on Cricket's phone and breathed a sigh of relief.

Bags in hand, I followed Cricket back to the truck and stuck the purchases behind the driver's seat on the floor.

"Should we go up?" Cricket asked.

"Yeah, we'll see where she's at."

I climbed the stairs behind Cricket, her amazing backside at eye level. I almost groaned. We walked into the doctor's office.

"Hey, Perdi, is she ready?"

The beehive receptionist stood and took Cricket's hand. "Not yet, but I think the baby is just fine." We both breathed out whatever pent-up stress we were carrying. "How are *you*?" Perdi asked, her eyes narrowed in that pitying expression people always adopted when they just found out you fell into a big pile of shit or, I guess, cow dung in Cricket's case.

"I'm fine," Cricket said, sliding her hand out of Perdi's. She looked up at me and I furrowed my brows.

"What's she talking about?" I asked when Perdi went to check on Bridget.

I was so relieved to hear that my little niece or nephew was fine, but the way Perdi acted sent huge red flags in the air.

"Oh, nothing, she's just nosy."

My gaze fixed on Cricket. She was fidgeting and

noticed I was watching her. She walked to the little sitting room area and plopped down onto a wooden bench, unfolding a magazine so outdated, the cover's model had decidedly crimped hair and a bright yellow baggy sweatshirt and headband.

I sat down next to her. Her arm touched mine, and that made my hands tremble a little. I played with fire by leaning into her and pretending to take in her magazine. "Think Reagan will get re-elected?" I asked. She grinned her clever little smirk and my heart began to thump in my throat. "Did you see that episode of *Punky Brewster* last night? Soleil Moon Frye is the bomb." More grinning.

You should stop, fool. This is borderline flirting.

"Don't watch a lot of television, but I do like films," she played along. "More of a Brat Packer myself."

"Molly or Ally?" I asked.

"Molly. Although, Ally was pretty rad in *The Breakfast Club*."

"Yeah, she had a whole who-gives-a-shit-about-what-you-think vibe. Like, I'm gonna toss my pimento loaf onto the top of this weird-ass modern sculpture then pound down this Pixy Stix-Cap'n Crunch sandwich and what are you gonna do about it?"

Cricket laughed, genuinely laughed. Loud. It caught me off guard but after a second, I became painfully aware of how amazing it was, how her whole face lit up, how her whole body shook. I was mesmerized by her.

A few minutes passed in silence then Cricket did something that made me crush so hard on her, I felt like I was going to crumble at her feet. She started whistling the theme to *The Bridge on the River Kwai*. It wasn't long before I joined in, but we didn't get to finish because Bridge finally emerged, looking a little green in the face, but otherwise intact.

I stood. "You okay?" I asked her.

"I'm fine, the baby's fine. I'm due June twenty-third."

"Congrats, Bridge," I said, hugging her.

She hugged back. "Thanks, Spence." She breathed deeply. "Pretty scared though."

"Well, it's a scary thing."

Cricket hugged Bridge when I let go. "I'm so glad to hear the baby's okay," she said.

"Thank you," Bridge answered. "You guys want to see the sonogram?"

She held out the glossy photo and I saw this tiny little peanut. Cricket aww'd and I just stood there absorbing the little thing, feeling proud and overwhelmed.

"Is this the head?" I asked her.

"No, that's its rear end," she laughed. "That's its head."

"Tiny little thing," I whispered.

"Dr. Harmon said it's about the size of a lime."

"That's hilarious," I smiled wide, tracing my fingers over the tiny outline.

I looked up and saw Cricket staring at me.

"What?" I asked.

She swallowed hard. "Uh, n-nothing."

CHAPTER EIGHTEEN

BEFORE WE went home that afternoon, we stopped by the local bank. I was forced to rely on Cricket's kindness once again when I asked if she would be willing to get the safety deposit box put in her name to store all the checks we'd gotten cashed right outside of Salt Lake City. She obliged, but if she was surprised by how much cash we had, she didn't say anything. Little did she know that was just the tip of the iceberg.

"You messed up again. You weren't careful. She knows how much you have," Piper told me, stretched on her side beside me on the bed. Her head rested in her hand.

"So what?" I asked, turning over onto my stomach away from her.

The bed covers slipped to my waist, so I tugged them up a little farther.

"Too bad," Piper purred in reaction, making me recoil.

"I like your back. I like your front even more. Turn over for me."

"Get out of here, Piper."

"She knows how much you have," she repeated.

"Again, so?"

"What if she tells the others? What if they want what you have?"

"She wouldn't do that."

"She could."

"Even if she did," I said, losing my temper, "they wouldn't take it."

"How do you know?" she asked.

"Because they're good people."

"There's no such thing."

"There is! You have no idea what you're talking about."

"Everyone has a little leech in them, Spencer. Don't be naive."

The alarm rang out at four thirty the next morning once more, and once again, I realized that I was indeed *not* dreaming. When I was dressed in my new clothing, I asked Bridge if she thought I looked like a tool. In perfect seriousness, she said, "Dude, you look like you belong here," which made me happy as shit. Jonah picked Bridge up again, but this time Cricket didn't meet me halfway down the drive, much to my disappointment. *This is good*, I kept telling myself over and over.

Jonah and I repeated cleaning out the stalls much as we did the day before but this time, we placed a bag of something called "bedding pellets" down. We laid the bags down in the corners of the stalls and with a knife, cut a cross section, tucking the flaps into the inside of the bag. What happened next fascinated me because we poured an entire bucket of warm water into the bag.

"Leave it," Jonah told me. "We'll come spread the bedding after breakfast."

GREED

"What will happen to the pellets?" I asked him as we made our way up to the main house.

"They spread. That entire bag will turn into at least twelve cubic feet of extra pine bedding. It has the consistency of sawdust, is soft on the horses, better for their allergies, and even increases the rate of urine absorbency, making it more sanitary. We use one to two bags a week, depending on how often the horses use the stalls."

"Cool."

"It is."

After breakfast, we spread the bedding. I was excited to get on a horse because it'd been at least a year, but Jonah informed me we needed to groom them before. I'd never had to do that. Shamefully, the stable hands did all that for us. Jonah taught me how to properly groom a horse so that it didn't chafe or get rubbed by any loose dirt during the workday. I asked him why they didn't do that when they put them away and he told me they did it any time a horse is ridden and any time they're put away.

"Damn, this is a lot of work," I told him.

Jonah laughed. "We haven't even started, greenhorn."

Ethan and Cricket came to stand in front of my stall with their horses.

"Ready?" Ethan asked me.

I nodded.

Everyone mounted their horses and I followed suit, a little bit nervous, and very unaware of what I was supposed to do. I had that same sensation you get when you were new to a school and had no idea who anyone was in your lunch period. You'd take your lunch tray and sort of stand around for a moment looking for a good spot to take a seat, but the entire time you're searching, all you can feel is everyone's eyes on you. That's a shitty feeling.

I sat there on my horse, completely clueless as to who I was supposed to follow. I heard a whistle to my left. It was Cricket.

"Yo, greenhorn, you're with me today."

My heart kicked into high gear. I trotted my horse to side by hers, relieved beyond belief. Not because it was Cricket. Because I had a destination. Yeah, that's it. "What are we doing?" I asked her beautiful face, unable to keep myself from staring.

"We're going to count head, get a reading on any stragglers in my section, direct them toward the herd again. We're bringing the entire herd in closer to the ranch."

"What for?"

"It makes it easier for us to prepare and react to births. We can keep a close eye on them." She turned away from me. "Eugie, come."

That old, cantankerous shepherd mix followed behind her.

We started for the pasture. The leather creaked and pulled beneath me. My horse's tail swished back and forth, its breath fogged the air in front of me. It was freezing out, but I felt comfortable enough thanks to Cricket's suggestions at the outfitters.

I followed her for a good fifteen minutes, mesmerized by her backside. She was so easy on a horse, not a single movement felt superfluous. She was born to be on that horse.

We were quiet, neither one of us knowing what to say to the other. It was awkward, yet I couldn't complain, not with the view it afforded me.

Finally, we reached our destination, a rise near the base of Bitterroot Mountain, above Lake Gossamer. We emerged between a wide copse of trees dusted with snow and I took in the sight before me. My senses felt overwhelmed, blasted with an intense beauty. The lake was so blue it didn't look natural and was so clear you could see all the way to the bottom. It was flanked by two sharp, rocky cliff sides that eventually graduated to peak after peak—a sea of daunting yet beautiful mountains. At the base stood hundred-foot pine trees. They littered the shoreline save for ten feet of varying gray rock peppered with a few red, yellow and green ones, smoothed by thousands of years' worth of running water. Round and perfect, I absently noted that my mother would have paid tens of thousands for them to line her drive.

"Yes," I said.

"I-I didn't say anything," Cricket responded, furrowing her brows in confusion.

"Yes, this is one of the most beautiful places I've ever been to. You were going to ask that, weren't you? How could you not?" I gestured to the nature surrounding us. My gloved hand creaked against the leather as I laid it back on the saddle's horn.

"Undeniably beautiful," she conceded as I stared at her. *No argument there.*

I continued to stare at her and my gut began to ache again. All I could think was the scene, the moment, would have made for the perfect first kiss. And my God did I want to kiss her. My eyes drifted to her lips and she licked them, sending me spiraling.

"Stop that," she said, biting them together, as if that would blunt her uneasiness.

"Stop what?" I asked, swallowing hard. This time wishing she was biting my lip instead of her own.

My lids felt so heavy, I very nearly closed them.

"That," she answered. "Whatever it is that you're doing. I-I...this was a bad idea," she breathed the last part.

"What is?" I asked softly, my tongue feeling as heavy as my lids.

"Us pairing off. Ethan didn't like it but Pop Pop insisted."

I waited a moment before asking, "Why?"

"He thought I could teach you the best. That you would respond best to me."

"Why would he think that, Cricket?"

"I'm not sure," she lied.

We sat silent.

"I think you know why."

Her eyes bored into mine, her chest rose rapidly with her breaths. "No, I don't."

"Oh, I think you do," I said, sidling my horse closer to hers and leaning over, grabbing her saddle's horn and bringing her within inches of my face.

She became flustered, turned away from me and started counting the cattle in the open pasture south of the lake.

"We're missing seven head."

I sat up in my saddle and took a deep breath, still staring at her. *You can't have her. Stop. Become her friend.* Only *her friend.*

I sighed and let her horse go. "Can you spot them?" I asked.

"There," she said, pointing her gloved hand just east of the lake. "There's five there."

"The other two?" I asked again. We searched the lake perimeter in silence. This time I spotted the remaining two. "There," I said, answering my own question.

"Come on," she said, her saddle protesting beneath her as she directed her horse back down the ridge.

I kept pace with her. "What's your favorite thing in the world?" I asked her.

She looked at me skeptically. "Why?"

"Cricket, I don't have ulterior motives. I just figure I'm going to be here a while, we're partners or whatever and it'd be nice if I knew a little about you."

She cleared her throat. "My favorite thing in the world? Let's see," she began, pulling a little at her bottom lip. I checked the gut ache yet again. "Besides my family?"

"Besides your family."

"Eugie," she said, smiling and glancing at the earth below her.

When she said his name, Eugie peered up at her, tongue lolling and eager to do her bidding.

"Not Ethan?" I asked, unable to help myself.

"Ethan is part of my family, Spencer."

"Fair enough. Do you have any hobbies?"

"I may dabble a little in sculpture," she said, her cheeks flaming red.

"Sculpture, eh? And your medium of choice?"

"I take scrap metal we used to recycle around the ranch and whatever I can find and make crazy things out of them."

"That's bad ass," I said, genuinely impressed. "What do you make?"

She looked on me strangely. "Do you really want to hear this?"

"Why wouldn't I?"

"I don't know. It's-It's just not a lot of people around here think it's an *efficient* use of time."

"Who are these *people*?"

"Oh, no one really," she evaded.

Ethan. Ethan was "the people" she was talking about.

"Why do they think this?" I asked.

We rounded the horses around the base of the ridge we'd traversed down and headed for the two cattle at the north of the lake.

"I guess because I could be, I don't know, doing necessary repairs or whatever instead." She looked at me with a smile. "There's always something to do on a ranch."

136

"Exactly," I agreed.

"Hmm?"

"There's always something to do here. Proof that life does not wait, so why not carve yourself out a little bit of happiness. Granted, I know this is fulfilling work because it helps your family survive." I sighed. "It's definitely *exhausting* work, but why does it have to be what defines you?"

"Trust me," she said, cryptically, "no one defines me by the work I do here."

I studied her, but her face gave nothing more away. I could tell it was one subject that was off limits with her so I kept my mouth shut.

"You never answered my question."

"Which one?" she asked.

"What do you make with this scrap metal you happen upon."

She smiled down at her hands then looked up at me once more. My heart stopped. She made my heart stop. "I make *unusual* things. For instance, I've always been fascinated by Churchill."

"Interesting," I said, laughing a little.

She ignored me. "So I created this exaggerated version of his head using odds and ends. I stamped his quote, 'If you're going through hell, keep going,' onto his forehead. I loved it. The others, not so much." She sat thoughtfully for a second. "Except for Jonah! Jonah loves my sculptures."

"And August?"

"Thinks they're a waste of time."

"And Ethan?"

She looked at me but didn't utter a word.

"I think I'd like to see these sculptures of yours, Cricket Hunt."

"Caroline," she corrected with a smile.

"Your real name?" I asked.

"Yeah, you can keep calling me Cricket if you want though, but if we're going to be partners, as you said, you should know my real name is Caroline."

"Caroline's a beautiful name."

"Thank you." She smiled that heart-stopping smile. "My dead mama picked it out."

"I don't know about that," I said. "I saw her picture in the main house. You seem to carry an awful lot of her likeness. Seems to me she lives on just fine."

She smiled at me. This time it reached glassy eyes. "Thank you."

CHAPTER NINETEEN

WE REACHED the two grazing cattle, both fat with calf, and began to lead them toward the five on the east side of the lake. Cricket and I tried to continue our conversation, but the heifers made it impossible—one or both of them getting skittish and trying to flee into the woods. It was hard to guide our horses, let alone the cows through the trees.

It took almost an hour just to reach the five on the east bank. We sat there with all seven for a moment to catch our breath.

"We've got to keep them out of the woods," she said. "I want you to keep the rear here and prevent them from turning around. I'll flank their left and prevent them from scaring off. We'll use the lake to our advantage. They'll avoid the deeper water."

I nodded.

My job was fairly easy, pulling left or right to prevent them from turning but Cricket? Cricket was like flipping

GREED

Houdini. One second she was casually setting a single heifer back into line, the next she was corralling all seven with what seemed like a single surge of her horse. Every single movement was calculated with not a single waste of energy, and she did it all flawlessly. She made it look effortless, when I know for a fact it was an orchestrated and anticipated dance. She was incredible. She was impressive. She was undeniably the most fascinating creature I'd ever known.

When we drew close to the herd, Cricket ran the strays toward the mass, and they seemed happy to be back. She turned around and met me.

"Is that Emmett on a horse?" I asked.

"Yeah, he always helps with the drives. No one save for Jonah has his instincts, and Jonah's are premature. He can practically draw out the herd's reactions on a piece of paper before we even set out."

As if he knew we were talking about him, Emmett came riding up, whistling at a stubborn cow. "How'd you do, greenhorn?"

"Ask your granddaughter," I answered with a smile.

The herd mooed, spooked and were altogether ridiculously noisy. That, coupled with the "ha's" and whistles from the ranch hands, and we had to raise our voices to hear one another.

"He didn't do too badly," Cricket told him, winking at me. I almost fell off my horse. "Is everyone in?"

"Ethan's still wrangling up five head pretty far from here. Somehow they got around that fence on the north side of the property."

"How many in all?" she asked.

"About ninety-three. We've got most of them though. Should be on our way soon."

Cricket nodded as Emmett headed back into the herd, then pulled her scarf over her mouth, making her look

140

like an old-fashioned bandit. I did the same. The warmth from my breath was a nice reprieve.

"Bonnie," I called to her.

"Yeah, Clyde," she deftly responded, making me laugh.

"How long will it take to drive the herd?" I yelled.

"It takes about four hours. There's a bit of road we have to cross to get to the main ranch. That's always a pain in the ass as the cattle spook easily by passing cars. They get confused."

"Why is there a public road running through the middle of your property?"

"It's thousands of acres, Spencer, and when the city comes knocking on your door with a paper stating 'eminent domain,' you don't really have a choice but to comply."

I nodded.

"Did they at least pay you for it?"

"Nope."

"Damn."

"Exactly."

A sharp whistle caught our attention. Emmett made a loop signal with his arm and everyone fell into place. Emmett up front, Jonah and a ranch hand I couldn't remember the name of to his left and right, Ethan and his dad behind them, ranch hands Pete and Drew behind them, and Cricket and me in the back. All the dogs were scattered around except for Eugie, and they were like little well-oiled machines, checking unruly cattle and keeping them in line. I was fascinated watching them work in sync with such incredible efficiency.

"Hope you feed those dogs well," I said.

"Oh, they eat like kings," Cricket laughed.

Suddenly, I saw Ellie ride up and join Jonah's side.

"Your grandma is helping?" I asked in disbelief.

"She's a tough old bird. Nothing could keep her from

this. Driving is her favorite part of the ranch. Grandma strives for adventure. She always rides point right behind Pop Pop."

"Point," I said.

"Yeah, if this were, say, a hundred years ago and we were driving the cattle for weeks, Pop Pop's position would be called 'trail boss,' Jonah and Joe would be 'point,' Ethan and Huck would be 'swing,' Pete and Drew would be 'flank' and you and I would be the 'drag.'"

"Cool," I said, interested in what she was talking about, possibly because I sat at the rear of five thousand cattle, or more possibly because it was Cricket talking and anything she said fascinated me. "How do you know all this?"

"I used to read my great-great-grandfather's journals. He used to ride the trails as a hired hand before he settled here."

We began the drive about an hour after sunrise, which was welcome, because it had already begun to warm us through. Halfway there, I was starting to sweat because I was working so hard to keep my section of cattle from going renegade. I would look over at Cricket and just the slightest movements on her horse would influence her cattle. I found myself studying her, learning how she anticipated their actions and trying to emulate her. About an hour into it and I thought I'd gotten the knack of it until one cow shot out of the herd like someone had smacked her. All the dogs were occupied, so it was left up to me to get her back.

I banked my horse left and chased after her but every time she would shoot right, I would overcorrect and miss her. She kept slipping out from my control, and I was starting to get frustrated. I heard Cricket come galloping behind me. I turned around to gesture for her to return to the herd, that come hell or high water, I was going to get this troublesome cow back to the group, but I was stunned silent when she pulled out her rope and started swinging it over her head. In one try, she roped the cow's neck. She turned to return to the group and I watched her slack-jawed, my gaping mouth refusing to close. *Damn.*

I had never seen anything sexier than Cricket Hunt roping a cow. I whistled low. *Still can't have her.*

She released the cow and we fell quietly in step with one another. The herd had slowed to a snail's pace and things became mellow.

"Didn't want to overstep," she offered in apology.

"No, it's fine," I said, still reeling from how talented she was.

"I just-we were getting ahead of you and I didn't want to lose you."

I read way too much into that and my heart leapt in my throat.

"It's seriously fine," I said with a smile.

She smiled back.

When we reached the road, Jonah and Emmett swung open the gates at the crossing. Ellie and Jonah stationed themselves in the road to prevent any cattle from straying and the herd quickly began meandering through. It was stressful because it thinned the herd out and it felt like an impossible task to keep the entire herd together.

Cricket and I watched as a truck began to approach, going too fast. We sat up in our saddles, our gloved hands gripping the horns of our saddle with serious tension.

"Stop," Cricket breathed under her breath, her chest rising and falling with the stress.

Ellie kept raising her hands above her head, but the fool made no move to slow down until it was almost too late.

"Slow down!" I yelled vainly, braced to jump from my horse, as if I was anywhere near them.

GREED

Cricket's hand wrapped around her throat. She looked panicked and unsure. I grabbed her shoulder in reaction and we sat helplessly waiting. There is nothing more pitiful than feeling that out of control.

Slamming on his breaks, he narrowly stopped himself from hitting Ellie. I heard Cricket inhale a sharp breath.

"Oh God, he missed her," she breathed, bringing her hand to her heart.

There was a split second of utter calm before pure chaos and all hell broke loose. The cattle spooked, most ran through the gate and dispersed into the pasture but at least seventy head lost route and followed the fence line in all different directions.

Jonah, Pete, Drew and Ethan scrambled to get as many as they could, while Cricket and I took care of as much of the herd as we could on our side, guiding them across the road and into the new pasture. Once all the cattle were through and the first gate was closed, Jonah dismounted his horse, wrapping his horse's lead at the closed gate. Before I'd had a chance to react, Jonah approached the driver's side, ripped open the door and started yelling.

"Shit," I whispered and dismounted, handing Cricket my lead and running over to Jonah's side.

Ethan quickly stood beside Jonah as well. The driver got out and got in Jonah's face, chest to chest and I pulled them apart, holding Jonah back. Ethan held the driver back.

"What in the hell is your problem!" Jonah yelled. "You had to have seen us!"

"Fuck you!" the guy responded, because he had nothing else to defend himself with.

Jonah surged forward and I had to use all my strength to hold him back. He was livid.

"You could have killed her!" he screamed.

The guy staggered back a little and it became apparent why his reaction time was so lethargic. Ethan let him go and joined Jonah's side.

I studied him. "You're drunk," I told him.

"You!" he yelled, not hearing me. He pointed at me. "Let's go!"

"I'm not gonna fight you, asshole, but I will fix your problem," I told him calmly, setting Jonah aside. I looked at him, letting him know to stay where he was.

I walked around the inebriated fool and removed his keys from the ignition. The guy tried to swipe them from me, but it was an exaggerated attempt, making him fall against the side of his truck.

"I'll be keeping these," I told him. I looked around for Cricket. She was still on her horse. "Call the cops?"

She nodded.

The guy stood upright, but it took his door to help him do it. "I'm gonna kick your ass," he slurred.

"I don't think so," I said. "You're going to wait right here and when the cops show up, you can explain why you're plastered at eleven in the morning and *driving*."

I turned and began to follow Jonah back to the fence to retrieve our horses but felt a tug on my jacket. My head fell back in reaction. *Oh, shit.*

I spun around and ducked as the idiot took a swing. *Don't hit him. Don't hit him.* He took a swing again, but I stepped back quickly.

"Stop," I demanded.

He staggered forward. "Your ass is grass, pretty boy," he taunted.

"Sit your ass down in your truck, or I'll put you there."

His face flamed red and his eyes narrowed in hate. *Here we go.* He took a swing but I avoided it easily, then laid an uppercut that knocked the bastard clean out.

"Whoa!" Jonah yelled, dragging it out. "Awesome."

"Help me," I told him, panicking, pulling the guy by his jacket toward his truck.

I laid the guy down on the side of the road and had Jonah reposition the truck on the shoulder. I let down the guy's bed and we lifted him onto it.

"He'll be safe here until the cops come," I said.

I looked around. Everyone was gathering the herd within the field, but they still had one eye on us. I jumped the fence and took my horse by the reins, encouraging a gallop until I met up with Cricket.

"They're on their way," she told me.

"Cool," I answered, feeling anything but.

I'd just clocked a guy, in a rural town with rural cops who have nothing better to do than investigate an assault against a rural drunk driver in the middle of a rural fucking highway.

Cricket read my body language. "If they ask us what happened, we've all agreed we saw nothing. You were never here."

I smiled at her, relieved beyond measure. "Thank you."

CHAPTER TWENTY

WE'D GOTTEN the herd going again and were out of the view of the highway by the time we heard sirens. Regardless if they could see us, I was still paranoid as shit.

"You're quiet," Cricket stated.

"Yeah," I said, giving her a small smile.

"No one will find out you hit that guy, Spencer."

I took a deep breath. "I know. It's just-I knew better than to do it."

"I saw what happened. It was either you or him. You did what you had to."

"I could have left him there."

"Imagine you'd just done that. Then imagine his drunk ass was staggering around the road and got hit by a car."

I couldn't help my grin. "Trying to make me feel better. That's nice but not necessary."

"I'm not trying to make you feel better. Sometimes

you can avoid the conflict and sometimes it's just necessary."

I smiled at her.

When we finally arrived at the ranch, I was incredibly relieved and incredibly exhausted. I couldn't believe how much work it took to run a ranch. I was definitely earning my keep.

We fed and watered the herd, then cleaned up before sitting down to a big lunch courtesy of Bridge and Ellie and two other house workers, one they called Cookie. I assume because she could cook the crap out of a good meal, and the other I overheard someone call Roberta the first day. Roberta was more on an assisting level Bridge had told me. She said the kitchen ranked herself at the bottom, then Roberta, Cookie and Ellie. She also said it was pleasant working with the women, as they were all cheeky and hilarious. The only drawback was that the main house didn't have air conditioning and the kitchen could turn stifling.

I sat next to Bridge at lunch. "I heard about what happened," she said.

"How in the world?" I sat, bewildered.

"Jonah ran up to the house after he'd put away the horses."

"Is that so?" I asked, looking for Jonah, but he was nowhere to be found. *Lucky bastard.*

"Listen, I like Jonah and all, but you've got to nip this thing in the bud, Bridge," I spoke quietly. "I mean, for gosh sakes, does he not realize that you're pregnant with another dude's baby?"

"You're so clever, Spence," she bit sarcastically. "Let me check you because apparently you think I've forgotten why we're here. Stop reminding me that I'm pregnant. The constant nausea is reminder enough. Got me?" I nodded, feeling guilty already. "And furthermore, I'm

148

being *reasonably* kind to Jonah because he's kind to me. I don't know where you're getting this idea that he's interested in me. He's aware I'm *harboring a fugitive*."

"You're right, Bridge, again. I'm sorry, but I want you to make it very clear to Jonah that you're not interested."

She shook her head at me. "I don't care how screwed up you think it is. This is going to be my last opportunity to feel like a normal girl because in a couple of months I'm going to be smuggling a basketball up in here," she said, gesturing wildly at her stomach. "Let me just have this normal friendship with Jonah. Just...let me, Spencer," she added quietly.

I sighed. "Whatever, Bridge. Just don't set yourself up for disappointment, because as soon as you start showing, that guy is going to want nothing to do with you."

Her eyes turned glassy and she shrugged, looking defeated. "He's a very sweet guy willing to be my friend, Spencer. Don't make me feel any more an outcast than I already do."

I let it lie there, partly because I felt like an asshole and partly because I was worried about her and didn't know how to fix it. I wished my mom was there to help. I felt so alone, like there was a weight upon my shoulders and I had no one else to share the burden with.

I looked around the table and spotted Cricket. Despite everything, despite the fact I knew I couldn't have her, that I shouldn't have her, I still felt a desperate need to know everything about her. I never had that feeling for anyone else. Not even for Sophie Price. *Huh. Sophie.* I hadn't given her a second thought since L.A. *Funny, that.*

The day went by quickly. Jonah and I worked side by side when Ethan took Cricket into town for some reason. There were two new things I learned that day. One, Jonah was, despite loathing to acknowledge it, a pretty nice guy.

GREED

He was more innocent than any other guy I'd ever hung with, and he actually made me want to be a better person. Go figure. And two, I hated Ethan. Yes, I promised myself that Cricket would be my friend and only my friend, but that didn't mean I was going to pretend I wasn't violently attracted to her, and it sure as hell meant that I wasn't going to like when Ethan touched her, kissed her *or* took her into town. I couldn't watch them when he took her into town and that thought, selfish as it may be, bugged the shit out of me. I hated him for no other reason than he got to do those things with her.

That evening, after dinner, I walked back down to our trailer. I was beyond irritated because Ethan and Cricket didn't show at dinner. I wondered where the hell they were but was too afraid to ask because I didn't want her family reading too much into my interest.

The sun had long ago set, and the little dirt roads on the ranch had begun to ice back over from lack of use. I peered down my lane to see, what else, Jonah's four-wheeler setting at the base of the trailer.

I popped up the steps and blew through the door in attempt to discover something but, instead of the debauchery I expected, I found both of them on opposite ends of the banquette, laughing at something altogether innocent.

"Hello there, idiot," Bridge greeted.

"Nice," I said, rolling my eyes. "What's up, Jonah?" I asked him, raising one brow.

He startled. "Uh, I better get going. See you tomorrow," he called toward me and opened the door, but before he left, he turned toward Bridge. "Same time?" he asked her.

"Yup, see you then," she answered, smiling.

I shook my head and decided to ignore it. I was exhausted and sore and dirty as shit. I wanted a shower. I shut the accordion door to our "bedroom" and tore off my clothing, tossing it into the corner I kept my dirty stuff.

I was beyond pissed when the door wouldn't close to the bathroom. With more force than necessary, I slammed the thing closed. I started the water and waited for it to start steaming before attempting to get inside. A few days before, I jumped in without thinking and almost froze to death.

Stepping into the tiny stall didn't add to improving my mood, as the water was barely warm. I ducked as usual to wash my hair and considered plugging the damn tub just to get some semblance of normality.

I washed quickly and dried just as quickly. I was feeling incredibly restless. *You need to get out.* I dressed warmly and decided to walk the property, maybe check out the family's original buildings. I rummaged underneath the kitchen sink and found a flashlight.

"Where are you going?" Bridge asked.

"Out. I need to get out."

She nodded, accepting this.

I bounded out into the snow and almost turned back around. I trudged forward and came to the top of our lane, hooking a left toward the old buildings. It was a good mile walk, but I needed to rid myself the terrible itch I could feel rising in the pit of my stomach. That itch I got whenever I wanted to run away from something I didn't like. Except this time I had no idea what I wanted to run from. *Bullshit,* I told myself. *You know exactly why you want to run. The difference this time is you want to run toward the main house, up those stairs and into the room of that incredible girl.* I outwardly cringed, unable to hide how I really felt, especially not from myself.

I got lost in thought. Internal arguments demanding I get the hell over myself, that I forget her, distance myself from her only to turn around and ask what was the worst thing that could happen and asking myself if I could steal her away from Ethan. *You've done worse*, I rationalized. And I had. I had done terrible, awful, incredible things to people. People I didn't even know. *Maybe this is one person you should let be.*

I'd made my decision, convinced I wouldn't even try to become her friend. *Too complicated*, I thought. And before I realized, I'd stumbled upon the first small building. I noticed there was light inside and flipped off my flashlight before circling the front, curious. I found a window, but the glass was so old and cloudy, you could hardly see into the lit room. I pressed my face against the glass.

Oh...no. No.

Cricket was inside, blasting a few tunes in a light denim button-up that fit so snugly I almost fell over. The sleeves were rolled up to allow her to work, and the shirt was tucked into a pair of high-waisted denim shorts with two rows of brass buttons down the front panel. My gaze followed down her short but beautiful legs to knee-highs. Her hair was wrapped in a bright red headscarf. Like a modern day frickin' Rosie the Riveter. And so unbelievably sexy. I could not compare her to anyone. When I looked on her, I couldn't even tell you that other women existed.

My hand tugged down my face. Suddenly, I felt stifling and had to pull off my knit cap and scarf. I swallowed. *Turn. Turn and run and get out. Turn*, I ordered myself.

But that's not what I did. Oh no. No, I was a glutton for punishment, it seemed. Instead of doing what I should, I did what I couldn't help, and knocked. I watched her reaction through the window. She dropped the pieces of scrap metal she'd been rummaging through and came to the door.

I stood upright once more and checked myself. The

door swung open and the scented candle she was burning bowled me over. The smell of baking chocolate cake swarmed around me, and all I wanted to do was taste Cricket.

My mouth gaped open, ready to speak, but no words would come. Her face flamed red.

"I'm sorry," she said, her hands going to her naked thighs. "I thought you were my grandmother. She checks on me sometimes."

"I-I was taking a walk and saw the light on." I swallowed, my gaze raking her body. She was covered pretty much from head to toe, but no matter how hard Cricket tried, she couldn't hide her curves. "I'm not disturbing you, am I?" I asked.

"No," she said, taking a deep breath. She opened the door wider and invited me in.

Careful. Be careful, Spencer.

Inside, it was incredibly warm. In the corner sat a wood burning stove and it looked like she'd put on a fresh log. I absently noted that she intended to stay for a while. I removed my jacket and placed it along with my cap and scarf on a table near the door. I studied my surroundings and discovered there were shelves and tables scattered in disarray around the room and were full of fascinating sculptures. My eyes lingered on one. The head of Winston Churchill.

I turned to Cricket. "Your work?"

Her cheeks flushed an enticing vermillion. *Oh, Cricket. You would be so smart not to blush again.*

"Yeah," she answered simply.

She seemed embarrassed, adding to how attractive I found her, and studied the ground with her hands tucked behind her back. She fought a smile while I fought to keep my hands at my side.

She made herself busy by clearing a stool covered

153

in scrap metal. She cleared her throat nervously and presented the stool to me before rounding the table she'd been working at when I discovered her.

I sat, my legs spread and hung both my arms over the back of the stool. Her eyes widened when she turned my direction and I almost laughed out loud. I unnerved her. *Click*.

"Cricket Hunt, show me your stuff."

Her head whipped my direction. "*Excuse me?*"

"Your sculptures?"

"Oh," she giggled, "sure. Uh," she began and stiffened her back, "but first you have to promise not to laugh at any of them."

"Cross my heart," I told her, making the motion my thumb.

She sighed, deciding something then with conviction she marched over to a shelf tucked into a narrow corner of the cabin. She stretched high, trying to reach one on the top shelf but she was too short. She made a movement to find something to stand on, but I stopped her.

"I'll get it," I told her, slinking off the stool and stalking toward her.

She made a movement to make way for me, feinting left then right, but I blocked her in. She looked up at me and it set my heart racing. I studied her face for a moment, unable not to.

"Which one?" I asked softly.

"Th-that one," she explained, her eyes trained on the sculpture at the far top left.

I reached over her and our bodies grazed from the proximity, sending shivers up my spine. I had never felt shivers before, not before Cricket. Not like that. *Never* like that.

I picked the piece up and brought it down to chest

level for me, eye level for her. "This one," I breathed.

"That's the one," she confirmed, not even glancing at the sculpture.

Her eyes were trained on my lips. She irresponsibly licked her own before drawing her bottom lip under her top teeth. I winced at the pain it caused me, a shot of pure fire blasted from the tips of my toes to the top of my head only to settle in the hollow of my stomach. It was a good burn though. Too good.

I uprooted my weighted feet and somehow walked away from her, but not before glancing back once more. I found Cricket had briefly sagged into the wall beside her before finding her bearings again. *Click.*

The fire continued to burn in my belly, knowing that if I really wanted to, I could steal a kiss. I knew if I did, though, she'd be all in then, all passion and hands, but just as quickly she'd be all out, an iron door slammed shut over the one I'd built the day we'd taken Bridge to the doctor. The one I erected only to immediately search out the weakest part. The part I shoved a boot through the second I saw Cricket Hunt in knee-highs and high-waisted shorts. And the last thing I wanted to do was create emotional distance from the very girl who sent me flying to the moon every time she licked her lips, smiled or crinkled her nose.

I set the piece down on the table and found my seat and position, sitting as I had before, as if nothing with lightning-like intensity had just transpired in that small nook. She sat in the stool on the other side of the table and watched me for a moment.

Finally, she spoke. "So," she said, before clearing her throat, "this is, uh, one of the first pieces I made."

I sat up, already engrossed, leaning forward and casually placing my forearms on the table. I hoped I fooled her. She inexplicably inclined forward as well, as if incapable of doing anything else.

"Yeah, so, anyway, I had just learned to weld and the work is shoddy, but it's my proudest piece. I made it all by myself with no one's help, and I poured myself into it."

"It's stunning," I told her.

She smiled her clever smile and I almost lost my cool. "No, it's not, but thank you."

"It's visually stunning, Cricket."

Instead of continually denying it, like most girls do, Cricket said, "Thank you, Spencer."

That kind of confidence is unbelievably sexy.

"How did you learn to weld?" I asked her.

"Pop Pop taught me. We live on a ranch. It was an inevitability. There's always something to weld around here."

I smiled at her.

"Tell me something."

"What would you like to know?" she asked.

"Anything. Anything at all that you want me to know," I told her.

She laughed quietly. "I shouldn't care that you know anything about me, Spencer."

"And? Do you, or don't you?"

She shook her head. "This is dangerous," she said, uneasy.

"We're just talking," I lied.

She sighed, pausing for a moment, gauging whether she wanted to open up to me. In the end, she said, "I don't want to live here forever."

Her face bunched as if bracing for a hit.

I laughed. "And?"

She cracked open one eye and warily peered my direction. "I can't believe I said it out loud," she giggled, as if she couldn't help herself. She looked at me fully. "I've never told anyone that before."

"Where do you want to go?"

"I don't know," she said with thought. "I guess-I guess I've never thought about it past that. Is that strange?"

"No, I definitely understand that. There's a fear there. I know that fear very well." I narrowed my brow, searching her face. "In your case, I suspect it's a fear of hurting those you love. You don't want to leave them, but you want to find yourself. You want this," I told her, gesturing at the shelves filled with extraordinary creativity.

Her breaths deepened with each revelation and her eyes looked on me fiercely. She swallowed, her eyes turning glassy. "Yes."

"When Bridge has the baby, I could take you to New York. I know someone," I told her.

I couldn't believe what I'd just offered, couldn't believe what I was saying, what I was thinking, what I'd just promised.

She looked at me intensely, her hand going to her neck. I briefly observed her hands were nothing like Piper's. *Her* nails were short, unpolished. *Her* fingers were slender and dainty. They looked so delicate to me, as if made from paper. I wanted to wrap them in my own and keep their porcelain beauty all to myself.

"I can't," she said, giving me the out my brain was begging for, but confusing my heart, causing it to fall at my feet.

"Why?" I stupidly insisted.

"I just..." she started, her eyes growing glassy once more. "I cannot go," she told me gently, "and I beg you not to ask me why. Please?"

"I would do anything you asked me, Cricket," I told her quietly.

GREED

Her eyes closed then slowly they fluttered open. "Spencer," she breathed, slowly shaking her head.

I cemented my arms to the table, my feet to the floor. When she said my name, I very nearly pulled her into me just so I could hold her, just so I could feel her skin against mine, pull the scarf from her head, breathe in her hair. Cricket Hunt was doing things to me I never imagined I could feel.

"I know," I breathed. "I'm sorry."

"We have to tread carefully," she told me.

"I understand," I told her truthfully.

She began to dig through little pieces of metal, setting aside the ones that interested her and I examined every single movement, riveted to how graceful she was. She was the human equivalent to a butterfly. Light and airy, graceful...and defied logic.

"What are you making?" I asked her, genuinely interested.

She sported her clever smile once more to torture me. "I'm thinking three little birds in a nest."

"Like Marley's song," I commented, not thinking anything of it.

She looked up at me in shock and answered with a nod.

"I'm going to hide 'smile with the risin' sun' somewhere in the nest."

"I think that's brilliant."

She smiled at me.

"These will be small enough that I can solder them." She went back to studying the pile on her table and a few minutes of silence passed. "Would you like them when I'm done?" she asked, her eyes never leaving her scrap. She was insecure, wary.

I was taken aback by her offer. "I-that would be an honor, Cricket. Thank you."

She raised her face at me. "I've never given any of my sculptures away," she confessed.

"Why not?" I asked. She shrugged her right shoulder. "Have you even offered?"

"Lots of times," she confessed sadly. "After the hundredth 'no, thank you,' I stopped asking."

I was impressed she didn't let those rejections stop her from doing something she loved. I admired courage, especially in women.

"Well, I'm flattered you asked me."

"I know," she said. "That gives me such a high."

Because it's me, or because it was anyone? I wanted to ask but couldn't pluck up the mettle. I was afraid her answer might damage me.

"Well, happy to oblige," I said instead.

I watched her work for close to half an hour before she took these giant sharp scissors and started shaping pieces with such ease, I wondered if she truly could be that talented.

She assembled something that resembled the shape of a bird head, but I couldn't envision where she was going with it until, that is, she began to shape intricate feathers. One by one, she soldered them on before adding a delicate beak and eyes.

She held the finished bird head in front of me and I couldn't believe what I was seeing. The work was so detailed; I didn't think it was possible with a medium like metal.

"Cricket, I," I began but was struck dumb. Rather than prattle on, I took the bird head in my hands, careful not to damage it, and consciously memorized it.

I handed it back to her. "I'm floored...It's astonishing. You're very talented."

"Thank you," she said, studying it with a massive smile on her face.

"You dazzle me," I told her.

Her cheeks flamed and she bit her bottom lip, further staggering me. She checked her watch.

"Crap!" she exclaimed, breaking the moment. "It's nearly midnight."

I laughed. "I remember a time when midnight meant the beginning of an evening, not the decided end."

"I'll remember you said that when we're shoveling horse manure at five in the morning."

I groaned. "Definitely time to go."

I put on my jacket and cap while Cricket reached for her headscarf, pulled it down and ruffled her bangs before grabbing her own coat. She wasn't wearing her usual jacket but rather a floor-length brown suede one. I took it from her and helped her in it. I wanted very badly to run my hands down the curves of her coat, but I restrained myself.

"Come on," she said. "I'll give you a ride."

She put out the fire in the stove and I followed her around the side of the little building to another four-wheeler. She got on and started the engine. I hesitated a moment, knowing this would be the closest my body had ever been to hers. I straddled the seat behind her, my legs bracing the sides of both of hers. My hands itched to run the length of her thighs, so I tucked them into my sides.

"Hold on," she whispered, making me reel. I peeled my hands away from myself and wrapped them around her tiny waist. I nearly groaned at the feel of her.

We lurched forward and her hair whipped with the wind, sending the unlikely scent of her vanilla and grapefruit shampoo my way. It was such an odd combination but I recognized it immediately. *Oh God, can't I just run my fingers through it? Just once?* I breathed deeply and my eyes slid into the back of my head.

All too soon, we were at my door and I slid off, away

from her warmth, away from her scent.

I walked up the steps and turned back around. "Goodnight, Cricket Hunt."

"Goodnight, Spencer Blackwell."

CHAPTER TWENTY-ONE

I LAID down and tried to sleep. I knew I was going to be exhausted the next day as it was, but I couldn't keep my thoughts from straying toward Cricket.

I used to keep this obnoxious list of criteria for the girls I dated. I would often hang with my friends and we would amend it, sharpen it up, add a few things. I kept the list and used it, even after I graduated prep school. These were the basics.

1) She must be a minimum of five foot ten.

2) Her hair can never be cut above the shoulders.

3) No fatties, but she has to maintain enough curves to satisfy.

4) No smaller than a C-cup.

5) Private school educated.

6) She must run in our circle.

7) Minimum seventy-five thousand dollar vehicle.

Now for my more personal preferences:

8) Blonde.

9) Elegant features.
10) Perfectly symmetrical face.
11) Facial features must look balanced.
12) No nicknames.
13) Quiet.
14) No clingers.

I'd memorized the list. *Oh my God*, I thought, *what a douche I've been.*

Cricket had obliterated it, just annihilated my previous criteria. She only shared a few attributes on the list, but I'd discovered something that evening that startled me. It didn't matter to me what I wanted before, because I somehow didn't want that anymore. I wanted someone short, thin and wispy with chin-length dark hair. Someone with grit, with gumption, with personality, with character, with humor. Someone who represented feisty, capable and talented. Someone like Cricket.

Cricket was my new criteria.

I crossed my arms across my chest and fell to sleep with a stupid grin on my face.

"Well, she's disgusting," Piper said, filing at a nail.

"What?" I asked, spinning around in my stool to face her.

"This Cricket you speak of. She sounds dumb. She has no direction. She doesn't want to stay at her grandparents' ranch, but she's too afraid to tell them so. She has no direction. She doesn't share your dream. She's not meant for you. Besides, she's a frail little thing. Not very attractive, if you ask me." My blood was boiling at a dangerous level. I found myself panting to control the anger. My fists coiled at my sides. "She's going to take your money," Piper provoked.

I unexpectedly launched myself at Piper and wrapped my hand around her throat. Her nail file rang out as it hit the tile beneath our feet.

GREED

"Take. That. Back," I gritted.

My hand tightened and her face began to look purple but instead of desperation, Piper's eyes delighted in mischief and she smiled. I removed my hand and sat once more to calm myself down.

"Sensitive?" she asked, catching her breath and leaning against the subzero in her ridiculous silk gown.

"Don't ever talk about her like that," I ordered, still trying to tame my temper.

Piper laughed.

"You're losing sight of what you're doing. You're too distracted. You need to focus. Girls will come and go, but this opportunity you've been presented is a once-in-a-lifetime thing."

My eyes narrowed on her. "How-how do you know about that?" I asked. "No one knows about that."

Piper sprawled out over the large island and faced me, her crimson hair cascading all around her. "I know everything," she whispered. She ran a hand across the flat of her belly and patted it once. "Like when I knew Bridge was going to get pregnant...I orchestrated it!" she giggled insanely. "Just like I knew your mama would always stay with your father because she's too cowardly and lazy to create a new life for herself. She'd rather taint her children with your father's vile influence than save their souls." My teeth began to grit. "I know everything. Just like I knew that teller would offer her body to get a little piece of your fortune." Her voice dropped to a murmur. "Like I knew you would take those photographs. As I said, I know everything." She laughed. "It's almost too easy. People make it way too easy. No one has conviction these days. It's pathetic. It's not even fun anymore."

She began to cackle shrilly and it got louder and louder, so loud my eardrums felt like they would burst. I clasped my hands over my ears and shrank into myself. "Stop!" I *begged. "Stop!" I yelled again. "Stop!"*

"Stop!" I cried out. I shot up and sucked in a frantic breath, in violent need of oxygen.

My alarm pierced throughout the room and my hand trembled as it reached to turn it off. Sweet silence rang through my head once more. My body sagged against the wall adjacent to my bed as I tried to calm myself. I stared down at my hands and marked how badly they shook, stuffing them into my sides. My head lolled against the bottom of the window.

"Are you okay?" a groggy-voiced Bridget asked.

"Huh? Oh, yes, just a," I swallowed, "a bad dream."

She looked at me fiercely, a confused expression on her face. "That must have been one horrible dream."

"It was nothing," I told her, trying to smile.

I threw my legs over the side of my bed and stood. I needed to get out of that trailer. I needed to get to work. I needed...something.

As I brushed my teeth, I purposely thought of Cricket and her clever smile, trying to distract myself. These dreams were cutting too close. I hated them. I didn't understand them and I wanted them gone so badly. I spat and rinsed, my hands still trembling, when a knock came to the door. *Jonah*, I thought, but when I opened it, I was surprised to see Cricket.

"Cricket? Everything okay?" I asked, letting her in.

She stepped inside and immediately I was calmed by her presence.

"Yes, it's just, we're seeing too many calves dead in the field."

"What's going on?" I asked, tossing on my jacket and hat.

"We're not sure, but it's spreading quickly and we're afraid for the calves yet to be born," she explained as I followed her out and down the steps.

"How many are dead?" I asked, curious, as we wound our way up the lane.

"Eleven," she said, her breath billowing out in front of her. She looked nervous, her brows furrowed in concentration. "We've tried several different antibiotics so far, but we don't have the right combination." She seemed to be talking to herself then. "At first I thought it might be pneumonia and umbilical disease, but the antibiotics used to treat those aren't affecting them." She slammed a fist into her hand. "We can't afford to lose any more."

"Hey," I said, touching her shoulder briefly and bringing her back. "We'll figure it out."

She nodded. "Ethan," she began, making my stomach clench, "has been out all night with them with Jonah. He's resting now. I told him I'd get you to help me."

I bobbed my head, refusing to speak in fear I'd say something stupid.

"We can't afford to lose any more," she said gravely.

"Wait, with Jonah? Maybe I should drive Bridge up to the house."

She dismissed me. "Oh, no, he's still getting Bridget this morning."

My eyes narrowed at her.

"Is he?"

"Yes," she said matter-of-factly, deep in thought.

"Why does he do that for her?" I asked her.

She recognized my meaning and lifted her head cautiously. "Because Jonah is the nicest guy God ever made, Spencer."

"I don't disagree, but I believe he's more motivated than that."

She looked at the ground and tried to hurry before me. "I don't know what you're talking about."

I snatched the back of her coat and brought her back. She looked up at me warily. "Cricket."

"Honestly?"

"Honestly."

She sighed. "I don't know."

"Bull!"

"I'm serious! He's a very secretive guy sometimes. He hasn't said anything to any of us, that I know of, but we can see what you see."

I tugged off my cap and ran my fingers through my hair. Blond strands fell forward and almost reached the tip of my nose. I slicked it back and drew the cap back on. "Doesn't he recognize that she's pregnant?"

"He's not an idiot," she laughed. "Wanna know my opinion?"

"What's that?" I asked, as we reached the carriage house. I didn't know what we were doing there, but I opened the door for her anyway.

"I think he sees a kindred spirit in her."

I snorted.

"What? Don't believe me?"

"No," I answered simply as we rounded several tractors with massive blades in front.

"Jonah's a big guy," she started and I laughed which made her grin. "Okay, a *very* big guy.

"The guy should be a freaking linebacker."

"Exactly. He's always been that large and to girls, that's intimidating. In high school, he fumbled around like a goof, unable to control his massive frame. He's always been lean, muscular, but it wasn't until he hit his sophomore year, right about the time he became really interested in girls, that he became the Mister Universe we've all come to love. It didn't help matters that he was shyer than anyone I'd ever met."

I whistled low.

"Tell me about it. I would have to drag him around with me, practically speak for him if a girl was present."

I laughed out loud. The idea of itty-bitty Cricket acting as bodyguard to Montana's version of Tom Hardy was too hilarious.

"Shut up," she said, fighting a giggle. "He's a giant teddy bear and incredibly sensitive. I remember him telling me how he hated how people stared at him."

"Ah," I said, finally realizing what she meant. "The way the ranch stares at Bridge."

"Exactly. Like she's a novelty," she said quietly. "He wants to shield her from all that." She cleared her throat. "It doesn't hurt that Bridge is Barbie personified, a virtual Miss Sweden."

"Oh God, don't say that!" I cringed.

"Sorry to inform you, Mr. Blackwell, but your sister is like liquid gold around here, pregnant or not. She may slip through their fingers, but that doesn't mean they aren't going to try."

"Oh, jeez," I said, wincing.

"And Jonah's a gentle soul. He's not going to rip and grasp at your sister like these other boys would. He'll tenderly cup his hands and just wait for her to pour herself inside. He's a patient guy."

"Okay, just stop. Stop. The visuals you're giving me are pissing me off." She laughed loudly. "What's so funny?"

"You. You're funny."

I pulled my smile to one side and raised a brow.

We approached a room with a glass door, incongruent with the rustic feel of the remaining carriage house.

"What is this?" I asked.

"This is an operating room. Occasionally we'll have to do emergency C-sections."

"Whoa. Who does those?"

"Pop Pop," she said absently, searching through large cabinets.

"Cool."

"It really is," she said, briefly gracing me with that clever smile. "I help him with each one. I have since I was little. Well, as long as I wasn't in school."

"Get out." I studied her. "Ever done one by yourself?"

"Never," she admitted. "I've only done three, but Pop Pop was there talking me through it."

"Still," I said, more than impressed.

"Got it!" she said, pulling out a large bottle of something.

I edged near her. "What's that?"

"Ceftiofur crystalline free acid. It's a sterile suspension. I'm going to try it on a few of the cows in the barn. See if we get a positive reaction. Doc suspected pneumonia from the symptoms we told him over the phone." She looked at me. "He's out of town. It's respiratory for sure, I'm just not sure it's pneumococcal."

She grabbed a few more vials and we trekked it out to the barn. She readied syringes and stuck the bovines with ease, rubbing out the muscles where she pricked them, and moving from cow to cow, like she played doctor every day, talking about nonsense all the while. She floored me.

"Done," she said, disposing of the vials and the syringes.

"What now?" I asked.

"The boys have probably already mucked out the stalls. Let's mount a few horses and check the fields for any more sickly calves or cows."

I nodded, invigorated by her determination. I almost forgot about my insane dream. *Almost*.

Piper invading my dreams brought forth the memories of all my detestable sins—ending with Lola and the photographs and Las Vegas. They ran through my thoughts on a never-ending cycle and completely deflated me. I recognized a goodness in Cricket that appeased those haunting reflections and knew from then on, I would always want to be surrounded by her. Something in her staved them off, and I was determined to find out her secret.

We saddled up and rode out into the field nearest the ranch. It'd snowed over a foot throughout the night and Eugie was having trouble lifting his joints through the height, so I lifted him onto my saddle and he sat cradled in front of me. Cricket shook her head at me.

"You'll spoil him," she said with a smile.

"So?" I challenged.

She rolled her eyes in jest and trotted forward toward a calf laying down.

"Oh no," she quieted under her breath.

"What's wrong?" I asked her, confused.

She dismounted. "They shouldn't lie like this," she explained. "They get hypothermia and die quickly this way. She must be sick too."

"What should we do?" I asked, dismounting myself.

"We'll have to take her back with her mama. Put her in the barn with the others. If the new mix of antibiotics works, we can start treating the herd and prevent more deaths."

We took the calf back to the barn then headed right back out into the blistering cold, Eugie all the time cosseted in my lap. We discovered three more in the herd like the last and two more dead calves.

"This is bad, Spencer," she said when we happened upon the second corpse. She threw her leg off her horse and settled her boots into the deep snow. I followed suit, dropping Eugie beside me. She looked on me for a moment.

"If I could fix it for you, I would," I told her, feeling beyond helpless.

She smiled softly. "I know," she said. She looked at the

lifeless calf and sighed. "Pop Pop will not be pleased." I shook my head in response. "We're relying heavily on this being an excellent year for us. We're depending on it."

This felt beyond foreboding. Cricket was confiding in me her family's secret fears.

"What will happen if you don't make it what you need it to be?" I asked bluntly.

She looked at me with glassy eyes. "I couldn't even begin," she said.

"Then we will make this year what you need it."

She smiled sadly. "Easier said."

We skipped breakfast that morning, too busy with the crisis of the ranch, but lunch was a requirement. We'd burned so many calories working and because of the cold, Cricket started to look ill.

"Come on," I told her when she locked another calf and its mother in a stall.

"No," she said, heading back toward the carriage house.

I tugged on her jacket. "Nope, I insist. Lunch. Now."

"I can't, Spencer, I've got—" she began but I cut her off by dragging her through the barn doors against her will.

I had to admit, manhandling someone so small delighted me to no end. She couldn't even put up a decent fight. Although her bony hands did annoy just a tad when she feistily punched at me, but I only laughed at her monstrous effort and the tiny effect it truly had. She laughed as she fought me down.

"I can't get a grip," she complained.

"Yeah, that's it," I laughed before turning to a mock seriousness. "Quiet," I ordered. "Ellie will kill me if I let you go any farther. You look pale."

"Uh," she said, staring up at me as I tossed her tiny figure around like a rag doll. "I hate to break it to you, but my skin is naturally this transparent."

GREED

"You're pale, I grant you, but your face always has a bit of rosy in its cheeks, and I've never seen your eyes this dull." She stared at me and I stopped abruptly, setting her down for a moment. She haughtily adjusted her clothing. "I mean, from what I've observed. You know, in passing," I told her, continuing on again. My neck started to heat under my bandana.

"You, uh, notice those things about me, do you?" she asked, as we ascended the staircase and began to round the deck toward the dining hall.

"It's no secret I'm attracted to you, Cricket."

Her face got a little bit of its color back. "Don't do that," she breathed and considered the ground.

"I won't do anything about it, Cricket. I fully recognize you're with Ethan."

Her head whipped my direction. "You-you won't?" she asked. *Did I detect a hint of disappointment? Click.*

"No, I won't. I'm not in the habit of breaking up relationships," I informed her before amending the statement. "Well, not anymore." I winked at her and she shook her head.

"Good," she asserted, but it felt weak and that made me happier than I could possibly say.

"Good," I repeated with strength.

"Good," she said again, but this time with a hitch.

"Great," I challenged, stopping and peering down at her.

"Excellent," she said, facing me, her hands on her hips.

"Outstanding," I declared, a brow raised.

"Wonderful," she hesitated.

"Brilliant," I nearly shouted.

"Peachy," she countered, but her hands fell at her sides.

I leaned into her and whispered, "Phenomenal."

She swallowed. "S-super," she stuttered, staggering back a bit.

"*Sensational*," I responded, inching closer.

She glanced to her right, toward the door, then back at me, licking her lips.

"You want to kiss me right now, don't you, Cricket Hunt?"

Her eyes blew wide. "I-I do not," she insisted, stepping back from me.

I leaned closer, inch by slowly painstaking inch, and her eyes began to flutter close, making me smile, pausing outside her lips when they fell slightly apart. My stomach clenched. I closed in farther, but instead of kissing her, I spoke into her ear. "Good."

Click.

CHAPTER
TWENTY-TWO

The third combination of antibiotics ended up working, but not before seventeen more calves perished over the course of three days, much to the ranch's discouragement. The workload tripled during the calving season, and I could not believe how tired I was at the end of the day, not that that stopped me from visiting Cricket every night to talk and watch her work.

We didn't speak about our expectations or lack thereof since the day on the deck. She knew we were playing with fire and although I wouldn't have minded getting burned, she was taking every precaution to keep clear of the flames. Whenever I would get near her, she would not so subtly steal away from me. If Ethan was around, she was particularly clingy to him, all the while staring at me.

Jonah, Ethan, Cricket and myself shared a schedule and stayed fairly inseparable. Much to my dismay, I was really starting to like and respect Jonah. And much to my absolute horror, I was finding Ethan more than tolerable. To be honest, I found him to be a much better person than I was, which pissed me off beyond belief even if he was entirely too serious for someone like Cricket.

Two weeks after calving season began, we were finishing our Friday off by breaking down the horses and cleaning out their stalls, readying them for a night's stay. The weather had turned bitter, and I was grateful to be indoors.

"Dude, I am so exhausted I could fall over and sleep right here next to Patches," I told Jonah.

He laughed. "That's too bad," he said.

I made a face. "What are you up to, dude?"

He leaned on his rake handle. "Every once in a while during calving season, Grandma makes us leave the ranch for a few hours. Tonight is one of those nights."

"Why?" I asked him, spreading pellets out with my own rake.

"She says it's not normal for young people to be this worked without at least a little bit of mischief."

This made me laugh because it sounded *exactly* like something Ellie would say.

"Well, what does everyone end up doing when she demands this?"

"We drive into Kalispell while the older hands watch the fields."

I laughed to myself. "What do you all do for fun around here? Do you drive the strip? Visit the malt shop? Split an Eskimo Pie?" I said in my best impression of Kenickie.

"Nah, too much snow, and sometimes, if Rizzo has a couple of quarters."

I glanced up at him in disbelief before I realized he was joking with me and he chuckled. "You're an idiot."

I smiled. "All right, so say I go with you into town?"

"There's a little pub-like grill off Main that we like to frequent. It's laid back and plays a few tunes. They've got a jukebox, sometimes the girls get up and dance on the peanut shell-covered floor."

"Girls?" I asked, mockingly looking around me. "What girls?"

Cricket and Bridge were the only young women on this ranch. It was a wonder the guys there didn't trip over themselves to get to them. It probably helped that they'd grown up with Cricket and that Bridge had her own personal bodyguard in the linebacker we all knew as Jonah.

"There'll be girls," he said quietly, almost fearfully, which made me want to burst out laughing. "They come from the nearby little towns. Also, Kalispell has enough of them to go 'round."

"I'm convinced," I jested, thinking back on L.A.

"Good," he said.

"Good," I countered, thinking on Cricket and smiling secretly to myself.

I spread the pellets around my feet again, even though it was unnecessary. I cleared my throat. "So, uh, will Cricket go?"

"Yeah," he said, thinking nothing of my question and my heart jumped. "Ethan takes her," he finished, and my heart sank to my feet.

Heavy-ass heart.

When the day was done, I went back to the trailer and decided to catch some Z's before everyone met up to drive out to Kalispell. I showered and fell to sleep in a blur of ten minutes. It had been several weeks since we'd come to the ranch, but it didn't seem to matter. My muscles felt like they were ripped apart, healed with a night of sleep, then viciously ripped apart once more the next day. This had gone on day after day, week after

176

week, and I was starting to feel the effects of it. I felt like a modern-day Prometheus.

And yet, though I was more tired than I had ever felt, I felt all the more accomplished for it. Life didn't feel like I was merely existing from one droning moment to the next. I felt effective, useful and altogether worthy. I had never felt that before, not once my entire life had I ever felt truly valuable. I had earned the right to be proud, but being enlightened in that way only exacerbated the fact that I had so much further to go before I could ever deserve someone like Cricket.

"And so what?" Piper asked me.

"So what, what?" I replied, annoyed.

I stepped out of the shower and wrapped a towel around my waist.

"You think this sensation will last?" she asked, almost desperate. She was pacing behind me and I could see her wild reflection in the mirror. "This supposed merit? You will grow tired of the tedious days, you know. You will grow in resentment." I scoffed at her as I began to shave. "You think to dismiss me so easily!" she asked hysterically.

I stopped what I was doing and narrowed my eyes at her. "If I could do that, you'd be gone completely," I told her before returning back to my task.

"Spencer," she said softly, remembering herself. She slithered across the marble floor to my side and leaned back against the bathroom countertop. "You're losing your motivation. You're dropping your guard." I shook my head, casting off her statement. "You're going to lose it all because she is going to take it!" she practically screamed, her cool facade breaking like weak glass.

I pulled away from her slightly and gauged her. "And what the hell is it to you, Piper?"

She smiled sweetly, but it felt frantic, forced. "I only

want what's best for you," she hummed throatily.

"Why?" I questioned her.

She looked affronted. "Don't ask stupid questions, Spencer," she said before turning and fleeing the bathroom.

I woke having no real recollection of my dream, but I knew Piper had made an appearance because my hands shook. They always shook when I woke after a nightmare starring Piper.

I laid in bed staring at the window. The stars were gleaming. I picked up the alarm clock and glanced at the time. *Eight o'clock.*

"You going?" I heard a voice ask me from the direction of the little living area.

"Yeah, Bridge, I'm going."

She sat on the uncomfortable banquette, watching the small television we'd bought. It was the only thing that would fit and not take up the entire trailer. I laughed when we bought it, remembering the forty-eight inch in my *bathroom* at home.

A knock came at the door. Bridge made a motion to stand, but I stayed her with a hand and got up to answer it myself. I swung the door open to see a very different Jonah than I was accustomed to.

"Who the hell are you?" I asked with a smile.

"Dang, what are you talking about?" he asked, mock dusting off his shoulders. "I always look this good."

"No, Jonah, you look like a disheveled linebacker on a horse, that's what you always look like."

He dug his size five hundred shoe in the ground and ducked his head, his cheeks burning a bright red. He swung his head left then right and avoided my stare.

"You really are a massive goof, aren't you? Come in, dude."

He bounded up the steps like a five-year-old instead

FISHER AMELIE

of the titan he was and ducked inside, removing his
cap inside and smoothing his hair out with his hands.
I followed behind him and noticed his face burned
something close to the color of brick.

"Hey, Bridget," he said with a lopsided grin.

I rolled my eyes and went to the sink to brush my
teeth. I pretended to be distracted with the stars outside
while they spoke.

"What's up, Jonah?" Bridget coolly replied, though I
could tell she was affected by how well he'd cleaned up.

"Nothin' much. Whatcha doin'?" he asked, sitting on
the banquette, a cushion between them.

"Oh, just watching a little TV. Same old, same old," she
offered with a smile, but her eyes lingered a little too long
on his face.

"Great," I mumbled around my toothbrush. I rinsed
and spit. "I'll be right out, Jonah," I said.

I entered the bedroom, and I use that term loosely, of
the trailer and shut the accordion doors separating me
from the living area. I picked out a few casual things—a
pair of worn jeans and a worn button-up. I shook my
head at the choices I had. Thinking back on how I used
to dress just made me depressed. I still had those things
with me, but I couldn't sport an Armani in this town or I'd
call some serious attention to myself, which was the last
thing I wanted to do. As I dressed, I listened to Jonah and
Bridget talk.

"You look very nice, Jonah," Bridget offered.

I rolled my eyes.

"Really?" he asked, and I could just imagine his face
blowing up a bright red.

"Yes, very handsome."

"Thank you, Bridget. You look very nice too."

To this, Bridget laughed loudly. "How would you
know, silly! I'm covered in this blanket."

179

There was a slight pause before he answered as if he was working up the nerve to say something. *Don't do it. Don't do it.*

"I don't have to see what you're wearing to know you look nice, Bridget."

A longer pause and my hands found my face then dragged painfully slowly down.

"Th-thank you, Jonah. I think that's the nicest thing anyone has ever said to me."

I couldn't take it anymore, so I tucked the accordion doors back.

"Ready?" I asked him.

Jonah appeared startled by my sudden appearance and stood too quickly, bumping his head on the ceiling of the trailer, inciting a giggle from Bridget.

"Sorry," Jonah said, his face bright red.

"Come on," I said, practically shoving him out the door.

"Wait," he said, turning around, "are you not coming, Bridge?"

"Uh, no," she said, standing herself. "I," she sighed, "well, I thought it would be weird if I went."

"*What*?" he asked, outraged. "*Why?*"

"Because, well, *you know*," she said glancing down at her belly.

"You can't even tell, Bridget, and no one with us is gonna feel any differently about you," he said to her quietly before pausing. Then he said, "*Trust me*," and all the anxiety on her face melted.

"Oh, um, okay. I'd love to go then."

She peered her head around Jonah. "Mind waiting just a second?" she asked.

"Of course not," I said, leaning against the door and gesturing toward the bedroom.

She ran back, giddy, and closed the doors. I watched

Jonah and he had a shit-eating grin on his face. He looked over at me and the grin dropped. He swallowed hard before turning to sit on the banquette. I sat across from him and only had to raise a single brow. Jonah eyes popped wide and he began to squirm, fiddling with the cap in his hand, wringing it over and over.

Fifteen minutes later, Bridget emerged in a simple pair of jeans and long sleeved t-shirt and I nodded my approval at her, to which she rolled her eyes. I did notice she had curled her hair, though, and applied makeup, but her choice in clothing, which had always left something to be desired in my opinion, impressed me to no end. Mostly because it covered every inch of her. *Good girl*, I thought.

Jonah helped her on with her jacket, even going so far as to playfully spin her around as he wrapped her scarf around her neck and making her giggle like a little girl. I got into the driver's seat and Jonah opened her door for her. She got in the backseat then he slid in behind her.

"You're not going to ride up front with me?" I asked, confounded.

He looked at me like I was crazy. "We're taking Cricket and Ethan up with us," he explained before looking at Bridge.

Bridget's eyes crinkled. "Uh, oh yeah! Um, you're taking Cricket and Ethan to Kalispell with Jonah and, well, now myself. I volunteered you. Is that okay?" she asked, shrinking into her seat a little.

"Fine," I gritted, trying not to look as pissed as I sounded.

I turned and put the truck into drive. Jonah and Bridget giggled and I whipped my head around to look at them, which plastered them into their seats. Bridge cleared her throat to fight the laughter, which earned her a look that could kill.

I parked outside Ellie and Emmett's and honked the

horn, my windshield wipers were at full blast as well as the heater and defrosters, but I still couldn't see more than ten feet in front of me.

"Think it's a good idea for me to be driving in this?" I asked Jonah, who had leaned up and almost over the console to check out the dash and the radio.

"Yeah, this is pretty standard this time of year."

Kill me if I'm in Montana this time next year, I thought.

Just then two dark figures appeared in the foggy headlights. One immediately went to the back to sit next to Bridge and the other toward the passenger door. *Please be Cricket. Please be Cricket*, I thought, staring at the figure at the passenger side window.

The car door opened and my stomach sank. Ethan. He climbed in and shut the door. The door behind me opened and in popped Cricket. I couldn't see her because she was so small and her head was hidden by the headrest. She kept fiddling with her coat and cursing the thing for being too long. I was desperate to see what she looked like but when she finally sat back, the cabin lights had gone dull and only the dash lights lit the interior, leaving Cricket in the dark, only the shadow of her face visible to me. *Damn*!

I meandered the long drive from the Hunt Ranch to the main road but barely. I kept stopping short thinking there was something in front of me. The truck was quiet except for the occasional snort from Ethan's side, which really angered me. I was making everyone uneasy and that pissed me off because I was a flipping awesome driver when snow wasn't involved. I looked over at Ethan, who was eyeing me. *Not everyone can grow up in Montana, asshole!*

"Do you want me to drive?" he offered, emasculating me in front of his unbelievably wonderful girlfriend.

"No," I said, staring him down. "I'm a fast learner."

He nodded his head but looked unsure, pissing me off further.

The highway was easier to navigate as there were lamps lighting up the way as well as a clearer path. The tension in the car eased to a tolerable level eventually and a conversation started between the three in the back. Ethan and I hadn't even glanced each other's direction since his stupid offer, and I could tell from his body language, rigid spine, crossed arms, that he did not like me.

"...and that!" Bridge said. I'd missed their entire start of conversation. Bridge whined a little. "I wish I had dressed up now too!"

"I am not dressed up, Bridget," she laughed. "You're just so used to seeing me in dingy ranch clothing, you now think it's the norm, but it's really not. I'm actually kind of a clotheshorse. I just have no occasion to wear them," Cricket replied.

"How do you even get pieces like this around here?" Bridge asked, genuinely curious.

I glanced back in my rearview and couldn't see anything, frustrating me to no end.

"I order them online, baby. There is no better invention than the Internet."

I kept glancing back in my rearview at Cricket, hoping somehow her face would magically light up and I could stare at her.

"Do you have any hobbies?" Ethan asked me suddenly and I jumped. He sat coolly in his seat. No movement, not a single twitch or shift. "Nervous?" he asked, narrowing his eyes at me.

I swallowed. "What?"

"I said, *do you have any hobbies?*"

I collect money. Lots of it. "Not really. I was on the row team at Brown, but I wouldn't call that a hobby," I told him truthfully. "How about you?"

"Cricket's my hobby," he said possessively under his breath.

183

GREED

I looked over at him as he stared me down with a fierceness I had rarely seen in another man. I stared back as savagely as he eyed me, my jaw clenched and eyes narrowed. We stayed locked like that until he broke the contact, satisfied I understood what he meant, and I turned my attention back to the road. What he didn't understand is that I wasn't afraid to bruise his face or my knuckles. I'd never shied away from a fight. Ever.

I was notorious in high school as the guy you didn't mess with because if you talked shit and acted like you wanted to fight, I'd give you the fight. It was easy to separate the talkers from the doers. And there were *always* more talkers than doers. I didn't know Ethan well enough to know if he was one or the other, but it didn't mean shit to me. I would throw down without a second thought. I wouldn't hesitate. Because if there was one thing I couldn't stand, it was people who tried to threaten bigger than they were willing to carry out. The only thing is, I thought Ethan was exactly the type of guy to follow through, not that I cared, like I said, I was willing, but I *did* care what Cricket would think. Very much.

The remaining drive to Kalispell consisted of Ethan and me seething at one another, Jonah riveted by Bridget, paying attention to nothing else, and the girls chatting, oblivious.

We parked in a gravel lot and my stomach fluttered thinking on Cricket, imagining her in something else other than jeans and chaps.

I turned off the engine and began to get out when Ethan stopped me. "I'll get Cricket's side."

I nodded my answer and I rounded the back of the truck, passing Ethan and trying not to feel too disappointed that I wasn't able to open her door for her. *What are you doing?* I asked myself. *She's not yours. She's not yours!* I felt so stupid and, frankly, I was appalled at myself. I'd kept trying to convince myself that I needed to be her friend and only her friend, but I wasn't acting like it.

I promised myself that there would be no outward or inward thoughts toward Cricket that weren't entirely friendly and nothing more. *Yeah, good luck with that.* I awkwardly stationed myself at the back of the bed, my hands stuck in the front pockets of my jeans, bunching my coat around the tops of my hips. The cold seeped through to the bone there, but I didn't care, whatever distracted me. I briefly pulled my cap down a bit to hide my eyes, then stuck my hands back in my pockets. I stared at the ground and toed the snow outlining my boots. They'd stuck down into six inches' worth. I kicked the mound around my toes and shook the remaining from my boots. I did this for no other reason than I *knew* I didn't want to look at Cricket.

I looked up quickly toward the passenger side and was forced to watch Jonah exit the back, then hold the door and offer his hand to Bridget to help her out. Much as I hated to admit it, I was going to be the fifth freaking wheel in that night's scenario. Despite what Jonah and Bridget defined their "friendship" as, I knew what was blossoming and felt powerless to stop it. I just wanted to guard my sister from pain. Pain I knew was coming. Pain that would make an already burdensome life more difficult, but sometimes you have to let live.

I stared hard at the ground when everyone gathered around me, then followed them, my eyes trained on their tracks.

How you gonna pull this off, dude, huh? I asked myself as I stumbled toward the front of the pub. *Eventually, you're going to have to look at her.* I decided it was best if I saw her in a controlled situation, one where, say, if I fell from my damn stool, no one else, particularly Ethan, would notice.

GREED

As soon as we got through the doors, I ripped off my jacket but left my cap on to shield me. "I'll be at the bar," I told everyone and left their questioning glances behind before anyone could object.

I was finally able to look up and sat at the back corner of the bar top, steadying my hands on the flat of the surface and trying hard to settle my breathing.

"What can I get ya?" the hot bartender asked. I say "hot" like that was unexpected, but aren't they all hot?

I smiled. "I'll take a Coke," I told her.

"Careful, it'll go straight to your head," she teased, making me laugh.

I dangled my keys in front of me. "Driving."

"Good boy," she said, winking.

She poured me my soft drink and slid it over playfully before making her way to the other end of the bar to help someone else.

I took a small sip, wishing to everything it would've been something stronger. I drummed my fingers on the bar, mentally preparing myself. I took three deep breaths and decided I'd waited long enough. I picked up my head and deliberately scanned the bar. Surprisingly, something with an amazing beat rang through the air causing my blood pressure to rise in anticipation. I placed my palm over my rapidly beating heart. *You're just looking*, I told myself. *Just. Look.* I took another deep breath and kept searching.

I spotted Bridge being goofy, looked like "the lawnmower," I think, and Jonah laughing his ass off at her. I spotted Ethan sulking in the corner, nursing a beer. My heart sped to an uncomfortable pace as I searched but couldn't find her. I half stood half sat and peered over the heads of the crowd but still no sign.

"Whatcha doin?" I heard over my shoulder, and I stilled.

My shoulders stiffened at the ringing bell that was
Cricket's voice, and I closed my eyes briefly. I was both
apprehensive and expectant. I couldn't torture myself
anymore and opened my eyes. My breathing labored as I
started to turn around.

Oh. My. God.

There she was. *Gosh damn it!* So gosh damn beautiful
I didn't think I'd ever recover from the sight of her. I
sort of staggered back into a sitting position and raked
her from head to toe. I barely recognized her, and that
astonished me.

Her face.

I wondered why she had to be so unbelievably
beautiful, torturing myself as I memorized every inch,
every centimeter, every millimeter of her resplendent
face. She sported her clever grin, but this time her lips
were painted a bright red and I ached to kiss them,
catch them between my teeth and claim the color on
my tongue, smudges be damned. The fact that Cricket
probably wouldn't have cared less made her all the more
enticing to me.

Her pitch-black hair was curled, reminiscent of a
forties pin-up, including her short bangs, which she'd
swept to the side and pinned up.

I would remember what she wore until the day I
died, down to the miniature buttons on the ankle straps
of her black heels. Underneath a thin, form-fitting cream
floor-length cashmere sweater coat she'd buttoned just
the center of, exposing her incredible legs, she wore a
tailored black, shin-length spaghetti strapped dress with
a sweetheart neckline. Countless pearls wrapped around
her long, slender, alabaster neck and fell strategically
down to her breasts.

GREED

She was a comfortable mix of casual and dressy, looked incredibly French, and exuded an elegance that would rival any of my prep school girlfriends. She was everything I never imagined I could possibly want. She was...*devastating*.

She smiled sweetly at me, completely unaware she'd cemented me to my seat, shell shocked and itching to grasp her shoulders and pull her into my chest forever. I would have whispered into her ear that I couldn't understand why I felt such an omnipotent and inexplicable need to take her with me everywhere I went for the rest of my life, even though I didn't love her...*yet*. I'd beg her to let me do it, to put me out of my misery and just let me have her. I'd pray she'd accept my desperate, though seemingly baffling, request. I'd tell her I didn't deserve her, that I knew I'd never be able to, but every day would be a monumental effort on my part to strive to.

But I didn't say those things to her. Instead, I bit my tongue, feeling for all the world like the biggest coward. Instead, I let her lean to my left and brush my shoulder and committed the feel of her heat to memory. Instead, I let her order for herself because I'd completely forgotten my breeding and hadn't offered her anything. Instead, I turned my head toward her hair and leaned slightly, drawing in, basically gasping in, her heavenly vanilla and grapefruit scent. Instead, I ignored my instincts to own her and let her stand silently in front of me.

"I asked what you were doing?" she asked again, unaware of my internal struggles.

I shook my head slightly and cleared my throat. "Uh, just sitting here, people watching," I offered with a slight smile.

She gracefully tumbled into the stool next to me and faced the mingling crowd. "It's busy tonight," she said.

"Is it?" I asked, unable to think of anything else.

Suddenly, I felt severely depressed. I wished to tear myself away from the magnificent person seated next to me. I glanced behind me at the bar shelves and wished I could snag the only premium bottle of liquor I was able to spot and hunker down in the bed of my truck with it.

"Yes, I haven't seen this many people out in a long time. I'm guessing the season has got more than a few restless souls to come out of hiding." She turned and smiled at me, and I almost wished I could cleave out my eyes just so I didn't have to subject myself to her glaringly pleasing face anymore.

I cleared my throat yet again and braced my Coke between my hands to steady them. "Uh, you look very pretty," I purposely understated.

She looked down at herself as if she just remembered what she was wearing. "Oh, thank you so much," she said.

She crossed her arms into herself and regarded me from the corner of her eye.

Click.

Where so far our "clicks" brought me nothing but unimaginable pleasure, that night I felt only crestfallen.

"Hey," she said, interrupting my thoughts.

"Hmm?"

"You're awfully distracted."

I smiled at her. "I suppose I am. I'm sorry," I apologized.

"It's okay. Got a lot on your plate lately, I know." She had *no* idea. "I don't think the stresses of the ranch are very good for anyone, but especially for those with an already full plate."

"No, it's really okay. I actually love the ranch a lot," I said, surprising even myself with that statement.

"You should tell Ellie as much. She would be tickled pink."

189

I laughed. "Okay, I will."

We were quiet for a few minutes, just watching the crowd and laughing at a few.

"I, uh, I finished your sculpture," she told me, but her face never left the crowd.

My stomach plummeted to my feet then leapt into my throat. "Cool," I said, feeling anything but.

She turned and studied me for a moment before returning her gaze back toward the crowd. "I think I'm gonna join the others," she said, standing up and disappointing the crap out of me. I watched her take a few steps before turning back around. "Coming?"

I was surprised by her offer and stood to join her. I followed behind her and drank in her walk, determined to retain it so I could recall it for years to come. No one walked like Cricket Hunt. No one.

We joined the others, and just as I expected, I was the fifth wheel in that night's scenario. After an hour of pity conversation with Cricket, I decided I'd had enough, and surveyed the girls around me. Not a single one could hold a candle to Cricket, but I wasn't going to sit there and be miserable if I could help it, so I decided to ask a girl to dance, finally deciding on one from a group that had been staring at me all night.

I stood up and told everyone I'd be right back then headed the direction of the group. They did that stupid girl thing where they whisper frantically, then make a feeble attempt to be cool and collected when you're within ten feet, as if we are blind until that ten-foot mark. The move almost made me turn back around, but I remembered what awaited me and trudged on.

"Hi," I said to the blonde with the long hair.

She was tall and provocative and chose a more vulgar style compared to Cricket. Essentially, she was the antithesis of Cricket. She was what I needed to distract myself from the one I really wanted but couldn't have.

"Hi," she said in an irritating baby voice. I crinkled my nose a little in annoyance, but she didn't catch on.

"I was wondering if you'd like to dance?" I asked.

She popped off her stool and unattractively tugged at her short skirt, then adjusted her breasts so that optimal cleavage was exposed. Girls, another little clue here: Only skanky guys want skanky girls. You'd be surprised what a little bit longer hem can get you in the long run.

She awkwardly tiptoed on her ridiculous heels to my side and leaned in way too close. I had to slant my head away just to talk to her.

"So, uh, are you from around here?" I asked.

"Uh-huh. I live in town."

"Cool, cool," I said wondering if that was all the answer I was going to get.

"I don't even have to ask if you're from around here. I can tell you're not."

We'd arrived at the dance floor and I placed a hand at the broad of her back to guide her, but she took my hand and pushed it to the top of her ass. I moved it up to the small of her back and sighed in exasperation.

"Uh, how do you know I'm not from around here?" I asked her as we swayed to the slow song.

"Because I know all the local boys," she said, pressing her breasts against my chest.

"I bet you do," I said under my breath.

"What's that?"

"Nothing."

I felt like I was fighting a slithering snake. She was all hands, legs and breasts, and it was irritating as she attempted over and over to touch me with them at all times.

I was uncomfortable. Before Montana, this was the type of girl I searched for in the clubs. To my friends and me, these were the expendables. The girls we had fun with and cast aside. The thought of the guy that cast aside Bridge burned a hole in my gut. *I'm such an asshole.*

I felt a heated stare bore into the back of my neck and I rubbed it to rid myself of the sensation. I turned around and found the eyes the stare belonged to. Cricket sat glaring at me—a look of utter dejection graced her face. I found myself questioning her with my eyes, but she noticed herself then and turned her face toward the ground.

I looked to her left and right and saw that she was alone. I studied the dance floor and saw Jonah and Bridge dancing. I looked over at the bar and saw Ethan talking to what looked like a friend of his.

"So, what are you doing after?" the blonde asking me.

"What?"

"I was asking what you were up to later. I have my own place just up the road and..."

"I'm sorry. You seem like a, um, *nice girl*? But I'm not interested. Thanks for the dance," I told her, leaving her there stunned, but I didn't care.

I felt a magnetic pull to Cricket and immediately made my way to her. She noticed me coming and awkwardly contemplated the ceiling above.

"Cricket?" I asked.

She met my eyes. "Hmm?" she asked with an attempt at cheery.

"What are you doing here?"

"Oh, nothing." She cleared her throat. "Why aren't you dancing?"

"Because I saw you here alone."

She swallowed. "You didn't have to do that," she said sweetly.

I sighed and fell into the stool next to her. "Yes. Yes, I did."

We sat in silence for five minutes and the songs changed twice. When a slow song came on, I stood and held out my hand.

"Dance with me?"

"I don't think that's such a good—"

"Excuse me, but Ethan is a fool if he doesn't take every opportunity in the world to hold you closely."

She smiled and stood. "Thank you," she whispered.

I led her to the dance floor and swept her into me. She was so polished, so refined, so unlike the blonde. I was baffled at her upbringing. I had no idea someone so elegant could come from such an interesting place like a cattle ranch. When I actually thought about it, though, every single one who worked on Hunt Ranch, down to the ranch hands, were polite, genteel and humble, even more so than the circle of wealth I grew up around.

I held her gallantly, respectfully, the way her demeanor, her confidence, her dress called me to hold her. I found myself gulping for air whenever she and I shared personal space. She stole away my sanity, every bit of my control and I felt frenzied, frantic whenever she was near and grieved the loss severely whenever she was not. The sensation was so new to me. She was more than lovely to me. She was painfully interesting, the best conversation I had ever had and I found myself wondering what she was thinking at times, instead of what she was wearing beneath her clothing. No one had ever affected me as she had. No one.

My left cheek rested against the side of her head as we swayed to the melody. We stayed completely quiet. I was unable to speak, too engrossed in making sure I learned her by heart. I felt so damaged holding her. My chest felt bruised, sore and hurt. "Hurt" was the perfect word to describe that misery of not belonging to her. My head kept calling out to me to save myself, to stop the torture, but I couldn't, just could not, let her go.

"Cricket," I whispered.

"No," she spoke into my ear, then sniffed, her voice breaking at the end. "Don't say it," she ordered, taking a buried, raspy breath. "I-I can't tell you why, but I can't leave Ethan." I nodded against her head and pressed her face into my shoulder. "I'm going to tell you something, but this can only be said once," she began, and took another shaky breath, "I suffer for you," she barely got out. "I want to be near you always. I'm falling in love with you and it's-it's a *sweet agony*, however, it's still an agony."

Instead of torturing myself by begging for more, I continued to dance with her, teetering on the verge of just throwing my forearm below her knees and stealing her away, taking her home, to a home, any home, *our* home... forever.

The song was too short and that cut to the bone. In just a few short weeks, I was almost in love with Cricket Hunt. In just a few more, I'd be a goner but couldn't convince myself to protect my heart.

I leaned into her face and kissed her cheek, relishing in how soft her skin was, how sweet she smelled. My eyes closed and I decided to keep that kiss forever.

A tap on my shoulder shattered my perfect world, and I hesitantly left the warmth of her skin. I rose, fully ready to accept my fate, expecting to find Ethan, but instead I found a tall, broad-shouldered man in a fine, black suit and odd glasses. There was something familiar about him, and I studied him a moment before placing it. I remembered August's words "weird old-fashioned spectacles."

Suddenly, my world crumbled at my feet.

"Who are you?" I asked the man, frozen in fear.

"Mr. Blackwell?" he asked, confirming my worst nightmare. "My name is Dominic Griffin," he explained, sending me spiraling. He removed his glasses and began polishing the lenses with a handkerchief. "I represent your father."

When he mentioned my father, Cricket leaned closer into my side and grabbed my forearm.

I reached into my pocket and removed my keys, discreetly placing them in the palm of her hand. She looked up at me, nodded and left. I turned back to the man.

"What do you want?" I asked, trying to control my voice.

He smiled chillingly at me and placed his glasses back on his face. "He wants you ruined," he said candidly, sending a chill up my spine.

I opened my mouth but couldn't respond. He placed his hands in his pockets and continued.

"He wants you to know that he's going to ruin you *and* your sister."

My blood began to seethe underneath my skin. "You tell him that if he so much as comes near us, I will take every documented piece of evidence I've kept against him and I will turn it into the authorities."

The man looked surprised. "I don't think you'll do that," he said after a moment's consideration.

"You don't?"

"No, that means you'd be incriminating yourself."

"Believe me, I would be more than happy to rot in jail right beside him if it meant he couldn't hurt my mom or Bridge ever again."

The man thought on what I said before nodding. "I'll tell him what you've said."

He turned to walk away, but I stopped him. "And?" I asked.

He pivoted my way once more. "And *what*?"

"How will I know if he's decided to back off?"

GREED

"Oh, you'll know," the man said, laughing. He walked out into the cold, still chuckling as if Bridge's and my lives were playthings to him. I suppose they were. If he worked for my father, he would be devoid of morals. *Says the pot.*

I ignored my inner jab and rushed out to the truck. It was running and near the door. I got into the driver's side quickly. The interior lights were on, and I could see everyone, including Cricket.

"What-what happened?" Bridge asked, scooting to the edge of her seat.

Her eyes were red from crying.

I glanced up at Cricket through the rearview and she looked nervous.

"Uh, well, Dad's found us," I said.

"No," she cried, slumping into her seat.

Jonah wrapped his arm around her, and I couldn't muster up an objection. She bent into him and cried into his shoulder.

"What does this mean?" Jonah asked.

I drove out of the pub parking lot and started to make my way back to Hunt Ranch. "Honestly, I don't know. I say this because I threw something at him I don't think he was expecting that might tie his hands."

Bridge raised her head and wiped below her eyes. "What?" she asked tearfully.

I looked straight at Cricket. "I shouldn't really say," I said, afraid to admit something so heinous in front of her. "Let's just say, if he were smart, he would leave us be."

Bridget nodded, thankfully accepting my vague answer, and laid her head back down on Jonah's shoulder. I looked up and noticed Cricket's narrowed brows, then quickly glanced back down at the road. She wanted to know but she wasn't going to press.

Guess we all have our secrets, Cricket Hunt.

CHAPTER TWENTY-THREE

Weeks went by and the calves started making an appearance by the droves. Jonah and I worked side by side a lot, and although I was still visiting Cricket at night, we barely said a word to one another, both of us afraid to come clean. I didn't care though. I had to be around her if for nothing else than she appeased my nightmares at night, but we all know it was more than that. It was more than that because I was falling in love with Cricket Hunt, and I was finding it increasingly more difficult to keep that fact to myself.

It had been weeks since Piper had made a manifestation, and I was so grateful. She was starting to eat at my soul. After the nightmares, it would take at least two days to shake her completely. Cricket was a balm to my disturbed spirit.

Cricket still hadn't given me the sculpture she'd promised me. I wanted to ask her about it, but it felt clumsy between us, and I couldn't force myself to demand it. Though so many times I wanted to. So many times.

Bridge was about five months along by then and starting to show. Much to my surprise, Jonah wasn't distancing himself as I had thought. In fact, he was even more attentive which, frankly, shocked me. I had decided the night we had an appearance from my dad's lackey Dominic that I was going to keep my mouth shut and just let things play out.

Dominic had not made a single attempt at contact. Neither had my father or my mother, which made me think my dad hadn't told her. The fact that he hadn't reached out in any capacity left me more than a little nervous, but with each day that passed, my uneasiness subsided more and more. We were fast approaching Bridge's eighteenth birthday, which also made me more comfortable.

There were also a few serious things going on at the ranch, but any time Bridge and/or myself would walk into the room, the conversation would turn silent. It wasn't our business, and we decided to respect their wishes. Although it did make us extremely curious.

About mid-February, Emmett assigned Cricket to be my partner because he needed Jonah to work with him more closely as they began to plan their new season, when they would inseminate the cows in April, etc.

On a random Wednesday, as we spread pellets out in the horse stalls, I broke down with Cricket. Ethan continually took her into town for hours at a time, and I was finding myself green with envy. I wanted answers.

"Hey, Cricket," I began.

"Mmmhmm?" she asked, throwing her rake back and forth with practiced ease.

"Where do you go with Ethan so often?"

She stopped raking and studied her hands a moment before going back to work at a furious pace. "Nowhere really."

"You're lying," I said, knowing her well enough then to know when she was indeed being untruthful.

I stopped and leaned on my rake. She did the same.

"I am not," she insisted.

"Cricket," I said, exasperated. "Why won't you just tell me where you go?"

She pushed her rake back down and avoided looking at me.

"Cricket," I pushed.

"Jeez, Spencer, can you just let it go?"

"No, I have to know."

She dropped her rake.

"No, you *don't*," she gritted, wounding me.

She picked her rake back up and we finished the stall, moving on to the next.

"Eugie," she said out of nowhere.

Instinctively, I opened the gate for him as I usually did when Cricket and I would have our one-word conversations.

"Eugie, come eat," I ordered into the dark path, knowing what she wanted of me and laying out his food as one of us always did.

We'd perfected those one-worded conversations, really. At night, when she worked, all she had to do was mention one word: "please," "that," "here," etc. and I would know exactly what she meant or wanted. It got so that we were so good at it, Ellie would often tease us because we found ourselves doing it around the group, much to Ethan's dismay, I might add.

Another thing that infuriated me about Cricket was that she obviously hadn't told Ethan about our late-night sessions. I found myself constantly frustrated, toggling between wondering if she was ashamed of me, or if she was afraid Ethan would put a stop to them.

When Eugie was done eating, I let him into the stall

with us and picked him up as if he was a lapdog, kissing his neck and setting him down. Cricket bent down and kissed the top of his nose then stood and went back to work. I piled a corner with a little bit of hay as usual and he laid on top. I did this in each stall we visited, and he would follow us from stall to stall.

When the pellets were done, we bathed and brushed down the horses, combing out their manes and tails. We'd put them all away for the night except one. We began to shampoo him together, working in sync as we always did, moving together as a cohesive unit.

"Six?" I asked, pointing at the horse we were cleaning.

She nodded her head that it had been six weeks since his last shoe change, so I grabbed the farrier tools.

Cricket was teaching me the trade because she was amazing and knew pretty much everything you needed to know to run a ranch because Emmett had taught her. I loved the lessons because it meant I would be close enough to her I could feel her warmth and smell her hair. I also hated the lessons for the same reasons.

"You want a go?" she asked.

"Sure," I said quietly.

I picked up the right hind leg and wedged the hoof between my legs right above my knees. I grabbed the nippers and carefully started to wedge the shoe back and forth to loosen the nails, hitting it to provide room between the top of the shoe and the nail itself and used the nippers to pull the nail. I did this slower than Cricket ever had because I wasn't as practiced, but she wasn't impatient with me at all. In fact, she was really encouraging, nodding every time she approved of something I did, another thing I liked about her.

She bent beside me and our shoulders touched, a fact she was probably unaware of but I was acutely perceptive of. She leaned forward a bit when I dropped the used shoe and began using the hoof knife.

This was the part I was always most nervous about because if you hit the frog of the hoof just right, you could hurt the horse and I was deathly afraid of causing any pain to the gentle giant.

"Perfect," she soothed, and I made an attempt toward the heel.

She stopped me with a cool, slender hand on my own when my tool drew closer to the bar and we both stilled, stood motionless, neither looking at the other, but the deep drawing of our breaths told us everything we needed to know.

She lifted her hand, pulled it into a fist at her side, and cleared her throat. "Uh, see this, um, angle of the wall right here?"

I gulped. "Yeah."

"This is where the painful part of the frog starts," she explained. "Just take care on this part."

I nodded and continued the job until she was satisfied with the rasp filing I'd done, and we let the leg rest a bit before fitting the shoe. I grabbed the hoof and put it back between my legs and placed the fitted shoe over the bed. I had a handful of nails in my hand and was losing control of them trying to balance the shoe as well as the hammer.

Instinctively, I went to put a few in my mouth to hold until I needed the next one.

"No," she said, placing her hand on my forearm. I peered down at her hold then back up at her slowly. "That's not a good idea."

She held out her hand and I dropped the nails in her palm.

"Why?" I asked, staring again at her hand.

"Because," she breathed quietly, "horses' hooves have a lot of bacteria. Pop Pop never lets us put the nails in our mouths."

GREED

I nodded and watched her beautiful hand slide back down and finished shoeing the horse, dropping the foot back down.

"Now come here," she said, leading me toward the front of the horse and bent down. I followed her lead and she inspected the final shoe, giving her approval with that clever smile and a thumbs up.

"Good," she said, standing.

"Thanks."

She finished the rest in half the time, but I didn't care. I enjoyed the hell out of watching how beautifully she worked without thinking. It was so second nature to her. She didn't notice that I was staring and I followed her every move, from the elegant swing of the hammer, how easily she cinched the nails and filed them down, the way her hands smoothed their way down the hoof to check her own work, down to the way her hair swung over her cheek.

When she was done, she let the hoof fall and stood, stretching her back and flipping her hair out of her face. She always gave the horses she shoed an apple for their troubles and would secret lovely things into their ears. She was so unbelievably attractive.

She clicked her tongue and led the horse out and toward its stall. I followed closely, memorizing the way her hips swayed. Inside, I kept the gate open just long enough to let Eugie in and closed it, letting the metallic clang break the silence.

Refusing to look at her, I gripped the top of the gate and grasped the wood so forcefully, I could feel tiny splinters break skin.

"Where?" I asked her.

She sighed. "I can't say."

My hands fisted and I slammed them on top of the gate, making my hair slide into my face. "Damn it, Cricket, it's eating me up inside."

"Stop," she said. I could feel she was on the verge of tears.

I faced her and ran my fingers through my hair, holding it back and sagged against the stall door. "I don't think I can take this anymore," I admitted.

"Spencer, I can't," she began, sounding exhausted.

"No. No, Cricket, *I* can't. *I'm* the one who can't take it anymore. You're so confusing to me. One minute it feels apparent that you're *at least* attracted to me, the next, you're chillingly distant, afraid to even come near me, especially when Ethan's around."

"Don't bring Ethan into this," she said, sliding down to sit in the hay next to Eugie. She rubbed the back of her neck in attempt to rid herself of our already wearying day. I knew I wasn't helping, that she and her family were stressed beyond belief, but I was miserable, more miserable than I had ever been in my entire life, and I was ready to bust the thing between us wide open. I was tired of pining, tired of feeling like she wanted me but not doing anything about it.

"Why not bring Ethan into this?" I asked.

"Because he's an incredible guy."

The jealousy burned deep with her answer. "There's no doubt he's a great guy," I admitted bitterly, "but he's not *your* great guy, Cricket. He's not *your* fate, Cricket."

She crossed her legs in front of her and tucked her hands between her thighs, resting her head against the wall and peered at the ceiling. "There's no such thing as fate, Spencer."

"Like hell there isn't!" I exclaimed emphatically. "I can recognize fate when I see it...*unlike you*," I said, breathing the last part.

She lowered her head and looked straight at me. "What are you saying?" she asked recklessly, unlike her usual very carefully planned statements to me.

I stood at my full height. "Are we doing this?" I challenged, my hands on my hips.

She stayed silent but eventually said, "Yes."

The butterflies in my stomach attacked in multitude. I called her bluff but realized that I might not want to hear what she needed to say. "Why are you with Ethan?" I asked first.

She turned her head, afraid to look at me.

"Don't do that," I told her.

"Do what?" she asked, fiddling with a bit of hay that laid at her hand.

"Avoid looking at me when I bring up Ethan? When all I'm asking is for a simple declaration from you telling me that you love him. That you're with him because you love him."

"I do love him," she said, still playing with the straw.

"Look at me."

She lifted her gaze and stared straight through me. I wanted to fall on my knees and beg her to deny it, but I didn't. I stood as still as a statue, waiting.

"I do love Ethan," she spoke.

I narrowed my eyes at her. "Say it like you're not talking about any one of your family."

Her head dropped quickly, then picked it back up. Her mouth opened and shut like a fish out of water.

"What I thought," I said.

Tears streamed down her face. "You don't understand," she explained. "He's so loyal to me, and right now I cherish that more than anything. I rely on him so much."

"I can give you loyalty," I told her softly, honestly.

She shook her head. "His loyalty is fifteen years old, Spencer. And that's kinda the point of loyalty, isn't it? When someone shows it to you, you have an obligation to return the favor."

"That's bullshit and you know it! You can't base the rest of your life off of that, Cricket! Loyalty is commendable, yes, necessary, yes, but it's not what makes a marriage *happy*." We both paused for a moment, only our breathing present. I watched her carefully. "And that's what you're going to do, right? Marry him?"

"Maybe...eventually. I don't know!" she exclaimed.

"*What*?!" I asked, frustrated beyond belief. "Cricket, I just-you're not making any sense to me. That's so illogical. In marriage, there has to be love. Trust me," I said, thinking on my parents. "If you don't want to be miserable forever, if you want to carve out even a small *niche* of happiness for yourself in marriage, you have to love the other person. And passionately. If-if you don't have that, you have nothing," I finished, sagging back against the wall.

"I think I could learn to love him," she said, trying to convince herself, I thought, more than me.

"Cricket," I begged, "if you haven't done so yet, it's never going to happen."

"You don't know that!"

"I-I don't know what to say to you right now. You seem so afraid, but you won't tell me why."

"We're not together, Spencer. You deserve no answer from me."

My jaw clenched. "No, we're not together. You've made that quite clear, and for no reason whatsoever it seems. You're not the drama type, Cricket, so I don't get why you're fighting this so much."

"I can't do this," she said, standing up but instead of leaving, she just watched me, practically pleading for me to take her.

I rushed her and pinned her body against the wall. Only our foreheads touched, our hands hung at our sides. She closed her eyes; both our breathing was strained, ready to burst with desire. It felt too heavy to breathe, too difficult. I closed my eyes as well, wanting to grab her in my arms and kiss her so hard, but I didn't. I hadn't been given permission.

"I know you're falling in love with me," I told her.

She nodded her forehead into mine, our noses almost touching; our lips mere centimeters apart. It was such a dangerous game, but I didn't care if I lost. I just wanted to play.

"Please," I begged her, my tongue heavy and thick. "Tell me it's okay to kiss you."

She moaned, pinching her lids tighter together as if in anguish. She wanted me just as badly as I wanted her.

"Just say one tiny word, Cricket. Just one word and I'll have you. I'd be so good to you, Cricket," I told her. She groaned deeper and shook her head back and forth against mine. "I'd adore you forever," I promised. "Just one word, Cricket, and we'd be so good together, perfect really. One word," I breathed again. I could feel her breaking down. Her face lazily pitched toward mine, imploring me to take her lips with mine, to explore her mouth with mine. I wouldn't budge, though. I needed permission. She needed to say it. "Cricket," I exhaled. "Jump with me."

"Oh God," she sighed and pressed her body against mine.

I shoved her farther back and pinned her tighter against the wall, my arms on either side of her head. She threaded her fingers through my hair and my eyes rolled into the back of my head. She brought my face into her neck and I inhaled her scent, my knees nearly buckling underneath me. I wanted her legs to climb up mine, but she sat there frozen, breathless, frustrating me to no end.

My nails dug into the wood a bit, furious at me for not touching her. I took the pain. It was a good pain, a pain I needed.

"Tell me," I ordered her.

She shook her head even as she panted with the same hunger I had.

I raised my head and looked at her face. She opened her eyes and I was almost completely lost at how beautiful they were. "Cricket, say it."

She bit her bottom lip, sending me into a near panic. "Oh, Cricket Hunt." I shook my head to clear the delirium. I pressed my lids tightly. "Now, Cricket, say it now."

Instead, her hands slid out of my hair and onto my shoulders. She immediately went distracted as her fingers felt the muscles in my shoulders and back up my neck, then back down my shoulders, all the way down my arms. She picked up my right hand and held it in hers while exploring it with the other. Her slender fingers repeatedly stroked the palm. I stayed completely still, though she was driving me crazy. I was afraid to scare her off. She was thinking, contemplating me.

"Callused," she uttered, then met my eyes. She brought the hand to her lips and delicately kissed the palm before running her fingers back over it.

As if I couldn't help myself, I gripped the back of her neck with that same palm, making her gasp. My other hand instinctively went to the small of her back and pressed her deeper into me.

"Cricket Hunt, I want you so badly."

Something in what I said woke her up. Her previously dreamy stare cleared and she shook her head slowly. Just as languidly, she stumbled away from me, staggering toward the gate.

I turned toward her. "Cricket," I called gently.

"I-I have to go to bed," she stuttered, pretending nothing had happened and leaving the stall.

I stood, immovable, listening to her retreating steps. I felt something nudge my leg and looked down. She'd left

GREED

Eugie and he'd stood, looking up at me. I slid down the wall and sat in the hay with him. He laid back down, his head on my leg and fell to sleep quickly. My hand went to his neck and rubbed there. I loved him as much as he loved me.

"So why can't she get that same concept, huh, boy?" I asked a sleeping Eugie.

I fell asleep right there in the stall with Eugie, still waiting for the one word from her I was never gonna get.

CHAPTER TWENTY-FOUR

VERY EARLY the next morning, I woke startled in the horse stall with Eugie still in my lap. I stood and stretched, the muscles in my back screaming at me.

"Come on, boy," I told him. He followed me out the barn and into the lane. It was bitterly cold and I wanted to sprint down to the trailer but poor Eugie was too stiff from old age to go any faster than a soft trot.

"Okay, old man," I told him and picked him up. I wrapped him in my coat and we headed for the trailer. Inside, he immediately curled up on the banquette and I let him, even throwing a blanket over him before patting his head.

Too cold to just lay down, I showered and warmed up as best I could. My bed felt uncomfortably small for some reason and I tossed and turned for two hours, obsessing over what had gone down with Cricket, wondering what the hell was going to happen with my dad, if he was even going to do anything. I thought about the possibility of

GREED

going to jail for a very long time for the "errands" I ran for him. I contemplated all of it and came to one conclusion.

No matter what the hell happened, the idea of Cricket marrying anyone else other than me made me sicker to my stomach than every awful scenario I could think of.

My eyes were wide open when my alarm went off, but I let it beep over and over, a welcome distraction from my thoughts.

"Dang, dude," I heard a groggy Bridge complain.

My palm, the same palm Cricket had kissed, slammed down on the off button.

"Sorry," I said, bringing that palm to my chest, desperate to rub out the ache she'd put there.

"Where were you last night?" she asked, rubbing her eyes.

"Oh," I cleared my throat, "I fell asleep in the horse barn."

She giggled a little and sat up. "Oh really?" she teased. "Did you, perhaps, fall asleep with anyone else?"

"Yes, as a matter of fact, I did."

Her eyes widened and she swallowed. "What? I was only teasing! She wouldn't do that."

I couldn't help my chuckle. "It was Eugie. I fell asleep with Eugie."

Her shoulders sagged in relief. "Good."

At the mention of his name, Eugie climbed off the banquette slowly and stretched before making his way over to me. He rested his head on my shoulder and watched me.

"What's up, dude?" I asked him.

"He probably needs to pee," Bridge explained.

"Probably," I said, standing up and opening the door for him.

Eugie found the least snow-covered grass he could and relieved himself. I stood at the door, freezing my ass off in only my track pants and waiting for him to come back inside when he unexpectedly took off down the lane. I narrowed my eyes and saw Cricket walking toward us.

Without thinking, I bounded out into the cold snow, no shoes, no shirt and bed head. "Cricket," I said, when I reached her.

Her eyes widened. "Oh my God," she said, looking down. "You *have* to put on a shirt."

"Why did you leave like that last night?" I demanded, ignoring her request.

She peered at my feet. "You'll lose your toes," she said and started walking toward the trailer.

I followed her. "Answer me, Cricket."

"Not here," she said, scanning around her.

I quieted down with the assumed promise she would eventually talk and we entered the trailer just as Bridge was emerging for the day. She kissed Cricket's cheek hello and winked at me then left to meet an already approaching Jonah.

I shut the door.

"What are you doing?" she asked. "We can't be in here alone."

"Why?" I asked, narrowing my eyes.

She stood tall. "Because it's disrespectful to Ethan."

I happened to agree with her. "Then we're in unison," I told her, which surprised her.

"We-we are?"

"Most definitely. And it's also why you should leave him and be with me."

Her jaw clenched. "I swear, Spencer, if you mention that to me one more time, I'm gonna to smack you."

"Do it," I challenged.

She narrowed her eyes. "I should."

I leaned casually against the counter next to the door and crossed my arms across my chest. "You know what I think?" I asked her.

"Why ask? You'll tell me anyway," she cheekily replied.

This made me smile. "I think you hate to hear the truth."

"Pshh, you are *so* wrong."

"No," I laughed, "I'm really not. Think about the way you practically melted into me last night, that seething kiss on my palm, the tangible heat smoldering between us. It tells me so much." She shook her head. "It lets me know," I continued, "that you're only in your relationship with Ethan because he's giving you something you think you can't live without, and you're too scared to give up."

She gasped, nearly choking on the draw and slapped her trembling hands over her mouth. Tears overflowed and my gut began to ache. I reached out for her.

"Cricket," I said, racking my brain, trying to figure out why my words wounded her so badly. "I'm so—" I began, but she shoved past me, sobbing and pushing through the trailer door.

I chased after her, but she ran with purpose, frantic to get away.

I caught up with her and grabbed her arm gently. "Cricket, tell me what I've said..."

"Stop," she bawled, refusing to look at me. "Please, just let me be."

I nodded and let her go. Every foot she stepped took her farther and farther away from me, and my chest throbbed with the pain I'd never really meant to cause her. I felt like such a fool. I'd pushed her too far. I ran my hands through my hair and decided I would go apologize to her immediately. I hustled to the trailer and got ready for the day then left, heading straight for the horse barn, hoping she was in there, where we usually met.

Inside, the ranch hands Pete and Drew were brushing down and saddling the horses, readying for the day.

"Hey, you guys seen Cricket?" I asked as nonchalantly as possible.

"Heard she's still up at the main house," Drew answered before going right back into the conversation he was having before.

I nodded and tried not to appear too eager to reach the house. Once out of sight, I nearly sprinted for the deck. In the dining hall kitchen, I found Bridge stirring something in a bowl and Jonah draped on the fridge next to her.

"Seen Cricket?" I asked.

They shook their heads no and I left the kitchen, making my way to the main living. I spotted Ellie in there.

"Ellie!" I said a little too anxiously.

"What's wrong, honey?"

"Oh nothing," I said, trying to calm myself a little. "Have you seen Cricket? She wasn't down at the stables this morning."

I shifted my body back and forth.

Her facial expression dropped a moment but quickly picked back up, shielding herself. "Honey, you'll probably be working with Drew and Pete today. Cricket's gone into town unexpectedly with Ethan."

The words "with Ethan" echoed through my head again and again. I nodded. "Thanks."

I walked back into the dining hall and lowered myself on the bench; my head fell into my hands. I yanked off my cap and ran my fingers through my hair.

CHAPTER TWENTY-FIVE

I WORKED the entire day with my eyes peeled for Cricket and even Ethan, but they never showed. That is, until dinner that night. I'd gone back to the trailer and showered just in case she showed up to dinner. I was determined to pull her aside and apologize for whatever I'd done. Seeing her in pain was eating me to my core, and knowing I was the one that caused it made me sick to my stomach.

Bridge, sporting a little bit bigger bump than the week before, sat next to me.

She sighed. "I look pregnant now."

I laughed a little. "Yeah, I mean, kinda, I guess. It's just this tiny little bulge. I thought you'd be a bit bigger than this, actually."

"Dr. Harmon said he's not that surprised and that first pregnancies take a while to show, especially in someone as slim as I."

"Ah, I see."

"So, uh, what's going on with you today?" she whispered.

"Dude, I f'ed up royally."

"What happened?" she asked, taking a sip of water.

"I don't even know, to be honest. I said something to Cricket, you know, to push her, really, and she reacted completely differently than I thought she would."

"What the hell did you say?"

"I told her that I thought she was Ethan because she was afraid to leave him."

"What did she do when you said that?"

I turned toward my sister. "Bridge, she broke my heart, reacted like I'd slapped her. She was trying really hard not to sob and ran as fast as she could."

"Damn, Spence, you really know how to push a girl."

I rolled my eyes. "Thank you for that."

"What are you going to do?"

"I don't know. As soon as I can, I need to get her alone and try to convince her to let me apologize."

Just then, yelling erupted from the living, and Bridge and I looked at one another before leaping up to see what was going on. We raced down the corridor where a small crowd had gathered. At the end of the hall, Jonah heard us coming and turned toward us. He immediately tucked Bridge behind him as if to protect her, which made me nervous.

I pushed through the other hands and stood up front. It was Ethan and Cricket at the bottom of the large log stairwell in the center of the room, and Ethan was yelling at her at the top of his lungs. I made a move toward them to stop him, but Emmett stayed me with a hand so I obeyed. Ellie and Emmett stood very near Cricket.

"This can't be happening!" Ethan yelled at the ceiling. His long black hair had fallen from its leather strap and shook with each word.

"Ethan, listen, I—" Cricket began to say but he stopped her.

"No! You don't understand! I need to do this for you, Cricket!" he practically screamed in her face, making my blood boil.

I clenched my jaw as well as my fists.

"I'm not going to ask you to do this for me, Ethan. It's too much of a sacrifice."

"Cricket," he said, his voice shaking. He fell to his knees and hugged her waist, then looked into her face. "I don't understand this at all. How could you consider this a sacrifice, if I don't? I love you."

"I love you too," she told him sweetly. Although the words matched, their meanings were completely different.

"We were on schedule," he said, not realizing it. "Everything was so perfect. What's changed?"

Cricket fell to her knees and held his face in her hands. "Ethan," she said, then broke down crying. "It's too much to ask. It's just too much."

"It's not. I've offered because I'm in love you. I want to marry you, Cricket. What better reason to do this than that?"

"I can't," she said, explaining nothing else and stood.

She pried Ethan's hands from around her waist, but he fought her, begging her to reconsider whatever it was they were arguing about. The tears streamed, but she had made her decision and shook her head twice before bounding up the stairs. It took everything in me not to chase after her, but I knew it wasn't my place, so I held back.

Ethan slumped into himself, his hair falling forward, shielding him.

Surprising me, Ellie fell to the second step on the bottom of the stairwell, buried her face in her hands and wept openly. Emmett sat with her and held her hand but didn't say a word.

The other hands had dispersed back to the dining hall, realizing they'd overstayed their welcome from the beginning. I turned around and went to Jonah and Bridge.

"What's going on?" I asked him.

He looked down at his feet. "I'm, uh, not really sure."

"Bull, Jonah. Just tell me what's going on?"

He looked at me with sympathy. "You're in love with her, with Cricket," he stated.

"I'm not."

"Then it seems you shouldn't worry about it," he told me. "It seems to be a private matter to me."

He led Bridge off toward the dining hall and left me there speechless. I turned when I saw Emmett pass me and follow Bridge and Jonah. Ellie still sat on the steps but she'd stopped crying, though her head hung low, thinking. I looked around and saw that Ethan was nowhere to be found.

"Ellie," I said softly, and sitting next to her.

She looked up and smiled genuinely at me. "Yes, son?"

"I'm not sure what's going on, and I'm not asking, but I do want to know if you're okay."

She patted my knee. "You're a good boy, Spencer Blackwell. You're still a little confused about life, but you'll figure it out yet."

She kissed my cheek and headed for the hall with the others, leaving me bewildered.

I wished I had asked her what she meant, but I didn't want to bother her. I was so confused because I thought I had life down better than anyone I knew. I chalked it up to old age and dismissed what she said.

I joined the others and sat at the table next to Bridge. We talked about the pregnancy and what we thought the sex of the baby was going to be. She'd decided that she would wait until the birth to find out. That drove me crazy, but there was nothing I could do about it.

"What about names?" I asked her.

"I have no idea, honestly. I can't decide on a single one."

"Oh, come on, Bridge. You have to be leaning toward a few."

"I'm serious," she laughed. "I think I'm going to have to look in the baby's face and decide then."

I smiled. "Wow, gutsy."

"I like to live dangerously."

"I know," I said, exasperated a little.

She huffed and rolled her eyes. "Get it out."

"Well, I mean, you and Jonah. What's really going on there?"

She looked at the next bench down from ours and eyed the subject of my question. "I-now don't get mad…"

I sighed. "Bridge, any time someone prefaces a sentence like that, I most *definitely* get mad."

"Well, just listen then," she began before taking a deep breath. "I like Jonah."

"I had that kind of figured out already."

"A lot," she said, agony written all over her face.

"I think he likes you a lot too, Bridge."

"I think so but, well, I'm so perplexed. I'm having someone else's baby. I'm not quite eighteen. I know it should feel inappropriate but I-I just feel so lost because I don't feel that way."

My heart went out to her. "You're punch-drunk."

"Extremely."

"Why don't you just follow his lead?"

She furrowed her brows at me. "Are you seriously talking to me about this?"

"Yes, Bridge, he's a good friend to me and, to be

honest, you have to be a rare kind of person for your friends to be okay with them dating your sister. You feel me?"

"Yeah, he's a gentleman. And I know that sounds so stupid in this day and age, but Jonah is so kind to me, so considerate and thoughtful. I don't think I've ever felt uncomfortable around him, and lately I've found myself watching his every move when he's around or wondering where and what he's doing when he's not."

I considered everything she was saying. "Just tread carefully," I advised. "Follow his lead, don't rush, and guard the shit out of your heart, Bridge."

She nodded, taking everything I said seriously. I wondered why I couldn't follow my own advice.

Halfway through dinner, Cricket shocked me walking into the hall. Her hair was back in one of her hair scarves and her eyes were red from crying, although I could tell she tried to cover them up.

My hands stilled on the table as she made herself a plate. I wanted to jump to my feet, run to her and pick her up. If I could have, if she would have let me, I would have carried her away. I wanted to kiss every inch of her swollen eyes and promise her that everything was going to be all right. *Oh God, she makes my chest ache.*

It took everything in me not to jump up when she approached the table. She made a move to sit next to Ellie, who happened to be sitting next to me, but changed her mind and sat at the complete opposite end of the table.

Damn it!

I watched her every single move, not caring at all if people thought I was psychotic. It wouldn't have bothered me if they did, not when she was so obviously hurting.

When dinner was over, everyone sat and chatted for a while when the phone rang. Emmett got up to answer and Cricket used the opportunity to try and sneak off, but I followed her and caught her in the main living area.

"Cricket," I said tenderly.

Instead of brushing me off, as I anticipated, Cricket faced me. "Yes?"

I didn't know what to say. I hadn't expected her to be receptive at all, so I just went with the first thing I could think of. "I'm sorry about this morning."

She smiled delicately. "It's not a big deal, Spencer," she said politely, making me feel uneasy.

"No, it was. I'm not exactly sure what I said, but I realize now that I pushed you too far and I'm sorry for that."

"You just helped me understand what I was too blind to see, and I fixed it. So, I should be thanking you, really." She smiled affably and turned toward the staircase.

She was acting so strangely, too politely, not at all the easygoing Cricket I was accustomed to. "Okay," I said, following her. "Can we talk some more?"

"If you'll excuse me," she said, putting me in my place, "I have a few things to do, but I'll see you around." She ascended the remaining staircase and hooked a right down the long hall to her bedroom.

I followed her anyway, not satisfied with the cold, apathetic conversation she'd just given me.

"Cricket, why are you acting like this?" I asked. My hand settled on her forearm as she reached for her doorknob.

She looked down at my hand and I removed it. "I'm not acting like anything. I'm with Ethan. I'm not using him or afraid to leave him anymore, and I think our friendship is improper. I think you and I should be fellow ranch hands and nothing more."

I felt like she'd punched me in the gut. "Anymore? You're not broken up? What was earlier all about?"

She sighed. "Of course not," she explained. "And earlier was just my fixing something that needed fixing. I'm setting boundaries between us, Spencer. You'll be gone in a few months, and it's not worth wrecking fifteen years of my life all because I'm starting to feel things for you."

"But if I was sticking around? What then? Would you be with Ethan then? It feels like you're settling."

She shook her head. "It's not settling. I've just made a decision. I made a promise and I cannot go back on it."

And with that, she left me in the hall, stunned.

I staggered back a little and headed back toward the stairs. "Still with Ethan?"

I felt more shocked than I thought I would.

"Yes, does that bother you, Blackwell?" I heard from the end of the hall.

Ethan stood, leaning against the wall, his eyes boring through me. He wanted a fight, I could feel it, but I'd already decided not in the Hunt house, not when they'd been so kind to us.

"Yes, it does," I told him.

"Finally, some honesty for a change," he said, standing to his full height but leaving his arms crossed. He walked closer to me and I found my fists naturally tightening. "You better watch yourself," he continued.

"Oh yeah? Why?"

"Because I'll catch you when you least expect it."

"What the hell is that supposed to mean?" I asked him.

"It means I see right through your shit and you don't want to provoke me."

"Is that a threat?"

"Damn straight," he said, lingering a moment before rounding me.

He knocked on Cricket's door.

"Who is it?" she asked.

"It's Ethan," he said, eyeing me.

"Come in," she invited.

He opened the door but before he went inside, gave me a triumphant smile.

"Asshole," I muttered and headed back downstairs to get my jacket and head back to the trailer, but the dining hall was unusually full.

I found Bridge sitting next to Jonah talking so I joined them.

"What's going on?" I asked.

"Emmett's on the phone with the McAllen family a town over," Jonah explained.

"Friends of the family or something?"

"Not really, but apparently something major happened. Pop Pop's asked us to stick around for a minute."

"Okay," I said just as Emmett walked in.

He sat at the front of the table. "Well, that was Amos McAllen's son. He's flown into Yellow Creek. Amos was in an accident last week and they've had to amputate his leg."

"Poor man," Jonah said, shaking his head.

"He's in pretty serious condition and his wife is suffering without him. As you know, calving season is in full swing and their ranch is small." Lots of hands started nodding. "She relied on Amos for a lot."

"I can go over and help them," Jonah offered quickly, shocking me.

"I was hoping you would say as much," Emmett said.

"Can we afford to lose Jonah?" I asked Bridge under my breath.

She shrugged. We were strapped for hands as it was. Jonah nudged my shoulder and I looked at him like he was crazy. The death look he gave me confirmed it.

I raised my hand like a fifth grader. "Uh, I can go too," I volunteered.

"Thank you, Spencer," Emmett said. "That's about all we can spare, I believe."

A few days away from Cricket might help clear your head a little too, I thought.

That night, I practically toppled into bed, tired all the way down to my bones by so many different things.

"*You look pathetic, you know that, right?*"

"*Shup up, Piper," I said, locking the villa door and heading toward the elevators.*

I pressed the button for the bottom floor. She followed me when the doors opened.

"*You look desperate to her and she's probably lost all respect for you.*"

"*Shut up, Piper!*"

She sighed and leaned against the glass in her satin gown. "I tried to tell you, Spencer. She's not good for you. She's nothing but trouble."

"*Piper, shut up, or I'll shut you up.*"

"*And she's going to take all your money," she sang.*

My blood burned in my veins and my hand found her throat and squeezed. "Shut. Up."

She smiled and I let her go. She gasped, then started laughing. "You hate to hear the truth," she said, borrowing my own words. "And what about your deal?" she asked.

"*What deal?*"

"*The deal your friend made you. The phone call you got on the way back from Vegas?*"

"*How do you even know about that?*"

"*You forget, Spencer, I told you I know everything. I know he offered you the chance of a lifetime on an inside trade involving an innovative technology. I know you have every intention of taking it because it would set you and your sister up extravagantly for life. I also know that you're two million dollars short."*

"Yeah, no thanks to you."

She pouted. "Trust me," she said, "if I had known the offer was coming and that you'd take it, I'd have kept your money safe."

"And now I have no way of obtaining that two million! He's going to need that soon! How am I supposed to get it now?"

"You'll find a way. Borrow it."

"From who?"

"One of your prep school boys should have that liquid easily."

"Maybe."

She paused and watched me. "You could blackmail someone," she added slyly.

I narrowed my eyes at her. My stomach began to turn because I was considering it. "Who?"

"That married executive in Chicago. You could contact him and blackmail him."

"My dad already did that!"

"Right. Your dad. Not you. You don't think he would pay to keep you quiet as well?"

I considered it. "Maybe."

"Good boy," she said as the doors opened to the lobby.

GREED FURY LUST IDLE BINGE ENVY VAIN

CHAPTER TWENTY-SIX

I woke the next morning with no real idea why Jonah and I were driving an entire town away to help a guy the family barely knew when the ranch couldn't afford to lose any more hands, but then again, they helped Bridge and me out so who was I to judge?

We pulled up to the ranch and noticed it was a little bit outdated and not as kept as the Hunt Ranch.

"Amos is almost seventy," Jonah explained. "He used to keep a better ranch, but I suspect he's gotten a little old and can't keep up."

"Where are his kids?"

"His kids went to college and never came back. They built lives in the city."

Can't blame them, I thought.

We pulled toward the main house and took in the sights. Parts of the barn roof were falling in. The fences need immediate restoring. I suspected a few cows had probably escaped through them. Amos McAllen was too old to keep up with his ranch.

"Why doesn't he just retire?" I asked as we came to a stop.

Jonah gave me that look again. "Retire on what? Most ranches around here don't necessarily take in a huge profit. We survive from year to year."

I nodded but couldn't fathom how people lived like that.

An older but fit woman emerged on her porch and met us by Jonah's truck.

"You must be from the Hunt Ranch," she said, extending her hand.

Her smile reached her eyes as she squinted in the sun.

"Mrs. McAllen?" Jonah said, taking her hand.

"Oh, please, call me Faye!"

"Faye, I'm Jonah Hunt and this is another of the ranch's hands," Jonah said discreetly.

"Spencer," I said, offering my hand and she took it.

"So nice to meet you boys," she said cordially. "Come on in for a moment."

We followed her up the creaky steps of her porch and I briefly noted that needed repairing too. Her house was small but comfortable and clean.

"I've got something special planned for your lunch today," she said, beaming.

"Don't trouble yourself, Miss Faye, we're here to help you, remember?" Jonah said.

She grabbed his hand in both of hers and patted them gently. "I know, son, and I cannot tell you how grateful we are," she said, nearly shedding a tear and pulling on my wound tight heartstring.

"This is what we do for our neighbors," Jonah said smiling.

She patted them once more then let them go.

"If you don't mind," Jonah began, "we'd like to get

straight to work if that's okay?"

"Oh, by all means, don't let me keep you, love."

He smiled once more and I followed him out and onto the porch.

"They've only got a hundred cows here," Jonah said, scanning the field near the barn and applying his gloves. I pulled mine from my back pocket and followed suit.

"Oh, good, we should be done pretty quickly," I said, feeling a little invigorated. Jonah looked at me. "What?" I asked.

"We've got a ton of work to do here. We'll be here until late, I think."

"What? Why?"

"Have you seen the state of this ranch?"

"Yeah, so?"

"So? We'll have to make all these repairs for them."

"What in the hell, Jonah? I thought we were just here to help with the herd."

"We are," he said, bounding off the front porch and heading toward the barn. "But we're gonna leave this ranch better than how we found it."

I shook my head. "That is ludicrous."

Jonah stopped in his tracks. "Spencer, you afraid of a little work?"

"No," I said, affronted.

"Then quit your bitching," he replied, cursing for the first time I'd heard since I met him.

I laughed. "Fine."

We tended the herd, just like we did at the Hunt Ranch, but in a fraction of the time. Then Jonah made me clean and organize the barn because it was a cluttered mess. We could tell Amos left the tools he needed at a level for easier access so we hung all the tools he didn't frequently use on the barn wall and did the same for the tools he used often at a level he could reach them.

GREED

That took more than three hours alone. I thought we were done, but Jonah decided the floors needed cleaning so we grabbed a broom and a hose, much like we did in the horse stalls when we would clean out the pellets. We scrubbed and rinsed the concrete floor. When all was said and done, it looked like a brand-new barn, save for the holes in the roof where patches of snow were coming through.

"We're gonna have to tackle that roof," he said, eyeing the damage.

"How are we going to reach it?" I asked, looking around.

"There's a ladder built on the outside. We'll have to gather materials and climb up."

We searched the barn and found what we needed, then rounded the building searching for the ladder.

"Dude, that looks sketchy," I said, inspecting the rungs of the old attached ladder. I placed a foot on the first rung and tested my weight. It held. "How are we going to get the wood up there?"

"Tie it up, I guess, and heave it over."

"Okay," I said, heading for the barn in search of rope.

We tied the wood and tucked our hammers and nails in our back pockets and hauled the heavy load up and onto the roof.

We were both out of breath when we reached the top. "Damn," I said, looking down. "That fall would hurt."

Jonah peeked over the edge. "Can't disagree."

We trekked across the snow-covered roof and I almost slipped twice, my heart pounding in my chest. We sat at the first bit that need patching and started working. After five minutes, I broke the silence.

"It's cold as shit up here."

I rubbed my gloves back and forth and slapped them together a few times to bring the feeling back into my fingers.

"Duh," he said.

"Smart ass," I laughed.

"Jackass."

"Bridge lover," I tested.

He looked at me, shocked, his mouth and eyes wide open before busting out into the loudest guffaw.

"Cricket lover," he bit back.

"What the hell!" I said.

"Oh what? You can dish it out but you can't take it?"

"I don't love your cousin, dude."

"Sure," he said, rolling his eyes and hammering another nail.

I cleared my throat. "So, do you?" I asked.

"What are you talking about?"

"Do you like my sister?" I asked.

His face flamed red. "I do," he stated simply.

Hearing it from his own lips made it so much more real to me.

"How much?" I asked, finishing the patched sub-roof.

He looked at me as he dragged over the pile of wood shingles. "Honestly?"

"Yeah," I said, reaching for a shingle.

He scratched the back of his neck, afraid to spill.

"It's okay, dude," I told him.

He sighed. "Too much. Way too much."

This confused me. "So, uh, do you wish you didn't or something?"

"No way," he claimed emphatically.

"What do you mean by 'too much' then?" I asked, my big brother side coming out full force.

"I just meant that I'm in love with your sister, and I don't think she feels the same way and that...that eats at me."

I let the news sink in, feeling a combination of impressed with Jonah, bewildered and confused.

"I think," I began carefully, "that she may care for you more than you think."

Jonah's head shot up, his eyes wide. "Shut up," he said seriously.

"I'm very serious, Jonah."

"Oh my God," he said, sitting up and back on his heels. His hand went to his chest and he turned to sit, as if he couldn't believe what I'd told him. His head hung low as he studied the tops of his boots. He removed his wool cap, then put it right back on, as if he was unsure of what to do with his hands.

"You okay? I asked.

He smiled, but one corner turned up more than the other, like he was embarrassed. "I think so."

I cleared my throat. "So, what are you going to do?" I asked, hammering another shingle in.

The noise brought him back to the present and he joined me once again.

"I don't know. I guess I'm going to have to talk to Bridget."

"That's a good idea," I said but hesitated.

"What?"

"You're okay with her being pregnant?"

His face softened. "I'm definitely okay with it."

"How can that be?" I asked, astounded but grateful nonetheless.

"You don't choose who you fall for, Spencer. Either you do or you don't," he said, stunning me.

Bridge had said something strikingly similar to me the day we left.

"Ain't that the truth," I chimed in.

"See. I knew you liked my cousin."

"How do you figure that?"

"Your previous statement, for one. Two, the fact that she comes in the room and not a single one of us can break your attention from her. And three," he said, "Ethan can't stand you and Ethan likes everyone."

The mere mention of Ethan made my skin crawl.

"You know," he continued, "we all love and respect Ethan like he was part of our family."

"Yeah, yeah," I said, starting to get pissed off.

"Wait a minute! We all love him, Spencer, but we also want what's best for Cricket."

I regarded him, puzzled. "Speak plainly."

"I just mean," he said, finishing up the last shingle, "that sometimes Cricket doesn't make the best decisions when it comes to herself. She has these ideas of what's best for her family and friends, and she's constantly sacrificing herself for them."

"For example, sticking around the ranch when she so obviously wants to explore the world a little?" I asked.

"That."

"And staying with Ethan because she thinks it's what her family wants?"

"Maybe," he answered.

"And, *maybe* denying that she's falling in love with me, even though I know in my gut, in my heart of hearts, that she's supposed to belong to me?"

He paused. "*Perhaps.*"

CHAPTER TWENTY-SEVEN

OVER THE next few days, Jonah and I made that ranch so clean, so organized, so efficient that I couldn't help but be a little proud of myself and the jobs we'd completed. Faye was so appreciative, by the third day, she was sending home enough baskets of baked goods to feed a small army. We kept trying to insist that it was not a big deal but she would have none of it.

Other ranches had followed our lead and sent hands to help out on the McAllen Ranch. We were all toggling a week at a time, and Jonah and I weren't due back there for another six weeks. Although, the McAllen's son suspected they'd have a permanent hand there by then.

The following Friday morning, I had to admit it was nice to wake up and not have anywhere to be but the Hunt Ranch. The day went by uneventfully. I hadn't seen Cricket or Ethan for more than a week, and the separation from Cricket was a torment, but I was happy for it all the same. I needed to clear my head, and Jonah helped me do that by keeping me busier than I'd ever been in my life.

Before dinner, Ellie dragged Jonah and me over to the old Hunt buildings, the ones Cricket worked out of. I tried not to let that affect me, but being near her sculptures hurt my stomach.

"Here," Ellie said, prying open a large sliding door to an abandoned-looking barn.

"What are we doing out here, Ellie?" I asked.

"There's an auction tomorrow evening in Yellow Creek for Amos McAllen."

I looked at Jonah, addled. *What more could they need?* I thought.

"Amos needs a prosthetic," Ellie explained, rummaging through a carefully organized shelf at the back. "We're going to see if there's anything in here worth donating."

"Isn't this all family heirloom-type stuff?" I asked

"Yes, sir." She winked.

"You're going to give a family heirloom to strangers?"

"Does this surprise you, baby?" Ellie asked, setting aside a tool that looked very old.

"Frankly, I'm shocked, Ellie."

She smiled at me and patted my cheek. "This is what we do for our neighbors, honey. We take care of each other."

But they're strangers! I thought, then I remembered the day Bridge and I came to ask for their help, how open and generous they were with us, how they welcomed us without any expectations of a return, and how they didn't judge us. I felt utterly ashamed.

"I see," I said, lifting something off the wall for Ellie.

Just then, the doors slid open behind us and Ethan and Cricket walked in. I smiled kindly at Cricket, then turned back to helping Ellie.

"Hi, Grandma," Cricket chimed, and Ellie turned around.

GREED

"Hello, darlin'." She smiled. "Hi, Ethan honey."

"Ellie," Ethan greeted, making my fists clench.

Ellie picked up a pile of old papers and a photograph slid out from underneath. She gasped and we all turned her direction.

"Oh my word," she said, bending down and picking it up. She dusted it off and studied its subject with glassy eyes. "It's my mama," she said, running her fingers reverently over the surface. She turned it toward me and I almost choked.

The woman in the photograph was petite and slender, bobbed black hair, stylish and looked exactly like Cricket. She wore a flapper-style dress and a headband with a jaunty feather at the side. Her arm was raised and in her hand was a champagne glass. She looked beautiful and happy. Her smile looked as clever as Cricket's.

"What was her name?" I asked, taking the photograph and trying not to feel crazy, like I was looking at a picture of Cricket.

"Caroline," Ellie said, looking over at Cricket.

I did the same, and seeing her so close up made my chest throb, but I turned back to the task at hand.

Ellie picked several nice things for the auction, and I couldn't believe how generous she was being.

She picked up my hand and squeezed it. "Would you mind using your nice truck, Spencer, and taking this over to Yellow Creek for me? I think you're the only one here who knows your way around there, besides Jonah, and I need him."

"Not at all, Ellie." I smiled.

"Thank you, baby." She turned toward Cricket. "Grandbaby, will you go with him and see that Faye's sister Helen knows all she's getting from us and what they are worth?"

Cricket's eyes widened and she looked panicked. She

turned to Ethan and his face was expressionless.

She swallowed. "Of course," she answered.

"Thank you, baby," she said. "Ethan? Jonah? Will you come help me in the horse stalls for a minute. There's some readjusting I need done and it's driving me crazy."

"Yes, ma'am," Ethan responded, narrowing his eyes at me.

Jonah and a reluctant Ethan followed her out, leaving Cricket and me alone for the first time in a week. It was beyond awkward.

"I'll get the truck," I said, making my way out of the barn.

I thought I was alone until I heard the faint crunch of Cricket's boots in the leftover snow. I twisted my head just enough to see her behind me but didn't acknowledge her more than that.

When we reached the truck, I held open the door for her and helped her in as respectfully as I could, still not saying a word. I rounded the front and hopped into the driver's side, starting the engine. My hand instinctively used the back of her headrest as I backed out, and that made her flinch. I wanted to laugh, but I checked it quickly. *Goofy girl.*

I slowly made my way toward the old barn and the silence felt deafening. I hopped out and began to gather the things Ellie wanted to donate to the auction, fitting them into the back of the extended cab. At the end, I let Eugie jump in on my side.

The half-hour drive to Yellow Creek was so restrained, the sexual tension so palpable, I almost demanded she roll down her damn window, anything to relieve the strain. I had to drive around the stupid town for five minutes longer than I'd anticipated because I was having trouble finding the old schoolhouse they were using for the auction and dinner.

"Thank God," we both breathed at the same time when we pulled in.

Click.

We hid our smiles and went inside as Eugie followed. We looked for Faye's sister Helen, but it didn't seem she was around.

"Truck," I said and she nodded.

We began unloading everything and laid it next to all the offerings. I hoisted myself up to sit on the edge of the old stage and wait for Helen. Cricket made a move to do the same but she was so short, she couldn't get her leg over the edge.

"Oh my God," she said, laughing.

She was giggling so hard she couldn't get a grip and kept struggling to get up.

"'Oh my God' is right," I teased.

I jumped off and tossed her by the waist onto the edge, making her squeal. Trying hard not to snicker, she adjusted her clothing.

She sighed. "Thank you."

"You're welcome," I said, setting Eugie next to her.

I leaned back on my elbows but she stayed sitting, her hands wedged between her bouncing knees.

"Nervous?" I asked her nonchalantly.

Her knees stopped bouncing. "Uh, no. Are you?"

"Not even in the slightest," I said coolly.

"That's good," she replied.

"It's *great*," I said, teasing her.

She shook her head but didn't say anything.

"You look just like your great-grandma," I said, changing the subject.

She faced me and smiled. "Thank you."

"I'm sorry. Was that too intimate a compliment for work colleagues?" I needled. "I wouldn't want to cross any boundaries."

She pursed her lips, huffed and faced the open space again.

"How do you think Patches is doing today?" I baited. "I know Ellie found an abscess in his right hind hoof."

"He's fine. Pop Pop treated him. He's resting."

"That's good news. Who is Drew riding then?"

"I don't know," she puffed.

"When do you think we'll be able to turn the cows out to summer pasture?"

"If we're lucky, the end of April."

Her short, bland answers were cracking me up.

"That's superb," I answered sarcastically.

She nodded.

"Hey," I began.

"Spencer! Stop talking to me about the ranch!"

"Oh, so I guess we can't talk about anything at all then? Awesome! What awesome company *you* turned out to be."

She sighed and her head fell. "I'm sorry. I-I just needed some boundaries with you. We were getting *close*, if you catch my drift, and it was disrespectful to Ethan." She faced me. "I just needed you to know that it needed to stop."

"That's fine," I lied. I mean really, really lied.

She regarded me and opened her mouth to say something, but a loud clang came from the front of the schoolhouse.

"What the hell was that?" I asked. "Stay here," I ordered her.

I jumped down and made my way toward the front, Eugie tight on my heels. No one was there, but when I made an attempt to look outside, the weather had taken a drastic, dangerous change. The wind was so strong I couldn't open the door more than a foot. Snow blew so strongly and so heavily, I couldn't see but a few inches in front of me.

GREED

I shivered from the cold that had seeped through and met Cricket back at the edge of the stage. "You should probably come see this," I told her.

She hopped down and she beat me to the door. "Holey. Moley."

"Will it calm down any?"

"Uh, um, I don't think so. This, Spencer, is a blizzard in Montana."

"Should we try to book it out of here?

She gawked at me like I was daft.

"So, we're stuck here then," I concluded.

"Uh, that's a big yes."

"For how long?"

Her eyes widened as if she just realized something. "Um, awhile," she said vaguely. "Excuse me," she said, pulling her cell from her back pocket.

I stayed planted by the door with the little glass windows and watched the white attack every inch of Yellow Creek with Eugie at my feet.

"Are we going to be here all night, boy?" I asked him, to which he licked my hand.

"I take that as a yes then."

"Hey," she spoke into her phone, "yeah. Yeah, I *know*, Ethan." She blew at her bangs. "Let me talk to Pop." There was a brief pause. "Hey, yup. No, I didn't see it coming. We were in the old schoolhouse waiting for Faye's sister Helen." Another pause. "I know. We're not going anywhere." She looked around. "It still has power, but we'll start rummaging for provisions here in a second, just in case. Uh-huh. Okay, yup, tell her I said I loved her too. Yeah, sure." A longer pause. "I know, Ethan. I *know*." Her voice dropped to a whisper. "You're just going to have to trust *me* then, Ethan, all right? Okay, I will. Love you too. Bye."

She hung up then rounded the foyer. "Got anything in

your truck worth retrieving?"

I thought about it. "Uh, I've got a new comforter Bridge just bought. Also, there's an emergency kit that came with the truck. I think there's a bag of peanut M&M's."

"You had me at M&M's," she said, making me smile.

"Stay here," I said and wedged myself through the door.

Eugie tried to follow, but Cricket held him back.

A blast of blistering cold permeated me to my bones within a second. My body began to shiver, and I had to fight the strong, chilling wind the five feet to the truck. I hit the key lock in my pocket and jumped inside.

"Oh. My. God." I shivered.

I didn't want to waste any time, so I found an old trash bag that had laundry in it and tossed the clothes inside and started tossing anything I thought we could use inside, including the comforter, the emergency kit and the M&M's. I also found a lighter, an old metal flashlight that belonged to Jonah, and a bag of candy bars hidden underneath the passenger seat so frozen they could break a window. No doubt put there by Bridge because her doctor told her to start watching her carbs.

I ran as fast as I could back into the school with my loot. Cricket had pushed the door open as far as she could, and I wedged myself through with the bag.

Once inside, I jumped up and down and shouted, "Hooo!" making Cricket howl with laughter.

"Cold, city boy?"

I returned her earlier look. "Um, excuse me? But you're skinny ass would be a solid Popsicle five feet outside this door."

"Hey! I've got some insulation, buddy."

"Oh yeah, Skeletor, sure you do."

Her jaw clenched. "Come on. We have to search the

building in case the electricity goes out."

I followed her, reveling in my Skeletor reference because

A) Masters of the Universe rocks

B) It got under Cricket's skin.

The schoolhouse wasn't very big, hence the reason it was called the "old" schoolhouse. Basically, it was three rooms total, a stage area that probably doubled as the cafeteria and two classrooms.

We checked the classroom closets, but there was nothing worth pulling out.

"Hey," I said, pointing to what looked like a janitor's closet.

I pried open the door and dust came billowing out. I let it settle before stepping inside. "Here's an old candle," I said, picking up a red pillar candle probably used at Christmastime fifty years ago.

"See anything else worth using?" she asked.

I checked the shelves. "Score!"

"What is it?"

"A bottle of whiskey," I said, dusting off the label. "Unopened from about twenty years ago." She didn't say anything. "Cricket?"

"Yeah?"

"Did you hear me?"

"Yeah, a bottle of whiskey, cool," she said, unenthused.

I pocketed the whiskey and shut the door to the closet.

"Not a fan of whiskey?" I asked.

"You could say that," she said vaguely.

She started walking back toward the stage area. "You could force down a shot if it got too cold. It'd warm you up."

"Yeah, I couldn't do that even then," she explained, or didn't explain.

"Okay," I sang, letting it lie.

"I wonder if there's anything behind the stage."

Eugie had stayed behind and was pacing the end of the stage waiting for us. I sat our meager findings on the edge and helped Bridge back up. I didn't have the heart to tell her there were stairs hidden behind the curtain. I helped myself and began our way to the back when the lights went off and the electricity powered down.

"Dang," Cricket said.

It was pitch dark, so I grabbed the flashlight I'd tucked in my jacket just in case that very scenario played out.

"Oh!" she said, when I turned on the light. "Good. A flashlight."

"Yes, a flashlight."

"Shut up."

I smiled and led the way.

There was nothing to the left of the stage but the pulley system and the stairs, so I led us back over to the right side. There was a tiny stage room tucked in the corner, and inside there were rows of Christmas costumes.

"That's it then," she said. "What we see is what we've got."

"Let's grab a couple of these wise men beards." I snatched one off a shelf and put it over her head. "Got to keep that mug warm, Thumbelina."

"Hey!" she said, laughing and tugging off the beard. She placed it back on the shelf.

"How about these capes," I suggested seriously.

Cricket ran her hands along the length of a crushed velvet one. "Yup, these are our best options."

I tossed them over my arm and we retreated back to the stage. I layered them on the floor for some nice cushioning and Eugie immediately curled up at the end

241

and fell fast asleep. I emptied the bag on top and we went through my findings. I lit the candle to conserve the flashlight.

I held the candle under my face. "Once upon a time, there was a devastatingly handsome young man and an *okay*-looking girl and they were stranded...in a blizzard... in Montana," I bellowed menacingly.

She rolled her eyes.

"The devastatingly handsome young man hid a deep, dark secret," I said, dropping an octave. Cricket shook her head. "At," I began and looked down at my wristwatch, "exactly nine thirty-seven in the evening every evening, he turned...into a vampire! He *knew* that the *okay*-looking girl didn't stand a chance against him, so he did the only thing he could," I said, setting down the candle. "He cut off his hands!" I cried, pulling the sleeves of my coat over my hands.

I held the stumps up and Cricket eyed them for a second before bursting out laughing.

When she caught her breath, she said, "How would cutting off the hands of a vampire stop him from eating her?"

"I don't know," I said. "I didn't think he could overpower her at that point. Have you ever tried to do anything without hands?"

"Do you know anything about vampires? They're super strong. Hands or no, he could still pin her down."

"Oh my God," I exaggerated. "I'm so sorry! Excuse me!" I shouted to the empty room, causing Eugie's head to pop up then back down. "I have the world's foremost leading expert on vampires in my midst! Alert the papers!"

"Shut up," she laughed.

"I still think she could throw him off," I tested, holding up my fake stumps and examining them.

"No," she insisted, having no idea where I was going. "He could definitely overpower her."

"Hmm. We should definitely test that theory," I said, tossing myself on top of her and flapping my handless cuffs at her.

"Stop," she laughed, trying to roll me off, but I pinned her beneath me.

She fought me, giggling uncontrollably and causing me to roar with laughter.

"Stop," she sighed but her laughter was dying.

It suddenly got very quiet and we both stopped squirming. I was very aware that I was laying on top of Cricket Hunt. We watched one another, our chests rising and falling against each other. My hands found the pile of capes beneath us and I pushed myself up, rolling to my side and sitting up.

I cleared my throat. "Sorry," I rasped, refusing to look at her.

She sat up as well and fixed her mussed hair. "It's, uh, okay," she acknowledged, staring at her lap.

"M&M? I asked, pulling the bag out.

I poured a few in her hand, careful not to touch her. "Thanks."

I laid down on the capes and tucked one hand behind my head while tossing M&M's in the air and trying to catch them. I only missed one and only choked on two.

"How long do you think before the storm blows over?" I asked.

"Not sure," she answered, laying down beside me.

"Think they'll cancel the auction?"

"Nah, they'll clear the roads and we'll be out and about in no time at all."

"You've lived through these often then."

"Hundreds of them."

"Cricket?" I asked after five M&M's.

"Yeah?"

"Do you ever talk about your mom?"

She studied me. "Not really."

"Cool."

It was silent for seven more M&M's.

"I was young when she died."

"Sarah, right?" I asked, thinking on the first day I met Cricket Hunt.

She gazed at me, surprised. "Yeah. Sarah."

I kept silent.

"I was seven, but I remember it like it was yesterday."

"How sad. How old was she?"

"Twenty-four."

"Too, too young."

"Too." She grabbed a handful of M&M's. "She got sick when I was about five. For the longest time, I had no idea what was going on. Then, one day, she came to me and told me she would be in the hospital for a few days but she would be back and I would be with Grandma and that Grandma would bring me up to see her in two days.

"I cried and begged her not to go, but she convinced me she'd come back, so we marked my calendar for two days ahead and she promised me Grandma would take me to see her."

My breathing got deeper, heavier, sadder.

"So, the next day I made a big X on the calendar when the day was done and the day after that, I woke very early and dressed in my Sunday dress and shoes. I packed a bag because I didn't understand that she was actually in nearby Kalispell, and I waited very patiently for my Grandma to come upstairs so we could go visit Mama.

"But breakfast passed, lunch, and we were approaching dinner and I still hadn't gone to see my mom. So I grabbed my suitcase and found my grandma's room and knocked on her door.

244

"She said it was okay for me to come in, so I did, and when she saw my face she broke down crying. I had no idea what she was crying for, so I asked if she was okay. I asked if she was crying because we wouldn't be able to visit Mama that day."

"Oh my God," I couldn't help but breathe.

Cricket looked at me and gave me a half smile.

"Grandma said that we wouldn't be visiting Mama and sat me down at the edge of her bed." Cricket turned thoughtful. "I still remember the feel of the weight of my dress shoes as they dangled." She shook her head to clear it. "She set my suitcase on the ground next to her knees and grabbed my face as she so often does, even still, and she said, 'Cricket, I have something to tell you.' I had no idea what she was saying. I had an idea of what death was, but I had no idea how permanent it was.

"I nodded that I understood, but after a few days, I started to feel sick without my mother, and I told my grandma that I was ready for her to be alive again, that I wanted to see her."

"Cricket," I said, turning on my side.

Tears cascaded down the sides of her face.

She turned on her hip and faced me. "Yes?"

"I am so sorry."

"What for?"

"I'm sorry that she was taken from you so early. It wasn't fair."

She reached her hand out on the cape we laid upon but didn't quite touch my hand. She was just near enough for me to feel the heat of her fingers and my heart beat sadly for her.

"Spencer," she said, studying both our hands then piercing my eyes with her bright blue ones. "Life on Earth is fleeting. It's a gift, but when God wants you, He will take you. It's not meant to be a punishment to you or to your loved ones. In fact, it's truly an extra incentive for you to do His will, for you to serve Him so you can strive to be with Him as *well* as the ones you lose. There's a peace in that, Spencer."

She stunned me with that statement. Absolutely stunned me. Because I had never *ever* thought of death as anything other than a punishment. I feared it with utter dismay, with complete abhorrence, with despair and foreboding.

"And death," she continued, "is a beautiful thing for those destined for God's world. How could I possibly begrudge her that happiness?"

She considered my expression and laughed a little through the tears.

"It took me a long time to come to terms with that, but when I finally did, it clicked." She smiled. "Now, that doesn't mean I'm not selfish sometimes and miss her, but that's okay because I'm human." She smiled wider. "And I love being human. What a gift it is to be human."

I stared at her in the candlelight. "You're beautiful," I said.

Her eyes closed tightly. "Spencer," she breathed.

"I'm saying that as a co-worker, Cricket."

She snorted. "Shut up," she laughed.

"I'm serious. As a fellow ranch hand, I feel it within the realm of appropriate to tell you that I think you're the most beautiful girl I've ever had the pleasure to meet."

"Spencer," she said, her eyes going glassy.

"And as your co-worker, you should also know that I find you talented, smart as a whip, capable and sweet."

"Spencer," she whispered, the tears more evident now.

"And-and I don't think it's at all improper, as your co-worker, mind you, to tell you that, in my humble opinion, you're settling for the life you have."

She squeezed her eyes closed. "Spence, stop," she wept.

246

"I don't think it's a bad life, the life you've chosen, not by any means, but I do think you should give yourself a try."

She shook her head no.

"I think you could have a hell of a time finding out what you really want, that you'd discover some pretty incredible things about yourself. You said yourself you didn't really want to be here. I don't think you meant that you wanted to leave forever, but I do think you wanted to explore while you're young."

She sobbed a bit but shook her head more emphatically.

"Cricket, your family wouldn't die if you took off for a little while."

She sobbed harder. "You don't understand."

"Help me to, then."

She sucked in a breath then exhaled. "You can't fathom the unimaginable sacrifice they've all made for me, Spencer."

"Because they took care of you? Cricket, they did that because they wanted to."

"No," she said, grieving something terrible, "it's more complicated than that."

"Then *tell me*, Cricket."

She broke down. "I don't wish to burden anyone else anymore. I'm so tired of being a hardship."

"Cricket," I said, grasping her hands, "whatever it is that you speak of, it's not. I can promise you that it's not a burden to those who love you. Trust me."

She was crying so hard, she couldn't answer, so I did the only thing I could think to do. I pulled her across the capes and held her while she lamented and that was exactly what she was doing, she was mourning. What, I didn't know.

I pulled out Bridge's new down comforter from the

bag and tossed it over the both of us as it was starting to
get cold and I let her cry, I let her unburden herself of all
the heavy sacrifice she decided to walk around with for
her family and I suffered to carry it for her instead.

Ethan may have felt as if he was in love with Cricket,
but I thought he was more in love with the idea of what
they were. Anyone truly and genuinely interested in her
would have seen this side of her. This sad, taxed soul.

"Cricket," I spoke into her hair as her breathing
steadied into my chest, but she didn't answer, worn out
from a heavy life she didn't want to speak of.

Her cell rang from underneath the blanket, but I
couldn't find it in plain sight. I ran my hand along her hip
and felt the vibration. I nearly laughed at the temptation.
I carefully wedged it from her back pocket and brought it
to my face.

"Hello?" I whispered.

"Where's Cricket?" Ethan asked.

"She fell asleep," I bit.

"Where?" he asked, suspicious.

I sighed audibly. "Ethan, I made her a pallet on the
stage floor. She's resting comfortably."

"Why are you whispering? Are you-*are you laying next
to her*?"

"No," I lied, "sound travels in this place. I'd rather not
wake her. She seemed really tired."

"Fine," he conceded, exasperating me.

"You know, you should trust her," I told him honestly,
unable to help myself.

"I do trust her. It's you I don't trust."

"Do you?" I asked, becoming aware that he truly
didn't. "I don't think that you do. I don't mean that
you *can't* trust her, but I think you're frightened she'll
discover what you've known all along."

"Shut up!" he shouted.

"I almost feel sorry for you, Ethan."

"Shut up!" he shouted again, incensed.

"Fine, I won't say another word," I told him and hung up. "Because I don't need to," I revealed to the empty line.

I laid the phone above our heads and blew out the candle.

At three in the morning, we were startled awake by Eugie barking.

"What is it, boy?" I asked him before realizing he was barking at a loose shutter flapping in the wind.

We both laid back down. "Eugie, hush," a raspy-voiced Cricket ordered him and he quieted down.

I began to stretch when I felt that Cricket's body was on mine. Her leg was hooked around mine, her head resting on my chest, her hand around my waist.

"I'm sorry," she said. I couldn't see her face flame red, but the heat on my chest told me all I wanted to know.

She scrambled to her side of the pallet. I stood up and stretched once more.

"I'm gonna check the roads."

The snow had ceased to a light dusting and the plow trucks had already gone through the town, which meant they'd done the same thing for the highways. As I studied the winter wonderland before me, I debated whether I should tell Cricket we could leave.

Sleeping next to her, even if was for a few hours, was so incredible it made my heart pound just thinking about it. I didn't know how I'd gotten as far as I had since meeting her. I went from wanting to know what her body felt like to sleeping next to that body but only being able to think about how I was dying to know what her heart felt like.

An intense, burning pounding hit me in the chest and my hand shot to my heart and stayed there. I waited for the sensation to subside but it didn't. At first it hurt, but then it scorched me so sweetly I begged for God never to take it away. It blistered my soul, imprinted in my skin, and seared my lips.

It was the exact moment I fell in love with Cricket Hunt. The point in time I knew my life would never be the same again. My hand shot out and rested flatly against the cold window and the ice melted beneath it.

But the next moment I acknowledged I could do nothing about it, and the pain was so intense I felt like punching that window through. Because I couldn't claim her lips whenever I felt like it, I couldn't change the oil in her truck for her, I couldn't leave a note on her mirror for her whenever I felt like it, or find pieces of scrap metal on the side of the road and instinctually pick them up for her. I couldn't help her catch Eugie for his bath, touch her hip because I just felt like it, or *drive her into Kalispell*. I couldn't do those things because she wasn't mine to do those things for, and that was pure agony for me.

"Cricket," I said, walking back to the stage with purpose.

She sat up, devastating me, and my hand clenched at my chest.

"Uh-huh?" she asked.

"Um, the roads are clear. We can leave if you want."

"Oh," she said, pushing the blanket down her legs, "that's great."

I nodded but I didn't agree.

CHAPTER TWENTY-EIGHT

THE AUCTION that night was to happen as scheduled. The entire ranch went into a frenzy in attempt to get as much done as possible so just a few hands could stay behind and watch things.

Although I was exhausted, I headed back to the trailer to shower and found Bridge curled up on the banquette.

"What's up, dude?"

She sat up. "Jonah," she said and started crying.

"Shit," I said, sitting next to her.

"No," she laughed, still crying. "It's these damn hormones. He told me something today and I just ran off."

"Oh yeah?" I asked.

"Yeah, I'm just—I'm having trouble with it."

"Why?"

"Because I feel like I don't deserve him, Spencer."

"Oh, Bridge," I said shaking my head. "How in the world could you possibly think that?"

"He's such a good guy, Spence. And, I mean, the only

251

reason I even know him is because I put us here," she explained gesturing to her growing stomach.

"Bridge," I said, emphatic. "We're here because our father put us here." She leaned back and looked up at me. "We're here," I continued, "because you couldn't stand the idea of not having your baby, and you didn't care that it meant you would have to live an entirely different life to do that. I think that is the bravest shit I have ever heard of, Bridget. That courage makes you worthier to Jonah, to me, to these people, than anyone. Your baby does not define you, but your courage to keep it does."

Her bottom lip trembled and she nodded with backbone.

"I think you finally get it."

"I have to go," she said, tossing on her jacket and wrapping her scarf.

She ran out the door and I got up to see her head to the road from the window, but at the top of the lane I saw Jonah coming down the drive, wringing his hands and worrying his lip. When Bridge saw him, she started running to him, sprinting, her hair escaped its ponytail and the blonde mass spread out behind her.

Jonah stopped walking, looking stunned and opened his arms for her. She jumped into them and he hugged her tightly, making me want to cry a little, but if you repeat that to anyone I will personally come kick your ass.

He began to kiss her and I'd decided I'd seen enough. I was still careful not to put too much stock in their fledgling relationship, but I couldn't help the very good feeling their mere existence put in my heart.

I dressed, showered and drove myself to the auction—just myself and no one else. Since realizing I was in love Cricket, I had never felt more alone in my life. I sort of felt myself spiraling, retreating into myself, but I had no idea how to crawl out of the hole.

I was in love with Cricket.

She was choosing to be with Ethan.

Ethan didn't really understand her, as cliche as that sounded.

So I, I was going to accept that, be as kind to both Ethan and Cricket as I could, get through the next few months for Bridge, set her up wherever she wanted to be, and get myself as far away from the Hunt Ranch as possible—not just for my own heart's sake, but also to protect them from my father because his eerie silence was starting to scare the bejezus out of me.

I'd also made the decision to come clean to the man I'd helped my father blackmail. That I'd do it when I could secure the safety of Bridge and all the Hunts.

The inside of the old schoolhouse was packed; hundreds of people gathered around, mingled and laughed while waiting for the rest of the comers and the auctioneer. My eyes went straight for the stage and I wished I'd never come.

"Hey," I heard from behind me.

My head hung low for a moment.

"Hey," I said, turning around and facing Cricket and an older man in a wheelchair.

His right leg was missing below his knee.

"This is Amos McAllen. He wanted to meet you just as soon as you got in. He insisted."

I smiled at him and extended my hand.

The old cowboy took it and shook it with a strength I hadn't expected of a seventy-year-old. "Mr. McAllen, it's an honor."

"Son," he said, patting our joined hands with his free one. "I needed you to know that what you and Jonah Hunt have done for my family will not go unpunished." He smiled. "My wife and I pray for you every day and your generosity is much appreciated. I'm humbled, young man."

This shamed me because I remembered complaining almost every moment of the day with Jonah. If I had put his face to the ranch, I would have been silent and worked twice as hard. "Sir," I said, "you give me entirely too much credit."

"Not possible," he said, unwilling to accept anything else.

I nodded and smiled and gave it to him. He was obviously the more generous one. He wheeled off and Cricket stood beside me.

"He's a very nice man."

I watched him struggle with the chair and it broke my heart. "Extraordinarily."

Around five o'clock, the auctioneer began the auction and things took off at an entertaining pace. I found a chair at a table near the back and sat.

"Can I roll in here?" I heard Amos McAllen ask me.

"Of course," I said, sliding out the chair next to me so he could wheel himself in.

"Faye tells me you liked her cooking."

I laughed. "Yes, I did. I miss her daily baskets, but I think my love handles are thanking me they're no longer around."

Amos chuckled.

"So how long have you been a rancher?" I asked him.

"I've lived on that property since I was born."

"No kidding. What a life you've had."

"You don't know the half of it," he said.

It turns out he was not seventy but seventy-nine and he'd fought in Korea when he was seventeen. He said he saw things no human should ever witness and to this day detests communism with every fiber of his being. He told me when he first got home, the slightest noise would send him back to Korea and that Faye was the only one who could bring him back to the present.

He told me that when he'd left for Korea, Faye was just a wispy fifteen-year-old with curly red hair and buck teeth, but when he came home, she was a steamy eighteen-year-old redhead with curves for days and the prettiest face he'd ever seen. He said he knew he had to have her five minutes after seeing her in town for the first time since he'd left. "I was smitten," he said simply.

He talked about marrying Faye. He put me in stitches when he said he thought he'd died and gone to heaven their very first time and how they didn't leave their bedroom for practically a year straight. He also told me it was how they got their first son. I was almost rolling on the floor by that point.

He talked about how he lost that first son in Vietnam, but that's all he mentioned of that. It was obviously too painful to talk about, so I didn't press. He spoke of hard times and good times, of feasts and famines, of disease and health. And before I knew it, two hours had passed and I had heard his life story.

I'd discovered that Amos McAllen was the kind of man whose name would never make the history books or national headlines, but there was something so extraordinary about him. It pained me that America would not know him personally. I imagined there were many people as incredible as Amos, but I would never get to know them. They would pass and their memories of people before them would die with them.

That seemingly short conversation with Amos told me that life is more than what the media wants you to think it is. He taught me that your world shouldn't be any bigger than the people around you, that you should serve those around you with fierceness, but we still had an obligation to care for those who needed our caring, even if they were half a world away.

It seems such a contradiction, but the way he

explained it made perfect sense to me. Basically, care nothing for celebrity, love only your God, your friends and your family, and be generous with your neighbors, even if they're very far away.

When Amos McAllen rolled away from that table, I felt my entire world shift and tilt and I knew I would struggle to find its balance for a very long time.

When Amos left, I went out to my truck, grabbed an envelope I kept in the glove box for emergencies and came back into the schoolhouse. Inside, I made sure everyone was good and distracted before I stuck one thousand seven hundred and thirty-seven dollars in the donation jar, wishing I had a whole hell of a lot more with me.

I began to walk away when that voice startled me again, making my heart pound in so many different ways.

"Spencer Blackwell," Cricket teased, "aren't you one big, giant softie."

I pursed my lips. "You weren't supposed to see that."

"I know." She winked. "That's what makes it all the more fun."

I shook my head and smiled.

"The auction's almost over, and they're about to serve dinner. Would you like to sit with me?"

I turned around and searched the crowd behind me before facing her once more. "Are you talking to me?" I joshed.

She smirked. "Yes, you."

"Where's Ethan?"

Her brow creased. "I'm not sure," she said, searching the crowd.

"I don't think he'd be pleased if he saw us sitting together."

"Well, that's his problem, not ours," she cheekily replied. "I'm tired of tiptoeing around him," she said, surprising me. "I can be friends with whomever I wish to be friends with."

At one time, this would have pleased me to no end, but that day of all days, I could not, would not, be her alternate.

"Cricket," I said, narrowing my brow. "I won't be your backup."

"What?"

"I refuse to be a backup," I told her. "I don't deserve it, and we both know we could never be just friends."

She looked wounded but I couldn't feel sorry for her. She made her choice, and I wasn't it.

"I-what are you saying, Spencer?"

"I'm saying that I don't just want to be friendly with you, Cricket. I want all of you. I want to be able to taste your lips whenever I feel like it, feel your skin, wrap my arms around your waist. I want to be with you utterly, and I won't take anything else but your entirety."

I turned and walked out the schoolhouse doors, got in my truck and headed back to Bitteroot.

"There," I told the steering wheel. "I made the declaration. It's up to her now."

CHAPTER TWENTY-NINE

Two months had passed.

It was mid-April, Bridge was huge, but she and Jonah were going strong. It helped to see her so happy when I was suffering so completely. Those words at the schoolhouse were the last I had said to Cricket, and she had yet to respond. I lost hope in getting one after the first week and was living day in and day out in a zombie-like state. The only relief I could get from how badly my heart ached was when Eugie would come stay with me.

He was my new best friend since Jonah and Bridge got together, and he was my little old stone. I noticed Cricket would let him stay with me often and that surprised me. I don't know why she did it but I didn't question it. I needed him. Dogs are funny little animals. They're such a curious thing. They give and give and give and expect nothing in return.

Calving season had come to an end, and the ranch had planted the hayfields in preparation for next winter. Branding season came and went, and we were exceptionally busy for almost two weeks. Apparently, the ranches helped one another out there. Each set of hands would pitch into each ranch's branding day, and we got all the ranches done in eleven days. I got to know a lot of the locals a little better and came to respect each one tremendously with how generous they all were with their time and opinion.

The people of Montana were some of the hardest working, genuine and charitable people I'd ever met.

Apparently, at the end of every calving season, all the young adults of the nearby ranches got together and camped in the mountains for two days. If you'd have asked me six months prior what I thought of the concept of camping, I'd have told you it was ludicrous. Now? Not so much. In fact, I was really looking forward to the fresh air, the burn in my legs from the hikes and just relaxing.

We left early on a Friday morning.

"Am I riding with you?" Jonah asked as I tossed my pack into the back of my truck.

"Hell yeah, dude. Load it up!"

I picked up his tent and launched it in with my own pack. I got in the driver's seat and Jonah opened his door.

"Hey, give me a second, I'm gonna say goodbye to Bridget."

I nodded.

He bounded up the trailer stairs and ducked inside. A minute later, he emerged and got in.

"I wish she was coming," he said.

"Yeah, pretty sure a heavy-with-child Bridge would annihilate us within the first hour."

Jonah laughed but he didn't disagree.

"You guys seem pretty happy," I observed.

Jonah grinned like a little kid. "Yeah, she's a fascinating girl."

GREED

"That's refreshing," I told him.

He looked at me. "Why?"

I shook my head at the memories. "All my friends back home couldn't describe Bridge as anything other than hot. I beat more than my fair share of asses."

"I'd be lying if I didn't say I wasn't a little bit pleased to hear that."

I nodded.

"So, uh, how have you been doing lately?" he asked with pity in his voice.

"Come on, Jonah, don't do that."

"What!? We're just worried about you is all." When Jonah used the word "we," it drove me nuts. Not because it was him and Bridge. Well, maybe it was a little bit because of that, but mostly it was because "we's" meant two people, and I very much felt like one person. "You're not acting yourself and it's starting to freak us out."

I exhaled through my nose. "At the McAllen auction I told her I didn't want to be her backup. I told her I wanted all of her or nothing."

Jonah swallowed. "And she didn't..."

"Are we together?" I shouted.

"Right, well, I'm sorry."

I tapped the steering wheel in frustration. "Yeah, me too."

The truth is, Bridge and I could have left Hunt Ranch if we'd wanted to, but she liked being there, and then there was the whole Jonah thing. Plus, the Hunts, well, all the Hunts except for Cricket, thought we didn't have money, and even then, Cricket didn't know exactly how much we really did have. I could have left almost immediately after my dad found out we were there, but I couldn't bring myself to leave a life where I could see Cricket every day. Even if it did mean it was torture.

The campsite was at Hungry Horse Reservoir and

was teeming with people; some had already pitched their tents and had fires going. I pulled in next to a few trucks and we unloaded the bed, deciding to set up our tents nearest to the water. When we were done, we gazed out into the reservoir.

"Jonah!" someone yelled from behind us making us twist around.

"Hi, Finley," he said, cheerfully.

Finley was a pretty girl, tall, around five foot eight. She had a sort of bronze complexion, even her hair was a rusty color. She gave Jonah a side hug.

"Fin, this is Spencer. Spencer, Finley."

"Nice to meet you," I said, offering my hand.

"A pleasure," she said, with a sweet smile, taking my hand.

That's when I noticed someone was playing some old school Our Lady Peace. I loved Our Lady Peace. My gaze traveled around the campsite to find the source. Cricket was rocking out to "Automatic Flowers," one foot perched on the bench of a picnic table and she was nerdily playing air guitar while singing at the top of her lungs. Four other girls about her age were singing along with her. *Oh my God, why do you have to be so freaking amazing?*

She was wearing worn cutoffs mid-thigh and shin-length combats with the tops unlaced and a baggy t-shirt. Her hair was bone straight and the edges looked razor fringed. She was so unbelievably sexy and obviously not trying at all.

"...around here?" I heard to my left.

My head whipped Finley's direction. "I'm sorry?"

"I was asking why I hadn't seen you around here before."

"Oh," I said, trying not to focus on Cricket. "I've been busy on the Hunt Ranch."

"Are you one of their hands?" she asked.

"You could say that," I said, feeling sort of proud to wear the badge.

"Cool."

"Um, are you from this area?"

"Yup, born and raised," she answered.

"Finley and I were classmates," Jonah added. "She was in Cricket and Ethan's class."

The mention of their names together made me want to jump in the reservoir and sink to the bottom. "Nifty."

Finley laughed. "Yeah, nifty."

I eyed her sarcastically.

"Ethan and I got along great," she said, "but Cricket hated my guts."

"Not this again," Jonah laughed, sitting down on a nearby rock.

"What?" I asked.

"Finley had, uh, well…"

"I had a crush on Ethan in high school," she admitted.

"Oh," I caught on.

"Anyway, so Cricket considered me her arch nemesis."

"She really didn't, Fin," Jonah corrected her.

"I know when a girl doesn't like me," she said, tucking her hands in the front pockets of her jeans.

Jonah shook his head.

"I know Cricket pretty well," I said, "and I seriously doubt she's ever hated anyone ever."

She nodded. "You're right. 'Hate' is a strong word. Let's just say, she wasn't a fan," she laughed.

We all looked over at Cricket and the group of girls. "Who are they?" I asked.

"Those are a couple girls from our class," Finley answered.

"Those five girls were the biggest troublemakers in our high school," Jonah said, shifting a foot onto the rock and resting his arm on his knee.

"Like how?" I asked, curious.

"Besides the random times they broke the law, they broke so many hearts in the halls of our school, I was surprised the walls didn't melt."

"That's hilarious," I said.

"Fin used to hang with them a lot too."

"Sometimes," she said.

"Come now, Fin, you've broken more than your fair share of hearts."

"Not really," she said, staring at Ethan.

Huh.

Finley brightened all of a sudden. "You guys going swimming later?" she asked.

"Swimming?" I asked, aghast. "In this weather?"

Jonah laughed. "There are a few hot springs nearby. We like to chill in there and throw back a few."

"Wow, hadn't expected that little bonus. The only shorts I brought are cargo shorts."

"You'll be fine," Finley said. "Trust me."

After dinner, everyone got their suits on and I put on my cargo shorts and we headed up to the springs with a cooler and a radio. I couldn't believe how rad it was that they had hot springs in Montana. I joined everyone a little late, and most were already in the springs, which made it all the more embarrassing because when I came strolling up with my towel, all the girls came to the edge of the pool to say hello.

"Spencer! Over here!" Finley said, leaning over the edge a little and waving me over.

My eyes searched the pools for Cricket, but I couldn't find her in the crowd of thirty or so. I walked over to where Finley was and set my stuff down on the rocky edge of the spring pool.

"These are some friends of mine," she said, gesturing to the gaggle of girls lining the pool with her. "They've expressed a desire to meet you," she said, winking and smiling.

I shook my head a little. "Nice to meet you all," I said, waving.

"This is Sarah," Finley began at the far left.

I bent down and shook Sarah's hand.

"Ava, Grace, Faith, Clementine, and Eliza."

I shook each hand in turn.

"Very nice to meet you all."

They all floated in silence as if waiting on something when it dawned on me that they were waiting for me to get in. I pulled off my shirt and tossed it with my towel. When I turned around their mouths were agape.

"What?" I asked.

"N-nothing," Finley said, her eyes wide.

I got in with them and they situated me in the center of their line, then fanned around me. They asked me question after question about life in L.A., if I was going to stay in Montana, etc.

"I can't stay," I told them.

"Why not?" Finley said.

"I just-I can't stay."

"Oh," Finley said, "you hate us," she teased.

"No!" I insisted. "I think Montana is one of the best places on Earth and I've been all around the world. The people here are so amazing. It's just that I, uh, need to finish school," I lied.

"Maybe you could come back afterward," Ava offered.

"Probably not," I said.

"You got a girl back home or something?" Faith asked.

"No, not at all. I could never date any other type of girl than a Montana girl," I charmed. "They will leave a lasting impression on me," I laid on thickly.

They all aww'ed which made me laugh.

"So it's settled then," Eliza ribbed. "Spencer will have

to come back to Montana."

"Yes," they all chimed in, clapping their hands and being very girly.

God, I've missed girls, I thought. Maybe that's all you need is a little feminine attention to help you get over Cricket.

Just then Cricket walked toward our pool and I almost sank completely into the hot spring muttering "hummina-hummina-hummina."

"Here comes Cricket," Faith said, waving her over.

Cricket smiled and made her way straight for our pool. She wore a vintage forties cherry red one-piece that tied in a bow at the breasts. Her hair was up in a scarf and tied jauntily just below the crown. I wanted to die. How in the hell can this girl rock a one-piece better than any string I've ever seen in L.A.? When she saw me, her face fell and there was a slight hitch in her step but no one but myself noticed. Her smile picked back up and she stood at the outline of the pool.

"Hello, ladies!"

They all blasted her with cheery hellos while I could only stare at her.

"Come in!" Faith said to her.

"Oh, no, that's okay," she said, looking at me. "It looks like you guys got a good thing going here. I'm just running back to the site for a few more drinks."

She turned and waved goodbye before they even had a chance to reply.

"See what I mean?" Finley asked, startling me.

"Huh?"

"She hates me," she explained.

"Oh, I'm most definitely sure that wasn't because of you, Finley."

"Yes, it was."

"No," I held, "it was because of me."

Finley furrowed her brows. "Why?"

Everyone broke off into private conversations by then so I proceeded to tell her everything I felt for Cricket, how badly I had fallen for her and how she rejected me.

Finley laid a hand on my shoulder briefly. "I know what that feels like," she said, smiling at me in understanding.

I squeezed her hand in camaraderie. "Thanks."

Her hand fell back into the water and we sat there in silence. "Do you still like Ethan?"

"Uh, yeah, I guess I never really got over him. Is that pathetic?" she asked.

"No, I don't think so. Actually, I was sort of in love with a girl in high school. Her name was Sophie. She was incredible," I said, thinking back on her.

"What was she like?"

"She had the most awful personality you've ever known," I said, laughing.

Finley looked at me like I was crazy.

"But she was so hot," I explained. Finley creased her brows in disgust. "Hear me out," I said. "I used to be totally shallow about shit like that, and Sophie was the ultimate prize. She was beautiful, like, supermodel beautiful."

"Whatever happened to her?"

"She got caught with drugs and was sentenced to work in an orphanage in Uganda for six months."

"Sounds like she got what she deserved," Finley bit.

I thought about the Sophie that came back and how extraordinary she truly became. "She definitely got what she deserved," I concurred.

The night carried on. Put on fast forward, people got in and out, ate, drank and left. I found a kindred spirit in Finley and thought she was a genuinely nice girl. We were the last two left that night at close to two in the morning when she excused herself. I walked her back to the campsite but decided to turn back and spend a little while longer in the springs while I had the peace and quiet.

The water was beyond warm in the chilly air, and I sank deeply into it down to my neck. I'd felt so lost lately when just months before I had such a definite course set ahead of me. My deadline to invest in my friend's stock came and went and I had to watch it take off exponentially, making my friend rich beyond his wildest dreams. I wasn't as jealous or angry about it as I thought I would have been, but it did help that I had millions stashed away for a rainy day just in case another investment came my way.

I felt sick without Cricket's rocky friendship and thought very seriously about just buying a little house nearby to visit in my future years of life. Just knowing she was nearby would have to be enough for me and I needed to come to terms with that.

I looked up at the deep blue sky scattered with glittering stars and was in absolute awe of the wilderness that was America. I sat up a little, trying to make out the constellations when I felt a nose on my back.

"Eugie?" I asked and he licked the side of my face.

"Oh, I'm sorry," Cricket's sweet voice rang out like a balm to my soul, making my eyes roll back into my head. "I was just coming for a late-night swim."

"It's okay," I said, sitting up even more, my heart beating rapidly.

Those words were the only I'd heard her address directly to me in weeks. She turned like she was going to leave, and I bolted out of the water.

"Don't go," I said, grabbing her forearm gently.

Her eyes followed up my hand and arm to my face.

"Okay," she whispered.

GREED

She peeled off her short robe and sandals and slipped into the water with me. We were deathly quiet for more than ten minutes and I felt so tempted to leave. It was getting awkward, and I never liked to feel awkward with Cricket. I made a move to get out of the water just when she spoke.

"Do you like Finley?" she asked, startling me.

"Yeah, she's a fine girl."

Her head bobbed up and down as she stared at the stars.

"She's quite beautiful," she said.

"I suppose so, yes."

"Was she interesting to you?" she asked.

I wasn't sure where she was going with her line of questioning.

"Cricket?" I asked.

"Yeah?" she said, running her hands over the top of the water.

"Are you jealous I talked to Finley all night?"

Her head whipped my direction. "No!"

"Then why are you so curious?"

She cleared her throat and looked back up at the night sky. "I don't know." She sighed.

I ran my hands through my wet hair.

"Thank you for taking care of Eugie for me," she said, changing the subject.

"He's been helping me through some stuff."

"He's good at that." She smiled.

I smiled back. "I know."

She stood up and the water reached just below her breasts, which made me laugh because it met my waist.

"Come here," she said, walking to the opposite edge of the pool.

I followed her and we peered over the precipice.

"Wow," I said simply.

Cascading down the mountains, in a stairstep pattern, were dozens of little hot springs reflecting the night sky. They were breathtaking.

"I can't believe how beautiful this is," she whispered. "I never tire of it."

"Agreed," I said as I looked upon her profile.

Our arms touched briefly but instead of jerking away as I'd expected, she let our skin linger together and the warmth drove me insane. Without looking at her, I pressed my arm deeper into hers. The reflection in the water showed me she pressed her eyes closed and encouraged me. I raised my hand a little and rested it beside hers, the sides of our palms barely touching, before wrapping my pinky finger around hers.

Her breathing deepened, her chest rose and fell faster with each finger I moved over her hand.

"Spencer," she exhaled, and I could no longer think.

I yanked her away from the edge and pressed her back into the larger rock in the pool. She gasped, and it did things to my stomach. I slowly inched my way closer to her and with each inch, she panted harder.

"Don't move," I sighed into her neck.

She frantically nodded and bit her bottom lip.

My mouth gaped open. "Oh, Cricket," I told her, my voice dropping an octave. "I told you never to do that."

She released her lip and I found my hand reaching for it. I ran my thumb across its glossy fullness, feeling her warm breath against the pad. I followed the plump line to the crease of her mouth then back.

Her hands reached for my shoulders but I stopped them, earning me another soft gasp. I pinned both her wrists above her head with one hand. With the other, I continued to explore her exquisite mouth before tracing my thumb down the line of her throat. She swallowed, making me smile.

"Your neck is delectable," I told her, studying it reverently. "Stay still," I ordered. I bent into the curve of her neck and inhaled. "My God do you smell incredible," I quieted into her skin, which earned me a soft moan. I stood once more but kept her wrists pinned. "Not another sound, Cricket Hunt, or I'll kiss you so hard your head will spin." Her mouth parted in disbelief but she obeyed.

I do believe she wouldn't have complained if I had, but she was enjoying our game as much as I was.

My free hand found the base of her throat and my thumb pressed between her collarbones briefly before running the length of each. My hand glided up the side of her neck before finding her jaw. I tilted her head up slightly and slowly inched my way closer until my lips met underneath the line of her jaw. I pressed the softest kiss there but delayed a little, letting my breath fan across her sensitive flesh before pulling away again. She exhaled when I did and sagged a little against my chest.

"Stand up, Cricket," I uttered against her skin.

She sagged a little farther before supporting herself once more. This was torture for us both, but it was such a good hurt.

I studied her body, trying to decide where to explore next. The flat of my hand found the top of her chest and stayed there while I felt her heartbeat, causing goosebumps to spread across her skin.

I pulled her hands down and let them fall into the water to warm her but then flattened her hands against the rock. "Keep them there," I instructed.

Both my hands met her hips and I pinched the bones between my forefingers and thumbs before sliding them up her sides, feeling every curve, learning every contour. When I met the undersides of her breasts, I slid them to the side, then up her arms and shoulders before coming back down, lingering at the swell of her breasts and meeting her hips once more.

Her eyes had drifted shut.

I shifted toward her ear. "Answer me this."

Her eyes fluttered open. "Yes," she barely breathed.

"Do you like my touch?"

"V-very much," she answered, sounding almost drugged.

My palm found the back of her neck and I angled her closer to me. I snatched her away from the rock and she breathed in sharply, pleasing me to no end. I sat her in the shallow end of the water, on its natural shelf underneath the pool, and wedged myself between her legs. I let my head fall at the base of her neck and let my lips procrastinate there, resting my forehead into her shoulder and driving myself crazy in the process.

I softly kissed up the base of her throat to the line of her jaw and lingered at the crease of her mouth. As if she were drugged, she tried to move her mouth toward mine but her movements were too heavy and I stopped her.

I chuckled. "No, no, Cricket. We'll kiss when I say we kiss." She nodded sluggishly and closed her eyes once more. "And when that happens, I want your tongue with mine. I don't want to know where you begin or I end." She groaned softly but nodded.

My lips found her throat again and I flicked my tongue out quickly and tasted salt, making my tongue swell in anticipation of the kiss.

"Cricket?" we heard Ethan call out.

Cricket let out a panicked gasp and pushed me away. She separated herself from me by sliding down the shelf. All I could do was stare at her in disbelief.

"I cheated," she said, placing her hand over her mouth as if in disgust.

"With who?" I bit, frustrated beyond belief that she was abandoning me yet again.

"You!" she whisper yelled.

"We haven't even kissed!" I yelled low.

"I'm an awful person," she said desperately. "I cheated."

"You are an awful person," I replied with acid and she began to cry. "But not because you supposedly cheated. It's because you haven't really been with Ethan for months now, yet you keep stringing him along. Just like me. You're cruel, Cricket Hunt. And I'm officially done with you."

"Wait!" she begged. "Please, let me explain. I'm ready to tell you everything. You have to understand!"

"Not a chance. I'm done with you," I told her and meant it.

I launched myself from the pool and headed straight for the campsite.

"Where's Cricket?" Ethan asked me.

"Back there," I told him. *With my heart.*

CHAPTER THIRTY

THE NEXT morning, Jonah "knocked" on my tent. I sat up and unzipped it for him.

"What!" I howled.

"Dang!" Jonah laughed. "What crawled into your sleeping bag?"

"Your cousin did."

"What?"

I laughed. "No, I just meant that I officially have decided to get over Cricket Hunt."

Jonah sat on his haunches. "What happened?"

"Nothing," I said, yanking my hair at the sides.

"I can see that."

"Bite me."

"Yowza. Sounds like she did a number on you. Is that where you were gone to last night?"

"Yeah, I was off getting tortured by your cousin."

"Now, wait a minute, did she, uh, tell you anything?"

"No! And I swear, I'm recommending you all for the CIA."

Jonah laughed. "All right, well, I'm taking Ethan hunting with Eugie for breakfast. You want to come?"

"Hell no! I want as far away from him as well."

"Fine, grumpy."

He zipped my tent shut and I fell into my pillow, pissed beyond belief. I don't know how it happened, I was so amped up, but I fell back to sleep.

"Spencer!" someone yelled, waking up.

My heart pounded. I unzipped my tent and discovered a panicked Cricket.

"What?" I asked.

"I'm, uh, sorry to bother you, but everyone went back down to the springs and I don't have anyone else to turn to."

"I'm always a last resort for you," I acidly replied.

"I deserve that, and I'm sorry, but right now I can't talk about that. Right now, you and I need to go out and search for Jonah and Ethan."

"What?" I said, my adrenaline spiking. "Why?"

"Because they took their bows to hunt and their rifles to protect and I just heard their rifles discharge."

"Oh my God," I said, already sliding my boots on.

I zipped my jacket up and grabbed my own rifle.

"Come on," I told her. "Where did you hear the shots?"

"In that direction," she said, pointing southwest.

"All right," I said, walking.

"Jonah!" I yelled and waited for a response.

"Ethan!" she yelled.

We traded back and forth that way for a good five minutes before we heard two shots. We stopped dead in our tracks before sprinting their direction, yelling their names at the tops of our lungs.

Finally, Jonah yelled back, "Spencer?!"

"Where are you!"

"This way," he said, blowing his air horn.

We found them and Eugie, their rifles cocked and ready and staring farther southwest from us.

"What happened?" Cricket asked, out of breath.

Ethan looked at her. "Are you okay?" he asked, concern in his eyes.

"I'm fine," she said, forcing a smile.

"Wolves," he answered.

"Oh no. Eugie!" she said, calling him to her side. She held his belled collar in her hand. "Stay here, boy."

"They ran off that way," Jonah explained.

"Good," Cricket said, "let's get back to the campsite."

He nodded but looked unsure.

We were halfway back to the site when Eugie began growling.

"Eugie?" Cricket said, uneasy.

All three of us cocked our rifles and lifted them.

"Where are they?" I whispered.

"They're circling us," Jonah answered.

"Quiet," Ethan said, scanning the woods around us.

Cricket's grip on Eugie's collar tightened and we moved in around her, sheltering her. Eugie growled even louder then started barking. Ethan and Jonah tensed.

"Shh, Eugie," Cricket ordered.

"Oh my God, there's five of them," Ethan said looking around.

I had no idea how he saw, but I knew how dangerous things had become.

"Each of us only has one shot," Jonah quieted. "Keep them in your sights. I've got this one here, Ethan far left. Do you think you could get the alpha, Spencer?"

"Yes," I said confidently, aiming at the glowing eyes a head above the rest of the wolves.

275

"Why can't we try to scare them off?" Cricket said, worrying her lip.

"They're ready to attack," Ethan said.

The alpha started stealthily made his way toward me. Eugie began to growl again and the wolf bared its teeth, his snarl grumbling menacingly. Eugie barked and the wolf leaped toward us.

My breath held as I aimed my rifle. I fired, hitting him in the chest and falling him midair. Two more shots rang out succinctly. I went to load the rifle quickly to get the other two but they leaped toward us before I could so I swung the butt of my rifle and pegged one in the head, but it did nothing but slow him down and he set his sight on Cricket with renewed fury.

"No," I breathed and threw myself on top of her.

Eugie ripped himself from her grasp and attacked the wolf.

"Eugie!" Cricket cried.

Jonah batted the fifth wolf with the butt of his rifle as well and we watched as Eugie chased both of them off into the woods, his belled collar ringing as he ran.

"Eugie!" Cricket yelled after him.

"We'll get him," Ethan promised. "Come with me," he said.

Cricket and Ethan followed the bell and Jonah and I fell in beside them.

"They could be so far away already," she said, worrying her lip again.

"We'll get him," I assured her.

She nodded.

We followed the bell as far as we could but out of nowhere the bell stopped abruptly so we did as well.

"No," she said, her hands going to her head.

"He probably just went out of hearing distance," Jonah tried to soothe.

"Eugie!" she called out over and over, her voice frantic.

"We should split up," Jonah told her.

"Okay," she said, without thinking and following Jonah, leaving Ethan and I together.

Jonah and Cricket went off toward the direction we last heard the bell, but Ethan and I just stood there staring at one another.

"Just follow me," he said, walking into the left side of the woods.

Silently, we walked, keeping our eyes peeled for Eugie, when we heard the wolves once more. Both of us having reloaded, we crept upon them. Their noses were pressed into something and they were working together to ravage it.

"No," I whispered running toward them. "No!" I yelled, my heart already shattering into a million pieces.

I raised my gun and shot one while Ethan shot the other and we stumbled upon Eugie, laying on his side, the only movement, the rustling of his fur in the wind.

"No," I said, falling at his side. I pressed my face into his snout and waited to feel his breath but nothing met my cheek and I almost broke down. My palm went to his side and I felt for a heartbeat but it failed to beat. "Eugie," I murmured, an overwhelming sadness already inundating me. My head whipped up. "Oh God, Cricket."

I picked him up and cradled him in my arms, burying my face into the side of his neck. I had no idea how we were going to tell Cricket. My whole body shook with the weight of having to relay such awful news to someone I loved so dearly. I didn't want it to be true. I would have paid my entire fortune in that moment to bring him back just so she would never have to know that pain.

I carried him the three miles back to the campsite and pulled out my sleeping bag, laying him inside and wrapping him up. I paced the side of the firepit, biting my nails while Ethan sat at the picnic bench, his head buried in his hands.

After half an hour passed, we saw Cricket and Jonah approach.

"Did you find him?" Cricket asked across the campsite.

Ethan and I stood by Eugie. "Cricket," we said in unison.

Cricket stopped at the edge of the site and began to shake her head.

"Please tell me you found him and he's okay," she pleaded. "Please."

I opened my mouth but couldn't find the words.

She began to sob and Jonah tried to soothe her. At first she let him, but quickly slid from his grasp and turned toward us, her eyes weeping. She knew where she wanted to be. All I wanted to do was console her, but she wasn't mine to console.

She started to run toward Ethan, run toward his comfort, her arms wide, anxious to be held, desperation written all over her face. My heart broke once more for her. I loved her so much. I wished so desperately to remove her pain. I would take it upon myself if I could.

She gained momentum, running as fast as she could, as if she couldn't get to Ethan fast enough, and my heart broke all over again.

But instead of running into Ethan's open arms as we both expected, she did something that shocked us both.

She ran into mine.

My heart began to pound when she neared me and I swooped her up into my embrace, hugging her so fiercely she could barely breathe.

"I'm so sorry, my love," I told her. Her tears drenched the side of my face so I kissed them. "So, so sorry."

"Me too," she sobbed into my neck. "I know how much you loved him, Spencer."

I couldn't answer, too choked up, so I just nodded into her neck. I kissed her face once more as the tears were still flowing, and I refused to put her down. I didn't think I'd ever put her down again.

"Why me?" I secreted into her ear.

"You were the only one I saw," she whispered back, making my heart burst.

"Let her go," we heard Ethan command at our right.

We broke apart and looked at him.

"Let. Her. Go."

"Ethan," Cricket began, suddenly aware of herself.

I tucked her behind me.

This move seemed to incense him. "You think I'd hurt her!"

"I don't know what you'd do, to be honest."

"Spencer Blackwell, let her go."

"No," I demanded.

"She's mine. Let her go."

"Ethan," Cricket repeated softly, stepping at my side. My hand instinctively held her from going any farther.

"Don't you dare, Cricket Hunt," he gritted, his jaw clenching.

"Ethan," she said, softer.

"Don't you fucking dare!" he bellowed.

"Don't yell at her, Moonsong!"

Ethan laughed before piercing me with his stare. "Are you kidding me right now?" He turned to her and ignored me. "Cricket, you're confused."

"I'm not. Ethan, I…"

"Don't," he said, his head hanging low. "Spare me this bullshit. This has been going on for so long, and I just put up with this shit. I should have known it was over when you took me off the list."

List?

"Ethan," she warned.

He faced me, the most furious, most livid expression in his eyes, and when he spoke, his voice dropped menacingly. "Spencer Blackwell, I warned you. I told you. Now I'm gonna get you...when you least expect it."

He eerily turned from us and wordlessly walked to his truck. He got inside, started the engine, but before he drove off, he watched me.

His eyes promised a furious revenge.

CHAPTER THIRTY-ONE

THAT SAME morning, we brought Eugie home. Jonah drove while Cricket and I rode in the bed with him, our hands petting his fur all the way home. Cricket kept saying that she couldn't believe it over and over, but I wasn't sure if she was talking about Eugie's death, Ethan's abrupt departure or both.

When we pulled up to the house, Ellie came bounding out to greet us, but one look at our faces and she knew something had happened.

"What's going on?" she asked in dismay.

Cricket hopped out of the bed and ran up to her. Ellie held her and stroked her head, still not understanding. I slid Eugie's body over in the sleeping bag and hopped out of the truck, letting down the tailgate, then picking him up. He felt so light to the touch; I could hardly stand it. For being such an amazing friend to Cricket and even to me, he should have felt more substantial. His weight should have been directly parallel to how he served the

Hunt family, but that would have made it impossible for me to lift him.

I carried him up the stairs and Ellie furrowed her brows, trying to decide what it was I was carrying when it dawned on her. She searched the truck, bed and ground quickly for him, but she wouldn't find him. Her hand went to her mouth.

"My darling girl," she told Cricket and hugged her tighter. When I came closer, her hand went to my shoulder. "Take him to the living room," she instructed. I began to walk away, but before I could take more than one step, she hugged my neck. "I'm sorry for you too, boy. I know you loved him very much."

I nodded, afraid to speak for fear I'd break down, and took Eugie to the main living room. I laid him on the plank flooring by the large windows and just sat beside him.

No one prepares you for the death of a pet. It's not quite like losing a human loved one, obviously, but you cannot help but feel a tiny bit of despair. After all, they serve you so loyally. I think they genuinely love you, and they're so protective of you. They do their jobs so instinctually and so exceptionally because that's how God made them.

I remembered stories from my childhood, when my mom used to take Bridge and me to church. They were the stories of St. Francis. Through St. Francis, we were reminded just how these creatures of God served humans, and by serving His humans, they served and praised God. I always thought of animals as nothing more than soulless creatures before those stories, never once thinking that they too had a purpose. I had seen a statue of St. Francis in a courtyard once and the image was of him bending down and scratching a dog behind his ears and I thought, if a man so close to God gave respect to even the lowliest of God's creatures, they must be worth loving.

Cricket came into the living room and sat beside me, taking my hand in hers.

"He was such a good boy," she said simply.

"He was," I agreed.

We sat, staring out the window, watching spring melt the leftover snow right before our eyes, coming to terms with the drastic turns our life had taken in the past few hours.

She squeezed my hand. "We'll have to bury him," she said softly.

"Of course."

"There's a little dogwood tree right at the bottom of our main homestead," she began.

"I know it," I told her, which made her smile.

"He liked to sleep there with me when we were both little."

"That's sweet, Cricket."

She nodded with a gentle smile. "The ground will still be too cold to dig by hand."

"I can get the digger."

She looked at me and smiled again. "Thank you."

I stood, ready to do what I needed to. "Stay here. I'll come get you when it's ready."

She stood up as well and reached for my hair, running her hands through the length before placing her palm on my cheek. "Thank you," she said, kissing the crease of my mouth.

The digger was in the carriage house, so I walked there with a heavy heart. I started the machine and drove it down to the dogwood she used to sleep under with Eugie as a little girl. I tried to imagine her as a small girl, as if she could be any smaller, with a puppy-sized Eugie. I pictured her again, older, recently, sitting on the bottom of the stairwell with a book in her hand and Eugie laid about at her feet. That's how I decided I'd always remember them together, and the thought made me warm through.

I dug a hole wide enough and deep enough to accommodate him and set the remaining dirt beside the grave. When I was done, I jumped from the digger and placed two shovels in the mass before heading back up to the carriage house, hosing off the digger and locking it all up.

The whole process took approximately an hour and in that time, all the hands had arrived, along with Jonah, and Bridge had joined them all at the house. We all walked to the bottom of the property. I carried Eugie with Cricket at my side.

We laid him inside and Jonah and I shoveled in the dirt while Ellie and Cricket held hands.

Afterward, Emmett said a little prayer asking God to give the family peace, and we went home to eat lunch. Everyone told their personal stories about Eugie, some funny, some hilarious, some sad and some silly, but all were heartfelt.

After lunch, Ellie asked where Ethan was. That was my cue to leave Cricket and take a shower back at the trailer. On my way down the lane, I passed an affectionate Jonah and Bridge, which made me simultaneously want to gag and smile. Go figure.

I had a plan, and now that I had an opportunity with Cricket, there was nothing that could stop me.

CHAPTER THIRTY-TWO

"Is a Miss Cricket Hunt here?" I playfully asked Ellie at the front door.

I handed her a small bouquet of flowers, which delighted her.

"Where did you get these?" she exclaimed.

"In town. I had to get a few things for our first date, which included flowers for one Miss Ellie Hunt."

"Charming," Ellie said, kissing my cheek. "Thank you. They're lovely."

I'd called Cricket from Kalispell, surprising her and asking her to dinner.

"Where are you going?" Ellie asked.

"Dinner, then who knows? I'm hoping to keep things casual. I know she's going through a rough time, and I just want to distract her a little."

"Thoughtful," Ellie said, her smile reaching her eyes.

Just then, Cricket descended the staircase, stunning

me speechless. Ellie nudged me with her elbow and winked.

"Caroline Hunt is sporting a black lace sheath with boat neck, cap sleeves and scallop-edge hemline," Ellie teased, her hands gesturing gracefully at Cricket as she descended the staircase. Cricket played the drama well and would stop to pose every few steps. "Notice the ankle-strapped black heels, accented quite nicely with a cluster pearl choker, and to top the ensemble off, a black beaded clutch.

"Caroline has decided to wear her hair down tonight and curled with a swept bang with simple makeup to accent her daring red lipstick," Ellie finished. She looked at me and winked. "Tell me we country folk can't clean up real nice," she added with an exaggerated accent, making me laugh, before kissing Cricket on the cheek. "Have fun. Be a good girl."

Ellie left the room to us and I found an overwhelming need to call her back. I had no idea what in the world I was going to tell the magnificent creature in front of me. She descended the staircase with ease and approached me with an easy smile, totally unaware of how unbelievably gorgeous she looked. She dazzled me, dazed me, stupefied me.

She had yet to realize she'd struck me mute and nonchalantly handed me her black cashmere long coat. I took it from her, my hands trembling, and she turned. I helped her into it and swept her hair away from the collar.

She turned her head, her back still to me, and whispered, "Thank you."

My mouth went severely dry when she turned toward me once more, still unaware and began fastening her buttons.

"Where are we going?" she asked, her face shining.

I opened my mouth but the words wouldn't come. I tried to swallow, but I wasn't able.

"Are you okay?" she asked. I shook my head like a fool. "Let me get you some water," she said, looking concerned.

As she began to walk off, I grabbed her hand and drew her to me. I curled both her hands into my chest and as she searched my face, I searched hers. I wrapped my arms around her tiny back and inhaled the scent of her hair, my eyes sliding to the back of my head.

The perfume sparked a memory in me, reminding me of that night I sat at her back and the wind whipped the bouquet of her hair at me. I recalled wishing so badly to run my fingers through her hair, so I sat back a little, ran my hands up her back and neck before cupping her cheeks in both my palms. My thumbs gently caressed her cheekbones briefly before I broke the contact and threaded her curls through my fingers. She closed her eyes and breathed deeply each time I would slide a strand between my forefinger and thumb.

"So soft," I quieted. She opened her eyes and we stared directly into one another. "You make it difficult for me to talk," I admitted.

"Do I?" She smiled.

"Very much so," I smiled back.

"Shall I needle it out of you?" she asked.

"And how would you accomplish that, Miss Hunt?"

Her heels gave her a few inches and she reached my neck easily. She kissed me tenderly at the base of my throat, making me chuckle low in my chest.

"That's not making it," I paused as she kissed that spot softly again, "any easier."

She pulled back. "Say what you need to say, Spencer," she said thoughtfully.

"I bought you something," I told her.

Her eyes widened and I placed a small orange paper

287

box with gold filigree on the top.

"It's a James Avery," I explained.

"I can see that."

She opened the box and emptied the gray leather pouch inside and its contents into her hand. Out slid a small charm bracelet with a single charm of a dogwood flower. Her hand went to her mouth and her eyes began to gloss. I fixed it on her wrist.

"Don't cry," I told her. "It kills me when you cry."

She let a tear slip. "Sorry," she giggled and I leaned down to kiss it away.

"This," she choked, examining the details of the charm, "is…" A few more tears escaped. "Now I'm speechless."

I laughed. "Cricket, you're so beautiful," I told her, referring to her massive heart.

"Thank you."

"No, let me finish," I told her, breathing in deeply. "You're more than beautiful. You're this bright, clean, exquisite light. Just being near you is a balm to my dejected heart."

At that, her hand found my heart and she pressed there.

"And," I continued, topping her hand with mine, "I've never met anyone as astounding as you. You're so fair it almost hurts if I stare too long. But-but I can't help it. If you're near, I have to watch every single movement, memorize every step, every gesture. You captivate me and I—" I declared, but she cut me short.

She looked around us.

"Spencer, save those words. Remember those words," she said, grabbing my hand and pulling me out of the main doors, we stumbled upon the rocky gravel to the moonlit hayloft and climbed the bales until we reached the top.

"What about dinner?" I asked.

"I just want to be alone with you."

Her words assaulted my senses. I removed my jacket and gently settled her on top.

I laid beside her, my arms on either side of her head and stared into her face.

"After prep school, a bunch of my mates and I backpacked around the world."

"Where did you go?" she asked, unbuttoning my cuffs and rolling up the sleeves.

I leaned forward and my hair fell into my face. She ran her hands through the mass and pushed the strands back for me.

"Uh," I said, shaking my head, "all over, but there's one particular place that reminds me so much of you."

"Where?" she murmured.

"Lake Maracaibo, Venezuela."

"What's there?" she murmured into my ear, bringing the side of my face to hers.

I spoke slowly, under the influence of her touch. "A, uh, a natural phenomena called Catatumbo Lightning." She lightly bit my earlobe and my head fell forward a bit. "Cricket," I mumbled.

"Hmm? Oh, yes, the Catatumbo Lightning."

"It occurs at the mouth of the Catatumbo River," I spoke into her neck. "Ceaseless, extraordinary bursts of lightning descend from a body of storm clouds that form a voltage arc more than three miles high. It's magnificent, Cricket. It's a constant barrage of remarkable light and it burns over and over. I sat at the outermost peak of the Andes nearest Lake Maracaibo and was dazzled for hours. If the sun had never risen, I couldn't have left it. I would have been a prisoner to its overpowering beauty." I sat up a little and looked at her. "You are Catatumbo Lightning, Cricket. You've caught me."

GREED

My hand covered her throat and I let my thumb circle the side of her neck over and over. Our breaths got heavier, cumbersome. My lids felt weighted and I closed them briefly when her hands found my shoulders.

Oh my God, you're going to kiss Cricket Hunt.

My hand slid to the back of her neck, my thumb smoothed across her jawbone. I drew near her, my heart pounding through my shirt. I let the weight of my body sink into hers.

"Am I too heavy?" I asked.

Her drowsy eyes found my own. "I like the pressure," she sighed, giving me a greater buzz, "the potency of it."

"I can't believe I'm going to kiss you," I confided. "Can you feel my heart exploding?"

She nodded. "Can you feel mine?"

My hand moved to a pulse point on her neck and I counted the beats.

"Nervous?" I asked.

She nodded again. "Overwrought, thrilled."

I forced myself to relax and ran my hand down her throat. Lazily, I unbuttoned the top of her coat and ran my hand over the lace across her breastplate. I breathed deeply in and out of my nose. My hand followed back up her neck and gently closed around her throat once more. I lowered my face and hovered just above her lips. Ever so lightly, I ran my bottom lip across her hers eliciting a shiver. I did the same thing once more, but this time I skimmed the tip of my tongue as well, just so I could taste her, just so I could know what I was in for, and my God did she taste extraordinary.

I pulled away and she objected, wrapping her arms around my neck and pulling me so close, I could taste her without touching.

"Kiss me," she ordered, and I was helpless to comply.

I crushed my mouth with hers and she moaned into

my throat, spurring me on. I moved with her and we kissed like we were made for each other. Her saccharine tongue melted with mine, and I found my hands pressing her back, pushing her deeper into me.

We broke to catch our breath and to gauge the other, to see if it was truly as powerful as it appeared. *Click.* It seemed it was. Her labored breaths fanned across my face and she grappled to get nearer. I drove my tongue into hers once again, and I felt intact once more, as if a piece of me hadn't gone suddenly missing.

"Blackwell," she exhaled into my lips.

"Hunt," I answered against her mouth.

But she forgot what she needed to say and showed me instead, sitting up, never breaking our kiss and tossing her jacket to the side, her arms now completely unconstrained. She threaded her hands through my hair, frenzied in her need to get closer, and pressed the kiss even deeper.

The kiss broke and my lips found her throat. "You belong to me," I claimed possessively, biting her carefully, reaping me a cottony gasp.

Her lips found mine again and we kissed with renewed fervor, eager to learn the other's lips and mouth and tongue.

We kissed for hours, no one curious as to where we were, more than likely because my truck was still outside the main house. When the sun started to make an appearance, I knew it was time to go, though I was loath to leave.

"Cricket," I pleaded between kisses, "I have to take you back or your grandmother will kill me."

"No," she defied, making me laugh against her lips.

"Please," I groaned, "for Ellie."

"Fine," she said, sitting back, before attacking me again, knocking me back.

GREED

My hands found the small of her back and I kissed her once again. I pulled her away and sat up once more.

She huffed and her mussed hair flopped in front of her face.

"You look beautiful after I've ravished you," I teased.

"You look awful, just awful," she ribbed.

"It won't work," I told her, laughing.

"What won't?" she asked, a brow raised.

"Taunting me."

She smiled her clever smile at me.

"Come on," I said, grabbing our coats and helping her down the bales.

Once on the ground, she sat on a bale and put her shoes back on that had found themselves somehow removed throughout the night.

"You have hay all over you," I told her.

"So do you," she said, giggling.

"Stand up," I ordered, and picked straws of hay out of her lace dress and hair.

She shook out her hair and swept her bangs. She looked flawless, like she hadn't just rolled around in a hayloft, as cliche as that sounds. She did the same for me and we put our coats back on.

I picked her up and she whooped when I swept her legs beneath my arm.

"How chivalrous," she said, smiling.

She was so light, I sort of manhandled her, bouncing her around in my arms. When she rolled her eyes, I kissed her nose.

"What a lovely first date," she commented.

"We didn't do anything but make out," I laughed.

She winked. "Exactly."

"You're a cheeky little thing."

"Um, you also got me a present. A very beautiful present, actually."

"It was nothing," I told her.

"It was not! It was so thoughtful!"

"I'm glad you like it," I said.

"How could I—" she began, but the smile on her face fell. "Oh God," she said, her back stiffening.

I set her down.

"What's wrong?" I asked. "Cramp?"

"Uh, n-no," she said, her hand at her back. "I need—" She stopped short, falling against me.

"Cricket?" I asked, worried.

"Home," she whispered, the color draining from her face.

"Cricket!" I yelled, scooping her up in my arms as she collapsed toward the ground.

"Cricket," I demanded, panicking, but she didn't respond.

I checked for a pulse but it was weak. She was breathing though, shallowly. I ran with her in my arms up the deck and into the living room, shouting.

"Ellie! Emmett!"

I laid Cricket on the sofa and reached for the phone, dialing nine-one-one.

"Ellie!" I shouted once more before the operator answered.

"Nine-one-one, what's your emergency?"

"Uh, my girlfriend just collapsed and I'm not sure what's wrong with her. Please," I pleaded, "send an ambulance immediately."

Ellie came bounding into the room, tying a robe around her waist. "What's wrong?" she began but took in Cricket on the sofa.

"Emmett!" she shouted and ran over to her. "Oh Lord! Cricket," she said, crying, "can you hear me?"

I hung up the phone and kneeled at her side. "I don't know what happened," I explained. "One minute she was fine, and the next she was grabbing at her back."

Ellie was crying and smoothing Cricket's hair from her face. "She, uh, she has kidney failure, Spencer."

It felt like a bomb had just been dropped, shattering my perfect world.

"What?" I asked.

"The past year, she's needed dialysis several times a week. She needs a transplant."

My chest felt constricted and I felt like I couldn't breathe. I didn't have time to worry about anything other than getting Cricket help.

"What can I do?" I asked.

"Are they sending an ambulance?"

I shook my head. "No, a medevac."

"Keep an eye out and guide them in?" she asked.

"Of course."

I felt so helpless. I paced the deck back and forth, praying harder than I ever had before, begging God to save her, to keep her here. An agonizing, seven minutes later, the helicopter made its appearance in the sky. I jumped on the balls of my feet in anticipation. It felt like they took forever to set down in the bit of driveway in front of the main house. Two EMTs emerged, and I led them into the house while the pilot sat ready to leave as soon as possible. They rushed past me and into the house. I followed them, panicked, on the verge of falling to my knees and yanking out my hair. I had no idea what was going on. Just an hour before she was normal, happy, in my arms. I was kissing her. Falling more and more in love with her.

In a whirlwind, they had her on a gurney, and had flown off with the love of my life. I was left standing alone on the deck wondering what in the hell I was supposed to do.

"Come on, son," Ellie said, wrapping her arm around

me. "The hospital," she explained.

I bounded down the deck stairs and opened Ellie's door for her. Emmett promised to follow within minutes after he informed Jonah, Bridge and the rest of the hands.

The thirty minutes it took to drive to Kalispell were the longest of my life. We drove in absolute silence, both praying, both hoping when we got to the hospital that she'd be fine. That it'd be a false alarm. That she would be walking, talking, being her normal, happy, funny self.

My hands gripped the steering wheel, the whites of my knuckles shining through. I periodically would run a hand down the length of my face in disbelief. I was so pissed at myself for not seeing the signs. Her multi-weekly trips to Kalispell with Ethan. Her refusing the alcohol. She told me on more than one occasion that the ranch, the people of her town, did not define her correctly. At Bridge's doctor's office, that receptionist asking how she was doing. Ethan and her "fight." Ellie crying at the bottom of the stairs. Cricket's profound thoughts of death. Her mother. Ethan and the list.

"Oh my God, Ellie," I said, my body starting to shake.

"Yes," she spoke quietly.

"Was Ethan Cricket's kidney donor?"

She looked at me. "Yes."

"Oh my God," I said, feeling the need to wretch. "Oh my God," I said again, my hands shaking so badly I could barely clutch the wheel.

That day, in the trailer, before their fight. *You're only in your relationship with Ethan because he's giving you something you think you can't live without, and you're too scared to give up.*

I pulled over, opened the door and vomited everything I had, which wasn't much since my stomach was empty. When I came back up, Ellie had found an old t-shirt on the ground and handed it to me.

GREED

I wiped my mouth. "Thank you," I could barely say. She nodded and I pulled back out on the road.

I was selfish. A selfish asshole who, no matter where he went, what his intentions were, wreaked havoc on everyone he got near. I was toxic, making good people around me pay for my past sins.

CHAPTER THIRTY-THREE

I PARKED quickly and Ellie, still in her bathrobe and slippers, and I headed directly for the E.R. We approached the check-in nurse.

"My granddaughter is here, love," Ellie spoke sweetly. "Name's Caroline Hunt?"

"Yes," she said, "she's with a doctor now."

"May we see her?" she asked.

"Just a moment," the nurse answered, standing up and heading through double doors.

I saw a row of seats near the desk and helped Ellie sit. She was so calm, so sweet, but she was leaning on me so heavily. I knew she was emotionally wrecked. My heart bled for her. I sat next to her and set her hands in my own.

We sat quietly, waiting for the nurse. It was taking forever. It always infuriated me when hospital staff took their time. I understood that this was the day-to-day of their jobs, but to us, to the family of the sick, it was a place where every minute, every second, felt like torment. I hated the casual "wait" attitude they possessed. It made me want to shake them. There was no sense of urgency when it came to their patients' families, and I thought that cruel. At a time where compassion should be priority, it fell so quickly to the wayside with the humdrum of their work.

The nurse finally strolled in with a "They're working on her now. I'll let you know something when I do."

"Is she conscious? Still breathing?" I demanded. "Can you give us anything?"

"I'm not sure," she explained and walked away.

Ellie and I prayed together and waited...and waited and waited and waited.

Two hours passed and we hadn't heard anything, making Ellie so nervous she was looking pale.

I stood and marched over to the nurse's desk. "Anything?" I asked as nicely as I could.

"Let me check," she said, incensing me.

I stood by the doors, my arms crossed, and waited, again.

She came back ten minutes later. "I'm sorry, but she was moved to the Critical Care Unit more than half an hour ago."

"What the hell?! Ellie," I said, turning toward her, "she's in CCU."

I ignored the nurse when she tried to give us directions.

"I'll just follow the signs," I told her.

I supported Ellie's arm in the elevator and guided her down the hall toward the Critical Care Unit sign.

"Can I help you?" a nurse asked as we approached.

"Yes, we're looking for a patient. Her name's Caroline Hunt."

"Oh yes, she's in room seven."

"Is she," I swallowed, "okay?"

"I believe so," she said, smiling.

Ellie fell a little bit against me in relief, breaking my heart. "Thank God," I said.

"Thank God, indeed," she smiled.

We approached the room slowly, hoping not to wake her if she was asleep, and slid the large glass door open. I slid the curtain back a little and took in Cricket.

She leaned forward a bit and smiled at the both of us, though she looked pale beyond belief and her hair was rustled.

"Hi," she said cheerfully.

"Oh God, Cricket," I nearly broke down, hugging her. I kissed the top of her head, side of her face and lips. "You scared us to death."

"It's okay," she told us. "I'm okay."

"You're not," I told her, gesturing to her bed.

She was hooked up to numerous machines, and it was overwhelming me.

I realized I had taken over Cricket when Ellie appeared at my side. "I'm so sorry, Ellie," I told her, making way for her.

"Granddaughter," she said softly, "which doctor have you spoken to?"

"Caldwell was here earlier but he left. He'll be back soon though and explain it all."

I'd forgotten that they probably knew the physicians there, that they'd been struggling with this for who knows how many years. I looked about the room and grabbed a chair for Ellie and she sat. I wheeled the doctor's chair over to the side of Cricket's bed and held her hand.

"I wish you'd told me," I said.

A tear escaped. "If I had told you, you would have seen the sick me and not the real me. I loved so much that you saw me for me. I loved that you didn't cut me slack or make excuses for me. I loved that you called me out."

"I'm so sorry," I told her, bringing her hand to my lips. "I am so sorry for the insensitive things I've done and said."

"Didn't you hear me?" she laughed. "I liked that you treated me normally, Spencer. I loved it."

A tall man with white hair approached the glass doors and knocked. "Can I come in?" he asked.

"Come in, Dr. Caldwell," Cricket instructed, waving him in. "Caldwell, this is Spencer Blackwell," she said, introducing me. "Spencer, this is my nephrologist, Dr. Caldwell."

I stood and shook his hand. "Nice to meet you."

"Nice to finally put a name to a face," he said.

I looked down at Cricket and she shrugged. "You came up a lot during dialysis."

I smiled at her.

I gave the doctor his stool but he refused it. "No, no, sit. I won't be long."

"Thank you."

He sighed, making my blood pressure spike. "Well, it's happening, and frankly, sooner than I thought it would."

Ellie and Cricket nodded but my blood ran cold. I didn't understand.

"We ran a screen," he continued, "and your levels were through the roof, Cricket."

She nodded as if she expected this.

"I want to do an ultrasound within the hour or so."

"Okay," she said.

He squeezed her foot and waved to everyone else. "I'll be back," he said. "Hang tight."

Ellie looked at Cricket and sighed. "I know," Cricket said, smiling. "Everything will be okay," she told Ellie, who began to cry. "Oh, Grandma, things are different now."

"They feel the same," she said, swiping beneath her eyes.

"Medicine has improved, Grandma. This is not a death sentence."

Ellie reached forward and grabbed her other hand. Cricket squeezed her hand, then turned to me.

"This is how my mother died," she said, shocking me to my core.

I swallowed, my mouth bone dry. "How old was your mother?" I rasped.

"My age when she was diagnosed," she answered.

I nodded, my eyes burning. "And this?"

"Yes, she died of advanced kidney disease." She squeezed my hand tightly. "Did you hear what I said?" she asked. "This is not a death sentence."

"What does this all mean then?"

"Well," she said, turning away from me, avoiding my eyes, "I'll need a transplant more than likely."

"And, uh, do you have one in mind?"

She looked at me but barely. "I'm on a list."

Ellie stood when her cell phone rang. "It's your Pop Pop. He'll be downstairs with everyone and he brought clothing for me. Will you be okay?" she asked Cricket.

"Yes, I've got Spencer."

Ellie smiled at me. "I'll be right back."

She left the room and slid the door shut.

A few minutes later, a nurse came in and took Cricket for an ultrasound, returning her in half an hour.

When they settled her back into place, I leaned up and pressed my face into Cricket's neck. I smelled her, felt her warmth, listened to her inhale and exhale and kissed her throat then sat back down. I needed all my senses to recognize her.

"Tell me the truth," I said, my voice shaking. "Was Ethan your living donor?"

Her body went still and she studied me for way too long.

"Cricket," I pleaded.

She audibly sighed. "He was. No one matched me except Pop Pop, and he was denied because of his age. Ethan was willing."

My eyes stung severely. "I caused that."

"You didn't," she said, palming my face. She bent forward and kissed my mouth. "I chose to release him, Spencer. It wasn't fair for me to ask that of him when I wasn't in love with him the way he was in love with me."

"Oh God," I lamented, kissing her hand. "I've ruined your life."

"Spencer," she spoke quietly, "you haven't ruined my life. You've awakened me."

I shook my head.

"Don't argue with me, Spencer. I know the truth when I see it."

"How long does it take to get a kidney, and when do you need it?" I asked.

"I'm not sure. It all depends on what Dr. Caldwell finds."

I nodded, ready to hear the truth, and if push came to shove, I'd crawl on my hands and knees to Ethan and beg him to consider donating.

She turned silent, reflective. "What's up, buttercup?"

"I was just thinking about Eugie," she said sadly.

"Cricket," I sighed, "he was a good boy, a very good boy."

"Yeah," she said, smiling. "He was old reliable."

"Definitely," I agreed.

She started telling me pleasing and hilarious stories of times she and Eugie got into mischief, how Ellie would punish her, which would indirectly punish Eugie, and how he would complain to her grandmother by whining at her door at night.

I laughed with my whole gut when she recalled a particular incident in which she had decided at eight that she wanted an ice cream. She said that Ellie told her they didn't have any and that they'd have to go into town later to get some because she was busy.

Well, apparently Cricket figured it was not at all unreasonable to take Pop Pop's truck out to drive into the town for her grandparents.

"You know, because they were busy and all."

Anyway, she said she got to the top of the hill at the end of the drive and she had to come to a stop because she saw Eugie running alongside her, jumping at her window and barking.

Thinking he wanted to join her, she opened her door, and he dragged her by her britches out into the road.

"That breed," she declared, "or rather, that particular mix," she amended, "is entirely too smart for its own good."

"I think that was half breeding, half Eugie," I said, laughing so hard, tears were streaming down my face.

"I believe you're right."

We immediately calmed when Dr. Caldwell entered the room. The expression on his face made me want to hurl, and no matter how obvious it was that he tried to school it, it wasn't happening. My hands began to tremble inside Cricket's, but I stilled them almost at once.

"Give it to me straight, doc," she said, squeezing my hand.

"Well," he said, scratching the back of his neck, "we can't explain the rapid decline of the kidneys, but we recognize acute renal failure. You need a kidney, Cricket."

She sighed. "Okay, how much time?"

"A few weeks?" he said, gutting me.

My heart began to hammer, to clobber my rib cage in overwhelming devastation.

"How," I said, clearing my throat to keep from sobbing, "long does it take to get a transplant?" I asked.

Dr. Caldwell got that look on his face again, shattering me. "It's a process," he began, but I stopped him, shaking my head and holding up a trembling hand. Cricket already knew the details, no need making her hear them all over again for my benefit, not when I could very clearly understand what he meant.

I breathed deeply in and out of my nose to keep from vomiting. Ellie came in the room, dressed and with Emmett. I left the room so Cricket could tell her grandparents the bad news. I waited outside the room and broke down a little when I heard both her grandparents begin to cry quietly.

Dr. Caldwell, left Cricket's room and I called after him. "Dr. Caldwell!"

He turned around. "Yes?"

"I-how quickly can you see if you qualify as a living donor? I'd like to give a kidney to Caroline."

His hand found my shoulder. "It takes around two weeks, son."

"I'd like to begin the process as soon as possible, please."

"Have you thought this through?"

"I don't have to," I told him.

"Listen, Spencer?"

"Yes, sir."

"We not only have to run several grueling tests on you, we also have to give you a psych eval, etc."

"Whatever. I'll do it. Also, I'll pay whatever needs to be paid to rush lab work. I'll pay whatever."

He narrowed his eyes. "That can be quite costly, and it does nothing but move the paperwork a little bit further. Once all is done, an executive panel makes the final decision."

"Like I said, whatever needs to be done. Whatever they need."

"All right," he said, nodding, making me feel like I was accomplishing something, doing anything other than nothing.

"Also," I added, "I don't want Cricket or her family to know about it. I'd like it to be anonymous."

"Won't they think it's suspicious that you are gone or missing during her surgery and recovery?"

"I just meant, Cricket doesn't find out until after the surgery and her family doesn't find out until the day of."

He furrowed his brows once more. "Okay."

"Thank you."

"No, thank you."

CHAPTER
THIRTY-FOUR

A WEEK and a half of secret lab work, tests and evaluations, and I was done with my part. I was done with all I could do and the waiting for the results was daunting. I was told that even if I was a match, the executive panel still made the final decision and sometimes they didn't approve, which infuriated me to no end.

Every day and every night I spent with Cricket. The nurses let me shower in her room and took care of me as if I was another patient, which I appreciated more than they could know. I bought them lunch one afternoon and you would have thought I'd given them a million dollars. They were so grateful, which shamed me knowing I could have done just that.

But I didn't know what Cricket was going to need later, and I wanted to save every penny just in case.

I'd discovered that when the most precious thing in your life could slip through your fingers, investments, money, those things suddenly meant absolutely jack. All I could focus on was keeping her alive and with me, damn the cost or the consequences.

I was asleep in my chair on the morning of the eleventh day when I was woken by shrill beeping and loud voices. I bounded up and took in my surroundings.

"She's flatlining," I heard a nurse's voice echo through the room as she flipped on the light.

I fell into the wall behind me as six more people entered the room, including Dr. Caldwell. I watched them all work, calling out orders and performing chest compressions.

My hands clasped on my chest and I begged God to help her, begged Him to give us just a little bit more time. I knew it was selfish, but I hadn't gotten to live with her at my side yet. A day of normal life with her felt too little, too brief. Tears cascaded down my face as their movements turned exaggerated, slow.

I hadn't gotten to show her His world yet. I hadn't gotten to give her the moon or the stars or a ring. I hadn't gotten to marry her, have a honeymoon or children with her. I hadn't gotten to experience life yet and I couldn't see a life without her. I didn't want to know a life without her.

I knew I was young, we were young, but it didn't matter to me. When you know, you know. I knew Caroline Hunt was supposed to grow old with me. I foresaw nothing but misery without her.

Life on Earth is fleeting. It's a gift, but when God wants you, He will take you. It's not meant to be a punishment... Cricket's words hung in the air above me like a tangible weight.

I nodded, ready for whatever God wanted. "I won't question you," I told Him. "I accept it, always."

And then a beep rang through the room, indicating

her heart was beating. She was alive, barely, but she was alive. I thanked God and sat against the wall, waiting as they stabilized her, intubated her and hooked her to a ventilator.

When most everyone was out of the room, except for her personal nurse and Dr. Caldwell, I finally spoke.

"What happened?"

"Her body is starting to shut down, Spencer."

I nodded.

"Can you still operate? If I'm a match, can you still operate on her in this condition?"

"It's riskier but yes, it's her best bet at life."

Again, I nodded. Words were escaping me.

"When do I find out if I'm a match?"

"The panel meets this afternoon. We should have an answer then."

"Good," I said, tired beyond belief.

The nurse and Dr. Caldwell left me with her, and I finally used that time to break down. I buried my face in her limp palm, kissed the top of her hand and memorized every pore. I spoke into her ear, not sure if she could hear me, but I did it anyway.

"I love you, Caroline Hunt."

I sat back down and breathed deeply, resting my head by her leg and keeping my hands on her skin. I just wanted to be near her. I just wanted to save her, and I couldn't do that by myself.

No amount of money could save her entirely. Nothing I really had worth giving could save her, except my kidney and a faith that God would save her if it was His will.

Ellie came into the room crying and I stood and hugged her fiercely. Emmett, Jonah and Bridge as well as a few of the other hands like Pete and Drew sat with us. We had too many in the room, but the staff there didn't have the heart to kick us out.

We all sat with her and watched a machine breathe for her. We watched her because she was too beautiful not to.

CHAPTER THIRTY-FIVE

"Mr. Blackwell," we heard outside Cricket's room at three in the afternoon.

My heart raced faster than it ever had and I wondered if I would go into cardiac arrest before I even a chance to save her.

I stood and left the room, sliding the large glass door shut behind me. Dr. Caldwell stood before me. I breathed deeply, trying to compose myself.

"And?"

"I stood outside the panel doors and just heard some news. It's decided that you are a suitable match as a living donor for Caroline Hunt, and you have been approved for transplant."

I couldn't answer him, couldn't respond. I collapsed on my knees, unable to support myself. I buried my face in my hands. Dr. Caldwell bent over me and patted my back.

"Son, this is very good news."

I stood and braced a hand on the wall next to me. "This is wonderful news," I said simply.

"We'll prep you both for tomorrow."

"Of course," I said, a confusing combination of happy, sad, worried, ecstatic and overwhelmed.

I sighed and ran my fingers through my disheveled hair before sliding the doors back open.

"I just talked to Dr. Caldwell and Cricket will get a kidney tomorrow," I told them.

"What?" Ellie asked, stunned.

"She will?" Bridge asked, sobbing, then hugged Jonah.

"Yes," I told the room, unable to stop my own tears.

Everyone jumped up and hugged, cried and the relief on their faces made the sacrifice all the more sweet.

Ellie looked at me and her face contorted in pain, but she also looked hopeful. She hugged me tightly around the neck. "It's your kidney, isn't it?" she asked, stunning me.

I pulled her away from me and answered her with a simple nod. She hugged me tighter and cried a little bit harder. "I love her, Ellie."

"I know," she said and kissed my cheek.

We all sat and reveled in our good news, talking and in such a hopeful mood.

"You know," I told Ellie softly, "I hadn't even gotten a chance to tell Cricket."

"That you love her?"

"Yes," I said, a little bit sad.

"Spencer, my darling, she already knows."

I shook my head, looking at her beautiful face.

"Spencer," Ellie repeated, "she knows, my boy."

"How?"

"Oh, I knew it before you did and so did she, though she was too stubborn to admit it," she laughed.

"You're not upset about Ethan?" I asked her.

"Spencer," she said, "I love Ethan like a son. He's a very good boy, but I never thought he was right for my granddaughter. Ethan is very consistent, he's got very set ideas about things, and Cricket is the very opposite of that. She's impetuous and very open and Ethan tried to stifle that. Now, I never disliked him, ever. He was patient and kind and he did love her very much, but he was not meant for Cricket."

I breathed a little easier. "I was so afraid you would hate me for taking her away from him."

"No one here does. We're not blind, boy. We see things as they really are."

"Thank you," I told her.

"Everyone can see the way she looks at you. The way you look at her. Everyone knows how much you love her. Everyone recognizes a good fit when they see it."

It was so comforting to hear her words.

A knock came at the glass door and Jonah told them to come in.

A man walked into the room, towering over us in our chairs, the smile on his face was so malevolent, so malicious, my hands shook violently. I stood quickly.

"Get out," I ordered. "Get the hell out of here right now. Get out."

The man chuckled. "Not happy to see me, I see," Dominic said, cocking his head sarcastically.

"What's going on?" Ellie asked, confused.

Bridge's hands went to her mouth. Jonah stood in front of her, beside me.

"Who's this?" Emmett asked politely.

I shook my head in disbelief. I charged at him, my chair screaming in protest as I pushed it behind me. I grabbed his throat while he smiled. "Get out of here. Right. Now."

Emmett stood and pulled me back. Not wishing to upset him further, I let him.

"But I have news," Dominic offered, holding up a manila envelope.

"Please, get him out of here," Bridge nearly shouted. "Get him out of here."

Jonah turned and held her but kept an eye on us both.

"We don't want anything you have. Keep your news to yourself. Get out!"

"But this news can't wait." He beamed, delighted in the horror he was causing the room.

"Can't you see what we're dealing with right now?" I asked him. I changed tactics. "Please, whatever it is you have, just give it to me on my own. These people have too much on their plates right now. Here," I said, walking toward the door, "let's step outside."

"I guess," he said, "but this news concerns them too. Well," he said, a sinister laugh escaping his lips, "it really only involves them."

"What-*what*? Why? My dad's business is with me, not with them."

"But you made it their business when you decided to live on their property."

My breaths became labored. "*What has he done?*"

Without another glance my direction, he turned to Emmett. "Emmett Hunt?" he asked.

"Yes?" a baffled Emmett answered.

He handed the envelope to him and Emmett took it before I could snatch it from Dominic's hands. "You've hereby been served with an eviction notice," he told them, a blackhearted smile on his evil face.

Emmett's and Ellie's faces dropped.

"No!" I screamed, moving to attack Dominic.

Jonah held me back.

"Go on," he said, laughing. "I'd love to press charges."

"I don't understand," Ellie said, stunning me. "We still had sixty days to come up with the money. We would have been fine after we took the cattle to market."

"You guys were in foreclosure?" I asked.

She nodded, ashamed. "We were. We mortgaged the ranch to pay for Cricket's medical fees. She needed it but we overextended ourselves. We were relying on the ranch's profits to put us in the black again." She turned to Dominic. "The bank said we had sixty days."

"My employer," he said, righting himself and fixing his tie, "otherwise known as Spencer's father, has purchased the bank to which you owe. He's decided, as a matter of discretion, that it would be best to cut our losses now and try to sell the ranch on our own. He feels it would be most prudent to recoup the loan." He smiled cordially, making me want to kick his teeth in. "It's all here in your eviction papers." He gestured toward Emmett. "Well," he said, taking a deep breath and turning toward me. His eyes burned with poison. "Maybe next time you won't try to screw over your father."

Dominic left the room and we all sat silently, numb.

"Oh my God," I said, feeling ill.

I sagged against the wall. Next to me was a trash can, and I bent to vomit into the bag, emptying the contents of my stomach and heaving in disgust with my father.

I sat back up, walked to the sink, rinsed out my mouth and slid against the wall, sitting on the hospital floor.

"I'm going to fix this," I told the deathly hushed room. "I'm going to fix this somehow," I kept repeating over and over.

Emmett read the start of the eviction notice. "We have ten days."

"I'll fix it, Emmett," I told him.

"I don't think you can, son," he told me kindly, making me want to wretch again.

"I will. I will fix this." I looked at the shocked faces around me, including Bridge's. "I am so sorry that we tainted your lives like this."

"Stop," Ellie pleaded. "You aren't responsible for your father's actions, Spencer."

"If I'd never shown up at your doorstep, you would have been fine," I said, dumbfounded. "I never should have contaminated your lives."

Bridge started crying. "I'm so sorry," she grieved, and Jonah hugged her tighter.

"Spencer?" I heard to my side. I turned. It was Dr. Caldwell. "We need to admit you."

"What?" Bridge asked, sitting up.

"I'm, uh, I'm giving Cricket a kidney."

I stood and squeezed Emmett's shoulder. "I will fix this," I told him. He clasped my hand so kindly that I almost lost it.

"I can't believe you're doing this for my granddaughter," he said. "Thank you. With everything I have, thank you."

I shook my head at him. "No, Emmett, thank you for allowing me to."

I hugged Ellie and she whispered a prayer into my ear. She too thanked me for my sacrifice. I couldn't believe them, these people I had ruined the lives of. They were so unbelievably generous that it humbled me.

"Jonah, Bridge, if you'll see me soon. I'd like to arrange for a few things? I'll need your help."

"Of course," Bridge answered.

I walked to Cricket's side and pressed my hands into her skin. I leaned over and kissed her mouth before whispering in her ear. "I love you. I'll see you tomorrow. I hope to save your life the way you have saved mine."

Dr. Caldwell led me to an admitting desk. An orderly made me sit in a wheelchair, which I thought ridiculous, but since I was officially a patient there, they didn't want to take the risk of my falling or something else inconceivable. They wheeled me into a room a floor below Cricket's.

As soon as I was in the room, I picked up the phone and dialed my father.

"Spencer," he greeted coldly, having no idea how he knew it was me.

"What can I do to get you to call this off? I'll pay for the ranch. Anything you want I will do."

He laughed. I could hear him in his office chair as it creaked. I imagined him getting comfortable. He loved this part of the game.

"Spencer, there is nothing you could do, beg, offer that would change this decision. I'm doing this solely for my own pleasure. To screw you over as you've screwed me."

"How?" I asked, calmly. "What I have I even done to you?"

"You defied me," he stated. "And now you must pay."

"And this is just to teach me a lesson?"

"No, not to teach you a lesson. Lessons are for people I plan on keeping around. This is, like I said, only for my own pleasure. I want you to suffer."

Suddenly my hate for him seeped out in a muddy, vicious river and was replaced with pity.

"Dad," I said with mercy, "I forgive you."

He didn't respond. I had mystified him.

"I will let you do these things to people you've never met before because I hope beyond all hope that you will discover the cruelty and hate that has taken up residence in your heart and soul and you will change yourself."

He inhaled loudly. "Listen, you little—" he began, but I hung up before he could finish.

I made one more phone call.

An hour or so later, Bridge and Jonah arrived. I was so amped up that Dr. Caldwell told me they may have to postpone surgery if I couldn't get my blood pressure in check. I knew as soon as I could get Bridge and Jonah to help I would be able to calm down.

"I have seven million, two hundred ninety-three thousand, eight hundred fifty-nine dollars and seventeen cents stashed away in a bank account in Zurich," I began, shocking them. "And a few hundred thousand more sitting in a deposit box in Kalispell in Cricket's name. My attorney in New York is aware of what I want and he's put all the funds in Zurich in your name, Bridget."

Her eyes blew wide. "Me?"

I laughed. "Yeah, you. Here's the phone number," I said, handing her a pad of paper. I had written all the information she needed. "I'll be in surgery and recovery and we have a limited amount of time before Dad closes the doors on the Hunts for good.

"Jonah, I'm so, so sorry that my family has harmed yours so egregiously, and I know my father has stolen a hundred years' worth of land that was your legacy." I sighed, afraid I'd break down. "But I am asking you and your family to forgive mine and accept this money, however much you need, to buy yourselves another ranch."

"We can't take this," Jonah answered.

"Jonah, this is not up for negotiation. You will take this money, or when I get out of here, I will buy one anyway and move all your stuff there. This way is better because you can choose what's best for your family."

"I'm-I don't know what to say," he said. "Thank you."

"No, no thank you's. This is the best way I know how to right a wrong."

"Bridge, all you have to do is call this number."

Bridge nodded, pocketed the pad of paper, kissed my cheek and she and Jonah set out to fix what our father had done.

I had done all I could do. Now it was time to let Dr. Caldwell do what all he could.

CHAPTER THIRTY-SIX

THEY ROLLED me down the hall and into the elevator and pushed the button for the third floor. My heart beat wildly with nerves and anticipation of seeing Cricket. The letter I'd written her was tucked into an envelope entitled "just in case" and I clutched it in my hand tightly.

They wheeled my gurney down the hall toward number seven, and I gripped the letter so tightly I almost crushed it. The doors opened and they backed me up a little to make room for her. I sat up a little to get a good look at her and I couldn't believe how valuable she looked. She was priceless.

They spun me closer to her side, and even though she was unconscious, I took her hand and kissed it. I didn't care that everyone was looking. "You're so amazing," I whispered into her neck. "And I love you."

I laid back down and they moved us both down the hall. As I passed Cricket's family, they all touched me. Only Ellie spoke though, after she kissed my cheek.

"We're so grateful."

"So am I," I told her, folding the letter in her hand.

Inside the operating room, the anesthesiologist introduced himself and described what he was going to do, but my pulse rang so loudly in my ears that I didn't hear him.

"Count down for me," he said.

"One hundred," I started. Cricket's face. "Ninety-nine." Cricket's smile. "Ninety-eight," I slurred. Cricket's kiss...

"Spencer?" someone, a man, asked me. "Can you hear me?"

I felt someone, a nurse perhaps, rearrange some tubing. I winced when I tried to open my eyes, so I closed them again.

"Spencer? Can you respond to us, please?"

I attempted to open my mouth, but I couldn't find the energy or the desire, so I decided I didn't care and welcomed the black again.

"Spencer?" my sister asked.

I sluggishly opened my eyes and saw her face. She looked so tired.

"How is she?" I rasped. She looked up at Jonah. "How is she?" I repeated.

"How are you feeling?" she ignored me.

I opened my eyes farther and cringed when I tried to sit up a little. "Answer me."

Tears fell down her face. "Spencer," she said cautiously.

"Why are you crying?" I asked her. "Why is she crying?" I asked Jonah, terror-stricken.

"Calm down," Jonah said, trying to make me lay back down. "You're recovering."

"Why in the hell is she crying?" I asked.

"Spencer," he spoke, readying me.

And my blood ran cold. "No, she's fine. She has to be. She's got to be," I said, sitting up, ignoring the blinding pain.

I started pulling tubes out of every part of me and swung my legs over the side of my bed. They both stood and tried to restrain me, but I pushed them with the leftover strength I had. I stood up and nearly passed out. I started to walk out of the room when three nurses came in, shouting about my sensors.

When they saw me they pushed a button and a few seconds later, a male orderly came in. It took all six of them to put me back on the bed. A random guy in an overcoat came in and administered something in my arm, making me drowsy, and I fought them until the black consumed me.

It turns out they kept me sedated until I'd recovered fully.

And they woke me the day of the funeral.

Bridge walked in the room with a black suit. "I don't believe you," I told her.

She turned around, her baby belly looking pretty in her black dress.

"I know," she said, her voice sounding like sand. Her face looked like she'd scrubbed it with the same.

"I'm not putting that on," I explained.

"You don't have to," she said, cleaning off the material with a lint brush.

My chest suddenly weighed a million pounds. "How can you clean that when...when..."

She turned around. "I feel useless otherwise." Her

tears fell quietly. "I can't do anything for you that would actually help you feel relief. I'm useless to you, my sweet Spence."

I turned toward the window. The sky was gray and it looked like it would rain.

I dressed but had to use a cane to walk. I was a walking zombie, in complete disbelief. People cried around me, but I didn't register it. I could only stand by her God-awful casket because I was still recovering and wasn't allowed to carry a handle.

Emmett held Ellie as they followed behind us. They insisted I travel with them in the family car and I wasn't in the mood to argue. I wanted to shout, "But I killed your granddaughter!" or "My kidney wasn't good enough for her."

And I should have known too. I should have kept my wretched life away from her beautiful one. I should have kept myself clear of her. I should have...but I didn't. And now I was burying her. I was going to bury her and never see her lovely face or her clever smile again. I felt ill to my stomach, and I could tell it was going to be permanent. No amount of time was going to heal me. My wounds would close, but my scars would remain forever—they were deep and they were painful and they were endless.

The cemetery felt like such a ridiculous place to put someone so bright and lovely. Cricket was too astounding, too astonishing, too mine to be laid there.

They set the casket on the rollers above the grave and the priest performed the ceremony. He blessed the casket using holy water and incense.

Many drew roses from the arrangements setting by the gravesite and threw them on the casket. The entire family and friends stood in line to say goodbye, but I couldn't go near her. I didn't want to believe it. She couldn't be in there.

GREED

The smell of the incense, the wind in the trees, the feel of the sun on the back of my neck, the low soothing words of the priest. They calmed me and I closed my eyes.

But when the priest stopped talking, the family stood, confusing me. Two men in gardener's jumpsuits approached the casket and I froze. They began turning their levers and I felt horrified.

"Stop!" I shouted, my whole body rejecting the idea. "Just stop!" I insisted and the family stilled. "She's not there. She can't be," I said, approaching the casket. I started panting. "Cricket," I demanded, trying to open the casket. "Please, you can't be there!" I shouted. The lid was nailed shut and I dug my nails so deep in the wood that they started bleeding. "She's not there!" I swore. "She's not here! She's not here! She's not here!" I said over and over.

"Spencer," Jonah said, throwing an arm around my chest.

"No," I sobbed. "She's not there. She's not there."

A few more hands came forward and held me back as the cemetery workers lowered her to the concrete slab beneath her casket with a resounding thud, making me howl with grief.

I longed for her. Longed so deeply. She was my happiness and she was gone in the ground. I would never get her back.

I sank on my knees to the grass and sat back. I wept into my hands until every pair of hands that had held me was no longer present. I looked up and the gravesite was empty. I looked around me, their cars disappeared.

The empty grave beckoned to me.

It began to rain so densely I could barely see around me. I crawled on my hands and knees through the mud and sat at the precipice. My hands went to my hair and

I pulled as hard as I could to distract me from the pain. I wanted to be in there with her.

"Take me with you," I begged her, staring down into the abyss.

"Do you feel alive yet?" I heard a shrill voice ask me.

My heart pounded and I stood, my body covered in mud. She laughed, making my teeth grind at its deafening sound. She approached my back and my body tensed. She never touched me, but I could feel her breath on my neck and I shuddered. She circled around the grave and faced me from the other side.

"What-what are you doing here?" I gasped, fear crawling up my legs.

"What are you going to do now?" she asked, walking to and leaning against a tall tree at the corner of the grave.

"I-I don't know."

She sighed and shook her head. "Spencer, you have nothing left now."

"I don't care," I said, staring into the black hole.

"Didn't I warn you that she'd take all your money?"

My head whipped her direction and my teeth gritted. "She didn't take it! I gave it to her!"

"And look what it got you in return," she said with a severely frightening smile, gesturing toward Cricket's grave. "You're alone. No money. No prospects."

I shook my head.

"What do you have to live for now?" she asked.

"I-I don't know."

"You have nothing to live for now, Spencer! Nothing. You shame me." She stood from her position and slinked over to my side of the grave. "And after I tried to help you," she whispered in my ear. "That's the only future worth having," she said, kneeling down and peering into the grave. "What a sweet release that would be from your pain," she thought out loud. She looked up at me. "Don't you think?"

I didn't answer, could only contemplate jumping in with Cricket.

"It'd be the best thing for you," she explained and stood. She turned her head to look at me. "Stop your misery," she breathed over me.

I nodded and made a move to step in, my foot hung over the edge.

But suddenly something tangible fit inside my hand and I couldn't quite make out what it was but it prickled warm. I studied my palm but it appeared empty. A fierce wind blew through the tree and the most intoxicating scent swarmed my senses.

Vanilla. Grapefruit.

"Cricket." I smiled and set my foot back down on solid ground.

"Huh?" Piper asked, her eyes narrowed. She looked down at my feet. "Cricket's gone," she desperately plied. "She's there, remember?"

"No," I told Piper.

"Go to her," she coaxed.

"No!" I yelled more emphatically.

"Spencer," she frantically bid, taking my hand.

"No," I said, shrinking out of her grasp.

I stepped back from the grave.

"Spencer," she panicked, "what are you doing?"

"I choose life," I told her, suddenly seeing her for who she really was.

The side of the grave began to crumble and she slipped, falling to the ground.

"Spencer!" she demanded, as the ground washed away further. "Come with me. This is the way to happiness, to relief."

Her red nails dug into the mud, grasping for purchase, but they kept slipping.

"No, it's not," I looked down on her. "All that awaits me there is death and not a happy one. No. No, Piper. I choose life."

"Spencer!" she begged feebly, her arms flailing about her, but there was nothing to hold her there.

"Goodbye, demons. I will carry you no further. You will never plague me again," I told her as she slipped into the black chasm, screaming her shrill cry for the very last time.

CHAPTER THIRTY-SEVEN

I GASPED awake, my chest felt sorer than I could imagine, but I was alive.

"Oh thank God," I heard Bridge say through tears.

"Mr. Blackwell," I heard to my left.

I turned my head their direction and heard gasps of their own.

"He's awake! He's awake!" Jonah said, but his voice grew distant as if he left the room.

A man peeled back my lids and shined a light in them. I cringed from the light. He started examining me and asking me questions.

"Mr. Blackwell, can you open your eyes?"

I tried to peel them open but the overhead light was too much. "The light," I tried to say but felt something down my throat. My hands went to my mouth and I tried to pull them out. I was starting to gag.

"No, Mr. Blackwell, don't pull that. We had to intubate you."

This confused me.

"Don't worry. We'll get the doctor to examine you quickly to take it out."

My head lolled back and forth, too heavy to pick it up.

Bridge approached my side. I could tell it was her because I recognized her perfume. "Spencer," she told me, holding my hand, "you've been out for a week now. You were in a coma." She sucked in a breath, trying to compose herself. A week? How's Cricket! I wanted to shout. "You didn't react well to the removal."

I tried to nod or open my eyes but I wasn't able to, so I squeezed her hand as best I could.

She wept into my shoulder. "Spencer, this has been the hardest week of my life."

I squeezed slightly once more.

"Spencer," I heard a new voice ask. It was Dr. Caldwell.

He examined me and confirmed it was okay to remove my tubes. On the count of three, he pulled them out and I fought for air, finding relief about ten seconds later. My eyes opened slowly and I took in my surroundings. Though it was too bright, I could see all the people who cared about me.

Most of Cricket's family and my sister were there, as well as my mom.

My eyes watered at the sight of her. "Mama?"

"Yes, baby," she said, kissing my face. "You really had us worried."

I smiled at her.

"Where's Cricket?" I asked the room.

"She's in physical therapy," Jonah said. I tried to get her out, but the lady at the desk wouldn't let me past the doors. "She is doing so well, Spencer. She's like a brand-new person."

"Thank you, God," I said, relieved beyond belief.

"And thank you," Ellie said, walking into the room. She

was bawling and hugged me tightly.

"Ellie," I said.

"Spencer," she said, smiling. "You scared the ever living stuffing out of us!"

I laughed. "I didn't mean to," I told her.

She stood up and I looked all about me. "I love you all."

"Yes, yes, they love you too," Dr. Caldwell said, smiling. "But you need rest, and I need all of them out."

They all filed out of the room except for Bridge and my mom.

"Mom!" I said when the door shut. "I can't believe you're here."

"When you didn't wake up from surgery, Bridget called me." Her head hung low. "She told me what your father did."

I squeezed her hands. "It's okay, Mom." I looked at Bridge. "It is okay, right? Everything got worked out?"

"Oh, it's fine," she said. "In fact, it's more than fine. Jonah found the most spectacular working ranch for sale a few miles south of Bitterroot."

"Does the family like it?"

"The family loves it," Bridget admitted warmly. "They've already moved the ranch and drove the cattle south."

Thinking back on Hunt Ranch made me so incredibly sad, but I was happy I was able to provide them the life my father stole.

"Your money helped," she said. "There's still a million left," she said.

"That's yours, Bridget."

"What?" she asked, her eyes wide.

"It's for you and the baby."

"And what are you going to do?"

"I'm leaving," I told them, shocking Bridge.

"What? Why?"

"As long as Dad is alive, is around, he will stop at nothing to ruin me. I can't risk the Hunts. I can't risk you or Mom."

"Spencer," Bridge said softly, "what about Cricket?"

"I'm doing this all for Cricket, Bridge. I did all this for her."

"She's not going to stand for this," she said.

"She'll have to. It's to keep her safe, Bridge. Do you promise not to tell her? At least until I've left."

"Yes," she complied, though she hated to.

We talked about my plan to leave and I agreed to take a few thousand dollars to keep myself afloat for a bit. I would return to Brown and continue going to school there. I would talk to the administration about the rowing scholarship I had and what it meant for me in the long run. I also promised Bridge I would return when the baby was born.

My mom was moving to Montana and planned on living with Bridget until she was done with her education, including college.

I had done everything I could for the family that did all they could for us, and I was more than satisfied.

Now, if I could only muster up the courage to leave Cricket behind.

Early in the morning, I discharged myself, much to Dr. Caldwell's dismay, but I promised him I would see a nephrologist as soon as I got to Providence and would report back to him. I thanked him and grabbed the bag Bridge hesitantly packed for me.

I kissed my sister and mother goodbye and caught a taxi to the airport.

I was going to keep Cricket Hunt safe if it killed me... or tried to...again.

CHAPTER THIRTY-EIGHT

IT HAD been nine days, seven hours and three, no, four minutes since I'd left Montana and I was in torment. I was getting shit sleep, not just because I was recovering from surgery, but mostly because I kept dreaming of the night I kissed Cricket.

I laid in bed, in my new apartment with bars on the window, with my new furniture I got at the Goodwill. I didn't buy anything upholstered there though. I drew the line there. Instead, I splurged and bought one sofa at Ikea as well as a mattress from one of those monster warehouse places that also sell gallons of nacho cheese.

But it wasn't the apartment I had a problem with. It was the fact that my home was two thousand five hundred fifty-six miles away, because my home was Cricket.

My alarm clock started beeping, indicating it was five-thirty in the morning and I did, indeed, have to start my first day of work at the campus coffee shop.

My summer semester wouldn't start for a few more weeks, but I had to do something to pay bills. I was basically miserable without Cricket, so why not tack on the added bonus of smelling like I'd been marinating in a coffee bean bag for twelve hours a day, right?

You can do it, I told myself. Just take it a day at a time. I sat up. Okay, maybe a minute at a time.

Since I'd gotten back, I'd seen a doctor several times and I was recovering well. He'd given me a clean bill of health to return to work. I called and talked to Bridge every day. She was getting bigger, staying healthy, things were going strong with Jonah, which I was glad to hear. When she tried to talk to me about Cricket, I would stop her before she could continue.

"No sense in torturing myself," I'd tell her.

I'd also written a very detailed apologetic letter to Peter Knight and his wife for my part in my dad's scandal. I explained everything to him and his wife but hadn't gotten a response, not that I expected one. I was just glad I told him the truth. I wasn't sure if it would help the man, but I hoped it gave him the evidence he needed to prove his innocence to his wife if my dad did the unthinkable.

I stood and took a shower in my three-by-three-foot bathroom, brushed my teeth before dressing in my uniform of jeans and a t-shirt. I grabbed my starched apron and keys and left, locking the door behind me.

I left my truck with my mom and Bridge, but got a place close enough to campus that I could walk without any issues. I passed a guy I remembered from my freshman year and waved. He looked surprised I'd done so but waved back. It made me think of the impression I gave off when I was here as the "other" Spencer.

The little coffee shop had an outside kiosk during the warmer months, so I was assigned to it since it didn't get quite as busy as the shop inside the campus. I was

331

greeted by a senior named Jason. He showed me the ropes, taught me how to make the more difficult drinks, where the supplies could be found and everything else. I could run the kiosk by myself just with an hour's worth of training.

After he showed me the entire kiosk and their procedures, he leaned against the counter.

"Is there nothing else to do?" I asked him.

"Nothing, man, just chill and wait for people is all."

Coming from the grueling day-to-day of the ranch made it feel like I was being lazy just setting back.

"Wait a minute," he said, snapping his fingers. "I know you."

"You do?"

"Hell yeah, you're that rich bastard who takes all the girls." He narrowed his gaze at me. "What the hell are you doing here?"

"I'm, uh, I'm not rich," I laughed.

"Bullshit. You're filthy rich, dude. I saw the cars you drove around here."

I held up my hands. "I need to clarify. I was just using my dad's money and he cut me off."

"Oh, shit! Got in deep with daddy, huh?" he ribbed. "What? He made you slum it with us lowlies to teach you a lesson?"

"Nah," I said, ignoring his attempt at getting a rise out of me. "It's a little more complicated."

"Yeah?"

"Yeah," I told him and relayed everything that had happened to me during the past six months, since we had the time.

When I was done, the guy's mouth gaped wide open.

"What?" I asked, uncomfortable.

"That's harsh, dude. What he did to you is messed up."

"Nah, I helped a lot of people and changed myself in the process."

"That's pretty righteous."

"Thanks."

When my first shift was over, I yanked off my apron, folded it and stuck it in my back pocket. I cut toward College Hill and stopped in at Louis Restaurant for some dinner. Although I had always loved the place, I found myself wanting the ridiculous food of the ranch. I looked up from my seat and called it what it was. Homesick. I was homesick something awful for Cricket.

I sat back and recalled all the times I made myself memorize her, utterly grateful that I had. Vanilla. Grapefruit. Clever smiles. Ballet walks. Swishing hips. Witty conversation. Humble attitude. Talented. All-around perfect. I sighed, leaving my food as it was and left enough for a generous tip.

I walked home, determined to trudge through it all, determined to give the Hunts a life free of any drama, and that was not going to happen if my dad had anything to say about it.

The night air felt thick. It was starting to get really warm and humid and I was ready for school to start, ready for the distraction. Summer bugs began chirping in the trees on my walk home. I studied the sidewalk, wishing it was field and snow.

I swung open the iron gate to my complex and let it slam shut behind me. I descended the walkway that led to my door and pulled my keys out of my front pocket. I swung them in my fingers, whistling "Yoshimi Battles the Pink Robots."

"That's my jam," someone beside me said.

I stopped walking, my keys dropping to the sidewalk below me. My heart started racing.

"You like The Flaming Lips?" I asked her, the same question I had that day she delivered the calf.

She sat on the retaining wall in front of my

apartment, one knee against her chest, and watched me. She made my blood furiously pump through my veins. I wanted to seize her.

"Why did you go?" she asked.

"I had to."

"No, you didn't."

"My dad won't stop trying to destroy me, Cricket, and he'll take down everyone in my path, including your family."

"You are my family, Spencer."

My eyes closed at her drugging words.

"Did you mean it?" she asked, holding up my crinkled letter. It looked so worn, like she'd read it over and over.

"Every. Word."

"Come here," she said.

I walked toward her.

She had a soft canvas bag beside her. She reached her hand inside and pulled her hand out. Perched on her palm was the sculpture of the three little birds. On a ribbon of metal, it read "Smile with the risin' sun."

"Take it."

I held it in my hand and studied its brilliancy. It was the most beautiful thing I had ever seen.

"You're the sun for me, Cricket."

"You're the sun for me, Spencer."

"I hate life without you, Cricket."

"I hate life without you, Spencer."

"I want you so bad. I can taste you already."

"I'm yours to taste, love."

"But my dad…"

"You're dad is not invincible, Spencer. We will cross those bridges when we come to them."

I studied her face. "You look good." I swallowed. "Healthy."

"Caldwell said I took my transplant without one

single complication. It was like it was made for me."

"It was."

She nodded.

"Cricket?"

"Yes?"

"I'm so in love with you."

A tear escaped her, cascading slowly down the side of her cheek. I ran the back of my index finger up the trail before I licked the tear.

"I'm so in love with you."

My hand went to my chest right over my heart and my eyes closed. It beat so wildly. Her words floored me.

"Don't ever leave me again," she said quietly.

"I couldn't if I tried," I said, setting the sculpture near her hand, purposely grazing her fingertips with mine. She gasped softly.

"I've been miserable without you," she said, another tear falling.

I leaned in and kissed that tear away and her breath hitched.

"I've been practically catatonic without you," I admitted.

That earned me her clever smile and I almost fell backward.

"Then what are you waiting for?" she asked.

"I have no idea," I breathed, rushing her in that moment.

She wrapped her arms around my neck and I picked her up off the wall. She locked her legs around my waist and I kissed her like our lives depended on it. That same drugging, intoxicating sensation rushed over both of us. The one that told us we were made for one another and that the chemistry between us couldn't be created with any other human.

Cricket Hunt, part owner of my kidneys, the girl who

called me on my crap and the girl I was gonna marry someday. She was the girl that could bowl me over with one smile. She was the girl who consumed my thoughts and my heart.

Cricket Hunt was my fate.

EPILOGUE

FOUR YEARS *later...*

"No, no. Her dress is getting dirty. Just pick her up."

I picked up the little girl with the halo of bright blonde curls and set her on my hip. I made a goofy face and she laughed.

"You're so funny, Uncle Spencer!" she giggled, her little hand going to her mouth.

"Your Aunt Cricket doesn't seem to think so," I whispered conspiratorially.

Cricket rolled her eyes but fought a smile.

"We better hurry or your mama is going to be so mad!"

Her bright green eyes widened and she nodded.

We entered the double doors and I set Savannah down. Cricket bent down and straightened her skirt for her.

"Is this the flower girl?" a random woman asked.

"Uh, yup," I answered.

GREED

She spoke into a handheld device and soon another woman came bustling forward with a ring of flowers for Savannah's hair. It was set low on the crown of her head.

"This itches."

"Leave it on and I'll let you have a giant piece of cake."

She settled down until she discovered the bell of her dress and then she twirled around.

"Bribery. I like it," Cricket commented.

I tapped my temple. "Future reference."

She winked.

Cricket had grown out her hair and it almost reached the small of her back. She curled it, and all I had wanted to do was run my fingers through it since she'd walked out of our bedroom.

My lids felt heavy and I rushed her side. I kissed her throat and moved up to her ear. "Wait until we get home," I growled.

She gave me her clever smile. "Why go home when we have a perfectly nice car back at the ranch?"

I stood, slack jawed. "Cricket Blackwell, you saucy minx."

She winked.

"We need all bridesmaids and groomsmen, please," the woman with the device shouted.

Cricket shoved pulled my arm to where she stood and I resisted, snatching up my wife by the waist and swinging her around. "Spencer," she laughed. "You are a troublemaker!"

The woman gave us the stink eye, so I placed Cricket back down. We both snorted into our hands.

"We need the maid of honor and the best man in the back here," she said and we stepped in the far back of the line.

I took the opportunity to pinch Cricket's butt. She gasped, inviting everyone to turn around and stare at us.

I shrugged my shoulders at them like I had no idea what was going on. They turned back around and she hit my arm. "You're gonna get us in big trouble," she giggled.

"I hope so."

"What a thing to say."

"Time to get serious, people," the woman announced, but she looked directly at us, inciting another laugh from us. "In a moment, the bride will come through here. The groom's up front already. Remember, just like rehearsal! This is go time."

The door to the cry room opened and out came my sister and she was breathtaking. A lace top and dupioni silk skirt. I know this because she and Cricket would tell me about it, like I gave a crap. I was glad they did though. Looking at her in that moment was one of the proudest of my life.

She strode forward and I stopped her before she met our mother's side.

She smiled wide. "Bridget, you look stunning."

"Thank you, brother," she said, kissing my face.

I hugged my mom. "You too, Mama."

She palmed our cheeks. "I'm so proud. So very proud of both of you."

Bridget leaned down and kissed her daughter. "You look very beautiful too, Savannah. Very grown up."

Savannah beamed and bounced on her heels.

I walked back to the end of the line and stood beside my wife. I tucked her dainty hand in my arm and laid my own on top of it.

The piano started and Savannah bounded forward, radiant and bursting with happiness. She gracefully laid lavender down on the stone floor of the church and made it all the way to the end of the aisle, but when she saw Jonah standing at the front, instead of standing to the side like she was told, she ran up to him and held his hand.

GREED

The wedding planner tried to get her to come down, but Jonah stayed her with a hand and kept Savannah with him.

The wedding party descended down the aisle couple by couple until it was our turn. I twisted around and winked at my mom and Bridge.

When it was our turn, I strode down the same aisle I had with Cricket just two years before for our own wedding.

"This bring back memories?" she whispered.

"I believe we did it in the car then too," I whispered back, making her bite her bottom lip and nod.

I shook my head at her. Cheeky.

We reached the end of the aisle and we were forced to separate, which I hated, but I knew I'd be able to look at her through the whole ceremony, so it was my only consolation. The piano stopped and a string quartet began to play "Jesu, Joy of Man's Desiring" as my mom and Bridge started to walk the aisle.

As I watched them, I looked upon my wife, down at my incredible Savannah, then Jonah, Ellie, and Emmett, and I couldn't help but wonder how I deserved such a preposterously happy and beautiful life. They were my family. They were my everything. I looked over at Cricket and the tears slipping down her face told me she felt the same way.

My mom and Bridge had reached the end of the aisle and I watched my mama give my sister to Jonah. I'd never seen either of them look happier than that moment. The moment where they, all three of them, became an official family. Savannah already called him daddy. She had from her three hundred and sixty-third day and he was. He truly was her father.

During the four years since Savannah's birth, Bridge had finished high school, gone to college, earned a bachelor's in agriculture, raised Savannah with my mom and Jonah and had carved herself a niche of perfect life, not because life was perfect, but because it was perfect for them.

Cricket and I had moved to New York briefly after graduating college to pursue Cricket's sculpting career, which she was hugely successful at, but we missed our family too much and decided to trek back to Montana.

Now, she ran a successful gallery of her own work in town and she shipped all over the world. She was well known in art circles and much sought after.

I was in my second year in law school, studying immigration law, working closely with my friend Sophie Price in Uganda. We were hoping to make a streamlined process to help the orphans there and get them homes here on the American side.

My mom won the Hunt Ranch in the settlement when my dad filed divorce years ago and she gave it back to the Hunts. They returned to their homestead and it was as if they never left. Jonah and the girls stayed back on the new ranch and ran that as a second homestead, a continuation of the Hunt Ranch, if you will.

Some of those profits helped Cricket and me complete school, and it supported us while I finished law school as well. It also helped fund many projects in the Congo, where a friend of Sophie and Ian Aberdeen's opened a second Masego.

All in all, God had been very good to us. Generosity is one of those traits rarely used, but it is, by far and away, one of the most rewarding gifts one could ever possess. I lived by many things, but my top motto was "give." Give, and you shall see the incredible rebound of it. The more you give, the more you get. It's a staggering notion, but the truth nonetheless.

GREED

Now, if you'll excuse me, I have a date with my wife in our car.

Click.

Boom.

ETHAN MOONSONG IS

FURY

AND HE'S COMING FOR YOU 2014

PREGNANT?

NEED HELP? PLEASE CALL

1.800.712.HELP

YOU ARE NOT ALONE

GREED'S

PLAYLIST

CONNECT WITH FISHER AMELIE

SIGNUP

FOR FISHER'S NEWSLETTER

Useless Eugie

MORE
OF FISHER'S
WORK

SOPHIE PRICE IS
VAIN

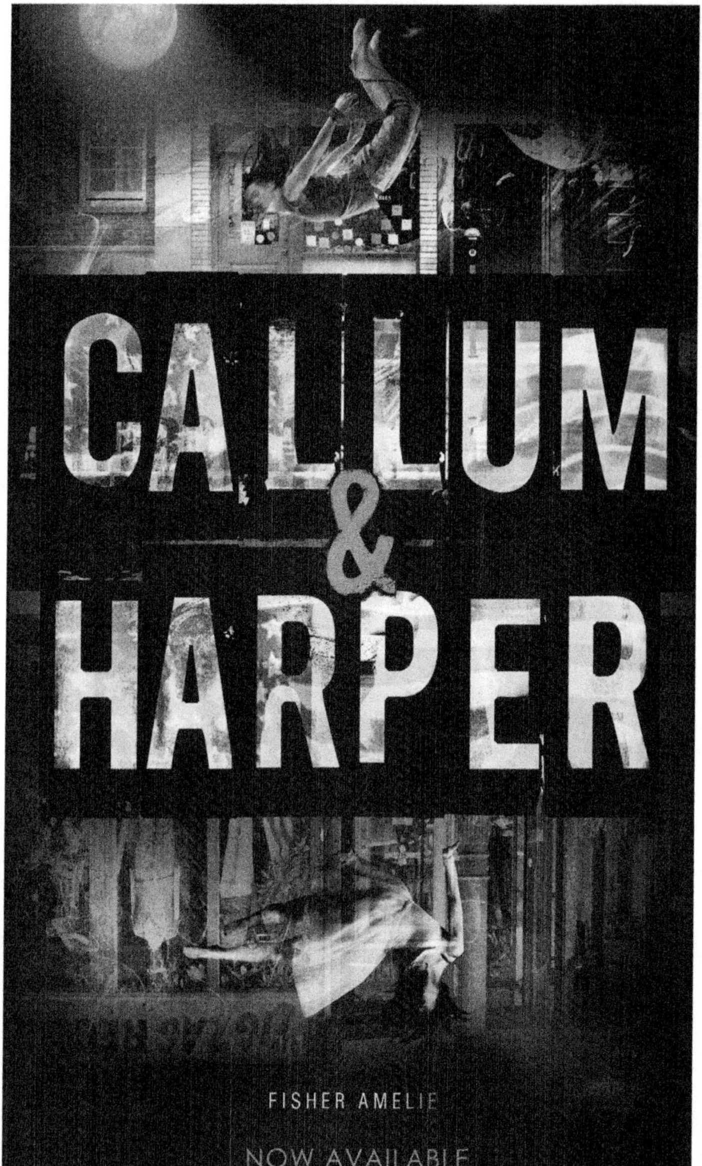
CALLUM
&
HARPER
FISHER AMELIE
NOW AVAILABLE

THOMAS & JANUARY

FISHER AMELIE

NOW AVAILABLE

ACKNOWLEDGEMENTS

I'd like to say thank you to my incredible editor Hollie Westring. Your work ethic is outstanding. Your ability to lift me up, the same. Thank you for your constant support. Plus, you're like Martha Stewart meets Grace Kelly meets Uma Thurman. That's pretty impressive. p.s. I cannot WAIT for your first book!!!

I'd like to thank my formatter, E.M. Tippetts. You were kind enough to take me in at the last minute, endure my unorganized chaos, and still, you pulled it off with grace. Thank you.

M. Leighton and Courtney Cole, what would I do without you guys? I've seen the both of you sky rocket to the top and where many would have left me behind, you didn't. You have both been so supportive, so generous, so compassionate. You're beautiful and generous on top of that. Thank you for being so incredible.

To my little ones, I don't do anything if it's not for you. Ever. I would die for you. I would declare war for you. When all is said and done, when all is over and nothing is remembered, all I can hope for, all I can pray for, is that I was the best mother to you.

Other half, we have had nothing but the harshest things happen to us this past year. Death after death, worry after worry, shock after shock...and yet, here we are, strong in our alliance, our friendship, our devotion. We're happy in our beautiful life. Yes, it feels bittersweet at times with the suffering and the trials but there was never, for one moment, that I felt alone. Ours is a forever kind. Ours is the enduring sort. I love you very much if you couldn't already tell. Very much.

PREVIEW

VAIN'S FIRST

CHAPTER

GREED FURY LUST IDLE BINGE ENVY VAIN

CHAPTER ONE

Six weeks after graduation and Jerrick had been dead for three of them. You'd've thought it would've been enough for us all to take a breather from our *habits* but it wasn't.

I bent to snort the line of coke in front of me.

"Brent looks very tempting tonight, doesn't he?" I asked Savannah, or Sav as I called her for short, when I lifted my head and wiped my nose.

Savannah turned glassy eyes away from her Special K laced o.j., her head wavering from side to side. "Yeah," she lazily slurred out, "he looks hot tonight." Her glazed eyes perked up a bit but barely. "Why?"

"I'm thinking about saying hello to him." I smiled wickedly at my pseudo-best friend and she smiled deviously back.

"You're such a bitch," she teased, prodding my tanned leg with her perfectly manicured nail. "Ali will never forgive you for it."

"Yes, she will," I said, standing and smoothing out my pencil skirt.

I could've been considered a dichotomy of dressers. I never showed much in the way of skin because, well, my father would have killed me but that didn't stop me from choosing pieces that kept the boys' tongues wagging. For instance, everything I owned was skin tight because I had the body for it and because it *always* got me what I wanted. I loved the way the boys stared. I loved the way they wanted me. It felt powerful.

"How do you know?" Sav asked, her head heavily lolling back and forth on the back of the leather settee in her father's office.

No one was allowed in that room, party or no but we didn't care. Sav's parents went to Italy on a whim, leaving her house as the inevitable destination for that weekend's 'Hole', as we called them. The Hole was code for wherever we decided to 'hole up' for the weekend. My group of friends were, at the risk of sounding garish, wealthy. That's an understatement. We were filthy, as we liked to tease one another, double meaning and all. Someone's house was always open some random weekend because all our parents traveled frequently, mine especially. In fact, almost every other weekend, the party was at my home. This isn't why I ruled the roost, so to speak. It wasn't even because I was the wealthiest. My dad was only number four on that list. No, I ruled because I was the hottest.

You see, I'm one of the beautiful people. That truly sounds so odd to have to explain but it's the truth, nonetheless. I'm beautiful and it's not because I have a healthy dose of self esteem, though I have plenty of that. It's obvious in the way I look in the mirror, yes, but even more obvious in the way everyone treats me. I rule this roost because I'm the most wanted by all the guys and all the *girls* want to be my friend *because of it.*

"How do you *know*?" She asked again, agitated I hadn't yet answered.

This made my blood boil. "Stuff it, Sav," I ordered. She'd forgotten who I was and I needed to remind her.

"Sorry," she said sheepishly, shrinking slightly into herself.

"I *know* because they always do. Besides, when I'm done with their boys, I give them back. They consider it their dues."

"Trust me," she said quietly toward the wall, "they do not consider it their dues."

"Is this about Brock, Sav?" I huffed. "God, you are such a whiny brat. If he was willing to cheat on you so easily, he wasn't worth it. Consider it a favor."

"Yeah, you're probably right," she conceded but didn't sound truly convinced. "You saved me, Soph."

"You're welcome, Sav," I replied sweetly and patted her head. "Now, I'm off to find Brent."

I stood in front of the mirror above her dad's desk and inspected myself.

Long, silky straight brown hair down to my elbows. I had natural blonde highlights throughout its mass. I'd recently cut my bangs so that they fell straight across my forehead. I ruffled them so they lay softly over my brows. I studied them and felt my blood begin to boil. The majority of girls at Jerrick's funeral suddenly had the same cut and it royally pissed me off. *God! Get a clue, nimrods. You'll never look like me!* I puckered my lips and applied a little gloss over them. My lips were full and pink enough that I didn't need much color. My skin was tanned from lying by the pool too much after graduation and I'd made a mental note to keep myself indoors for a bit. *Don't need wrinkles, Soph.* My light gold eyes were the color of amber and were perfect but I noticed my lashes needed a touch more mascara. I did this only to darken them up a bit not because they weren't long enough. Like I said, I was practically flawless.

"He won't know what hit him," I told myself in the mirror. Sav mistook this for speaking to her and I rolled my eyes when she responded.

"You play a sick game, Sophie Price."

"I know," I admitted, turning her direction, a fiendish expression on my unblemished face.

I sauntered from the room. As I passed the throngs of people lined against the sides of the hall that lead from the foyer to the massive den, I received the customary cat calls and ignored them with all the flirtatious charm that was my forte. I was the queen of subtlety. I could play a boy like a concert violinist. I was a master of my craft.

"Can I get you boys anything?" I asked as I approached the elite group of hotties that included Ali's Brent.

"I'm fine, baby," Graham flirted, as if I'd *ever* give him the time of day.

"You look it," I flirted back, just stifling the urge to roll my eyes.

"Since you're offering so nicely, Soph," Spencer said, "I believe we could all use a fresh round."

"But of course," I said, curtsying lightly and smiling seductively. I purposely turned to make my way towards the bar. I did this for two reasons. One, to make them all look at my ass. Two, to make them believe I'd only just thought of the next move on my playing board. I turned around quickly and caught them all staring, especially Brent. *Bingo.* "I'll need some help carrying them all back," I pouted.

"I'll go!" They all shouted at once, clamoring in front of the other like cattle.

"How about I choose?" I said. I circled the herd, running my hand along their shoulders as I passed each one. Spencer visibly shivered. *Point, Soph.* "Eenie, meanie, minie, *moe,*" I said, stopping at Brent. I followed the line of his throat and caught a glimpse of him swallowing, hard. "Would you help me, Brent?" I asked nicely without any flirting.

"Uh, sure," he said, setting down his own glass.

I linked my arm through his as we walked to the bar. "So how are you and Ali doing?" I asked him.

He gazed at me, not hearing a word I'd said. "What?" he asked.

Exactly.

Three hours later and Brent was mine. We'd ended up sprawled out on the ancient Turkish rug in Sav's parents' bedroom, our tongues in each other's throats. He threw me underneath him and hungrily kissed my neck but stopped suddenly.

"Sophie," he breathed sexily in my ear.

"Yes, Brent?" I asked, ecstatic I'd gotten what I wanted.

He sat up and gazed down on me like he'd never really seen me before. I smiled lasciviously in return, tonguing my left eye tooth. "Jesus," he said, a trembling hand combed through his hair, "I am such a fool."

"*What?*" I asked, sitting up, stunned.

"I've made a horrible mistake," he told me, still wedged between my legs. No need to tell you how badly that stung. "I've had too much to drink," he said, shaking his head. "I'm sorry, Sophie. Your being the most gorgeous girl I've ever met's clouded my judgement, badly. I've made a terrible mistake."

At that most fortunate of moments, we heard Ali calling out Brent's name in the hall outside the door and he tensed, his eyes going wide. I could only inwardly smile at what was to come. Before he'd had a chance to react to her calling to him, she'd walked into the room.

"*Brent?*" She asked him. She saw our position and

the recognition I'd seen in all the others before her was so obviously written all over Ali. She wasn't going to fight it. "I'm sorry," she said politely, like I wasn't in a compromising position on the floor with her boyfriend. *She's so pathetic*, I thought. She closed the door. We heard her pounding the floor to the stairs, running toward Sav no doubt. Sav would have to pretend she had no idea.

He threw himself to his feet, abandoning me half-hazardly on the carpet and immediately began chasing her. *Well, that's a first*, I thought to myself. Usually they went right back to business but I suppose we hadn't gotten far enough. *Yeah, that's why he left you lying here, half-undressed, chasing after his girlfriend, Soph.*

I balked at my own idiocy and stood up.

I walked to Sav's parents' bathroom and leaned over her mother's side of the double sinks. I fixed my bristled hair and ran my nail along the line of my bottom lip, fixing any gloss smudges. I tucked my form fitting black and white v-striped silk button up back into my pencil skirt and stared at myself.

A single tear ran down my cheek and I grimaced. *Not now,* I thought. I was my own worst enemy. That was my secret weakness. Rejection. Rejection of any kind, in fact. I hated it more than anything.

"You're too beautiful to be rejected," I told the reflection in front of me, but the tears wouldn't stop.

I ran the tap and splashed a little water on my face before removing the small bag of coke I'd hidden in my strapless. I fumbled with the little plastic envelope, spilling it onto the marble counter and cursed at the mess I'd made. I scrambled for something to line it with, finally stumbling upon her father's medicine cabinet. I removed the blade from her father's old fashioned razor and made my lines. I remembered her mom kept small stacks of stationery paper in her desk in the bedroom and I went straight for that, rolling the paper into a small roll.

The tears wouldn't stop and I knew I wouldn't be able to snort with a snotty nose. I went to her parents' toilet and tugged at a few squares of toilet paper, blew my nose then flushed it down. I swiped at the tears on my cheeks and bent over my lines just about the time a policeman came rushing in, catching me right before the act for the second time that night.

"What are you doing? Put your hands on your head," I heard a man's deep voice say.

I languidly stood from my unfinished lines and stared into the mirror. Sharing its reflection with me was a young, rather hot cop. *Shit*. I dropped the rolled up stationary that smelled like old-lady lavender potpourri and lazily put my hands over my head.

"Turn around," he said, fingering the cuffs on his belt.

I turned around and faced him, his eyes widened at the full sight of me. He stumbled a little, a hitch in his step, as he progressed my way. He brought my right hand down slowly, then my left and swallowed just as Brent had earlier. *Gotcha'*.

"What's your name?" I whispered, his face mere inches from mine. Beats Antique's *Dope Crunk* rang loudly from downstairs. *No wonder I hadn't heard them come in.*

"That's none of your concern," he said but the hesitation in his voice told me he thought he'd like it to be.

"I'm Sophie," I told him as he clicked the first ring around my wrist.

He kept narrowing his eyes at me but they would drop to my breasts then back up.

"N-nice to meet you, Sophie."

"Nice to meet you, too...," I drug out, waiting for his name.

"What are you doing?" He asked me, throwing glances over his shoulder, no doubt worried if more officers would be joining us.

"Nothing. Cross my heart," I appraised, taking my free hand from his and crossing my heart, which just so happened to be at the crest of my cleavage. His gaze flitted down and he started breathing harder.

"Casey," he told me.

"Casey," I said breathily, testing out his name. He fought a drowsy smile, apparently liking the way I said it and I smiled.

"L-let me have your hand," he said.

I gave him my unconstrained hand without a fuss. He took it and restrained it with the other.

"All tied up now, Casey," I whispered, raising my fisted hands just as he closed his eyes, almost drifting forward a bit.

"Come with me," he said, pulling me from the counter. His eyes glanced down at my lines and he shook his head. "What makes you do that shit?"

"Because it feels good," I told him, turning his direction and seductively running my tongue along my top teeth.

"Don't even," he said, "or I'll get you on propositioning an officer as well as possession."

"Suit yourself," I told him, shrugging my shoulders. "It might have been nice," I leaned forward and sang in his ear.

"I'm sure," he said. I could see the surprise on his face at his unexpected and candid response. I decided to run with it.

"I bet if you handcuffed me to the closet bar just beyond those doors, I'd be quiet as a mouse until you came back for me," I said, letting the double meaning sink in.

"Stop," he said. The breath he'd been holding whistled from his nose.

"How old are you, Casey?" I asked, leaning into him.

"Twen-Twenty-two," he stuttered.

"Huh, I just happen to be into twenty-two year olds. They're currently my thing," I lied.

His eyes came right to mine and held there.

"Really?" he asked, skeptical, yet inadvertently leaned into me. The grim line that had held his face before turned into a slight grin. *Seal the deal, Sophie.*

"Mmm, hmm," I said. I pushed further into his chest, my breasts mashed against his armor plate.

I tentatively kissed the pulse at his neck, knowing full well that if he really wanted to, he could definitely get me on propositioning.

I just couldn't go to jail. Not again. I'd already been once for possession when Jerrick died and the judge told me if I showed back up in his courtroom, I'd be toast. This was worth the risk.

"Jesus," he murmured.

I threaded my fingers through the belt loop at his waist and brought him closer to me. He fiercely took my face in his and kissed me like he was dying. *What an amateur*, I thought. *Thank God I got a dumb one.* His hands grappled all over my face as he had no grace whatsoever. If the guy wasn't so sexy, I don't think I could have put up the charade as long as I did.

"Officer Fratelli!" we heard come from downstairs and he broke the kiss. "Fratelli!"

"I'm-I'm up here," Casey said, flustered. He adjusted himself and wiped his mouth.

"Uncuff me," I said, almost panicked.

"I can't," he said.

"Yes you can, Casey. Do it and I'll repay you exponentially."

He groaned but looked at me apologetically. "When you get out, come find me," he said quietly as the other officer entered the room.

"The rest of the upstairs is secure," Casey said as if he hadn't just kissed my face off. "She was the only straggler."

"Fine," the older officer said. I thought he was going to leave but instead came through and examined the bathroom around us. "What the hell is this?" he asked Casey.

"What?" Casey asked.

"This," the older man said, gesturing to the lines of coke.

"Uh, yes, she was attempting a line when I found her," Casey told his superior.

Fuck.

"I'll bag this up," the man said and waved Casey on.

"I'm sorry," Casey said when we were out of the room, "I had to tell him. He'd have known I was lying."

"It's okay, Casey," I said with saccharine ooze. I kissed his mouth then bit his lip playfully. "It would have been the best ride of your life," I whispered. His eyes blew wide.

"Wait, what? We can still see each other," Casey desperately plied.

"Sure we can," I lied again.

"I wasn't going to tell him about the drugs," he said again, his voice quivering. "I had only planned on getting you on the party. That would have only been a ticket, a misdemeanor."

"I know, sweets," I told him, "but you still messed up."

Casey led me down the winding staircase and I felt as if time was standing still. All my friends, cuffed themselves, looked up at me as I descended over them. I smiled down at them bewitchingly and they almost cowered in my presence. I'd been the one who brought the coke and my smile let them know that if they brought me down, I wouldn't be going down with the ship on my own. If they squealed like the pigs they were, I would make their lives miserable. There's a fine line between friend and foe in my world.

Casey placed me into the back of a squad car when we reached the winding drive and buckled me in.

"Tell me," I said softly against his ear near my mouth, "what exactly am I being charged with?"

"Sarge will probably get you on drugs but if it's your first offense, you should be able to get off lightly."

"And what if it isn't?"

"Isn't what?" he asked, glancing over his shoulder.

"My first offense."

"Shit. If it's not, there's nothing I can do for you."

"Oh, well, there's nothing I can do for you then either," I said coldly, the heat in my seduction blasted cold with a bucket of ice water at the flip of a switch. Casey's mouth grew wide and he could see that he'd been had. I turned my face away from his, done with my pawn.

Casey got into the front seat and I could see through the rearview that his face was painted red with humiliation and obvious disappointment in himself that he fell for my game. He stuck the key in the ignition and drove me to the station.

I was booked, processed and searched. I scoffed at the women who had to search me before placing me in my cell. Stripping naked for anyone of the female persuasion wasn't exactly what I'd had planned for the evening. They looked down on me, knowing my charges, like they were somehow better than me.

"My lingerie probably costs more than your entire wardrobe," I spit out at the short, stocky one who eyed me with disdain.

She could only shake her head at me.

"Well it'll go nicely with *your* new wardrobe addition," the dark haired one said, handing me a bright orange jumpsuit.

This made both the women laugh. I slipped the disgusting jumpsuit on and they filed me away into a cell.

I shivered in my cell, coming down from my high. I was used to this part though. I only did coke on the weekends. Unlike most others I knew, I had enough self control to only do it at the Holes. It was just enough to drown out whatever crappy week I'd had from being ignored by my mother and father.

My parents were strangely the only I knew of who married and stayed that way. Of course, my mother was fifteen years younger than my father so I'm sure that helped and she stayed in incredible shape. If you pitched a pic of her then and now, you wouldn't be able to tell the difference and she'd gifted those incredible genes to yours truly. That was about the only thing my mother ever bothered to give me. My mother and father were so absorbed into themselves, I don't think they remembered me some days. I was born for one reason and one reason only. It was expected of my parents to give the impression of a family.

My mom was a 'housewife' and I use that term loosely. My father was the founder and CEO of an electronics conglomerate, namely computers and software. His company was based in Silicon Valley but when he married my gold-digging mother, she insisted on L.A., so he jetted the company plane there when he needed to. It was safe to say that one, if not two or three, of my father's products were in every single home in America. I'd had a five thousand dollar monthly allowance if I'd kept my grades up during prep school and that's about as much acknowledgment I got from my parents.

I'd just graduated, which meant I had four years to earn a degree of some kind then move out. I would retain a monthly allowance of twenty thousand a month but I had to earn my degree first. That was my father in a nutshell.

"Keep appearances, Sophie Price, and I'll reward you handsomely," my father said to me starting at fifteen.

And it was a running mantra in my home once a week, usually before a dinner I was forced to attend when he was entertaining some competitor he was looking to buy out or possibly a political official he was trying to grease up. I would dress modestly, never speak unless spoken to. Timidity was the farce. If I looked sweet and acquiescent, my father gave the impression he knew how to run a home as well as a multi-national, multi-billion dollar business. If I did this, I would get a nice little thousand dollar bonus. I was an employee not a child.

"Sophie Price," someone yelled outside the big steel door that was my cell. I could just make out the face of a young cop in the small window. The door came sliding open with a deafening thud. "You've made bail."

"Finally," I huffed out.

When I was released, I stood at a counter and waited for them to return the belongings I had walked in with.

"One pair of shoes, one skirt, one set of hose, one set of...," the guy began but eyed the garment with confusion.

"Garters," I spit out. "They're garters. God, just give them to me," I said, snatching them out of his hands.

He carelessly pushed the rest of my belongings in a pile over to me and I almost screamed at him that he was handling a ten thousand dollar outfit like it was from Wal-Mart.

"You can change in there," he said, pointing at an infinitesimal door.

The bathroom was small and I had to balance my

belongings on a disgusting sink.

"Well, these are going in the incinerator," I said absently.

I got dressed sans hose, returned my ridiculous jumpsuit and entered the lobby. Repulsive, dirty men sat waiting for whatever jailed fool they bothered to bail. They eyed me with bawdy stares and I could only glare back, too tired to give them a piece of my mind.

Near the glass entry doors, the sun was just cresting the horizon and I made out the silhouette of the only person I would have expected to come to my rescue.

Standing over six foot tall, so thin his bones protruded from his face, but with stylish, somewhat long hair, reminiscent of the nineteen-thirties, clad in a fitted Italian suit, stood Pembrook.

"Hello, Pembrook," I greeted him with acid. "I see my father was too busy to come himself."

"Ah, so lovely to see you too, Sophie."

"Stop with the condescension," I sneered.

"Oh, but I'm not. It is the highlight of my week bailing you from this godforsaken pit of bacteria." He eyed me up and down with regret. "I suppose I needed to get the interior of my car cleaned anyway."

"You're so clever, Pembrook."

"I know," he said simply. "To comment on your earlier observation, your father *was* too busy to get you. He does want you to know that he is severely disappointed."

"Ah, I see. Well, I shall try harder next time not to get caught."

Pembrook stopped and gritted his teeth at me before opening the passenger door for me. "You, young lady, are sorely unaware of the gravity of this charge."

"You're a brilliant attorney, Pembrook, with millions at your disposal," I said, settling into his Mercedes.

He walked the front of the car and sat in the driver's seat.

"Sophie," he said softly, before turning the ignition. "There's not enough money in the world that can help you if Judge Reinhold is presiding over your case again."

"Drive, Pembrook," I demanded, ignoring his warning. *He'll get me off*, I thought.

My house, or I should say, my father's house, was built a year before I was born but it had since been newly renovated on the outside as well as the inside so although I may have grown up in the home, it barely resembled anything like it did when I had been small.

It was grotesquely large, sitting on three acres in Beverly Hills, California, it was French Chateau inspired and over twenty-eight thousand square feet. I was in the left wing, my parents' were in the right. I could go days without seeing them, the only correspondence was out of necessity, usually to inform me that I was required to make a dinner appearance, and that was usually by note delivered by one of the staff. I had a nanny until fourteen when I fired her for attempting to discipline me. My parents didn't realize for months and decided I was capable of caring for myself after and never bothered to replace the position.

Freedom is just that. Absolutely no restrictions. I abandoned myself to every whim I felt. Every want I fulfilled and every desire was quenched. I wanted for nothing.

Except attention.

And I got that, I'll admit, not in the healthiest of ways. I won't lie to you, it felt gratifying...in a sense. I was rather unrestrained with my time and body. I wasn't different from most girls I knew. Well, except the fact I was exponentially better looking but why beat a dead horse.

The only difference between myself and them was I kept them wanting more. I used many, many, *many* boys and tossed them aside, discarding them, ironically, like many of them did to so many other girls before me.

This is what kept them baited. I gave them but a glimpse of my taste and they tasted absinthe. They were hooked by '*la fée verte*' as I was so often called. I was 'the green fairy'. I flitted into your life, showed you ecstasy, and left you dependent. I did this for fun, for the hell of it, for attention. I wanted to be wanted and my word, did they want me. Did they ever.

This paperback interior was formatted by

www.emtippettsbookdesigns.blogspot.com

Artisan interiors for discerning authors and publishers.

Printed in Great Britain
by Amazon